KEN SANCHEZ

Shadowplay (Willowbrook Book Three)

Contents

Author's Acknowledgement

Hi there! Thanks for picking up this book. If you're enjoying my work, you can find more stories like this if you scan the QR code below. While you're there, consider leaving a review – it really helps a writer out!

Scan me!

1

Longing For More

Peter

Peter Naps jolted awake, his heart pounding as the blaring alarm clock shattered the early morning silence. Groaning, he reached over and slammed his hand down on the snooze button, silencing the intrusive noise. As he blinked away the remnants of sleep, the dreary view of his cramped studio apartment came into focus, reminding him that another day of monotony and unanswered questions awaited him.

With a heavy sigh, Peter dragged himself out of bed and shuffled to the small, dimly lit bathroom. He stared at his reflection in the mirror, taking in the hazel eyes that seemed to hold a lifetime of secrets he couldn't access. The face looking back at him was familiar, yet foreign—a constant reminder of the empty spaces in his memory.

Shaking off the lingering unease, Peter went about his morning routine, trying to ignore the nagging feeling that something was missing. He knew he should be grateful for the life he had built since waking up in that hospital bed ten years ago with no memory of his past. But the questions that plagued him—who he was, where he came from, and why he couldn't remember—gnawed at his soul, leaving him feeling incomplete.

As he stepped out into the bustling streets of New York City, he pulled his jacket tighter around him, a futile attempt to ward off the chill that seemed to emanate from within. He walked briskly, his head down and his eyes fixed on the cracked concrete beneath his feet, avoiding the curious glances of the strangers who rushed past him.

Lost in thought, Peter almost missed the sound of the cheery bell jingling above the door as he entered Cups 'N' More, the cozy coffee shop where he worked. The rich aroma of freshly brewed coffee and warm pastries enveloped him, providing a momentary respite from his troubled musings.

"Morning, Peter!" Jess, his coworker, called out from behind the counter. "Ready for another day of coffee-slinging adventures?"

Peter forced a smile, trying to match Jess's enthusiastic energy. "As ready as I'll ever be," he replied, tying on his apron and taking his place at the register.

As he fell into the familiar rhythm of taking orders and crafting beverages, Peter couldn't shake the feeling that something significant was on the horizon. Little did he know that a chance encounter with a mysterious flyer would soon set him on a path that would change his life forever, leading him to the enchanting town of Willowbrook and the answers he so desperately sought.

Lost in the monotony of his everyday life, his mind drifted back to the fateful day that had set him on this path of uncertainty and longing. He remembered the sterile white walls and incessant beeping of machines that had greeted him when he first woke up in the hospital room, groggy and disoriented, with no memory of how he had gotten there or who he was.

The kind-faced nurse who had been checking his vitals had tried to reassure him, her voice gentle and soothing. "Welcome back, hun.

Gave us quite a scare when they brought you in unconscious from that alleyway. Can you tell me your name?"

But when Peter had opened his mouth to respond, he found himself grasping at empty air, his mind a blank void where his identity should have been. The realization had sent a wave of panic washing over him, and he had clutched at the strange necklace that hung around his neck, the only tangible link to a past he couldn't remember.

In the days and weeks that followed, Peter had drifted in and out of a medicated haze, his waking moments filled with a revolving door of doctors and nurses who poked and prodded at him, trying to unravel the mystery of the man with no memories. He had woken up countless times from nightmares he couldn't recall, his heart pounding and his skin slick with sweat, only to find himself alone in the sterile hospital room, with nothing but the beeping machines for company.

With no family or friends to claim him, the hospital staff had taken to calling him Peter Naps, a name that felt as foreign and unfamiliar as the face that stared back at him from the mirror. And when he was finally deemed stable enough to leave, they had helped him transfer to a group home, where he had begun the long, arduous process of rebuilding a life from scratch.

It was there, working in the home's small cafe, that Peter had first discovered his knack for crafting beverages, a skill that had eventually led him to his current job as a barista. But even as he had settled into his new life, finding a small apartment and a measure of stability, he couldn't shake the feeling that he was a stranger in his own skin, forever detached from the world around him.

The bells on the door jingled merrily and took him out of his thoughts, prompting Peter to look up from wiping down the espresso machine. His face broke into a grin as Lyra bounced in, her dress tinkling with each step. She waved excitedly, her smile as bright as the sun.

"Lyra!" Peter signed, setting his washrag down. "What brings you by today?"

Lyra pretended to take a sip from an invisible coffee cup and gave him a questioning thumbs up.

Peter laughed, "Coming right up, one caramel macchiato!"

As he prepared her drink, Peter's mind drifted back to their first meeting, a decade ago, just after he had woken up in the hospital with no memories. Lyra had shown up at his motel door out of the blue, her notepad in hand, welcoming him to the neighborhood. Despite his confusion, her warm spirit had drawn him in, and they had quickly become inseparable.

Peter slid the caramel macchiato across the counter to Lyra, who immediately started gesturing excitedly.

"Whoa, slow down!" Peter chuckled. "Let's see… you want me to go out with you tonight?"

Lyra nodded eagerly, pretending to dance and pointing from herself to Peter.

"Go out dancing, huh?" Peter hesitated. "I don't know, Lyra…"

Lyra unleashed her secret weapon: puppy dog eyes and mimed pleading hands, complete with a quivering lip.

"Okay, okay!" Peter threw his hands up in surrender, laughing. "How can I say no to that face? A night out does sound kind of nice."

Lyra bounced up and down, clapping giddily. Her eyes sparkled with mischief as she eyed Peter's faded graphic tee.

"Wait a second," Peter narrowed his eyes. "Don't tell me you want to go shopping first…"

Lyra grinned slyly, nodding and motioning along her body like she was showing off an outfit.

"Why do I get the feeling you've got this whole day mapped out scene by scene?" Peter groaned jokingly. "Alright, I know when I'm beat."

Lyra giggled softly, blowing him a thankful kiss before settling in to wait for Peter's shift to end.

As Peter went about his work, steaming milk and brewing drinks, he couldn't help but glance over at Lyra every so often. She was animatedly chatting with a tall, muscular customer who seemed to be leaning in a little too close for Peter's liking.

"Looks like someone's trying to get your number," Peter teased as they left the coffee shop, arm in arm.

Lyra rolled her eyes dramatically, sticking out her tongue and patting Peter's cheek in an "oh you" gesture.

"Yeah, yeah, I know," Peter laughed. "You eat guys like that for breakfast!"

As they walked, Peter's smile faded. He turned to Lyra, his expression growing serious. "Hey, thanks for getting me out today. I've been in kind of a funk lately, you know? Feeling stuck, like I'm just going through the motions."

Lyra nodded, pointing to her heart and miming lifting a heavy weight.

"Exactly," Peter sighed. "It's like this weight on my chest I can't get rid of. I just wish I could figure out who I am and where I came from. Maybe then I'd finally feel whole."

Lyra stopped, turning to face Peter. She placed her hand on his cheek, her eyes filled with love and confidence. Pointing to herself and then to him, she nodded firmly.

Peter's eyes misted over, understanding Lyra's unspoken message. The past didn't matter. She knew and loved him for who he was here and now.

"You always know just what I need," Peter pulled her into a hug. "Now come on, let's shop 'til your credit card smokes!"

Lyra's laughter, though silent, echoed through the streets as they set off on their adventure, ready to tackle whatever the day had in store.

Peter and Lyra hit their favorite boutiques, their laughter echoing through the stores as they played dress-up with the latest trends.

"I don't know, Lyra," Peter held up a plaid flannel at Hipster Haven, his brow furrowed. "Am I really ready to go full lumberjack?"

Lyra scrunched her nose, shaking her head. She rummaged through the racks, pulling out a deep green v-neck tee. Holding it up to Peter's chest, she smiled encouragingly.

In the dressing room, Peter turned side to side, admiring his reflection. "Huh, this actually looks pretty good."

Emerging tentatively, he struck a pose. "What do you think?"

Lyra's eyes lit up, giving him two enthusiastic thumbs up. She mimed flexing her biceps, making Peter laugh.

"Alright, alright, I'll trust your judgment on this one!"

At John's Leathers, Peter's fingers traced the supple jackets reverently. Lyra grabbed a classic moto, whipping it onto his shoulders.

"Not bad," Peter admired his reflection, pleasantly surprised.

Lyra fanned herself teasingly, swooning in exaggerated approval.

Peter left with two jackets, his confidence growing with each step.

At Jean Scene, Peter moved through the racks with newfound intuition, selecting pieces that spoke to him. Lyra clapped proudly, watching her protégé come into his own.

Swinging his bags as they left, Peter signed a heartfelt "Thank you" to Lyra. She had awakened a courage he never knew existed.

Taking a break on a bench, they people-watched, creating humorous backstories for passersby.

Suddenly, a TV caught Peter's eye. "Welcome home to Willowbrook," a soothing voice declared over idyllic suburban images. "Turn your life around and fill it with mystery."

"Lyra, did you see that? Willowbrook? Ever heard of it?"

But the TV had already gone dark. Lyra just shrugged, pointing to a nearby smoothie shop.

As the afternoon waned, Lyra checked her watch, miming an apologetic errand.

"No worries," Peter assured her. "I'll head home and start getting ready. See you tonight!"

On the quiet subway ride, Peter missed Lyra's animated presence. Arriving at his modest studio, he murmured, "I know it's not much, but it's home."

The neighborhood was sketchy, full of boarded up windows and suspicious characters. Inside, the water-stained walls and dingy carpet showed the apartment's age. But it was the only place Peter could afford on his modest barista salary. He tried to make the cramped space feel cozy with thrift store finds.

Finally the time had come and after a quick shower, Peter carefully styled his hair, going for a purposefully tousled look. "Ooh, looking good!" he complimented himself with an exaggerated wink. "Hair on point for the big night out."

Next came the new designer jeans and slim fitted v-neck tee that Lyra had picked out earlier. Peter nodded approvingly, adding a spritz of cologne. "Dressing the part already made me feel braver," he acknowledged.

The final touch was slipping on the antique necklace he never removed, the tear shaped charm cool against his chest. Peter held it briefly, drawing comfort from its familiar weight. "My trusty relic from my mysterious forgotten past," he declared dramatically.

Peter checked his phone, seeing Lyra's text. "On my way! Meet you at the club!" His stomach fluttered with nerves as he approached the unfamiliar venue.

The pulsing music and flashing lights assaulted Peter's senses as he stepped inside. He lingered near the entrance, watching patrons flow past him onto the dance floor.

Wading into the crowd, Peter felt utterly out of place among the carefree, grinding couples. His own identity confusion resurfaced, watching friends dance together with an easy intimacy he envied.

A tipsy couple nearby began making out passionately, their raw affection stirring an uncomfortable longing in Peter.

Suddenly, a flirtatious man with spiky blue hair sidled up to him. "Hey sexy, your moves are working on me," he purred with a wink.

Peter stiffened, flustered and intrigued, but before he could respond, the man had disappeared into the crowd. Peter's racing pulse hinted at a buried truth about himself.

Just then, Lyra bounded in, her eyes lighting up as she spotted Peter. She rushed over, enveloping him in a tight hug. Peter exhaled, his unease melting away in her comforting presence.

As they danced, Lyra kept Peter anchored in the moment, quieting his circling thoughts. With her, he could forget his yearning for a greater purpose and simply enjoy their time together.

Later, as they rested, Lyra gazed at Peter intently.

"What? Do I have something on my face?" Peter joked.

Lyra shook her head, her expression growing serious. She mimed opening a book and pointed from it to Peter.

"Wait, are you trying to tell me something?" Peter asked and obviously confused.

Lyra patted her chest, pointed to Peter, and gave two thumbs up, her message clear.

Peter sighed, the weight of uncertainty heavy on his shoulders. "I wish I could skip straight to the happy ending," he confessed wistfully.

Peter stumbled out of the club into the cool night air, his ears ringing from the booming music. The pulsing energy of the dance floor already felt distant as he headed home alone. Lyra had slipped away earlier with a wave and mysterious smile, off on another of her solo adventures.

Hands in his pockets, Peter let his thoughts wander as he walked under the streetlights. The evening had unlocked something within him. For the first time, he felt ready to explore the missing pieces of his identity, even if the answers scared him.

Rounding a corner into a crosswind, a large piece of paper suddenly plastered itself across Peter's face. "Bleh, what the…" he spluttered, peeling the flyer away.

When Peter saw what it was, his eyes widened. In glossy print, it advertised: "Willowbrook - the perfect place to find yourself." Below was a picture of town homes nestled around a glistening central park.

Peter's pulse quickened. This was now the second time he had randomly encountered mention of this mysterious town called Willowbrook. The coincidental flyer reignited the tempting pull he had felt seeing the mall advertisement earlier that day.

Peter studied the flyer closely, searching for any clue whether it was some kind of sign. The fine print listed a sales office downtown. Before he could overthink, Peter snapped a picture of the address on his phone.

2

A New Venture

James

James Crane sat in his lavish corner office, the Manhattan skyline stretching out before him through the floor-to-ceiling windows. He leaned back in his plush leather chair, rubbing his eyes after hours of staring at inventory reports.

"Another day in paradise," he muttered, his voice laced with sarcasm.

He gazed around the sleek space, taking in the dark wood furnishings and bookshelves lined with business classics. A crystal decanter of Scotch whisky and tumbler glasses stood at the ready, a testament to the success he and his friend Simon had built.

Despite the numerous industry accolades and photos of ribbon-cutting ceremonies adorning the walls, James felt a hollow ache in his chest. He reached for the bottom drawer of his desk, retrieving a small key from the chain around his neck.

Unlocking the drawer, James gently pulled out a worn leather wallet. He traced his fingers over the image of a laughing young man with mischievous eyes.

"Oh, Peter," he whispered, a wistful smile tugging at his lips. "What

I wouldn't give to be back in Tír na nÓg with you."

Memories of their carefree days in that enchanted realm flooded his mind—frolicking with fauns and nymphs under endless summer skies, exploring the lush landscapes, and reveling in the innocence and joy of eternal youth.

A knock at the door jolted James from his reverie. Simon poked his head in, concern etched on his face.

"Everything alright, James? You've been holed up in here for hours."

James sighed, running a hand through his hair. "Just thinking about the old days, Simon."

Simon entered, settling into the chair across from James. "I miss it too, James. But we've built something good here, haven't we?"

James nodded, gesturing to the office around them. "We have. But sometimes, I can't help but feel like something's missing. Like a part of me was left behind when we were cast out."

"I know what you mean," Simon said, his voice softening. "But we'll find Peter, James. We'll bring him home."

James met Simon's gaze, a flicker of hope in his eyes. "You really believe that?"

"I do," Simon said firmly. "We've come this far, haven't we?"

Another knock at the office door interrupted their conversation. One of their scouts entered, holding a steaming mug that read 'World's Best Boss'.

"Thought you could use a pick-me-up," Simon said, setting the coffee on James' desk.

James smiled, taking an appreciative sip. "You know me too well, my friend. This new blend is superb. Well done sourcing these unique roasts for our headquarters."

Simon waved off the compliment. "Just doing my part to keep morale up. Can't have the big boss getting burnt out, can we?"

James chuckled, leaning back in his chair. "Things certainly have changed from our Tír na nÓg days, haven't they? Seems like another lifetime ago we were frolicking with Peter and the others without a care in the world."

"Who would've thought we'd end up as stuffy corporate executives?" Simon grinned. "But somehow, running this company gives me the same satisfaction as our old escapades did."

"I must admit, building something successful here does fulfill me in ways I didn't expect," James said, gazing out at the New York skyline. "Still, I hope Peter has managed to find his own happiness in this realm."

Simon patted James on the back. "Speaking of Peter, I have some news for you."

James turned to him, curiosity piqued. "News? What kind of news?"

Simon lowered his voice. "Word from our network is that Peter may have been spotted at a nightclub downtown two nights ago."

"Wait, what?" James' eyes widened. "You found him? Who exactly did you find?"

"Now, don't get too excited," Simon cautioned. "One of our scouts saw a young man matching Peter's description with a blonde fairy. He wasn't able to get photographic proof before they slipped away, but it's the first promising lead in ages!"

James leaned back, stunned. "After over a decade without a single trace of him, Peter could really be here in the same city?"

"I knew you'd want to be informed," Simon said. "We're tracking down any other sightings and will update you the moment we confirm anything concrete."

James stood up, pacing the room. "We need to be cautious, though. If Peter is out there, we can't risk spooking him or drawing unwanted attention."

"Agreed," Simon said. "We'll keep this under wraps for now and continue our search discreetly."

James paused, looking out at the city skyline once more. "To think, after all these years, Peter could be within reach. It almost feels too good to be true."

Simon placed a reassuring hand on James' shoulder. "But it is true, James. And we'll do everything in our power to bring him home, just like we promised."

With renewed determination, James and Simon began to plan their next steps, the prospect of reuniting with Peter fueling their every move.

Just then, James' cell phone buzzed loudly, jolting him from his thoughts. He glanced down to see an unexpected name lighting up the screen - Adrian Belmont. James hadn't heard from the venture capitalist in years. He stepped out to take the call privately.

"Adrian, well this is a surprise," James answered. "To what do I owe the pleasure after so long?"

"James, great to hear your voice," Adrian replied smoothly. "I know it's been a while, but I have an intriguing business proposition if you have some time to meet up."

James raised an eyebrow curiously. Adrian was known for his lavish but sometimes risky investments. James would have to hear him out cautiously.

"I'm certainly open to discussing new opportunities," James replied diplomatically. "Why don't you send over some details and we'll set up a meeting."

After finalizing plans to reconvene, James clicked off the call, his mind spinning. An unexpected update on Peter and now a new venture on the horizon - things were certainly picking up.

Returning to Simon, James quickly regaled his friend with the call. Simon nodded thoughtfully as he listened.

"Adrian Belmont, wow that's a name I haven't heard in a long time," Simon mused. "But with your business acumen, I'm sure you'll vet any proposal wisely."

James smiled, grateful for his friend's faith in him. He knew Simon would help him analyze the upside versus risk rationally.

"Who knows, maybe this new opportunity will even aid our quest to find Peter," James added. "As a wise friend once told me, we must be open to all possibilities."

Simon chuckled. "Sounds like someone's been taking my advice to heart." He gave James a playful nudge. "Now how about celebratory drinks? The day's developments call for a toast!"

* * *

James arrived at the upscale steakhouse they frequented for client dinners, having received word from Adrian that he wanted to meet while they were all in New York. James spotted Simon already seated in the bar, sipping a whiskey.

"Started without me, I see," James teased, taking a seat.

Simon grinned, pouring James a glass from the bottle he had ordered. "You know me, always prepared. To new ventures bringing opportunity?"

James raised his glass, clinking it against Simon's. "To new ventures, indeed."

As they savored the smooth whiskey, James suddenly let out a surprised laugh, nodding towards the entrance. "Well, well, well. Look who just walked in, and with quite the handsome companion."

Simon turned, his eyebrows shooting up. "Is that Adrian Belmont? And he's actually smiling? I don't think I've ever seen him look so content."

"Let's go say hello," James suggested, already standing.

They made their way over to Adrian's table, James announcing their presence with a jovial, "Fancy seeing you here, Adrian!"

Adrian looked up, his usually stern face breaking into a warm grin. "James, Simon! Good to see you." He stood, clasping their hands before turning to his companion. "Allow me to introduce my husband, Benjamin. Darling, these are old friends, James Crane and Simon Clarke."

Benjamin smiled politely, shaking their hands. "Pleasure to meet you both. Adrian has told me wonderful things."

As they all sat down, James couldn't help but comment, "I must say, Adrian, I'm surprised to find you not only socializing but married! Last I knew, you were quite the brooding loner."

Adrian chuckled, lacing his fingers with Benjamin's. "Yes, much has changed since our world-wandering days. Meeting Benjamin lifted my curse of solitude. We helped heal each other."

James felt a pang in his chest, watching their easy intimacy. It reminded him of the bond he once shared with Peter, and he couldn't help but hope that his own story held a redemptive romantic arc ahead.

The conversation flowed easily as they caught up, James and Simon getting to know the thoughtful, sensitive side of Adrian that Benjamin had brought out.

Eventually, Adrian leaned forward, his expression turning serious. "I know you're both wondering why I wished to meet. The fact is, I have an intriguing business proposition if you'd be open to discussing it now."

James and Simon exchanged a glance. "Certainly, let's hear your thoughts," James replied.

Adrian folded his hands on the table. "As you know, I've been investing strategically in development projects that align with my values around community, sustainability, and innovation. One venture in particular near my estate holds great potential - a planned neighborhood called Willowbrook Heights."

Pulling out a glossy brochure, Adrian continued. "It's designed for today's residents who want an integrated, environmentally-friendly living space for humans and supernaturals alike. I'd like to get shipping and logistics established there early to support the long-term vision."

James and Simon exchanged a subtle glance as Adrian described Willowbrook catering to both human and supernatural residents. Having lived as supernatural exiles themselves for many years, this was not a surprise to them.

"Providing a welcoming haven for all types of beings to live in harmony – it's a noble ambition," Simon noted diplomatically as he flipped through images of lush parks and modern homes.

Adrian smiled, reading between the lines of Simon's carefully worded response. "I thought the concept might resonate, given your own unique histories."

He took a sip of wine before continuing. "Willowbrook has existed as a sanctuary for supernaturals for centuries. But recent times have seen more of our kind seeking refuge here amongst humanity. We want to expand the community responsibly to accommodate those looking for a place to truly belong."

Benjamin chimed in, "Willowbrook represents a new phase where all beings can integrate seamlessly, without fear of judgment or persecution. But providing resources and opportunity for the influx requires visionary partners such as yourselves."

James nodded thoughtfully as he processed their words. "It's astute to address the need for inclusive spaces ahead of the curve. You're quite right, the concept does align well with our values."

Simon added, "From a business perspective, being part of building a mixed community from inception could be incredibly fulfilling. We would love to make it thrive for all its inhabitants."

"We understand firsthand the challenges faced by those seeking to blend their supernatural gifts with human society," James continued.

"Your vision speaks to the future we all wish to manifest – one of unity, empathy, and progress."

"There are lucrative partnership opportunities for your company as a founding business presence," Adrian concluded. "I know it's a lot to consider, so please review the materials, and we can discuss next steps."

James slowly turned the pages showing images of lush parks and modern homes. This aligned well with the expansion goals he and Simon had for their company. And being part of a new venture like this from the ground up was extremely enticing.

Simon seemed equally impressed, asking Adrian thoughtful questions about construction plans and potential tax incentives for partner businesses.

"You've certainly given us much to discuss," Simon said. "We will have our team analyze the numbers and opportunities closely."

James nodded in agreement. "Your insights are invaluable, Adrian. I have no doubt that with Benjamin as your partner, your visions are bolder than ever."

He extended his hand across the table. "We look forward to further discussions and exploring a partnership that benefits us all."

Adrian smiled broadly as he shook James' hand firmly. "Excellent! I'll have my associates send over all the relevant materials. Please reach out with any other questions. I hope this is the beginning of something groundbreaking for everyone involved."

James and Simon shared an eager smile as they left the restaurant. "Well, this evening certainly took an intriguing turn!" James exclaimed. "I have a very good feeling about what lies ahead."

Arriving back at his sleek modern penthouse, James loosened his tie and headed to the kitchen for a nightcap. There on the marble island counter sat a plain envelope simply marked "For Boss".

James's pulse quickened. Any communication left for him this way meant sensitive information from their underground network of supernatural informants and private investigators. It could only relate to one subject - Peter.

With slightly trembling fingers, James tore open the envelope. Inside he found a brief typewritten dossier, along with a candid photo of a young man in an apron arranging pastries. James stared intently at the grainy image. Though older, the playful glint in those hazel eyes was unmistakable.

"After all these years without a single lead, could this really be him?" James murmured in wonder.

According to the dossier, the subject went by Peter Naps and worked as a barista in the city. They had yet to gather intel on his personal history, powers, or relationships. But it was the first concrete step in locating their long lost friend.

James's first instinct was to rush out and find Peter immediately. But he paused, contemplating his next strategic move. Barging in could spook Peter. James decided keeping his distance to discreetly learn more was the wisest initial approach.

James retreated to his bedroom clutching the classified dossier. He carefully stashed it away in a concealed wall safe, ensuring this explosive intel never fell into the wrong hands.

If any of James' powerful supernatural enemies discovered Peter was alive, they would surely try to capture him for leverage. James had to shield his vulnerable friend at all costs.

3

Heart Goes Boom

Peter

P eter stood outside the grand entrance of the library, his eyes wide with determination. It was his day off, and he had decided to spend it researching the mysterious town of Willowbrook that had captivated his thoughts.

"Alright, Willowbrook," he muttered to himself, rubbing his hands together. "Let's see what secrets you're hiding."

He marched inside, his steps echoing through the cavernous lobby. The librarian at the front desk raised an eyebrow as Peter approached, a man on a mission.

"Excuse me," Peter said, leaning in conspiratorially. "I'm looking for information on a town called Willowbrook. Got any computers I can use?"

The librarian pointed to a row of ancient machines in the corner, their screens flickering like something out of a horror movie. "Those are the public computers. Good luck."

Peter nodded, his jaw set. He didn't own a computer himself, his modest barista salary barely covering the essentials in the city. The smartphone he used was a gift from his best friend Lyra, who had taken pity on him a couple of years ago.

He sat down at one of the computers, the chair creaking ominously beneath him. The screen blinked to life, and Peter cracked his knuckles, ready to dive in.

Hours later, Lyra found him hunched over the keyboard, his eyes bloodshot and his hair standing on end.

"Peter!" she exclaimed, rushing over. "What are you doing? You look like you've been through a war!"

Peter looked up, a manic grin on his face. "Lyra! I've just been researching Willowbrook."

Lyra held up a hand, stopping him mid-sentence. She grabbed his notebook and scribbled furiously: *Peter, this is ridiculous. You need a real computer, not these ancient relics!*

Peter shook his head, his eyes wide. "No, no, I'm fine! I don't need a fancy laptop. I'm making do, see?"

He gestured to the stack of printouts beside him, the pages crumpled and smudged. Lyra rolled her eyes, writing: *STOP being so stubborn! Let me buy you a laptop, something nice for once!*

Peter laughed, pushing the notebook back. "Lyra, c'mon. You know I can't accept something that expensive. I'm doing just fine with these classics."

Lyra glared at him, underlining the word "help" three times. She clasped her hands together, giving him her best puppy dog eyes.

Peter sighed, running a hand through his disheveled hair. "I promise, it's not about pride. I just don't really need it. I'm a simple guy, you know that."

Lyra threw her hands up in exasperation, scribbling: *Fine, be difficult! But don't come crying to me when you strain your eyes on these dinosaurs!*

Peter grinned, pulling her into a hug. "I promise, when I'm a rich and famous researcher, you can buy me all the laptops in the world.

But for now, I'm happy with my old-fashioned ways."

Lyra shook her head, a reluctant smile tugging at her lips. She wrote: *You're impossible, you know that? But I guess that's why I love you.*

Peter laughed, the sound echoing through the library. The librarian shot them a stern look, and Peter ducked his head sheepishly.

"Oops, guess we better keep it down," he whispered. "But seriously, Lyra, thank you. Your friendship means more to me than any fancy gadget ever could."

Lyra rolled her eyes, but her smile was genuine. She wrote: *Just promise me you'll take a break before you go cross-eyed. And maybe invest in some reading glasses, grandpa.*

Peter chuckled, giving her a mock salute. "Aye aye, captain."

Lyra grinned, but then her expression turned apologetic. She scribbled a quick note: *Sorry, Peter, I've got to run. I promised to help a friend with a project. But don't stay here too long, okay? Get some rest, and we'll catch up later.*

Peter nodded, understanding. "No worries, Lyra. I'll be fine. Go be the amazing friend I know you are."

With a final hug and a wave, Lyra hurried out of the library, leaving Peter alone with his research. He turned back to the ancient computer, a determined glint in his eye. Willowbrook's secrets wouldn't unravel themselves, and he was ready to dive back in, one flickering screen at a time.

After coming up with nothing for a while, Peter got bored with the computers and wandered through the labyrinth of bookshelves, his fingers trailing reverently over the weathered spines. The scent of aged paper and leather filled his nostrils, a comforting aroma that felt like coming home.

"Ah, books," he sighed dramatically. "My one true love."

He gathered an armful of promising titles on local history and geography, the weight of knowledge both literal and figurative. With a grunt, he hefted the stack onto a nearby table, ready to dive into the mystery of Willowbrook.

Hours ticked by as Peter pored over the dusty tomes, his eyes straining in the dim light. He leaned back, stretching his stiff muscles with a groan.

"You'd think a town as weird as Willowbrook would have a neon sign pointing to its secrets," he muttered. "But no, I have to play Nancy Drew in the world's most cryptic library."

Determined, Peter hauled himself up to search for more clues. He reached for a particularly ancient-looking volume, his fingers grazing the spine just as another hand shot out, bumping his.

"Hey!" Peter yelped, spinning around. "Watch where you're-"

His words died in his throat as he found himself staring into the most startlingly blue eyes he'd ever seen. The stranger was unfairly handsome, with chiseled features and an air of mystery that made Peter's knees feel like Jell-O.

"I…uh…," Peter stammered, his brain short-circuiting. "I'm Peter. I mean, sorry. I mean, hi."

The stranger chuckled, a warm, rich sound that sent shivers down Peter's spine. "James Crane," he said, extending a hand. "Pleasure to make your acquaintance, Peter."

Peter took his hand, trying to ignore the electric tingle that raced up his arm at the contact. "Likewise," he managed, his voice an octave higher than usual.

James's gaze flicked to the book they'd both reached for. "Ah, 'Hidden Towns of the Hudson Valley.' A fascinating read. Planning a trip?"

Peter's heart leaped into his throat. "What? No! I mean, maybe? I'm just…researching. You know, for fun."

James raised an eyebrow, a smirk playing at the corner of his mouth. "Researching mysterious towns for fun? My, you are an enigma, Peter."

Peter felt his cheeks flush, but he couldn't help but grin. "Well, we all have our quirks."

"Indeed," James agreed, his eyes sparkling with mirth. "And what, pray tell, has captured your interest so thoroughly?"

Peter hesitated, biting his lip. Something about James made him want to spill all his secrets, but years of self-preservation held his tongue. "Oh, you know," he said casually. "Just a little town called Willowbrook. Probably nothing special."

James's eyes widened, a flicker of something unreadable crossing his face. "Willowbrook, you say? Now that is intriguing."

Peter's pulse quickened. "You know it?"

"I know of it," James said cryptically. "And I have a feeling, Peter, that your interest in Willowbrook is more than just idle curiosity."

Peter swallowed hard, feeling suddenly exposed under James's piercing gaze. "I…I don't know what you mean."

James smiled, a slow, knowing thing that made Peter's toes curl. "Don't worry, your secret's safe with me. But if you really want to unravel the mystery of Willowbrook, you might need more than just dusty old books."

He pressed the volume into Peter's hands, his fingers brushing Peter's in a way that felt entirely too deliberate. "Something tells me our paths will cross again, Peter. Until then, happy reading."

With a wink and a grin, James turned on his heel and strode away, leaving Peter gaping after him, clutching the book to his chest like a lifeline.

"What just happened?" Peter muttered to himself, his head spinning. "And why do I suddenly feel like I'm in way over my head?"

But even as the questions swirled in his mind, Peter couldn't help but smile. For the first time in a long time, he felt a flicker of something that might have been excitement, or even hope.

"Get it together, Peter," he muttered, shaking his head. "You're here to research Willowbrook, not daydream about handsome strangers."

With a determined sigh, he opened the book, his fingers tracing the ornate lettering on the title page. "Hidden Towns of the Hudson Valley," he read aloud, a thrill of anticipation running through him.

As he scanned the table of contents, a particular chapter caught his eye. "The Secrets of Willowbrook: A Town Shrouded in Mystery."

"Jackpot!" Peter exclaimed, earning a few curious glances from nearby patrons. He ducked his head sheepishly, lowering his voice. "Okay, Willowbrook, let's see what you're hiding."

He flipped to the chapter, his heart pounding as he began to read. The words seemed to leap off the page, painting a picture of a town steeped in intrigue and supernatural occurrences.

"For centuries, Willowbrook has been a magnet for the unexplained," Peter read, his eyes widening. "Ghostly apparitions, mysterious disappearances, and whispers of an ancient power that thrums beneath the town's quaint exterior."

He leaned back in his chair, his mind racing. "This is it," he whispered. "This is what I've been searching for."

"Looks like you found something interesting," a familiar voice said from behind him.

Peter jumped, turning to see James standing there, a knowing smile on his face.

"James! I, uh, didn't expect to see you again so soon."

James chuckled, pulling out a chair and sitting down across from Peter. "I had a feeling you'd still be here, nose buried in a book."

Peter felt his cheeks heat up, suddenly self-conscious. "Yeah, well, when I get caught up in something, it's hard to stop."

"I know the feeling," James said, his gaze drifting to the open book. "The Secrets of Willowbrook, huh? Find anything juicy?"

Peter hesitated, his instincts warring with his growing trust in James. "Maybe," he said slowly. "But I'm not sure what to make of it all yet."

James leaned forward, his eyes intense. "Peter, I'm going to let you in on a little secret. Willowbrook isn't just some quaint little town with a few ghost stories. It's a place where the impossible becomes possible, where the lines between reality and fantasy blur."

Peter's heart skipped a beat, James' words echoing his own thoughts. "How do you know all this?"

James smiled enigmatically. "Let's just say I've had my own experiences with the unexplained."

Peter swallowed hard, his skin tingling where James touched him. "I don't understand. Are you saying...are you saying you've been to Willowbrook?"

James nodded, his gaze distant. "I have. And it changed my life in ways I never could have imagined. But that's a story for another time."

He stood up, his hand lingering on Peter's for a moment longer. "Just know that when you're ready, Willowbrook will be waiting for you."

With that, he turned and walked away, leaving Peter breathless and more determined than ever to uncover the truth about the mysterious town.

As the library's closing bell tolled, Peter jumped, nearly toppling out of his chair. He'd been so engrossed in the book, he'd lost all track of time.

"Closing time already?" he muttered, glancing at his watch. "But I was just getting to the good part!"

With a sigh, he closed the tome, his mind still reeling from the revelations within. One thing was crystal clear - he had to get to Willowbrook, and fast. The answers he'd been searching for his whole life were waiting for him there, he just knew it.

Peter gathered his things, clutching the book to his chest like a precious artifact. He approached the front desk, where a bespectacled librarian was waiting with a knowing smile.

"Find what you were looking for, dear?" she asked, her eyes twinkling.

Peter grinned, tapping the book's cover. "And then some! This little beauty has more secrets than a high school diary. I don't suppose I could check it out?"

The librarian chuckled, shaking her head. "Oh, that one's special. It's not meant to be cooped up on a shelf, collecting dust. No, I think it's meant to be with you."

Peter's eyebrows shot up. "Wait, what? You're just giving it to me?"

"Call it a hunch," the librarian said with a wink. "Something tells me you and that book have a destiny to fulfill."

Peter clutched the tome tighter, his heart racing. "I…I don't know what to say. Thank you, really. You have no idea how much this means to me."

The librarian patted his hand, her smile warm and understanding. "Oh, I think I do, dear. I've seen that look before - the look of someone who's just had their world turned upside down in the best way possible."

Peter laughed, shaking his head in wonder. "That's one way to put it. I feel like I've just woken up from a long, weird dream, and now I'm finally seeing things clearly."

"Then my work here is done," the librarian said, shooing him towards the door. "Now go on, get out of here. Willowbrook's waiting for you, and trust me, you don't want to keep destiny waiting."

Peter grinned, saluting her with the book. "Yes, ma'am! I'm on my way."

He paused at the door, turning back to face her. "Hey, I never got your name. Who do I thank for this life-changing literary experience?"

The librarian smirked, pushing her glasses up her nose. "Call me…a friend. A friend who knows that sometimes, the greatest adventures start in the most unexpected places."

With that cryptic statement, she disappeared into the stacks, leaving Peter staring after her in bewilderment.

"Okay, that was weird," he muttered, stepping out into the cool night air. "But then again, what about this whole situation isn't weird?"

He looked down at the book in his hands, feeling a thrill of anticipation. "Alright, Willowbrook," he said, his voice ringing with determination. "Ready or not, here I come. Let's see what kind of trouble we can get into together."

Checking his watch, Peter realized he was about to be late meeting Lyra for dinner at their favorite diner. Quickening his pace, his mind swirled with thoughts of how to tell his best friend about the revelations today's research had brought.

Arriving at the retro diner, Peter spotted Lyra already seated in their usual booth by the window. She was engrossed in something on her smartphone but looked up and waved when Peter entered.

Chrome accents on the stools and tables reflected the glow from red glass lampshades hanging overhead. Black and white checkered tiles lined the floors. Along the counters, swiveling stools with cracked leather seats awaited patrons.

The scuffs and innate imperfections only added to the warmth and character of the space. Outside, neon signs beckoned people inside with promises of the best burgers, shakes, and slices of pie in the city. This had been a second home for Peter and Lyra for years.

"Hey! Sorry I'm a little behind, got caught up at the library," Peter explained breathlessly as they hugged.

As Peter slid into the red faux leather seat, Lyra tilted her head quizzically. She pantomimed opening a book and reading, eyebrows raised.

"You won't believe it, but I finally found some key info about Willowbrook!" Peter explained excitedly. He had been talking to her about it since he found out about the town.

He regaled her with the obscure book's accounts of Willowbrook's supernatural past, and the personal draw many felt to visit it throughout history. Lyra listened intently, eyes wide.

"So I was thinking, it's probably time I check this place out myself," Peter concluded, sipping his milkshake. "It just feels like something is calling me there, you know?"

He studied Lyra hopefully, waiting for her reaction. Her brow furrowed thoughtfully as she tapped her chin. After an extended pause, she finally nodded and gave a hesitant thumbs up gesture.

Peter sensed her lack of enthusiasm. "You're welcome to come with me of course," he offered. "Make it a fun road trip?"

Lyra bit her lip, glancing away uncertainly. She mimed looking at an invisible calendar, grimacing and shaking her head no.

"Hey, no worries if you can't get away from work or had other plans," Peter said understandingly. "I know it's pretty last minute. I can just go solo this time."

Lyra reached over to squeeze Peter's hand apologetically. Then she wrote on a napkin note: *Just be safe please! But I know you have to follow your heart.*

Peter smiled affectionately. "Thanks for understanding. I knew I could count on you." Lyra had always supported him figuring out life on his own terms. It was one of the reasons their friendship flourished.

After the waitress dropped off their cheeseburgers, Lyra tilted her head thoughtfully. She scribbled a note and slid it over: *What's the real reason you want to visit Willowbrook so suddenly?*

Peter paused, caught off guard by the question. He took a sip of his milkshake as he contemplated his answer.

"I'm not totally sure," he began slowly. "I guess I've been feeling kind of restless lately. Like my life is missing something important that I can't name."

Lyra nodded, her eyes gentle and understanding as she waited for him to continue.

"It's crazy, but finding out about Willowbrook has sparked something in me," Peter tried to explain. "Learning it's a haven for people seeking purpose, I feel drawn there for some reason. Like maybe it holds answers I didn't know I needed."

He glanced down self-consciously. "I know that probably sounds nuts. I just have this intuition that Willowbrook is important somehow."

Lyra smiled and squeezed his hand reassuringly. Taking up her pen, she responded: *It doesn't sound crazy at all. I know you'll find what you're seeking there. Just trust your heart.*

Peter exhaled in relief. "Thanks for saying that. I guess I'm ready for a fresh start. Other than you, I don't have much tying me here."

He shrugged, picking at his fries. "Big cities like this just make me feel lonelier. At least in a small town like Willowbrook maybe I could really belong."

Lyra's eyes shone with empathy. She scribbled fiercely: *You're going to thrive in Willowbrook, I just know it! This is the perfect next step!*

Peter grinned, bolstered by her vote of confidence. "Well, with your blessing I guess my decision is made! Here's to new adventures." He lifted his milkshake in a toast.

They spent the rest of dinner talking casually about their weeks apart. But in the back of Peter's mind, an uncertainty nagged. He couldn't shake the feeling Lyra was hiding something regarding Willowbrook. He trusted her implicitly, yet sensed she was holding back for reasons unclear.

But Peter pushed aside his doubts for now. He didn't want suspicion to taint this celebratory night. There would be time later to diplomatically ask Lyra about her hesitations about his visit to Willowbrook.

"I'm coming, Willowbrook," Peter whispered up to the glittering sky.

Saying it aloud sent a thrill through him. He didn't know what secrets the town held, but he had faith it would guide him exactly where he needed to go, just as the mystical librarian had promised.

30

4

A Familiar Presence

James

He stood gazing out the floor-to-ceiling windows of his sleek penthouse, swishing the dark red wine in his glass pensively. Below, the city skyline glittered as dusk settled over Manhattan. But James's thoughts were far away, lingering on a chance encounter earlier that week.

Ever since crossing paths with Peter at the library a couple of days ago, James had been unable to shake him from his mind. The brief interlude kept replaying, like a song stuck on repeat. The brush of Peter's fingers as they both reached for the same book. His shy smile and the way he self-consciously tucked that unruly lock of hair behind his ear. And most of all, those hazel eyes that sparked instant familiarity in James's soul.

James took a long sip of wine, feeling the memory of Peter's touch linger like a phantom limb. After over a decade apart, fate had unexpectedly brought them together again when James least expected it. He had been so thrown in the moment to find Peter there within arm's reach, just as beautiful as James's dreams always painted him.

Though Peter had physically aged, his essence remained untouched by time. James was captivated all over again by his guileless warmth and the intrinsic goodness shining through. The years apart had only intensified the ache inside James.

Being close to Peter again brought all those buried feelings rushing back to the surface. Feelings that James had tried his best to suppress back in their Tír na nÓg days, scared of their forbidden nature. But he couldn't deny the magnetic pull between them, drawing him like a moth to Peter's pure light.

James knew acting on these impulses could ruin the most precious bond in his life. He would never jeopardize Peter's friendship for the sake of selfish desire. But resisting the romantic love blossoming in his heart grew harder each day.

With a conflicted sigh, James turned from the windows. He removed the skin-toned prosthetic hand concealing his right wrist. Attaching Peter's ingeniously crafted hook in its place, James instantly felt more anchored. Like Peter was there beside him, guiding him through the emotional tempest within.

"You always could see right through me, couldn't you Peter?" James murmured, a sad smile touching his lips. "Your friendship is more than enough. I'll silence these reckless wants, so nothing changes between us."

James was so lost in troubled thought that he didn't realize how tightly he was gripping the wine glass. It shattered abruptly in his good hand, making him flinch. Crimson rivulets ran down his wrist as James stared numbly at the shards littering the floor.

This emotional turmoil was so unlike him. James was always the pinnacle of steely composure, never revealing weakness. But where Peter was concerned, his armor cracked.

Footsteps approached, jolting James from his daze. He looked up to see Simon entering, assessing the messy scene with concern. Without a word, Simon fetched a broom and gently swept up the jagged pieces.

James sat heavily on the bed, overwhelmed by guilt. "Please Simon, allow me to clean up my own mess."

But Simon waved him off kindly. "No need, it's done. Are you alright my friend? Your mind seems burdened as of late."

James sighed, touched by his friend's perceptiveness and care when he deserved neither. "Forgive my distressed state. My thoughts have been…troubled."

Simon's eyes shone with empathy as he pulled up a chair. "This is about Peter, isn't it? Seeing him again after so long must have stirred up many emotions."

Trust Simon to read him like a book, James thought wryly. "I confess, finding him has consumed my every thought," James acknowledged. "I can scarcely focus on anything else."

He shook his head ruefully. "You must think me a fool, so preoccupied by the past."

But Simon just smiled. "Not at all. Peter was special to us both. Tell me, what was it like being with him again after so long?"

James gazed out the windows pensively as he gathered his feelings. "It was exhilarating, but also overwhelming," he began slowly. "At once, it seemed the years apart melted away. His eyes, his voice, his spirit - all exactly as I remembered."

Simon listened intently as James described their encounter in detail, conveying his jumbled emotions. It felt cathartic opening up about just how powerfully Peter's presence still affected him.

"He seemed timid though," James concluded. "Lacking that bold spark he once possessed. The years estranged from his origins have undoubtedly taken a toll."

Simon nodded thoughtfully. "Yes, awakening to a strange new world alone would dampen the most vibrant soul." He gave James a knowing look. "He will surely regain his spirit now that you've found him again."

James managed a small, hopeful smile at the thought. "Perhaps you're right. If this undeserved second chance is meant to serve any purpose, rekindling Peter's light must be it."

His phone buzzed with a text. Glancing down, he saw it was from one of the scouts he had tracking Peter's movements.

"Peter just arrived for his shift at the cafe," James informed Simon, unable to keep the eagerness from his voice.

Noticing his reaction, Simon suggested gently, "Why don't you go see him again? Even briefly. It may ease your mind, if nothing else."

James pondered this, hesitant to seem a lurking specter. But his desire won out. "You make a fair point," he conceded, reaching for his long coat. His hand once more in place, James felt braced to see Peter again.

Simon gave an approving nod. "I will always support anything that brings you peace, my friend."

James clasped Simon's shoulder warmly before heading out into the bustling city streets. The late afternoon sun glittered between skyscrapers as he wove his way toward the café. James wasn't sure what he hoped to achieve, but seeing Peter's face was like a siren call he was helpless but to obey.

Simon smiled knowingly. "Well you'd best get going then. Wouldn't want to miss your window."

James rolled his eyes in mock exasperation, but couldn't contain his smile. "I suppose you're right. I'll be back later." Simon just chuckled and waved him off.

Stepping outside, James joined the stream of pedestrians hurrying along the crowded sidewalks. He walked briskly, weaving around slow moving tourists and street vendors shouting out deals. Impatience quickened his pace as the café's location drew closer.

Within a few blocks, the towers of industry and commerce gave way to treelined streets flanked by brownstone apartments. The neighborhood had a relaxed charm, worlds away from the frenetic energy James just left.

At the corner, he descended the stone steps to the subway below ground. Mercifully, a train was just pulling in, saving him precious minutes. Settling into a seat near the door, James watched the dark tunnel walls speed by in a blur. He bounced his knee restlessly, willing the stops to pass quickly.

After what felt like an eternity, James emerged back into daylight a few blocks from the cafe.

Picking up his pace, James weaved through groups ambling along the sidewalk. He felt magnetically drawn to his destination now, Peter's presence calling like a beacon. The closer he got, the faster his heart raced with anticipation.

As he arrived, he immediately joined the queue. James observed Peter working the register up ahead, illuminated by a ray of sunlight. He was greeting each customer warmly, eyes crinkling with mirth when they exchanged a joke. His innate radiance still took James's breath away.

As the line moved along, James's heart raced faster.

Finally, it was James's turn, but Peter's gaze remained fixed on entering numbers into the register.

"What can I get started for..." Peter began automatically before glancing up. He froze, eyes blowing wide. "James!" he gasped. "I mean, hello sir, my apologies!"

Peter's cheeks flushed delectably as James removed his sunglasses, maintaining a casual air. "Hello Peter, fancy running into you again. I was just passing by and fancied a coffee."

"O-of course!" Peter stammered, clearly flustered. He fumbled adorably tying on his apron. "What, um, what would you like?"

"A cappuccino please," James requested smoothly. As their hands brushed exchanging payment, he savored the contact, letting his fingers linger. Peter shyly met his gaze before ducking his head.

James took his drink and selected a small bistro table nearby. Ideally positioned where he could admire Peter while remaining innocuously in the background. It thrilled him to have this stolen intimacy, seeing Peter's everyday habits and mannerisms.

As the crowd filtered out, Peter's shoulders gradually dropped in relaxation. His smiles came easier, laughter more vibrant. James observed the veil of self-consciousness fall away, allowing Peter's innate radiance to shine through.

James lingered over the dregs of his now lukewarm cappuccino, not wanting to miss a moment of Peter in his element. When Peter went on break mid-morning, his eyes immediately found James and widened in surprise, as if not expecting him to have stayed. James lifted his coffee mug in friendly salutation.

After a brief hesitation, Peter untied his apron and made his way over. "You're still here?" he asked, though a subtle pleased smile teased his lips.

"Of course, I was quite enjoying the view," James responded instinctively. He silently chided himself for the flirtatious remark. Keeping his true feelings buried grew harder whenever Peter was near.

If Peter noticed the double meaning, he didn't let on. "Well, you have impeccable timing. I was just about to go on break actually." He sank into the chair across from James.

"You seem pretty busy today." James said. "Why have they got you working so much?"

"This is my last day before some time off," Peter explained, a new lightness in his tone. "I decided I could use a change of scenery for a bit, to clear my head."

James leaned forward, intrigued. "Oh? Taking a holiday somewhere?"

Peter chewed his lip thoughtfully. "Not exactly a vacation, more just…trying to find some clarity I guess." He glanced down, seeming to wrestle with whether to elaborate.

James gently prodded, "Forgive my prying, but you appear troubled. Perhaps I could lend an ear?"

With a resigned sigh, Peter opened up. "Honestly, I've felt sort of lost lately. Like I'm just going through the motions each day without purpose." He shook his head ruefully. "Sorry, you probably think that sounds pathetic."

"Not at all," James countered. "I think many can relate to what you describe. Feeling unmoored, seeking one's place." His heart ached at Peter's unspoken pain.

Peter gave him a grateful look. "Exactly. So I'm hoping maybe getting away will offer some fresh perspective. It's just something I need to do for me."

James nodded. "An important journey to take. Will you be traveling alone then?"

"Yeah, just me on open roads," Peter said. "I have a destination in mind actually which is Willowbrook." He looked at James hesitantly, as if gauging his reaction.

James managed to keep his face neutral despite the shock jolting through him. Willowbrook was the last place he expected naive Peter to venture towards alone. But the coincidence confirmed fate had intertwined their paths not randomly.

"I hope you find what you're searching for there." James remarked carefully.

Peter's eyes took on a distant, melancholy look that made James's chest ache. "To be honest, I'm hoping Willowbrook may hold some answers about where I come from," he admitted quietly. "About who I am."

James stilled, unsure how to respond. Peter's amnesia clearly still plagued him, casting a shadow over his spirit. James yearned to illuminate Peter's obscured past, but knew the truth had to come from within.

"Your origins do not define you," James said gently. "But I sincerely hope your travels bring you the clarity you seek, one way or another."

Peter blinked gratefully. "That means a lot, thank you." He smiled then, soft and achingly familiar - a glimpse of the guileless boy James had known. "I don't know why, but I feel I can trust you, James."

Those simple words threatened to undo James completely. How he had missed that smile, that ceaseless faith Peter once placed in him. Their lost years apart suddenly felt unbearable.

Before James's emotions could overwhelm him, Peter's timer buzzed insistently. "Back to it," he sighed. "Enjoy the rest of your day!"

"And you as well," James managed. He lingered a few minutes more, knowing the next time he saw Peter, the journey to Willowbrook would be underway. The forces propelling them along converging paths would soon bring revelations neither were prepared for.

Stepping outside into the sunlight, James tilted his face skyward, emotions churning. Their encounter today confirmed Peter was still drawn to James, despite having no conscious memories of their shared past. An unbreakable bond still thrummed between them, humming just below the surface.

James strode briskly, renewed purpose fueling his steps. If Peter was venturing to Willowbrook, he needed protection, whether he realized it or not. James refused to fail him ever again. He had to ensure Peter arrived there safely, surreptitiously clearing any hidden dangers from his naive friend's path.

Steeling himself, James pulled out his phone to make a necessary call. Adrian answered on the second ring. "James! To what do I owe the pleasure?"

"Adrian, apologies for the short notice, but I wanted to take you up on establishing a Willowbrook location for the business after all," James informed him briskly.

"Excellent!" Adrian responded enthusiastically. "I'm delighted you changed your mind. I have the perfect site ready when you are."

"Then it's decided. Expect Simon and myself within a few days to finalize details," James confirmed.

After exchanging brief pleasantries, James clicked off the call, a plan formulating. If Peter was venturing blindly to Willowbrook, then James would pave the way. He refused to lose track of his vulnerable friend again.

5

Town of Smiles and Bagels

Peter

The crescent moon, its pale light barely illuminating the otherwise dark bus stop. He pulled his jacket tighter against the chill of the night air. According to the brochure he'd found, this midnight bus was the only way to get to the supposedly haven of Willowbrook.

He wasn't sure what he expected to find there, but something deep inside told him this trip would lead to answers about his forgotten past.

He wished Lyra could've come with him. Earlier, when she'd stopped by to see him off, her expressive face had told him she might try to follow after him soon. He hoped so. Her warm companionship would make this strange journey less lonely.

Peter checked his watch again - five minutes to midnight.

Out of the corner of his eye, he caught a flash of movement in the dark woods. He turned to see a pair of glowing eyes watching him from the trees. His heart skipped a beat. But then headlights cut through the night as the bus lumbered into view. The eyes vanished.

With a hiss of brakes, the bus rolled to a stop in front of Peter. He hoisted his backpack over his shoulder and climbed aboard as the doors creaked open.

As the bus lumbered along the darkened roads, Peter's thoughts wandered. Was he doing the right thing, traveling to this strange town on just the whisper of a feeling? He'd told his job this was merely a vacation, but part of him sensed this trip might turn out to be more permanent.

Unbidden, the image of James rose in his mind - those piercing blue eyes that seemed to see right through him. Peter's pulse quickened at the memory of James' handsome face. He chided himself for even thinking someone like James could want him. Peter was nobody, just a barista barely scraping by. And James was…everything. Sophisticated, successful, magnetic. Peter squeezed his eyes shut, willing away these foolish fantasies before they consumed him.

Outside the bus windows, the scenery began to change. The harsh neon lights and looming skyscrapers of the city faded into the distance. Rolling green hills and thick forests took their place, dotted with quaint farmhouses and grazing livestock. It was like stepping into another world where time moved more slowly.

As they passed through a particularly dense wood, fireflies winked in the shadows like fairies. Peter pressed his face to the glass, enchanted by their hypnotic dance. How long had it been since he'd seen such unspoiled natural beauty? The concrete jungle he called home suddenly felt light years away.

Eventually, the woods thinned out again into well-kept fields and orchards. They passed a charming little village with a windmill and candy-colored storefronts advertising fresh baked pies and local produce. Further along, larger buildings began appearing - a stately brick courthouse, a movie theater with a shining marquee, some shops and restaurants.

They were nearing the outskirts of Willowbrook proper now. Peter sat up eagerly, taking it all in. The driver called back over his shoulder, "Won't be long now! We'll be arriving in the heart of town shortly."

"Thank you," Peter said.

Though apprehension still nagged at him, a sense of rightness filled his chest. He just knew this was exactly where he needed to be.

At last the bus pulled up in front of a quaint redbrick station. With another blast of brakes, it shuddered to a stop. The doors wheezed open.

"End of the line, kid," the driver said cheerily.

Peter thanked him again and stepped out into the cool night air, the doors creaking shut behind him. The station stood on the edge of a vibrant town square. Even at this late hour, golden light glowed from the windows of charming shops and cafes lining the cobblestone streets. The tang of wood smoke and roasting nuts mingled invitingly in the air.

Peter hitched his pack higher on his shoulders, suddenly hesitant. The bus rumbled away into the night, leaving him alone.

Just then, the driver leaned out his window and called back, "If you're looking for a place to stay, there's an inn just down the way near the library called The Dreamery! Best rates in town!" He waved cheerfully as the bus turned a corner and disappeared from sight.

Bolstered by this kindness, Peter set off toward the heart of town. He passed an old-fashioned movie theater with a vintage marquee listing showtimes for classics like Casablanca and Singin' in the Rain. Next door was a cozy bookshop, its front display overflowing with leather bound volumes. Peter made a mental note to explore those treasures soon.

Peter wandered through the expansive town square, taking in the charming park at its center with the bubbling fountain.

He needed to find the hotel the bus driver had mentioned - The

Dreamery. Peter hadn't booked accommodations, wanting to simply see where the journey took him. Now fatigue from traveling was setting in. He hoped to secure a room for the night.

At last on the far side of the square, Peter spotted the quaint facade of The Dreamery beside the stately library. His heart lifted at the sight. Inside, the lobby exuded cozy charm with plush rugs and a crackling fireplace.

The receptionist, an elderly woman named Shelby, greeted him warmly from behind a polished oak desk. "Welcome to The Dreamery, dear! Will you be checking in this evening?"

Peter nodded, suddenly bashful. "I don't have a reservation, but I was hoping you might have a room available?"

"Of course! We always keep a few vacancies open for wayward travelers like yourself." Shelby peered at him kindly over her spectacles. "Now, how long will you be staying in our fair town?"

"Oh, um, I'm not sure exactly," Peter stammered, caught off guard. He hadn't planned that far ahead.

Shelby smiled reassuringly. "No matter. Why don't we start with one week and go from there?"

Peter sighed in relief. "That would be perfect, thank you."

After sorting out the details, Shelby handed him an ornate brass key. "You'll be in room eight, just upstairs on the left. Please let me know if you need anything at all!"

Peter thanked her again and made his way up the creaking staircase. His room was cozy yet far more spacious than his cramped apartment back home, with a canopy bed as the centerpiece. Leaving his backpack on the antique writing desk, he collapsed onto the plush mattress.

Though exhausted, Peter's empty stomach protested loudly. He hadn't eaten since lunch many hours ago. But he was wary of venturing out into the unfamiliar town at night alone.

A knock at the door made him jump. He opened it to find Shelby holding a covered basket, a knowing look on her face. "I thought you might be hungry after your travels, so I brought you some treats from our kitchen."

Peter's eyes widened. "That's so thoughtful, you didn't have to…"

"Nonsense! We want you to feel welcome." Shelby pressed the basket into his hands. "Have a good rest, dear. Let me know if you need anything else!"

He thanked her profusely before closing the door again. Lifting the cloth cover, he found fresh-baked blueberry muffins, apple turnovers, and even a small wedge of rich chocolate cake. His mouth watered as he devoured the feast.

Fed and warm in his cozy room, Peter's earlier worries seemed to fade away. This place already felt more like home than anywhere he'd been before. He drifted off to sleep feeling peaceful and protected.

* * *

Morning sunlight filtering through the curtains awoke Peter. For a moment he was disoriented, unsure where he was. Then it all came back - the midnight bus, the mysterious town, arriving at The Dreamery. It hadn't been just a vivid dream.

After washing up, Peter ventured downstairs to the lobby. Shelby sat knitting behind the front desk. "Good morning!" she called cheerfully. "I hope you slept well? There's coffee and breakfast in the sitting room."

The sitting room was all rough-hewn wood and overstuffed armchairs surrounding a sooty fireplace. A sideboard held baskets of baked goods, carafes of coffee and juice, and plates of fresh fruit. Peter filled a cup and plate before sinking into a cushy leather armchair.

As he ate, he overheard two men at a nearby table chatting. "Did you hear? The old Crawford place just got bought up," one remarked.

His companion gasped. "You don't mean that big manor house near the beach? I heard it's been abandoned for ages."

"Exactly. Word is some fancy big city types are turning it into offices. They got crews working on it soon."

Peter's ears perked up. Big city types here? How intriguing. Willowbrook clearly wasn't as cut off from the outside world as it first appeared. He wondered what else he might discover during his stay.

He approached the front desk where Shelby sat knitting. "Excuse me, Shelby? Could I trouble you for a recommendation on where to grab some bagels? Preferably somewhere close by." He was genuinely craving bagels.

Shelby set down her knitting needles and smiled up at him. "But of course, dear! Let's see, there's a lovely little cafe just around the corner called Glimmer. They have the best pastries and coffee in town. Just tell Dominic I sent you."

"Glimmer, got it. Thank you!" Peter said gratefully.

"Their blueberry scones are to die for," Shelby called after him. "Enjoy, and stop by again if you need anything!"

Peter soon located Glimmer's cheerful storefront down a side street. The aroma of fresh baked goods wafted out as he opened the door, setting his mouth watering. Inside was all polished wood and sun-filled windows. Mismatched tables were packed with patrons chatting amiably over steaming mugs. The comforting atmosphere reminded Peter of home, though he couldn't place why.

When it was his turn at the counter, the barista greeted him with a warm smile. "Welcome to Glimmer! I'm Dominic, the owner. What can I get started for you?"

"Um, just a coffee and one of those chocolate bagels would be amazing," Peter said, distracted by the case of tantalizing pastries.

"Coming right up!" As Dominic rang up his order, understanding dawned on his face. "You must be the newcomer staying over at The Dreamery. Shelby told me to keep an eye out for you."

Peter rubbed his neck self-consciously. "Is it that obvious I'm not from around here?"

"In a charming way," Dominic laughed. "But don't worry, we're a friendly bunch. Why don't you grab a seat and I'll bring your order over?"

Peter chose a table by the window overlooking the bustling street. True to his word, Dominic soon appeared bearing a foaming cappuccino and flaky croissant. "It's on the house today," he said with a wink.

"Oh I couldn't possibly do take that. I can pay." Peter said and start to pull out his wallet to pay for his bagels.

"No, I insist. Keep it. Call it the Willowbrook Hospitality." Dominic said.

Peter knew not to decline these things over the years. "Thank you. I appreciate it." He smiled softly at Dominic.

Dominic pulled up a chair opposite Peter before he could object. "Now, what brings you all the way to Willowbrook?" he asked, studying Peter over tented hands.

Peter wrapped his hands around the warm mug, gathering his thoughts. "Well, it's kind of hard to explain…" He trailed off, unsure how much he wanted to reveal.

"No need to rush," Dominic said kindly. "I'm always ready to lend a listening ear to a newcomer in need." His tone was open and non-judgemental.

Buoyed by Dominic's patience, Peter began slowly. "I guess you could say I've felt…lost for a long time. Haunted by this emptiness I can't explain. I'm hoping this town might have some answers about where I come from and why I can't seem to remember big chunks of my past."

He glanced up to find Dominic watching him intently, brow furrowed in concentration. "What kinds of things can't you remember?" Dominic asked.

Peter ran a hand through his hair with a shaky laugh. "That's the strangest part - it's almost like I'm missing huge chapters. Significant people and events that should be there are just...gone. I don't even know how old I am."

Dominic made a thoughtful humming sound. "That must be very difficult to cope with. Do you have any clues at all about your history? An object, a place?"

"Nothing concrete," Peter admitted. "But I've always had this necklace." He pulled out the pendant, its metal edges worn smooth. "I get the sense it's important, but I have no idea why."

Dominic gestured wordlessly to examine the necklace, and Peter passed it over. Closing his eyes, Dominic cupped it in his palms, concentrating.

After a long moment, he handed it back. "There is definitely powerful magic caught up in that pendant. I have no doubt it's tied to your past in some way."

Peter shifted in his seat, hesitant to contradict this friendly man who had listened so openly. "I appreciate you saying that, but magic? I've never seen any proof it actually exists outside of stories."

Dominic just gave an enigmatic smile. "I understand your skepticism. The workings of Willowbrook can seem far-fetched to outsiders at first. Not meaning any disrespect to your beliefs of course."

"No no, none taken," Peter rushed to reassure him. "It's just...talk of spells and mystical energy goes against everything I thought I knew. But I don't want to dismiss it either." He shook his head with a rueful laugh. "I'm probably not making much sense."

"On the contrary, your doubts are perfectly logical for who you are now," Dominic said gently. "Self-discovery takes time. The magic of this place manifests slowly, in its own way for each person."

Peter nodded, grateful for Dominic's patience. Whether or not magic was real, this compassionate man had listened and taken him seriously when he needed it.

"Thank you," Peter said sincerely. "For letting me unburden myself, and for keeping an open mind even if I remain skeptical for now. I appreciate you hearing me out."

Dominic patted his hand reassuringly. "Of course. We all find our way here when we're lost. But Willowbrook has a way of providing clarity, in time…"

Changing the subject, Peter gestured around the cozy cafe. "This is such a great space. Do you run it alone?"

"No, I have a wonderful woman who helps me around but she's currently on leave." Dominic said, handing the necklace back. "But I could always use extra help, especially with more newcomers stopping into town lately. If you're looking for something to keep you busy, I'd be happy to hire you on. No prior experience needed."

Peter blinked in surprise. He hadn't expected a job offer, since he was still technically employed back in the city. But the prospect of working somewhere so warm and welcoming tempted him. And he really didn't know how long he'd stay in Willowbrook.

"Thank you, really. I'll have to think on it," Peter said finally. "This town has already been so welcoming. I appreciate you looking out for me."

Dominic gave his shoulder a paternal squeeze. "It's what we do here. Now, finish your breakfast and enjoy exploring our little corner of the town. And stop by anytime if you have more questions!"

Peter spent the next few hours wandering along Willowbrook's charming streets, peeking into shops and nodding hello to the friendly residents he passed. The bookstore drew him in again, and he stocked up on additional tomes about harnessing energy and scrying for lost things. Just holding the volumes filled him with a sense of possibilities.

In a music shop, the eccentric white-haired owner insisted Peter take home an antique wooden flute. "A gift to welcome you to town!" he declared cheerily over Peter's protests. The instrument felt strangely familiar in his hands, and he found himself able to play a simple melody almost instinctively. Magic seemed to thrum through the very air here.

At a cart selling flowers, the vendor gifted him a small potted plant. "For clarity and focus," she explained with a dimpled smile. By now, Peter knew better than to refuse such acts of generosity. He tucked the fragrant herbs into his backpack carefully.

The sun was sinking toward the horizon when Peter's feet led him back to Glimmer. Inside he found Dominic wiping down tables and humming along with the radio. He brightened at the sight of Peter lingering in the doorway.

"Changed your mind about that job already?" Dominic teased. He gestured Peter over to sit, then bustled behind the counter to prepare them both coffees.

Peter laughed softly. "Not yet. But I did want to properly thank you for your kindness today. It really meant a lot."

Dominic waved away his words. "It's nothing, truly. Us outsiders need to stick together, especially in a town as unique as this." A shadow seemed to cross his face then, his earlier cheer faltering.

Peter wondered what Dominic's story was, how someone so warm and vibrant had ended up here like himself. But he knew better than to pry. "Well, either way, I'm grateful," Peter said simply.

Dominic studied him a moment, seeming to come to a decision. "You know what, why don't you help me out here and I can see where your skills are at? We'll be closing up soon, but folks still tend to wander in."

He raised his eyebrows in invitation. After a brief hesitation, Peter agreed. It would be nice to make himself useful after Dominic had shown him such kindness.

Dominic grabbed an apron off a hook and tossed it to Peter, who caught it reflexively. "Have any experience with baking?" Dominic asked.

"Um, not really," Peter admitted as he tied on the apron. "But I'm a quick study and happy to learn."

Dominic waved away his concerns good-naturedly. "No experience required. I'll show you the ropes. Just follow my lead."

He briskly showed Peter around the kitchen, demonstrating how to shape dough into neat rolls, mix up icing colors, and pull trays of golden-brown pastries from the oven. Peter paid close attention, determined to pick it up quickly.

Soon customers trickled in, and Dominic nudged Peter up to the register. Peter took orders and counted out change while Dominic assembled the drinks and treats. They fell into an easy rhythm. Peter found himself enjoying the work and the pride of creating something with his hands.

As they cleaned and closed up for the night, Dominic clapped a floury hand on Peter's shoulder. "You did fantastic for your first day! Let me know if you want to pick up more shifts."

As Peter untied his apron and said farewell to Dominic for the evening, he marveled at the unexpected turn of events. When he'd wandered into the cozy cafe this morning, he never could have imagined leaving with an impromptu job.

Yet somehow, helping Dominic serve customers and clean up had felt natural - as if no time had passed since he last worked in a busy kitchen. Muscle memory he didn't know he possessed had kicked in during the dinner rush.

Walking back to the inn under the glowing streetlamps, Peter shook his head in disbelief. He had come to Willowbrook hoping for answers, only to wind up with more mysteries.

But for the first time in forever, the questions swirling in his mind didn't fill him with dread. He felt buoyed by this unconventional new beginning. Dominic had offered not just a job, but kindness, companionship, purpose. More than Peter ever expected to find here.

He still wasn't sure how long he'd stay in Willowbrook. But suddenly the thought of building a temporary life here amongst people like Dominic didn't seem so strange. For now, Peter was exactly where he needed to be.

6

Ominous Shadows

James

After a week of finishing their affairs and business in New York, James gazed out the car window as they neared their destination, the quaint town of Willowbrook.

He'd asked Simon to arrange a small rental house for their stay. Simon could always be relied upon to handle the details. James preferred to focus on the big picture. It was a partnership that worked, ever since the two of them had arrived in this modern world so unlike the magical realm of their youth.

As the car rolled to a stop, James raised an eyebrow in surprise. The house Simon had secured was a stately two-story Craftsman, surrounded by lush gardens. James stepped out of the cab, impressed. "Well done, Simon. This looks perfect."

Simon grinned, looking pleased. "Only the best for us, boss. I know how particular you can be about your creature comforts." He stopped the car and took their bags while James examined the exterior. It really was ideal - charming yet with all the modern conveniences he'd grown accustomed to.

Once they were settled in, James pulled a bottle of wine from the fridge, pouring two glasses. He raised his in a toast. "To new ventures." Simon clinked his glass against James' before taking an appreciative sip of the bold red.

James sank into an armchair, the rich wine warming him from within. How long had it been since he'd allowed himself to relax and take things slowly? In New York, it was go go go from dawn till dusk. But perhaps this sabbatical in the countryside was exactly what he needed to restore some balance. Willowbrook seemed charming, untouched by the rushed pace of city life.

"We should call Adrian soon," James mused, swirling the wine in his glass. "Start setting up meetings about the new office space. But no need to rush it - we just got here, after all."

Simon gave him a knowing look but didn't argue. James had learned to trust his own instincts when it came to business. He hadn't built a thriving shipping empire by being reckless or hasty. Patience was key.

James gazed around the sunlit living room, the wine leaving him uncharacteristically sentimental about days gone by. He thought of his loyal crew back in Tír na nÓg , sailing the jewel-toned seas, full of camaraderie and purpose. Long buried memories surfaced, bittersweet, before he forced them away. The past was best left in the past.

Simon returned from making some phone calls, interrupting his reverie. "Adrian will be by soon to pick us up," Simon informed him. "He's eager to discuss business prospects over dinner at the manor tonight."

James nodded, passing his wine glass to Simon who took a sip. "Excellent. I'm looking forward to seeing him and Benjamin again." He raised an eyebrow at his friend. "You're welcome to join us, of course. Unless you had other plans?"

Simon laughed. "As much as I enjoy your business conversations, I was rather hoping to explore the town this evening." He gave James a knowing look. "I'm sure you two will manage just fine without me."

"Of course," James agreed smoothly, hiding his smile. Simon knew him too well. He preferred handling negotiations on his own terms. "Just try to stay out of trouble. I can't have you scandalizing the locals on our first night here," he added wryly.

Simon placed a hand on his chest in mock affront. "Who, me? I'm the picture of respectability." His eyes glinted with familiar mischief that made James briefly nostalgic for their youthful antics. How far they'd come from those carefree days.

Musing over his wine glass, James' thoughts turned to the real reason this town called to him. "Do you think he's settling in alright?" James asked quietly. "Peter?"

Simon's expression softened in understanding. "I'm sure our friend is just fine. This seems a welcoming place."

Privately, James hoped the same. Unbeknownst to Peter, he had contacted Adrian to discreetly watch over the Peter. Protect him from potential enemies who might seek to take advantage of his vulnerable state. Adrian had graciously agreed, for which James was immensely grateful.

Which reminded him - "Have our scouts reported back yet? Any signs of danger lurking near town?" James pressed. One could never be too cautious.

"All quiet so far," Simon reassured him. "But they'll keep vigilant watch. Rogues would be foolish to try anything with so many of us here."

Still, James resolved to stay alert. He would let no further harm come to the lad if he could help it.

The rumble of tires on gravel signaled a vehicle's arrival outside. James straightened his blazer and went to greet the new arrival.

A kindly older gentleman stepped out of the sleek black town car.

"Mr. James, pleasure to see you again," he said, tipping his cap. "Mr. Adrian sent me to collect you and Mr. Simon."

James recognized him as Mr. Johnson, Adrian's longtime driver. He smiled and shook the man's hand warmly. "Wonderful to see you as well, Mr. Johnson. Thank you for coming all this way."

Simon joined James with an enthusiastic greeting for Mr. Johnson, clearly also pleased to see the familiar face.

On the drive into town, Mr. Johnson stopped near the village square per Simon's request. Music and laughter drifted through the open windows as villagers congregated.

"This looks perfect, thank you Mr. Johnson," Simon said, clearly eager to join in the festivities.

"Try not to get into too much mischief without me there to supervise," James teased as Simon stepped out of the car.

"No promises!" Simon called over his shoulder with a grin. They watched him stroll off to mingle with the colorful crowd, immediately drawn into conversations with cheerful townspeople.

James shook his head affectionately. His friend had always been able to charm his way into any social circle. He was likely in his element among these celebrants of old traditions.

Mr. Johnson filled him in on the town's preparations for the upcoming Summer Solstice festival. "The villagers are all quite excited," he related. "There will be music, dancing, and plenty of old magic in the air."

James made a polite but noncommittal sound. Such festivities held little appeal for him these days. He was here for business matters, not nostalgic celebrations.

Mr. Johnson gave James an understanding look in the rearview mirror but didn't press the issue of his disinterest in the festivities. He well knew James' general avoidance of dwelling on the past or old traditions.

They drove on in comfortable silence, the music fading into the distance. As the village slipped from view, the scenery shifted to the dense forests and rolling green hills surrounding Adrian's estate.

When the stately manor came into view, James gazed up appreciatively despite himself. Trust Adrian to secure the most grandiose property around, even all the way out here. Some things never changed.

Mr. Johnson dropped him at the imposing front entrance. James straightened his blazer and knocked on the sturdy oak doors, awaiting a response.

The door soon creaked open to reveal Adrian's longtime butler, Mr. Prattle. Despite the years since James had seen him last, the man seemed ageless. "Good evening, Mr. James," Mr. Prattle intoned. "Please follow me. Master Adrian is expecting you in his study."

James greeted the butler warmly, allowing himself to be led through the manor's lavishly decorated halls. Mr. Prattle announced him at the study door before departing with a small bow.

Inside, Adrian was just finishing up some paperwork at his massive desk. He looked up with a grin as James entered. "James! Good of you to come, please have a seat."

James settled into one of the plush leather chairs across from Adrian. "Thank you for seeing me. You have a lovely home, as expected." He glanced around curiously for any other occupants. "Will Benjamin be joining us?"

"I'm afraid my better half is working late at the library this evening," Adrian informed him with an affectionate eye roll. "I swear he lives amongst those dusty tomes. But we'll all have dinner together soon."

James nodded. "Of course. Well, allow me to again express my sincere gratitude for accepting us here and giving us the offer of putting up a branch in Willowbrook. Opening a small branch here will help us tap new markets."

Adrian waved off his earnest thanks. "It's mutually beneficial. Your presence will bring some much-needed modern commerce to our little corner of the world." His expression turned serious. "But I know that's not your only reason for coming here."

James tensed slightly. Nothing got past his old friend. "You're right," he acknowledged. "I'm also here to check on Peter. I want to ensure no further harm comes to him in his vulnerable state. Have your sources reported back on his arrival?"

"At ease, my friend," Adrian said gently. "Young Peter is being looked after, just as we discussed. I have eyes all over town monitoring his safety closely."

He let out a breath he hadn't realized he was holding. "Thank you, Adrian. Your discreet assistance in this matter means everything, truly."

"Think nothing of it," Adrian said firmly. "We protect our own, especially those who cannot fully protect themselves." He studied James shrewdly.

"Does Peter know…everything?" Adrian asked. "From what I hear, he believes himself fully mortal now."

James tensed, hesitating how much to reveal. But Adrian had proven trustworthy with their secrets time and again. "No, his memories are gone." he said quietly. "He knows nothing of magic or his true origins."

Adrian's brow furrowed. "That must make life difficult for him here, not understanding the town's true nature."

"It's for his own safety," James insisted. "The shock of the truth could destroy the fragile equilibrium he's found. Peter can't know who he really is…" James faltered, emotion clogging his throat.

Adrian surveyed him closely but didn't pry further. "You don't need to explain more tonight. I understand many old wounds run deep." He squeezed James' shoulder. "Your secrets are safe with me, my friend."

James nodded gratefully. The curse that had stolen Peter's memories and magic also meant death if he learned the truth prematurely. But Adrian didn't need those worrisome details. This was James' burden to bear alone.

Sensing his discomfort, Adrian smoothly changed topics. "Why don't I show you the prospective site for your new offices? It's just a short drive." He pressed the intercom on his desk. "Mr. Prattle, please have the car brought around. Mr. James and I are going out."

The butler's affirmative response crackled through the speaker. James shot his friend a look of thanks for the distraction. Adrian had always been adept at redirecting conversations with subtle grace.

Soon James and Adrian were ensconced in the town car as Mr. Johnson drove them to the prospective building site. Adrian pointed out local landmarks and highlights as they went, keeping the conversation light.

James allowed the peaceful ride and his friend's soothing voice to settle his lingering anxieties. This place already felt more like home than anywhere he'd been since leaving Tír na nÓg all those years ago.

To James' surprise, Mr. Johnson directed the car out along the coast road, bringing the vast ocean into view. James drew a sharp breath at the sight of moonlight shimmering across the dark waters. It reminded him painfully of the sea he'd once sailed back in Tír na nÓg.

Adrian gave him a knowing glance. "I thought you might appreciate seeing this. I recall your tales of exploring the jewel-toned seas."

James nodded, momentarily too overcome to speak. His friend had remembered those wistful stories and brought him here to recapture just a hint of that lost past.

"There's an ideal site near the lighthouse that should suit your needs," Adrian continued gently. "With a view of the sea as a bonus."

He took in the charming white lighthouse perched atop craggy cliffs. He could picture an office building nestled just below without impeding the natural beauty.

"It does seem perfect," he managed finally, giving Adrian a grateful look. Building a new future didn't have to mean letting go of the past entirely. This thoughtful gesture was Adrian's way of bridging both in his own subtle manner.

They continued on down the coastal road, discussing potential layouts and materials for the new waterside construction. James felt his earlier melancholy ebbing away, replaced by building excitement.

Adrian turned to James. "So, tell me more about your vision for the new building. What sort of layout and design did you have in mind?"

James collected himself, focusing on the future rather than the past. "I'm picturing floor-to-ceiling windows to capitalize on the lovely ocean views," he described. "Simple but elegant materials - stone, wood, glass. We want it to blend with the natural beauty here."

"That sounds perfect," Adrian agreed enthusiastically. "We can use local timber for the wood elements. Oh, and perhaps a patio or observation deck overlooking the sea!"

"I love that idea," James said, growing more animated as he shared details about his dream workspace. The haunting encounter was forgotten as they bantered back and forth, planning and refining the details.

As they rounded a curve, however, James tensed. A lone figure stood on the road up ahead, half cloaked in shadow. Everything about the stranger radiated menace, from his wicked grin to predatory stance.

Before James could demand who he was, the figure strode forward, leering menacingly through the car window. "Peter will always be with me..." the stranger rasped cryptically, before dissolving into wisps of black smoke.

James jerked back, heart pounding. What had that apparition meant? Some enemy had found him already - someone connected to Peter's past? But no, looking again, the road was empty. There was no sign the ominous stranger had ever been there at all.

Beside him, Adrian looked equally puzzled by the strange encounter. He laid a steadying hand on James' arm. "Are you alright? I'm not sure what we just witnessed, but it clearly unsettled you."

James took a few deep breaths to slow his racing pulse. "I'm fine. It must have been my imagination playing tricks." He quickly changed the subject, not wanting to dwell on the unnerving incident or speculate on its possible meaning.

In truth, he was rattled to the core by the apparition's cryptic words.

Adrian eyed him with concern. James avoided his probing gaze, staring fixedly out at the passing nightscape. He should have known this place might conjure ghosts - both real and imagined. He would need to keep his emotions in tighter check.

They dropped dropped him off at the rental house after their eventful drive along the coast. "Get some rest, my friend," he said. "We'll be in touch soon about moving forward with the building plans."

James bid him goodbye and went inside, still unsettled by the strange encounter on the road.

7

Cornered

Peter

There was an insistent knock at his door. Still groggy, he glanced at the bedside clock - just past seven in the morning. Who could be visiting at this hour?

With a groan, he dragged himself out of the warm cocoon of blankets. Forgoing a shirt, clad only in pajama pants, he shuffled over to open the door.

Peering blearily into the hallway, Peter found it empty. No one lingering outside. Then a glance downward revealed a small package sitting on the floor. Plain brown wrapping paper, his name scribbled across the top in an unfamiliar hand.

Peter picked it up and quickly closed the door. No telling who had left this mysterious delivery.

Back inside his room, he sat on the edge of the mattress and carefully tore open the box. Inside was a single painting. A faded, worn painting of a group of boys, no older than teenagers, playing around a miniature pirate ship made of wood and painted in vibrant colors. One boy, in particular, caught his eye. He had a shock of messy hair, bright eyes that seemed to hold a mischievous glint, and a smile that could melt glaciers.

A strange feeling washed over Peter, a prickling sensation at the base of his skull followed by a sharp, throbbing pain that exploded behind his eyes. He doubled over, clutching his head, as images flooded his mind. Images of himself, younger, laughing with the boy from the photograph, building sandcastles on the beach, exploring hidden coves, secrets whispered between giggles.

Abruptly the vision cleared, leaving Peter breathless and disoriented. Too many questions swirled inside him. Who had sent this puzzling photo? What were they trying to tell him?

Peter's heart raced as he scrutinized the image anew. The smiling boy's features certainly resembled his own, though younger. And awakening those flickers of memories proved a connection existed. This was no mere coincidence - someone knew about his fractured past and was reaching out anonymously. But why the secrecy? What did they want from him?

Glancing at the nondescript packaging yielded no further clues. Frustrated, Peter tossed the box aside and began pacing the room, emotions seesawing between excitement and unease. He'd come to Willowbrook hoping for exactly this - concrete clues to his origins. But its unsettling arrival raised alarms he couldn't ignore.

Peter studied the photo intently, trying in vain to grasp the fleeting memories triggered by the familiar-looking boy's icy blue eyes. But the images evaporated like smoke, leaving him with only a lingering headache in frustration.

Collecting himself with effort, he set the photo aside and made his way to the bathroom on shaky legs. Splashing cold water on his face, Peter met his own eyes in the mirror. What had happened?

Those vivid flashes felt real, like he was truly reliving moments from his missing past. The boy in the picture somehow held answers, he was sure of it. But piecing together the puzzle was maddeningly just out of reach.

After taking a few deep, steadying breaths, Peter changed into comfortable clothes and pocketed his phone. Better to keep busy today to avoid obsessively dwelling on the bizarre delivery.

He texted Lyra, letting her know he was doing alright so far in this odd new town. She'd asked him to check in periodically to appease her worry for him.

Down in the lobby, he greeted Shelby before heading out into the morning sunshine, unsure of his destination. His feet carried him toward the lively downtown area to wander and explore some more.

Soon he found himself outside a cheerful diner named Willow. His growling stomach decided his next stop. Inside, cozy booths lined the windows looking out on the street. A curly-haired waitress waved him over with a friendly smile.

"Welcome! You can sit anywhere you like," she said, handing him a menu. "I'm Gemma, your server. Let me know if you need anything."

Peter chose a table by the window. "Thanks. This is my first time here. What do you recommend for breakfast?"

Gemma's eyes lit up. "Well, welcome to Willowbrook then! Oh, you have to try the cinnamon roll pancakes, our specialty! Our chef makes them from scratch and they're to die for."

The mention of a secret recipe piqued Peter's curiosity. He had always been drawn to anything veiled in mystery, a trait Lyra often teased him about. "Alright," he decided with a grin, "bring me your legendary pancakes then, and a cup of your strongest coffee, please."

"Excellent choice!" Gemma winked and headed off to place his order.

Peter settled into the booth, his gaze drifting out the window. The world outside moved in a blur of activity - people hurrying to work, cars zipping past, leaves swirling in the autumn breeze. He felt a pang of loneliness settle in his chest, a yearning for a connection that went beyond the fleeting interactions of everyday life.

Suddenly, the bell above the diner door chimed, announcing a new arrival. A man, with dark hair that seemed perpetually windswept, walked in, pushing a peculiar contraption - a stroller with a sleek, black cat perched regally inside. Peter couldn't help but chuckle under his breath at the sight. It was such an unexpected, yet strangely charming, combination.

The man greeted Gem, the friendly waitress, with a warm hug. Their easy familiarity spoke of a long-standing bond, a connection that Peter envied. The man then turned, his gaze landing on Peter, and a brief flicker of curiosity crossed his features before he turned back to Gem, their conversation continuing in hushed tones.

A moment later, the man approached Peter's booth, a gentle smile playing on his lips. He parked the cat stroller at a safe distance before sliding into the seat opposite Peter. He seemed younger than Peter by a few years, his features holding a boyish charm that softened the sharp angles of his jawline.

"Hi there," the man greeted, his voice warm and inviting. "I'm Benjamin. You must be new here. I haven't seen you around before."

Peter smiled back, his initial apprehension melting away under Benjamin's friendly demeanor. "I'm Peter," he replied, gesturing towards the cat. "And that, I presume, is your…companion?"

The black cat, seemingly unimpressed by Peter's presence, narrowed its golden eyes and let out a low, disgruntled meow. Benjamin chuckled, the sound rich and full-bodied.

"This grumpy fellow is Jimmy," he said, reaching out to scratch the cat behind the ear. Jimmy, however, remained unimpressed, swatting at Benjamin's hand with a disdainful paw. "Don't mind him," Benjamin continued, amusement dancing in his eyes. "He's just warming up to you."

Peter couldn't help but grin at the image of the dignified feline being described as "warming up." "He certainly seems like a character," he remarked, amusement bubbling in his chest.

"First time visiting Willowbrook?" At Peter's nod, he went on, "It takes some getting used to, but I think you'll find there's something special about this place."

"It does have a certain charm already," Peter agreed. "And everyone's been really friendly so far."

"So, Peter," Benjamin said, leaning back in his chair, "Are you just visiting, or thinking of settling down?"

Peter hesitated. The truth was, he wasn't entirely sure himself. He had come to Willowbrook seeking answers about his past, but the town, and its inhabitants, held an unexpected charm that was starting to weave its way into his heart.

"I... I'm not sure yet," he admitted, his voice laced with uncertainty. "I'm here to explore, to... well, to find myself, I guess."

Benjamin's eyes softened with understanding. "Willowbrook has a way of doing that," he said, his voice tinged with a touch of nostalgia. "It draws people in, makes them feel something they haven't felt before. Many come for a visit, but end up staying for a lifetime."

As their conversation deepened, their food arrived, served by two men who looked remarkably similar to Benjamin, only tinged with the silver of time. They both offered him warm smiles and a quick hug before doting on Jimmy, cooing over the disgruntled feline.

"Benny, you didn't tell us you were bringing a guest!" the shorter man chided playfully, pulling Benjamin into an embrace.

"Aren't you going to introduce us to your new friend?" The other guy said.

"Peter, meet my parents," Benjamin introduced, his voice filled with pride. "Steve and Larry, this is Peter, the new guy in town."

Peter shook their hands, charmed by their exuberance. "Nice to meet you both! You have a wonderful place here."

Steve and Larry, their faces etched with the warmth of countless smiles. "Welcome to Willowbrook, son," Steve boomed, his voice radiating genuine hospitality. "And consider this meal on the house. We own the diner, you see."

Peter blinked, his initial shock quickly replaced by a surge of gratitude. He knew his budget wouldn't sustain daily meals out, and their kind gesture warmed him from the inside out.

"Thank you so much," he stammered, a genuine smile spreading across his face. "That's very generous of you, truly."

"They're always trying to feed people," Benjamin said with an embarrassed but fond grin. "I hope that wasn't too overwhelming."

Larry winked, his eyes crinkling at the corners. "Don't worry about it, son. We take care of our own around here." Their unexpected kindness left Peter a little overwhelmed, but in a pleasant way. The entire town seemed to exude a warmth and friendliness he hadn't encountered before. He decided to roll with it, soaking in this newfound sense of belonging.

As they continued eating, Peter couldn't help but ask, "So, Benjamin, what do you do here in Willowbrook besides stunning everyone with your artistic talent?"

Benjamin chuckled, his eyes twinkling with amusement. "Well, Peter," he began, wiping a stray bit of syrup from his lips, "I actually work at the local library. You know, the one right across the street?"

Peter's eyes widened. The library. It was the perfect starting point for his search, a treasure trove of information waiting to be unearthed. A wave of excitement washed over him, a feeling he hadn't felt in a long time.

"That's perfect!" he exclaimed, a bit too enthusiastically, earning a raised eyebrow from Benjamin. "In fact, I was thinking of heading there after..." he trailed off, realizing the freeloader he might sound like.

Benjamin, however, simply smiled and placed a comforting hand on his arm. "Don't worry about it," he assured him. "I was actually heading there myself. How about we make an afternoon of it? You can ask me all the librarian questions you want, and I can introduce you to the wonderful world of Willowbrook's local history."

"I'd like that very much," he replied, his voice filled with a newfound optimism.

After finishing up at the diner, Benjamin gave him an impromptu tour as they walked to the library. He pointed out landmarks and relayed interesting bits of the town's rich history with infectious enthusiasm. Peter found himself drawn in, imagining this place coming to life decades and centuries past.

They soon arrived at the stately public library. Inside the grand entryway, an elder librarian peered at them over her spectacles.

"Benjamin, welcome back," she greeted warmly. "And who is this newcomer you've brought along?"

"Miss Ethel, meet my new friend Peter," Benjamin introduced. "He's going to be spending some time in Willowbrook."

Miss Ethel gave Peter a smile that radiated kindness. "Wonderful to meet you, dear. Feel free to explore the library to your heart's content while you're here."

"Thank you, that's very generous," Peter replied, already eager to dive into the resources around him.

They ventured deeper into the main rooms, a question that had been nagging Peter slipped out. "Not to look a gift horse in the mouth, but why is everyone so immediately welcoming and generous here? I'm essentially a stranger."

Benjamin's expression shifted almost imperceptibly before smoothing over with a polite smile. "It's simply our way with visitors. Willowbrook has a long tradition of hospitality."

Something in his studiously casual tone gave Peter the sense he was holding something back. But clearly Benjamin didn't feel comfortable elaborating further. "Of course, my mistake," Peter said quickly. "I really do appreciate the kindness."

Benjamin's shoulders relaxed as he continued the tour, now keeping the conversation focused on the library's architecture and contents. Peter paid close attention, while still mulling over the apparent universal desire to accommodate him specifically. Another mystery to file away.

After the overview, Benjamin left him to explore on his own for a while, saying he needed to get some work done. Peter thanked him again for his time and helpful introduction.

Alone, Peter allowed his feet to guide him, senses heightened in this sanctuary of knowledge. He trailed his fingers along the book spines, selecting a few titles on local lore, meditation and harnessing mental energy. Surely he would find something of use about recovering memories or identifying origins.

Settling at a table tucked away in a remote corner, Peter spread out the stack of books, suddenly feeling overwhelmed. Where did he even start in his vast sea of ignorance?

He wished Lyra was here to help him make sense of it all. She had always been his anchor in even the most chaotic times.

With a deep breath, Peter focused on the text in front of him, one passage at a time. He just needed to remain patient and trust the answers would reveal themselves at the right moment. This library likely held many secrets if he knew how and where to look. He would start by decoding whatever clues the books provided, then go from there.

Several hours passed in focused silence as Peter steadily worked through the small stack of books. But none so far revealed anything useful, only vague metaphysical philosophies. Doubts began creeping in that this library gambit had been pointless.

Rubbing his bleary eyes in frustration, Peter was ready to give up for the day. Just then, a meow drew his attention downward.

There was Jimmy, grooming himself a few feet away. As Peter watched, the cat stretched and lazily batted his paw against a lower shelf, as if beckoning him over.

Feeling only slightly foolish, Peter followed as Jimmy led him through the rows to a section on ancient mythology and magical places. With another insistent meow, the cat head-butted one volume until it tumbled from the shelf.

Retrieving the book, Peter inspected it curiously. The title was in an ornate script he didn't recognize, yet somehow the words made instant sense in his mind. As he read them aloud - *"Leabhar na Scáileanna agus na gCosán Caillte."* - the syllables flowed off his tongue, resonating with a long-buried familiarity.

"That's written in Gaelic, the ancient Irish language," came a hushed voice behind Peter, making him startle. He turned to find Benjamin watching him with barely concealed surprise.

Gathering himself, Peter asked tentatively, "Is it rare for people around here to read Gaelic?"

"No one can, Peter." Benjamin confirmed, scrutinizing him closely before seeming to catch himself. "My apologies, you're free to borrow that text if you'd like. Please let me know if you need help interpreting anything."

Peter thanked him, touched by the offer. As he checked his watch, he was shocked to find several hours had passed. The sun was already sinking toward the horizon outside.

Peter tucked the ancient book safely into his bag, his mind swirling with questions. How had he understood the inscription, spoken in a language he'd never encountered before?

Willowbrook seemed to be a place brimming with secrets and

hidden meanings. Bidding farewell to Benjamin and the ever-present Jimmy, he set off towards the inn, his steps echoing on the cobblestone streets bathed in the warm glow of the streetlamps.

His initial curiosity soon gave way to a growing unease. An unsettling feeling, like a prickling sensation at the base of his neck, began to creep in. He couldn't shake the sense of being watched, a pair of unseen eyes following his every move. Each rustle of leaves in the wind, each creak of a weathered signboard, amplified his anxiety.

Glancing back over his shoulder, he caught a glimpse of what appeared to be a large, hulking figure shrouded in the shadows. His heart skipped a beat. Was it just his paranoia, fuelled by the strange events of the day, or was there truly something stalking him?

As he quickened his pace, his breathing becoming ragged, the figure grew clearer. Panic clawed at his throat as he recognized the distinctive outline of a large canine, its eyes glinting in the dim light. It was a wolf, its powerful form stalking him with an unnerving stillness.

Terror surged through him, every instinct screaming at him to run. He sprinted down the deserted street, his legs pumping like pistons, the wolf gaining ground steadily. He could hear its heavy paws pounding the pavement behind him, closing the distance with an alarming speed.

Turning a corner, he found himself trapped, the narrow alleyway ending in a high brick wall. The wolf appeared before him, its imposing size filling his vision. A whimper escaped his lips as he backed away, his back pressed against the cold brick, the feeling of the rough surface a stark contrast to the rising panic within him.

The wolf crouched low, its eyes burning with an unnatural intensity. Peter braced himself for the inevitable attack, his hands instinctively raised in a futile attempt to shield himself. He squeezed his eyes shut, awaiting the sharp bite and the searing pain that would follow.

But it never came.

He cracked open an eye, blinking away the tears of fear that welled up. The alleyway was empty. The wolf, the source of his terror, was gone. Had it been… an illusion? He looked around frantically, his breath coming out in ragged gasps. Relief flooded his system, leaving him weak and trembling.

"Peter?" A voice startled him. He turned to see Benjamin standing at the entrance of the alleyway, his brow furrowed in concern.

"Are you alright?" Benjamin asked, his voice laced with worry.

"I… I thought I saw a wolf," Peter stammered, his voice barely a whisper. "It was right here, but… it's gone now."

Benjamin looked around the empty alleyway, his expression unreadable. "There's no wolf, Peter," he said gently. "There never was."

Peter stared at him, bewildered. Was he hallucinating? Had the stress and the strangeness of the day finally gotten to him? But the terror he had felt, the image of the wolf, it all felt so real.

"Are you sure?" Peter asked, his voice barely above a whisper.

Benjamin gave him a reassuring smile. "Positive," he said. "Why don't we get you back to your room? You look like you could use some rest."

Peter nodded, his mind still reeling from the encounter. As they walked back, he couldn't shake the feeling that something wasn't right. The wolf, the ancient book, the unsettling feeling of being watched – it all felt like pieces of a puzzle he couldn't quite grasp.

Reaching the inn, Peter turned to Benjamin, his voice filled with lingering uncertainty. "Thank you," he said, his words carrying the weight of his unspoken fear. "For everything."

Benjamin squeezed his shoulder gently. "Don't worry about it," he said, his smile warm and understanding. "Get some rest, Peter. And tomorrow, perhaps we can discuss these… visions of yours in more detail."

Peter nodded, unsure whether he was comforted or even more confused. He retreated to his room, the image of the wolf seared into his mind, a chilling reminder of the mysteries and dangers that lurked beneath the surface of this seemingly idyllic town.

72

8

Shadows and Doubts

James

James watched from the shadows as Peter exited the library, looking troubled. What had shaken him up this time?

He wanted to rush over and comfort him, but he held back. Revealing himself now would only alarm Peter, especially in his rattled state.

Peter hurried down the street, head down, nearly knocking over an elderly woman in his haste. He stammered an apology before breaking into a run. James' protective instincts ignited. Something had clearly spooked Peter. He moved to follow when a dark shape darted out from an alley ahead.

A massive black wolf with burning red eyes stalked toward Peter, its lips curled in a vicious snarl. Peter stumbled backward with a cry, pale with terror. James reacted on instinct, hand raised to summon his magic, but he paused. Using his powers would expose him.

Before James could intervene, the beast charged. Peter collapsed to the ground, arms shielding his head. Just as the wolf was about to strike, a brilliant flash of blue light erupted between them, throwing

73

the creature back with a pained yelp.

Benjamin stood there, arm extended, a glowing quill-shaped staff in his hand. With elegant sweeps of his staff, he warded the dazed wolf away until it retreated into the shadows. James let out a breath he hadn't realized he was holding, awed by the display of power and grateful for the intervention. Benjamin was clearly no mere librarian.

"Peter! Are you alright?" Benjamin helped the shaken young man to his feet. Peter nodded mutely, still stunned.

"Let's get you back to the Dreamery. We'll be safe there." Benjamin kept a protective hand on Peter's back as he guided him away. James hesitated, then stealthily followed at a distance, needing to ensure Peter's well-being.

Once the pair entered the cozy inn, James lingered nearby, concealed beneath a glamour spell. After a few moments, Benjamin stepped back outside alone, turning sharply in James' direction.

"You can show yourself now. I know you're out there."

James canceled the glamour, slowly emerging from the shadows. Benjamin eyed him warily.

"I mean no harm," James said gently. "I only want to help him."

Benjamin considered him a moment before replying. "We shouldn't talk here. Meet me at Glimmer in one hour." Before James could respond, Benjamin slipped back inside.

James paced the streets aimlessly until it was time, thoughts swirling.

At last, James arrived at Glimmer's, a cozy bakery nestled amongst the shops. The sugary scents of frosting and cinnamon enveloped him as he stepped inside. Benjamin waved him over to a table tucked in the back corner.

After they ordered tea and pastries, an awkward silence fell between them. James cleared his throat. "I know you're wary of me, but I mean no ill will, I assure you."

Benjamin nodded slowly, looking thoughtful. Before he could

respond, the bakery's bell chimed cheerfully as Dominic bustled over to their table.

"Here are your treats, gents. Cinnamon roll for James and a slice of our famous triple chocolate delight for Ben." Dominic placed the plates down with a wink. He then pulled up a chair to join them.

"I'm closing up early today with all this peculiar fog rolling in. Figured I'd keep you two company."

James studied the merry-faced man as he and Benjamin chatted. Another potential ally for Peter, it seemed. Dominic possessed an insightful nature. The more support Peter had, the better.

After Dominic headed off to close up the bakery, leaving just the three of them, James turned to Benjamin. "What exactly happened after Peter left the library earlier? He seemed quite shaken."

Benjamin nodded gravely. "Yes, I sensed something was wrong and went to find him. Jimmy warned me as well." He gestured to the cat, who had settled on the table, observing the two humans intently.

"Jimmy?" James raised an eyebrow.

Right on cue, the cat's eyes locked onto James' own. A deep, distinctly human like voice came out of Jimmy. "Peter was in danger. My mystical senses detected a dark presence approaching."

James stared, dumbfounded that this feline was communicating with him perfect diction. He collected himself enough to respond weakly. "You…you speak?"

Jimmy flicked his tail, looking amused. "Obviously. I am no ordinary cat, as you can see. I have been helping guide Benjamin in his duties here."

James shook his head in wonderment. Willowbrook was truly a place of magic if even the animals conversed so eloquently.

Jimmy continued seriously, "Something sinister forced Peter to flee the library in terror. Thankfully, Benjamin intervened, but it is clear the forces threatening the boy are growing stronger."

James gripped the table edge, anxiety rising. "Do you know precisely what he encountered?"

Benjamin shook his head. "I arrived only in time to protect Peter from a giant black wolf. But other dark forces surely lurk here too."

James' mind raced, imagining Peter utterly alone and terrified, fleeing that vicious beast. He should have stayed closer. He turned to Jimmy and collected himself. "Please, tell me everything you know. I only want to keep him safe."

Jimmy nodded. "Noble of you. As I said, an ancient darkness stirs here, drawn by the power Peter possesses, though it still lies buried. His magic begins to reawaken."

James' pulse spiked. "His magic is returning?"

"Gradually, yes. Your arrival, this town - it is eroding the blocks on his mind and magic. But this leaves him vulnerable to those who would exploit him."

James' hands curled into anxious fists. How he wished he could simply wave away the sinister forces threatening sweet, gentle Peter.

But Jimmy was already shaking his furry head. "It cannot be rushed. Patience and care are vital. The process has begun - guide it, but gently."

James forced himself to take a calming breath. "You're right, of course. His well-being comes first."

Jimmy gave an approving purr. "You are a loyal friend to him. Stay by his side through the trials ahead." His gaze took on a faraway look. "Strange days are dawning…"

A heavy silence fell. James' mind churned with questions. How much did the cat truly know about Peter's past, their connection? Sensing his curiosity, Jimmy refocused on him.

"Peter's mind remains shrouded, but light peeks through. He could read the Gaelic text - a promising sign. In time, as he finds answers here, clarity will come."

James' heart quickened. "So being in Willowbrook does help restore his memory?"

"It balances his energies. This place has a way on unraveling curses it seems like." Jimmy tilted his head thoughtfully. "Yes…your shared history is will come in handy in time and I could sense that you two have a really strong connection."

James leaned forward eagerly. "What do you mean?"

But Jimmy stood and stretched lazily. "All shall be revealed soon enough. For now, be patient. Guard him, guide him." He blinked his burning green eyes knowingly. "When the time comes, you'll know what to do."

"I know you have many questions. But Jimmy speaks truth - pushing too hard could damage Peter further. Stay close to him for now."

James wrestled down his rising frustration. Every protective instinct screamed at him to take action, find definitive answers. But he respected these kindred spirits who only wanted to help Peter heal.

"Very well," he conceded softly. "I will walk this path as you advise, even if the way forward remains unclear."

Dominic, who had been listening intently, spoke up. "If you don't mind me asking, Jimmy - how do you know so much about these mystical forces in our town?"

Jimmy glanced at him, eyes glinting. "As a Guardian of the Realms, it is my duty to monitor the balance of energies between worlds. This town has long been a crossover point."

James tensed in surprise. Guardians were the stuff of myths - yet here was a flesh-and-blood one, albeit feline.

"A Guardian, here in Willowbrook! Who would have thought?" James said in surprise.

Jimmy preened under the attention. "Yes, well, I try to maintain a low profile normally. But circumstances required I take a more active role guiding Benjamin."

"And helping Peter, it seems," Benjamin added. "We're fortunate for your wisdom."

Jimmy nodded before fixing James with an intense stare. "Now it falls to you, James, to take the next step. The time has come to properly reunite with Peter."

James' mouth went dry. The prospect of facing Peter, seeing no recognition in those gentle eyes, twisted his heart. But Jimmy was right - continued avoidance would not help.

"You're certain it is time?" he asked quietly. "What if I only cause him more distress?"

Jimmy's gaze softened slightly. "Your paths crossing again was inevitable. Have faith in your bond. It persists beneath his confusion." When James still hesitated, Jimmy sighed. "Honestly, you must get over this nervous fretting! Reveal yourself before the poor man thinks he's going mad."

James flushed, chagrined. Clearly he was being overcautious. "Point taken. I suppose I must simply trust in what we once shared."

Benjamin smiled encouragingly. "It will go smoothly, you'll see. We'll be right here for you both."

Bolstered, James took a steadying breath. "Very well. I shall seek him out tomorrow and try jogging his memory."

"Excellent. Oh, and do take that stick out of your behind while you're at it," Jimmy added cheekily. "He prefers your more relaxed side."

James coughed, caught between amusement and embarrassment at the cat's audacity. Perhaps he had been too somber since arriving. If Peter responded better to lightheartedness, he would oblige.

Eager to move forward, Benjamin suggested, "I've had an idea, actually. The Summer Solstice festival is soon. You two could volunteer together - give you plenty of time to interact while keeping Peter's mind occupied."

James brightened. "A marvelous plan. The cheerful atmosphere may soften his unease around me until memories resurface."

"Precisely," Benjamin agreed.

Jimmy nodded approvingly. "Then it's settled. Now go prepare what you'll say to him. And for heaven's sake, unwind a little! He'll sense your tension."

James nodded, though his brow furrowed with uncertainty. "I shall do my best. But establishing the business here is also demanding of my time."

Benjamin waved a hand reassuringly. "Let me handle things on that front. You focus on reconnecting with Peter."

"I can help convince Peter to volunteer too," Dominic added with a wink. "Just leave it to me."

James felt a swell of gratitude for his new allies. "Thank you, truly. I would be lost without your guidance."

After finalizing plans, James bid them goodnight and retired to his room at the rental. But sleep eluded him as worries swirled endlessly. What if Peter rejected him outright? Or worse, what if James' presence caused a setback in his recovery?

Restless, James stepped out onto his moonlit balcony for fresh air. The mist had cleared to reveal glittering stars, casting dark shadows across the garden below. James leaned upon the railing, heart heavy. Peter was so close now, yet still agonizingly out of reach.

James' thoughts spiraled back through the years, laden with regret. He should have defied everyone and stayed by Peter's side, no matter the cost. Instead, he had been a coward, leaving Peter to contend with controlling forces. And Peter had paid the price, stripped of memories and power.

Hot shame washed over James. He had failed the person who needed him most. Consumed by his own interests, blinded by toxic ambitions, he had missed all the signs of Peter's imprisonment and suffering.

Until it was too late.

By the time James escaped his family's clutches to search for his lost friend, the damage had been done. Peter was gone, fate unknown. James had scoured every corner of every realm since, but the search was vain. Until fate guided them both here, to the mortal realm.

Yet now that Peter was within reach, doubt paralyzed James. Did he even deserve a second chance, after such betrayal? Peter likely saw him as a stranger now. James' selfish choices had cost them everything.

As James agonized over his mistakes, a knock sounded at his door. He slipped on a robe and opened it to find Simon standing there, brow furrowed in concern.

"James, I heard about the attack on Peter today. Is he alright?"

James waved him inside wearily. "He's shaken but unharmed, thankfully. Benjamin drove the beast off before it could hurt him."

Simon let out a relieved breath as they sat. "Good, good. This town certainly has its share of strangeness." He peered at James. "But you seem troubled yourself. What's wrong?"

James debated how much to confess. He and Simon had been friends for years, but James had always kept his tangled history with Peter secret. But the time for full truth was approaching...

"Just worried for him," James said evasively.

Simon nodded. "Any idea who's behind it all?" At James' silence, Simon studied him a moment before asking gently, "James, what aren't you telling me? I know there's more going on here."

James hesitated, then slumped with a sigh, tension draining from his shoulders. "You're right. There are things about my past with Peter that I've concealed from everyone, even you. But it's time I fully explain."

Simon listened intently as James revealed the painful history - his and Peter's hidden magical realm, their once unbreakable bond, the controlling forces that had ripped them violently apart.

"I left him at the mercy of those who sought to use him," James confessed bitterly. "Now his mind and magic are damaged, and I must make amends."

He trailed off, dreading Simon's reaction, but his friend reached out and grasped his hand firmly. "I cannot imagine how difficult this has been for you both. But the past is done - all you can do is prove your devotion from here onward."

James's throat tightened with emotion. However would he have managed this without a loyal friend by his side?

"Thank you for understanding," he rasped. "I aim to protect him now, whatever it takes."

Simon smiled. "You won't have to do it alone. I'm here for you both." He squeezed James' hand. "Now, tell me everything I should know about these forces threatening him."

James paused, considering, before asking "First, would you mind telling me where you disappeared to so early today? You were already gone when I woke."

Simon looked hesitant. "I went to consult with someone who might help us understand what's happening here." At James' questioning look, he sighed. "I spoke with Wanda."

James tensed at the name. Wanda had been a mortal girl Peter brought to their magical realm long ago after she'd accidentally witnessed supernatural events. When her own latent power awakened, she'd become obsessed with learning more.

In particular, she'd developed an unhealthy fascination with Peter, drawn to his immense magical abilities. James had never trusted her underlying motives.

"Wanda?" James repeated tightly. "Did she give any useful insight?"

"Possibly. She seemed very interested that Peter was here and was eager to see him again." Simon quickly continued at James' scowl, "But I was careful not to reveal anything too sensitive!"

James forced himself to remain calm. As much as he disliked Wanda, she did possess her own magical knowledge. "Let's hear what she said then."

"Well, she wasn't surprised dark forces would pursue Peter, given how powerful he is," Simon explained. "She warned his latent magic reawakening could attract dangerous attention." When James stayed silent, Simon went on, "I know you dislike Wanda. But she just wants to help keep Peter safe. She cares for him."

James couldn't help a derisive laugh. "Oh yes, I know exactly what Wanda wants from him." At Simon's surprised look, he elaborated, "She desires Peter only for his power, nothing more. She manipulates her way into his heart, preying on his kindness."

Simon shifted uneasily. "Surely you misjudge her. She seems genuinely concerned for his well-being."

James' response was sharp. "Because his abilities fuel her own! She exploits his vulnerabilities." He took a breath, willing calm. "Just be cautious what you reveal to her about Peter or his returning magic."

"James, she cares for you too. Is she really so untrustworthy?" Simon asked quietly.

James bristled, anger flaring in his chest. "You know how little I've ever trusted her, yet you went behind my back?"

Simon held up his hands placatingly. "Please, hear me out. I know you dislike Wanda, but she does care for Peter. She could have insights to help us."

"Help Peter, or help herself to his power?" James snapped back. "She is obsessed with him for her own benefit!"

"James, calm yourself," Simon urged gently. "I know you feel protective of him, but lashing out will not help. Let's discuss this rationally."

James took a deep breath, clenching his fists and willing himself to relax. Simon was right - he needed to control his temper.

Finally, he ground out, "I apologize for my anger. But you know why I distrust her. Why seek Wanda out now?"

Simon hesitated before saying carefully, "Peter may have confided things in her that he did not share with anyone else."

James went very still, a cold knot forming in his stomach. The thought of Peter trusting that manipulative woman over him…it cut deeply.

"Explain, please," he managed tightly.

"Well…you and Peter were separated. He may have felt comfortable opening up to her in ways he didn't with others," Simon said helplessly. "I only want us to have as much information as possible to help him."

Logical perhaps, but the idea still stung. James had left Peter vulnerable and unsupported. He had no one but himself to blame for driving his love to find solace with someone so cunning as Wanda.

James closed his eyes, fighting back the ache in his chest. He drew in a quavering breath before replying hoarsely, "You may be right. I failed him, so he turned to those he should not have in my absence."

Simon gripped his shoulder firmly. "Do not torture yourself. Focus on what lies ahead, not past regrets."

James placed his hand over Simon's, taking comfort from the supportive touch. "You are a true friend. I shall take your advice and not allow jealousy or bitterness to guide me."

He opened his eyes, resolve renewed. "Please, just promise me you will exercise caution around Wanda. I do not believe she wishes any harm upon Peter, but her ambition makes her dangerous."

Simon nodded solemnly. "You have my word. I will keep any details about Peter or his returning power to myself."

James managed a small, grateful smile. "Thank you. That is all I ask."

He stood then, needing to move, to release the last remnants of turmoil still coiled within him. Tomorrow's meeting could not come soon enough.

As if reading his mind, Simon said bracingly, "Get some rest now. You've got a reunion to prepare for."

James walked him to the door, spirits lifting once more. With so much uncertainty ahead, he could not afford to dwell on past regrets or jealousies. He had to trust in the devotion he and Peter had once shared, and believe it could be rekindled.

Simon left James with an encouraging squeeze of his shoulder. As he readied for bed, James focused on remembering the joy he'd once felt in Peter's presence. That blissful emotion waited for them again over the horizon. He needed only to remain fixed upon that bright beacon of hope to guide him there.

The shadows of the past could not be outrun, but the light of their future still beckoned. James would follow it faithfully, wherever it led.

9

Some Light And Then Some…

Peter

Peter sat cross-legged under the spreading branches of an ancient oak tree in Willowbrook Park, the weathered Gaelic text open on his lap. He traced a finger along the cryptic symbols, brow furrowed in concentration. The ink seemed to shimmer faintly at his touch, sending a tingling warmth up his arm.

"What secrets are you hiding?" he murmured, squinting at the archaic lettering. The words danced teasingly before his eyes, always remaining just out of reach of his understanding. He sighed, running a hand through his tousled hair. Every page he deciphered seemed to lead only to more questions.

As he thumbed carefully through the brittle pages, a shadow fell across the book. Peter glanced up, startled, to see Dominic standing over him with a strained smile. The normally unflappable baker had a smudge of flour on his ruddy cheek and his apron was askew.

"Peter! Thank the heavens I found you. The festival preparations have sent the bakery into absolute chaos. I desperately need an extra pair of hands if you're willing." Dominic's eyes were pleading.

Peter hesitated for a beat, his gaze darting back to the perplexing text. The mysteries it contained pulled at him like a magnetic force. But the naked desperation on Dominic's face tugged at his heartstrings. The kind baker had welcomed him warmly to Willowbrook, always ready with a pastry and a smile.

"Of course, I'd be happy to help," Peter said, snapping the book shut decisively and standing up. Unraveling the secrets of his forgotten life could wait a few hours. "Lead the way, boss."

Relief washed over Dominic's face. "You're a lifesaver, Peter. I owe you one."

As they walked briskly towards the bakery in companionable silence, Peter's thoughts wandered treacherously back to the strange visions that had been plaguing him with increasing frequency - fragmentary glimpses of an otherworldly life, of magic thrumming in his veins, of a dark-haired man with piercing blue eyes...

He shook his head firmly, banishing the unsettling images. He had a job to do, a chance to lose himself in the comforting mundanity of flour and sugar and yeast. Baking was a blissfully uncomplicated alchemy compared to the esoteric secrets lurking in ancient tomes.

The bakery was a hive of barely controlled chaos. Baking sheets clattered, timers shrilled and the air was thick with the mouthwatering aromas of cinnamon, vanilla and caramelized sugar. Dominic tossed Peter an apron with a harried grin.

"Welcome to the madhouse. You're on muffin duty - blueberry and chocolate chip. Oven's already preheated." He clapped Peter on the shoulder before dashing off to rescue a tray of scones.

Peter took a deep, fortifying breath, inhaling the homey bakery scents. This, at least, felt solid and real beneath his hands, not like the chimerical tatters of memory that blew like wisps of smoke through his mind.

He threw himself into the work, measuring flour and sugar, cracking eggs and folding in plump berries and chocolate morsels with single-minded focus just like what Dominic thought him on his first day here. There was a soothing rhythm to it, a predictable chemistry. Cause and effect. Nothing like the maddening enigmas that dogged his every step.

Time blurred as he lost himself in the hum and bustle of the kitchen. Muffin after muffin slid into the oven and emerged golden-brown and picture-perfect, ready for the festival-goers.

As he slid the last tray onto the cooling rack, a wave of exhaustion hit him. He slumped against the counter, suddenly feeling the weight of all the questions he carried.

Dominic materialized at his elbow with a knowing look, pressing a steaming mug into his hands. "You looked like you could use this. It's my special blend - chamomile, honey, and just a touch of magic."

Peter laughed softly, cradling the warm ceramic. "Magic, huh? Feels like that's all there is in this town sometimes."

"You're not wrong," Dominic chuckled wryly. "But it's not all ancient curses and ominous prophecies, you know. Magic can be as simple as a perfectly baked muffin or a cup of tea made with love." He smiled gently at Peter. "I don't know what burdens you're carrying, but I've seen how the weight of them bows your shoulders. Just remember, you don't have to carry them alone. Willowbrook looks after its own."

Unexpected tears pricked at Peter's eyes. He blinked them back, returning Dominic's smile tremulously. "Thanks, Dom. For the tea and the talk. And for letting me make a mess of your kitchen."

"Anytime, my friend. Anytime."

As he sipped the fragrant, subtly spiced tea, Peter felt some of the tension unknot from his shoulders. Dominic was right - magic didn't have to be a looming, abstract threat. It could be as tangible as flour-dusted hands and the simple kindness of a shared cup on a trying day.

Peter fell into an easy rhythm working alongside Dominic, the physical labor a welcome respite from the ceaseless whirring of his thoughts. As they slid the last batch of muffins into the oven, Dominic turned to him with a considering look.

"You know, Peter, you're a natural at this. Have you finally considered working here?"

Peter laughed, dusting flour from his hands. "Honestly, I haven't had the time lately and I promise that I would think about it more."

Dominic nodded thoughtfully. "Well, I've been thinking. We could really use an extra set of hands around here on a more regular basis. Would you be interested?"

Peter's heart leapt at the offer, but he hesitated, old fears and uncertainties rising up to choke him. "I…I don't know, Dom. Like I told you before, I'm not sure I should commit to anything long-term right now. There's so much I still don't understand about myself, about my past… And besides, I still have my job back in New York."

Dominic laid a comforting hand on his shoulder. "Hey, it's okay. I get it. You can take it one day at a time, alright? No pressure."

Peter managed a grateful smile. "Thanks, Dom. I appreciate that."

"Of course. And while we're on the subject of temporary commitments…" Dominic grinned mischievously. "How would you feel about helping out with our booth at the Summer Solstice festival? It's just for a couple of days, and I have a feeling you'll be a hit with the customers."

Peter's pulse quickened at the mention of the festival. It would be the perfect opportunity to spend more time with James, to try to piece together the fragments of their shared history. He nodded slowly, a matching grin spreading across his face.

"You know what? I'm in. Sign me up for the festival gig."

Dominic clapped him on the back, beaming. "Excellent! I promise, it'll be a blast. Now, let's get these beauties out of the oven and ready for the display case. We need to feed the hungry volunteers."

They fell back into their easy camaraderie, trading jokes and stories as they arranged the fresh-baked treats. Peter felt a warm glow of contentment suffusing him. For the first time since he'd arrived in Willowbrook, he felt like he was part of something, like he belonged.

As the afternoon wore on, Dominic dispatched Peter to the storeroom to retrieve more supplies. Peter pushed open the heavy wooden door, fumbling for the light switch in the dim, dusty space.

As his hand brushed the wall, he felt a sudden, searing cold. He jerked his hand back with a gasp, staring in horror as tendrils of shadow seemed to coil around his fingers, merging with his flesh.

"What the hell?" he whispered, his heart hammering against his ribs. He shook his hand frantically, willing the darkness to dissipate. Slowly, the shadows receded, leaving his skin tingling and icy.

Peter stumbled back against the shelves, his breath coming in shallow pants. He took a deep, shuddering breath, trying to calm his racing thoughts. He couldn't let Dominic see him like this. Peter grabbed the supplies with shaking hands and made his way back to the front of the bakery, pasting on a smile that felt brittle around the edges.

Dominic glanced up as he emerged, his brow creasing in concern. "You alright, Peter? You look a little pale."

Peter waved off his worry with a forced laugh. "Yeah, fine. Just got a little lost in thought back there. You know me, always got my head in the clouds."

Dominic chuckled, shaking his head. "Ah, the curse of the dreamer. Well, don't let those clouds carry you too far away. We've got work to do."

Peter nodded, throwing himself back into the comforting routine of the bakery. The festival preparations were in full swing, and he and Dominic had volunteered to help feed the army of workers transforming the town square into a magical wonderland.

As they navigated the controlled chaos of the festival grounds, Peter's mind buzzed with anticipation. Every banner hung, every lantern strung brought him one step closer to unraveling the mysteries that haunted him.

Lost in thought, Peter didn't notice the figure rounding the corner until it was too late. He collided with a solid wall of muscle, stumbling back with a startled "oof!"

Strong hands gripped his shoulders, steadying him. "Whoa there, you okay?"

Peter's head snapped up at the familiar voice, his heart stuttering in his chest. "James! I...yeah, I'm fine. Just wasn't watching where I was going."

James grinned down at him, his blue eyes crinkling at the corners. "Well, I can't say I mind being run into by you. It's a pleasant surprise."

Peter felt a blush creeping up his neck. He took a step back, trying to regain his composure. "What are you doing here? Not that it's not great to see you, I just didn't expect..."

James chuckled, running a hand through his dark hair. "I'm actually here as a favor to a friend. They needed some help setting up their stall, and I figured I might as well pitch in with the rest of the preparations while I'm at it."

Peter nodded, a smile tugging at his lips. "That's really nice of you. I'm here with Dominic, helping to feed the volunteers. Speaking of which..." He glanced over his shoulder to where Dominic was waiting patiently, an amused expression on his face.

"Go on," Dominic said with a knowing smile. "I can handle the food for a bit. You two catch up."

Peter shot him a grateful look before turning back to James. "Looks like I've been granted a temporary reprieve. Want to give me a hand with some of these decorations?"

James' face lit up. "I'd love to."

As they worked side by side, stringing fairy lights and arranging garlands of summer flowers, Peter felt a sense of rightness settle over him. There was an easy rhythm to their conversation, a natural ebb and flow that felt both new and achingly familiar.

"You know," Peter said as he struggled to untangle a strand of lights, "I've been having the strangest experiences lately. Ever since I arrived in Willowbrook, actually."

James glanced at him, something unreadable flickering in his eyes. "Oh? Like what?"

Peter hesitated, wondering how much to reveal. But something about James' steady presence, the warmth of his gaze, made him feel safe. Understood.

"Visions, I guess you could call them. Flashes of another life, another...me. And then there was this moment in the bakery storeroom..." He trailed off, shaking his head. "You're going to think I'm crazy."

"I don't think you're crazy," James said softly when Peter had finished. "I think... I think there's a lot about this world, about yourself, that you're just beginning to understand."

Peter searched his face, looking for any hint of mockery or disbelief. But all he saw was earnest understanding and a flicker of what might have been recognition.

"You talk as if you know something about all this," Peter said slowly. "About me."

James dropped his gaze, a muscle ticking in his jaw. "I... It's complicated, Peter. There are things I want to tell you, things you deserve to know. But the time isn't right. Not yet."

Peter's brow furrowed as he studied James' face, trying to decipher the cryptic words. "What do you mean, James? What things do I deserve to know?"

James shook his head, a pained expression flitting across his features.

"I... I shouldn't have said anything. Please, just forget I mentioned it."

But Peter couldn't let it go. The questions that had haunted him for so long were too close to the surface, the yearning for answers too strong. "James, please. If you know something about my past, about who I am... I need to know."

James closed his eyes, taking a deep breath as if steeling himself. When he opened them again, there was a new resolve in his gaze, tinged with regret. "Peter, I care about you. More than you know. And because of that, I have to ask you to trust me when I say that now is not the time for those revelations."

Peter's heart clenched at the raw emotion in James' voice. He could see the internal battle raging behind those blue eyes, the desperate desire to share warring with a deeper, more primal need to protect.

"I do trust you," Peter said softly, his hand still resting on James' arm. "But I'm tired of living in the shadows of my own mind. I'm tired of not knowing who I am or where I come from."

James placed his hand over Peter's, his touch warm and steadying. "I know. And I promise you, when the time is right, when it's safe... I'll tell you everything. But for now, I need you to hold on just a little longer. Can you do that for me?"

Peter searched James' face, seeing the pleading sincerity etched in every line. He wanted to push, to demand the truth that hovered just out of reach. But something in James' expression, in the tender way he held Peter's hand, made him pause.

"Okay," he said at last, the word a soft exhalation. "I'll wait. For you."

Relief and gratitude washed over James' face. He squeezed Peter's hand once before letting go, the loss of contact leaving Peter feeling strangely bereft.

James covered Peter's hand with his own, squeezing gently. "Thank you. For understanding, for... for being you."

Peter's heart swelled, a lump forming in his throat. In that moment, he knew with bone-deep certainty that whatever trials lay ahead, whatever secrets the Summer Solstice held, he wouldn't face them alone. He had James, and that was enough.

They turned back to their work, the air between them charged with unspoken emotions. As they hung the last of the decorations, their hands brushed, sending a jolt of electricity up Peter's arm.

He glanced at James, seeing his own longing mirrored in those ocean-blue eyes. For a heartbeat, the rest of the world fell away, leaving only the two of them, poised on the brink of something vast and inevitable.

Then Dominic's voice cut through the moment, shattering the spell. "Peter! James! The food's ready, come and get it before this lot devours it all!"

Peter stepped back, a rueful laugh escaping him. "Duty calls, I guess."

James grinned, the tension broken. "Can't let the hungry hordes go unsatisfied. Lead the way."

As they made their way back to the food stall, shoulders brushing with every step, Peter felt a new sense of camaraderie and connection with James. It was as if the shared experience of decorating and their heartfelt conversation had forged an unbreakable bond between them.

Throughout the day, as they worked side by side to prepare for the festival, that bond only seemed to grow stronger. Peter found himself marveling at the way James seemed to anticipate his every need and movement, handing him a hammer before he could ask or steadying a ladder without prompting.

"It's almost like we've done this before," Peter remarked with a laugh as James passed him a string of lanterns, their fingers brushing in the process. "Like we're some kind of festival preparation dream team."

James chuckled, a knowing glint in his eye. "Maybe we were in another life. Or maybe we're just naturally in sync."

Peter's heart skipped a beat at the implication, at the tantalizing possibility of a shared history he couldn't remember. But before he could dwell on it, a booming voice interrupted his thoughts.

"Well, well, if it isn't my two favorite workers!" Benjamin strode towards them, his broad face split in a grin. "I hope you lads are ready for a break, because we've got a feast fit for kings waiting for you."

Peter's stomach growled on cue, reminding him that he hadn't eaten since the muffins he'd sneaked at the bakery. "Lead the way, good sir. We humble laborers are at your mercy."

Benjamin laughed, clapping Peter on the back with enough force to make him stumble. "That's the spirit! Come on, Dominic's outdone himself this time. You won't believe the spread he's put together."

As they followed Benjamin to the food stall, Peter couldn't help but marvel at the sense of community and camaraderie that suffused the festival grounds. Everywhere he looked, people were laughing, joking, working together with a shared sense of purpose and joy.

"It's something special, isn't it?" James murmured, as if reading his thoughts. "The way this town comes together, the way everyone looks out for each other."

Peter nodded, feeling a lump form in his throat. "It is. It's... it's everything I never knew I was missing."

James placed a hand on his shoulder, the touch both comforting and electrifying. "Well, you're a part of it now, Peter."

The words wrapped around Peter's heart like a warm embrace, filling a void he hadn't even known existed. As they reached the food stall and were greeted by Dominic's beaming face, he felt a sense of belonging wash over him, as tangible as the summer breeze on his skin.

The rest of the day passed in a blur of laughter, hard work, and the kind of easy companionship that felt like coming home. Peter found himself trading jokes with Benjamin as they hung streamers, learning the finer points of pie crust from Dominic, and always, always gravitating back to James' side.

As the laughter and chatter swirled around them, James leaned in close, his breath warm against Peter's ear. "I don't want this day to end. But I know it's just the beginning of something amazing."

Peter turned to meet his gaze, seeing the promise of a shared future reflected in those ocean-blue eyes. "Then let's make sure it's a beginning we'll never forget."

James squeezed his hand, a silent affirmation. "You can count on it."

And with that, they let themselves be swept up in the joy and camaraderie of the moment, the bond between them a shining thread woven through the tapestry of the festival.

As the day drew to a close and the happy crowd began to disperse, James pulled Peter aside, a nervous energy thrumming through his body. "Peter, I… I know we still have so much to do for the Summer Solstice. There's decorations to finish, stalls to set up, a million and one details to attend to."

Peter nodded, his brow furrowing slightly. "Of course. We'll tackle it together, just like we did today."

James took a deep breath, as if steeling himself for something momentous. "That's just it. I don't want to do this, any of this, without you. Not just the festival preparations, but… but everything."

Peter's heart began to race, hope and trepidation warring in his chest. "What are you saying, James?"

James reached out, taking both of Peter's hands in his own. "I'm saying that I want you by my side, Peter. Not just as a friend or a festival co-worker, but as… as something more."

Peter's breath caught in his throat, the world narrowing down to the earnest, hopeful expression on James' face. "Are you… are you asking me out?"

James laughed softly, a blush staining his cheeks. "I guess I am. I know it's fast, and there's still so much we don't know about each other, about your past. But I also know that I haven't felt this way about anyone in… in longer than I can remember."

Peter's heart felt like it might burst from his chest, a kaleidoscope of emotions swirling through him. Joy, fear, excitement, and above all, an overwhelming sense of rightness.

"James, I… I feel the same way. I don't know what the future holds, but I know I want you in it. By my side, hand in hand, facing whatever comes our way."

10

Mementos

James

He paced the length of his room, his footsteps echoing on the hardwood floor. The events of the day kept replaying in his mind, a whirlwind of emotions and doubts threatening to sweep him away.

"I can't believe I asked him out," he muttered, running a hand through his hair. "What was I thinking?"

He sank down onto the edge of his bed, head in his hands. The moment had felt so right, so perfect. Peter's hand in his, the sparkle in those eyes, the promise of a shared future stretching out before them.

But now, in the cold light of doubt, James couldn't shake the feeling that he'd made a terrible mistake. He'd let his heart override his head, let his longing for the connection they once shared cloud his judgment.

And then there was the slip-up, that careless mention of Peter's past. James groaned, flopping back onto the bed. He'd seen the flicker of curiosity in Peter's eyes, the unspoken questions hanging in the air between them.

"Idiot," he berated himself. "You just had to go and open your big mouth."

He knew it was only a matter of time before that little hint came back to bite him. Peter was too clever, too determined, to let something like that go. And when he started digging, when he started unraveling the secrets James had been so careful to keep.

James shuddered, pushing the thought away. He couldn't bear to imagine the betrayal on Peter's face, the hurt and anger that would surely follow.

A knock at the door startled him from his spiraling thoughts. He sat up, taking a deep breath to compose himself before calling out, "Come in."

The door creaked open, revealing the concerned faces of Benjamin and Dominic. Simon trailed behind them, a knowing look in his eyes.

"We thought we might find you here," Benjamin said, stepping into the room. "Figured you might need some company after."

James chuckled humorlessly. "That's one way to put it."

Dominic perched on the edge of the desk, fixing James with a sympathetic look. "Want to talk about it?"

James sighed, running a hand over his face. "I don't even know where to start. I just... I can't believe I asked him out like that. What if he only said yes because he felt obligated? Because he thinks I'm his only friend in this town?"

"James," Simon said gently, taking a seat beside him on the bed. "Anyone with eyes can see that Peter cares for you. Deeply. That kind of connection doesn't come from obligation or pity."

James shook his head, unconvinced. "But what if I'm reading too much into it? What if I'm just projecting my own feelings onto him?"

Benjamin snorted, crossing his arms over his broad chest. "Trust me, James. He looks at you like you hung the moon and stars. He's as gone on you as you are on him."

A flicker of hope ignited in James' chest, but he quickly tamped it down. "Even if that's true, I can't risk our friendship. I can't lose him again, not after everything we've been through."

"You're not going to lose him. I can already tell that Peter's not the type to run at the first sign of trouble. He's in this for the long haul, just like you are." Dominic said, his voice soft but firm.

James wanted to believe him, wanted to let himself be swept away by the promise of a future with Peter by his side. But the specter of the curse, of the secrets he still held close to his heart, loomed like a shadow over everything.

"There's something else," he said quietly, staring down at his hands. "I… I may have let something slip. About Peter's past."

The room went still, three pairs of eyes fixed on James with varying degrees of concern and exasperation.

Simon said carefully. "What exactly did you say?"

James flushed, the words tasting like ash on his tongue. "I don't know, exactly. It was just a passing comment, a hint that I might know more than I was letting on. But I saw the look in his eyes, Simon. He's not going to let it go."

Benjamin scrubbed a hand over his face, blowing out a long breath. "Well, that complicates things."

"You think?" James snapped, frustration and fear getting the better of him. "I'm trying to protect him, to keep him safe until he remembers on his own. But every day, it gets harder and harder to keep the truth from him."

"What if we used your magic?" Dominic suggested, a thoughtful frown creasing his brow. "Just a little nudge, to help him remember your bond?"

"No," James said immediately, shooting to his feet. "Absolutely not. We all know the risks, the dangers of interfering with the curse. It could kill him, Dominic. I won't put his life in jeopardy, not for anything."

Simon nodded, a grim set to his jaw. "James is right. We can't take that chance. But there has to be a loophole, some way to break the curse without putting Peter in danger."

Benjamin leaned against the wall, arms crossed over his chest. "Jimmy did say that just being around James would speed up the process. Maybe we just need to be patient, let their connection do the work for us."

James felt a flicker of hope at that, remembering the glimmers of recognition he'd seen in Peter's eyes, the inexplicable pull that seemed to draw them together.

"I think you're right," he said slowly, a small smile tugging at his lips. "I can see it, every time we're together. It's like… like some part of him remembers, even if his mind doesn't. Like our souls are reaching for each other, trying to find their way back home."

Dominic grinned, clapping James on the shoulder. "Then that's what we focus on. Giving you two every opportunity to connect, to let that bond grow stronger. The rest will come in time."

James nodded, feeling some of the weight lift from his shoulders. It wasn't a perfect solution, but it was a start. A path forward, lined with hope and the promise of a love that could conquer even the darkest of curses.

"Thank you," he said, looking around at the three men who had become his closest confidants, his family in all but blood. "I don't know what I'd do without you."

Simon smiled, pulling James into a quick hug. "That's what we're here for, James. To support you, to help you and Peter find your way back to each other. No matter what it takes."

James felt a warmth bloom in his chest at Simon's words, the unwavering support of his friends a balm to his troubled mind. As they settled back into their seats, a companionable silence falling over the room, James allowed himself a moment to bask in the glow of their affection.

But even as he savored the peace, the specter of the dark forces threatening Peter loomed in the back of his mind. He couldn't shake the feeling that time was running out, that every moment they spent in the dark was a moment too long.

After a while, he excused himself from the room. James knew there was one more thing he needed to do before their date. One more piece of the puzzle he needed to put in place.

He climbed into his car, the engine roaring to life as he pulled out onto the winding coastal road. The ocean stretched out before him, a vast expanse of blue that seemed to hold all the secrets of the universe in its depths.

James drove in silence, his mind churning with thoughts of Peter. He thought of the metal box hidden beneath the earth, that no one knew existed but only himself.

As he reached the secluded cove, James parked the car and stepped out onto the rocky shore. The salty breeze whipped through his hair, carrying with it the tang of brine and the whisper of ancient magic.

He walked to the water's edge, his eyes fixed on the horizon. With a deep breath, he raised his left hand, the prosthetic gleaming in the sunlight. A flick of his wrist, a pulse of his magnetic mastery, and the hand detached, revealing the hook hidden beneath.

James closed his eyes, reaching out with his senses, feeling the thrum of the metal in the earth, the pulse of the wards that concealed it. He raised the hook, a silent command, and the ground began to tremble.

Slowly, inexorably, a massive metal structure rose from the depths, the earth parting like water to reveal the box he had hidden so long ago. It was a storage unit of sorts, a repository of secrets and artifacts that James had never fully understood.

James stepped into the cavernous metal structure, the air heavy with the weight of memories and secrets. The lantern cast a soft glow over the shelves and crates that lined the walls, each one a treasure trove of a life lived long ago.

He moved slowly, reverently, his fingers trailing over the mementos and artifacts that he and Peter had collected over the course of their time together. A seashell from a stolen afternoon at the beach, a pressed flower from a picnic in the meadow, a scrap of parchment bearing Peter's looping handwriting.

Each item was a tangible reminder of the bond they had shared, the friendship that had burned so brightly between them. James felt a lump form in his throat as he picked up a small wooden carving, a gift from Peter on their meeting.

He remembered the way Peter's eyes had shone as he pressed it into James' hand, the way his smile had lit up the room like the sun breaking through the clouds. Even then, James had known that what they had was special, that the connection between them was more than just a passing fancy.

As James held the small wooden carving, memories of their tumultuous history flooded his mind. He and Peter had always been drawn to each other, even in the midst of their battles and disagreements. It was a push and pull, a constant dance of wills that somehow only served to deepen their connection.

He remembered the countless times Peter had thwarted his plans, swooping in with a mischievous grin and a glint in his eye. James had been so focused on his own ambitions, on the power he sought to wield, that he had failed to see the true treasure that lay before him. Peter had been a constant thorn in his side, a reminder of the humanity he had lost touch with in his pursuit of control. But even in their clashes, there had been a spark, an undeniable chemistry that drew them together like moths to a flame.

But it wasn't until this moment, surrounded by the evidence of their shared history, that James realized just how deep his feelings for Peter truly ran. It wasn't just affection or attraction, but a bone-deep love that had taken root in his heart and refused to let go.

"You really need to give him more credit, you know?" a voice spoke from behind him, startling James from his reverie. "Peter did what he did for you."

James whirled around, his heart pounding in his chest. Standing before him was a regal woman, her emerald robes billowing around her in an unseen breeze. Her face was ageless, timeless, with eyes that seemed to hold the secrets of the universe.

"Who are you?" James demanded, his hand instinctively reaching for the hook at his side. "And how did you get in here?"

The woman smiled, a serene curve of her lips that did nothing to calm the racing of James' heart. "I mean you no harm, James. I am simply here to offer guidance, to shed light on the path ahead."

James narrowed his eyes, his grip tightening on the table behind him. "You seem to know an awful lot about me and Peter. But I don't know a thing about you."

The woman inclined her head, a regal nod of acknowledgment. "I am known by many names, but you may call me Moriganna. I have watched over you and Peter for longer than you can imagine, waiting for the moment when your destinies would intertwine once more."

James felt a flicker of unease at her words, a sense of foreboding that he couldn't quite shake. "What do you mean, 'once more'? And what did you mean about Peter doing what he did for me?"

Moriganna's smile turned enigmatic, her eyes glinting with secrets untold. "All will be revealed in time, my dear. But know this - Peter's sacrifice was not made lightly, and the consequences of his actions will echo through the ages."

James growled in frustration, his temper flaring. "Enough with the riddles and the cryptic warnings. If you have something to say, just say it."

Moriganna laughed, a tinkling sound that seemed to fill the room with a soft, ethereal light. "Oh, James. You always were the impatient one. But very well, I will speak plainly."

She moved closer, her robes whispering against the metal floor. "The shadows are gathering, James. The forces that seek to keep you and Peter apart are growing stronger by the day. And if you are not careful, if you do not heed my warning, they will consume him utterly."

James felt a chill run down his spine at her words, a fear that he had never known before. "What do you mean, consume him? What are these shadows you speak of?"

Moriganna's face grew grave, her eyes darkening with a sadness that seemed to stretch across the ages. "The shadows are the manifestation of the curse that binds Peter, the darkness that seeks to claim his soul. They are the whispers in the night, the doubts that plague his mind, the fears that eat away at his heart."

James shook his head, his mind reeling with the implications of her words. "But how do I stop them? How do I keep Peter safe?"

She placed a hand on his shoulder, her touch warm and comforting despite the gravity of her message. "You must be his light, James. You must be the beacon that guides him home, the love that anchors him to this world. For only in the strength of your bond will he find the power to banish the shadows and break the curse that binds him."

James growled and felt a surge of determination at her words, a fierce protectiveness that burned in his chest. "I won't let them take him. I won't let the darkness win."

Moriganna smiled, a sad, knowing curve of her lips. "I know you won't, my dear. But the path ahead will not be easy. There will be trials and tribulations, moments of doubt and despair. But if you hold fast to what you feel for him, if you trust in the bond that ties you together, you will find your way through the darkness and into the light."

James nodded, his jaw set with resolve. "I understand. And I'm ready, whatever it takes."

Moriganna stepped back, her form beginning to shimmer and fade. "Then go forth. Go forth and claim the destiny that awaits you. And remember, even in the darkest of nights, the stars still shine."

With a final, enigmatic smile, she vanished in a swirl of emerald smoke, leaving James alone once more in the cavernous metal room.

He stood there for a long moment, his mind spinning with the weight of her words. The shadows, the curse, the trials that lay ahead - it was almost too much to bear.

He cast one last glance around the room, at the mementos and artifacts that told the story of their life together. And then, with a deep breath and a heart full of hope, he stepped back out into the world, ready to face whatever lay ahead.

For Peter, for their future, there was nothing he wouldn't do. No battle he wouldn't fight, no darkness he wouldn't brave.

Together, they would find their way home. And in the end, that was all that mattered.

*

11

Reunited And It Feels So Good

Peter

Wiping the sweat from his brow, he stepped back to admire the colorful banners he had just finished hanging. The town square was a flurry of activity, with volunteers bustling to and from as they prepared for the Summer Solstice celebration.

Despite the festive atmosphere, Peter couldn't shake the feeling of unease that had been growing in the pit of his stomach all morning.

He had woken up feeling slightly off, a dull ache thrumming behind his eyes and a strange heaviness in his limbs. At first, he had chalked it up to the late night he had spent poring over the ancient Gaelic text, trying to decipher its cryptic messages. But as the day wore on, the feeling had only intensified, leaving him dizzy and disoriented.

"Peter, are you alright?" Dominic's concerned voice cut through the haze, startling Peter from his thoughts. "You're looking a bit pale."

Peter forced a smile, waving off his friend's worry with a shaky hand. "I'm fine, Dom. Just a little tired, that's all. Nothing a good night's sleep won't fix."

Dominic frowned, his eyes searching Peter's face for any sign of deception. "Are you sure? Maybe you should take a break, sit down for a bit."

Peter shook his head, immediately regretting the action as the world tilted dangerously around him. "No, no. I'm good. I want to finish hanging these banners before I head out."

Dominic looked unconvinced, but he nodded slowly. "Alright. But promise me you'll take it easy, okay? Don't push yourself too hard."

Peter smiled, a genuine one this time. "I promise. Thanks, Dom."

As Dominic walked away, Peter turned back to the task at hand, determined to push through the strange malaise that had taken hold of him. He had made a commitment to help with the festival preparations, and he wasn't about to let a little fatigue stop him.

But as the minutes ticked by, the dizziness only seemed to worsen. The world swam before his eyes, the bright colors of the banners blurring together into a kaleidoscope of dizzying hues. Peter gritted his teeth, forcing himself to focus on the simple act of tying knots and hanging streamers.

Finally, after what felt like an eternity, the last banner was in place. Peter stepped back, a sense of relief washing over him. He had done it, despite the pounding in his head and the trembling in his hands.

As he turned to leave, a familiar voice called out to him. "Peter! Wait up!"

Peter's heart skipped a beat at the sound of James' voice, a flutter of excitement mingling with the unease in his gut. He turned to see the dark-haired man jogging towards him, a bright smile on his face.

"James, hey." Peter smiled, hoping his exhaustion didn't show too plainly on his face. "What's up?"

James' smile faltered slightly as he took in Peter's appearance, concern etching itself into the lines of his handsome face. "Are you okay? You look a little...off."

Peter waved a hand dismissively, forcing a laugh. "You know, if people keep asking me that, a guy might start to get a complex."

James chuckled, shaking his head. "Sorry, sorry. I just wanted to make sure we were still on for tonight. For our date."

The word "date" sent a thrill down Peter's spine, a spark of warmth that seemed to chase away some of the chill that had settled into his bones. "Of course we are. I wouldn't miss it for the world."

James beamed, his blue eyes crinkling at the corners in a way that made Peter's heart flutter. "Great. I'll pick you up at seven?"

Peter nodded, reaching out to take James' hand in his own. "It's a date."

But as their fingers intertwined, Peter felt a sudden jolt, like an electric current running through his veins. The world around him seemed to flicker and fade, replaced by a series of rapid-fire images that flashed behind his eyelids.

He saw James, but not as he was now. He was younger, his face unmarred by the scars that now traced his skin. They were in a place Peter had never seen before, a lush, green landscape that seemed to shimmer with an otherworldly light.

And then, in a blink, the scene changed. They were in a dark, cavernous space, the air thick with the tang of salt and the crash of waves. Peter was falling, his body plummeting towards the jagged rocks below. But just as he was about to hit the ground, a strong hand grabbed his wrist, yanking him back from the brink.

It was James. James had saved him, had risked his own life to pull Peter back from the edge of oblivion.

As quickly as they had come, the visions faded, leaving Peter gasping and disoriented. He blinked, the concerned face of James swimming into focus before him.

"Peter? Peter, can you hear me?" James' voice was urgent, his grip on Peter's hand tightening.

Peter nodded, swallowing hard against the lump in his throat. "I... I'm okay. Just got a little dizzy for a second there."

James frowned, his eyes searching Peter's face for any sign of pain or distress. "Maybe we should postpone tonight. If you're not feeling well..."

"No!" The word burst from Peter's lips before he could stop it, desperation tinged with something else, something he couldn't quite name. "No, I'm fine. Really. I don't want to cancel our plans."

James hesitated, clearly torn between his concern for Peter's well-being and his own desire to spend time with him. "Are you sure? I don't want you to push yourself if you're not up for it."

Peter smiled, squeezing James' hand in what he hoped was a reassuring gesture. "I'm sure. A little rest and I'll be good as new. Besides, I've been looking forward to this all week."

James' face softened, a tender smile playing at the corners of his lips. "Alright. But promise me you'll take it easy until then? Maybe head back to the inn and get some rest?"

Peter nodded, a wave of fatigue washing over him at the mere mention of rest. "I will. I promise."

James leaned in, pressing a soft kiss to Peter's forehead. The gesture was so tender, so intimate, that it took Peter's breath away. "Take care of yourself, Peter. I'll see you tonight."

With a final squeeze of his hand, James turned and walked away, leaving Peter alone once more in the bustling town square.

Peter watched him go, a tangle of emotions swirling in his chest. The visions, the flashbacks, the strange sense of familiarity he felt around James - it was all so confusing, so overwhelming. And yet, beneath it all, there was a sense of rightness, a feeling that he was exactly where he was meant to be.

As he made his way back to the inn, his steps heavy with exhaustion, Peter's mind raced with questions. Who was James, really?

And then there were the feelings, the undeniable pull he felt towards the dark-haired man. It wasn't just attraction, though that was certainly part of it. No, it was something deeper, something that went beyond the physical and into the realm of the soul.

Peter approached his room at the inn, his mind still swirling with thoughts of James and the strange visions that had been plaguing him, he noticed something odd. The door to his room was slightly ajar, a sliver of light spilling out into the dimly lit hallway.

Peter's heart skipped a beat, a frisson of fear running down his spine. He had always been careful to lock his door, to keep his few possessions safe in this strange new town. Who could have possibly gotten inside?

With trembling fingers, Peter pushed the door open, bracing himself for the worst. But as he stepped inside, his fear gave way to shock and then, overwhelming relief.

There, perched on the edge of his bed like a golden-haired model, was Lyra. His best friend, his confidante, the one person in the world who knew him better than he knew himself.

"Lyra?" Peter breathed, hardly daring to believe his eyes. "What… what are you doing here?"

Lyra's hands moved in a flurry of signs, her face split wide with a grin. "Took you long enough to get back! I was starting to think you'd forgotten all about me."

Peter laughed, the sound bubbling up from somewhere deep inside him. He crossed the room in two quick strides, gathering Lyra into a bone-crushing hug.

"Forget you? Never," he mumbled into her hair, breathing in the familiar scent of sunshine and wildflowers. "But seriously, what are you doing in Willowbrook? I thought you were back in New York."

Lyra pulled back, her green eyes sparkling with mischief. "I was. But I couldn't shake the feeling that you needed me. Call it best friend intuition."

Peter's heart swelled with affection, gratitude welling up inside him like a spring. "You have no idea how much I've missed you, Lyra. How much I've needed someone to talk to."

Lyra's expression softened, her hands moving in gentle, soothing motions. "I'm here now, Peter. And I'm not going anywhere. So why don't you tell me what's been going on?"

And so, Peter did. He told her about the strange visions, the flashes of a life he couldn't remember.

As he spoke, Peter could feel the weight of his confusion and fear lifting from his shoulders. Lyra listened intently, her eyes never leaving his face, her hands moving in occasional signs of encouragement or comfort.

When at last he fell silent, Lyra was quiet for a long moment. Then, with a gentle smile, she began to sign.

"Peter, I know you're scared. I know this is all new and confusing and overwhelming. But I also know you. I know your heart, your intuition. And if there's one thing I've learned in all our years of friendship, it's to trust that intuition."

Peter bit his lip, uncertainty swirling in his gut. "But what if I'm wrong, Lyra? What if these visions, these feelings, are just... just my mind playing tricks on me?"

Lyra shook her head, her expression fierce with conviction. "You're not wrong, Peter. Your heart knows the truth, even if your mind hasn't caught up yet."

Peter felt a rush of warmth at Lyra's words, a sense of validation that he hadn't even realized he needed. He raised his hands, ready to sign his thanks, to tell her how much her support meant to him, but what came out instead was, "I have a date tonight."

Lyra's eyes widened, her hands flying up in a flurry of excited signs. "A date? Peter, you sly dog! Who's the lucky person?"

Peter felt a blush creep up his neck, a giddy smile tugging at his lips as he signed back, "His name is James. He's… he's amazing, Lyra. Kind and funny and so incredibly handsome."

As he spoke, Peter pulled out his phone, scrolling through his camera roll until he found the picture he was looking for. It was a candid shot of James, taken just a few days earlier at the festival preparations. He was smiling at something off-camera, his blue eyes crinkled at the corners, his dark hair tousled by the breeze. The soft glow of the lanterns cast a warm light over his features, making him look almost ethereal.

Peter handed the phone to Lyra, watching her face closely for her reaction. But instead of the excitement he expected, he saw something else flash across her features. Something that looked almost like… recognition? Shock?

"Lyra? What is it?" Peter asked aloud, his brow furrowing in concern.

Lyra shook her head, handing the phone back to him with a smile that didn't quite reach her eyes. Her hands moved slowly, hesitantly, as she signed, "Nothing, Peter. It's just… are you sure this is James? "

Peter felt a flicker of unease at her expression, a sense that there was something she wasn't telling him. He signed back, "Of course I'm sure. Lyra, what's going on? You're acting strange."

Lyra hesitated, her hands twisting together in her lap. For a moment, Peter thought she might actually tell him what was bothering her. But then, with a shake of her head, she smiled and signed, "It's nothing, Peter. I'm just… I'm just worried about you, that's all. This town, these visions… I don't want you to get hurt."

Peter reached out, taking her hand in his and squeezing gently. "Lyra," he said softly, making sure she could read his lips, "you know you can tell me anything, right? If there's something going on, something you're not telling me…"

But Lyra just squeezed his hand in return, her smile turning reassuring as she signed with her free hand, "I know, Peter. And I promise, if there was something you needed to know, I would tell you. But for now, let's focus on the positive. Like the fact that you have a hot date tonight!"

Peter knew she was changing the subject, knew that there was still something she was holding back. But the excitement in her eyes, the genuine happiness for him, was enough to push his concerns aside for the moment.

"You're right," he said with a grin, signing along with his words. "I do have a hot date. And I have absolutely no idea what to wear."

Lyra laughed silently, the joy on her face chasing away the last of the tension in the room. Her hands flew in a flurry of signs, "Well, lucky for you, you have me. And I happen to be an expert in the art of date fashion."

As Lyra began to rifle through his closet, muttering soundlessly about color schemes and fabric choices, Peter's hand drifted to his chest, to the small silver pendant that always hung around his neck. It was a simple thing, just a flat disc engraved with a swirling pattern that reminded him of the wind. He had had it for as long as he could remember, though he couldn't quite recall where it had come from.

He caught Lyra's attention with a wave, then signed, "Hey, Lyra? Can I ask you something?"

Lyra glanced over her shoulder, a shirt dangling from her fingers as she signed back, "Of course, Peter. What is it?"

Peter held up the pendant for her to see, signing slowly, "My necklace. I've been wearing it every day, just like always. But I guess I never really thought about why. Do you... do you know where it came from?"

To his surprise, Lyra's face paled, her eyes widening with an emotion he couldn't quite name. She dropped the shirt, crossing the room in two quick strides to take the pendant from his fingers.

Her hands trembled slightly as she signed, "You've been wearing it? Every day?"

Peter nodded, confusion swirling in his gut as he signed back, "Of course. I never take it off. Lyra, what's going on? Why are you so worried about my necklace?"

Lyra closed her eyes, taking a deep breath as if to steady herself. When she opened them again, her gaze was fierce with intensity as she signed, "Peter, I need you to promise me something. Promise me that you'll keep this necklace on, no matter what. That you won't take it off for anything, not even for a second."

Peter stared at her, his heart racing in his chest. He had never seen Lyra like this, so serious, so… frightened. He signed slowly, carefully, "Lyra, you're scaring me. What's going on? What aren't you telling me?"

But Lyra just shook her head, pressing the pendant back into his palm and curling his fingers around it. Her signs were firm, unyielding, "I can't explain it, Peter. Not yet. But please, just trust me on this. Keep the necklace on, and everything will be okay."

Peter searched her face, looking for any hint of the carefree, mischievous girl he knew so well. But all he saw was a grim determination, a resolve that bordered on desperation.

"Okay," he said at last, his voice barely above a whisper as he signed along. "I promise."

Lyra nodded, some of the tension draining from her shoulders. Her signs were soft, apologetic, "Thank you, Peter. I know this must be confusing for you, but I promise, I only want what's best for you."

Peter believed her. He had to. Lyra was his best friend, his sister in all but blood. If she said that this was important, that he needed to trust her, then he would. No matter how much it scared him, no matter how many questions it left unanswered.

But even as he tried to push the concerns aside, to focus on the excitement of his impending date, Peter couldn't shake the feeling that there was something bigger at play. Something that Lyra knew, something that she was desperately trying to protect him from.

He thought of James, of the instant connection he had felt with the dark-haired man. He thought of the visions, the flashes of a life he couldn't remember. And he wondered, not for the first time, if they were all somehow connected.

But before he could dwell on it further, Lyra was grabbing his hand, pulling him towards the door with a determined grin and a sign that needed no translation.

"Come on, Peter. We've got a date to prepare for, and I know just the place to start."

Peter let himself be dragged along, a smile tugging at his lips despite the unease still churning in his gut. If there was one thing he knew about Lyra, it was that when she set her mind to something, there was no stopping her. And right now, her mind was set on turning him into the most irresistible date in all of Willowbrook.

As they stepped out into the warm summer air, the bustling streets of the town stretched out before them, Peter felt a flicker of excitement chase away the last of his concerns. Yes, there were still secrets to uncover, still truths to be told. But for now, he had his best friend by his side and the promise of a magical night ahead of him.

And really, what more could he ask for?

So with a laugh and a squeeze of Lyra's hand, Peter let himself be swept up in the moment, in the joy and the anticipation and the sheer, unbridled hope of it all. The future was uncertain, but one thing was clear.

12

When The Stars Align

Peter

He stood in front of the mirror, nervously adjusting his tie for what felt like the hundredth time. Lyra had worked her magic, transforming him from a slightly disheveled, confused man into a dashing date ready to sweep James off his feet.

At least, that's what she had assured him with a flurry of excited signs and a mischievous grin.

But now, standing alone in his room with the minutes ticking down to James' arrival, Peter couldn't shake the feeling of butterflies in his stomach. It was a sense of anticipation and familiarity that he couldn't quite place.

A knock at the door startled him from his thoughts, and he took a deep, steadying breath before crossing the room to answer it. And there, standing in the hallway with a bouquet of roses in hand and a nervous smile on his face, was James.

Peter felt his breath catch in his throat. James looked stunning, his dark hair artfully tousled, his blue eyes sparkling in the soft light of the hallway. He was dressed in a fitted suit that accentuated his broad shoulders and trim waist, the deep burgundy of his tie bringing out the flush in his cheeks.

"Hi," James said softly, holding out the roses. "These are for you."

Peter took the bouquet with trembling hands, a giddy smile spreading across his face. "They're beautiful, James. Thank you."

James ducked his head, a shy grin tugging at his lips. "Not as beautiful as you."

Peter felt a blush heat his cheeks, and he turned to set the roses on the nearby table before he could do something embarrassing like swoon. When he turned back, James was holding out his arm, a playful glint in his eye.

"Shall we?"

Peter nodded, slipping his arm through James' and letting himself be led out of the inn and into the warm summer night. As they drove through the bustling streets of Willowbrook, the twinkling lights of the festival casting a romantic glow over everything, Peter couldn't help but marvel at how right it felt to be by James' side.

They chatted easily as they made their way to the restaurant, their laughter mingling with the joyful sounds of the town.

As they approached the restaurant, Peter's eyes widened in surprise. The building was nestled at the base of a lighthouse, its whitewashed walls gleaming in the moonlight. He had never ventured this far out of Willowbrook before, and the sight of the majestic structure rising up against the starry sky took his breath away.

"James, this is… this is incredible," he breathed, turning to face his date with a look of wonder. "I had no idea this was even here."

James grinned, a mischievous twinkle in his eye. "Well, I may have done a little research to find the perfect spot for our first date. I wanted it to be something special, something you'd never forget."

Peter felt a warmth bloom in his chest, but it was tinged with a bittersweet ache. The gesture was so thoughtful, so romantic, but it also served as a reminder of all the things he couldn't remember, all the parts of himself that were still lost in the shadows.

As they made their way inside the restaurant, Peter tried to push the melancholy thoughts aside and focus on the beauty of the moment. The dining room was bathed in soft, romantic lighting, the tables adorned with flickering candles and delicate floral arrangements. Floor-to-ceiling windows offered a breathtaking view of the ocean, the waves crashing against the rocky shore below.

They were seated at a table by the window, the moonlight casting a silvery glow over everything. As they perused the menu, Peter found himself sneaking glances at James, his heart racing every time their eyes met.

"This view is spectacular," he said softly, gesturing to the expanse of sky and sea outside. "The moon and the stars… it's like they're aligned just for us."

James smiled, but there was a hint of concern in his eyes. "It's beautiful, isn't it? Almost as beautiful as the company."

Peter tried to return the smile, but he could feel the weight of his emotions pressing down on him, threatening to crush the fragile happiness of the moment. He looked down at his hands, fidgeting with the napkin in his lap.

"James, I… I need to tell you something," he said softly, his voice trembling slightly.

James reached across the table, covering Peter's hand with his own. The warmth of his touch was comforting, grounding. "You can tell me anything, Peter."

Peter took a deep, shuddering breath, trying to find the words to express the tumult of emotions swirling inside him. "I'm… I'm scared, James. Scared of how much I feel for you, I feel like… like I'm losing myself, like I don't know who I am anymore."

James squeezed his hand, his touch gentle and reassuring. "Peter,

I can't imagine how difficult this must be for you. To have these glimpses of a life you can't remember, to feel like a stranger in your own skin... it's a burden no one should have to bear alone."

Peter felt tears prick at the corners of his eyes, a lump forming in his throat. "I just... I don't want to drag you into this, James. I don't want my problems to become your problems."

James shook his head, a fierce determination blazing in his eyes. "Peter, listen to me. Your problems are my problems, because I care about you. Deeply. Whatever you're going through, whatever challenges lie ahead... I want to face them with you. Together."

Peter felt a warmth bloom in his chest, a flicker of hope amid the darkness. "You... you really mean that?"

James smiled, his thumb stroking gentle circles on the back of Peter's hand. "I do, Peter. I know we've only known each other for a short time, but I feel a connection to you that I can't explain. A pull that goes beyond just attraction or chemistry. And I'm not going to let fear or uncertainty stand in the way of exploring that connection."

Peter let out a shaky laugh, wiping at his eyes with his free hand. "I feel it too, James. Like... like we were meant to find each other, like our paths were always destined to cross."

James nodded, his eyes shining with emotion. "Then let's walk this path together, Peter. Let's take it one step at a time, and see where it leads us. I'm not going anywhere, and I'll be by your side every step of the way."

Peter felt a weight lift from his shoulders, a sense of peace washing over him. He knew the road ahead wouldn't be easy, knew that there were still so many questions to be answered and obstacles to overcome. But with James by his side, he felt like he could face anything.

"Thank you, James," he said softly, his voice thick with emotion. "For being here, for... for being you."

James smiled, lifting Peter's hand to his lips and pressing a gentle kiss to his knuckles. "Always, Peter. I'll always be here for you."

As they sat there, hand in hand, the moonlight casting a soft glow over their faces, Peter felt a flicker of hope take root in his heart. He didn't know what the future held, but he knew that with James by his side, he could weather any storm.

And for now, that was enough. More than enough.

* * *

As James escorted Peter back to the inn after their date, Peter's heart was a whirlwind of emotions. The evening had been perfect - the laughter, the shared glances, the warmth of James' hand in his - but beneath the giddy joy, a current of uncertainty tugged at his thoughts.

When they reached Peter's room, the air between them crackled with tension. Peter's hand trembled slightly as he unlocked the door, his mind racing with possibilities and doubts. He turned to face James, a shy smile on his lips.

"I had a wonderful time tonight," he said softly, his voice barely above a whisper.

James grinned, his blue eyes sparkling in the dim light of the hallway. "Me too, Peter. It was… magical."

They stood there for a moment, gazes locked, the space between them charged with unspoken longing. Then, slowly, James leaned in, his lips brushing against Peter's in a feather-light kiss.

Peter's breath caught in his throat, his eyes fluttering closed as he melted into the embrace. James' arms wrapped around his waist, pulling him closer, deepening the kiss until Peter's head was spinning with desire.

But even as his body responded to James' touch, Peter's mind couldn't fully quiet the nagging whispers of doubt. What if this was all too good to be true? What if James realized how broken, how lost Peter really was?

As if sensing his turmoil, James pulled back, his brow furrowed with concern. "Peter? Is everything okay?"

Peter tried to smile, but it felt strained, brittle. "Y-yeah. I'm fine. It's just…"

He trailed off, unsure how to put the tangled knot of his emotions into words. James studied his face for a long moment, then gently took his hand and led him to sit on the edge of the bed.

"Talk to me, Peter," he said softly, his thumb rubbing soothing circles on Peter's palm. "What's going on in that head of yours?"

Peter took a shaky breath, his gaze fixed on their intertwined fingers. "I… I'm scared, James. Scared that this, us… it's all too perfect. Too good to be true."

James frowned, tilting Peter's chin up to meet his gaze. "What do you mean?"

Peter swallowed hard, fighting back the sting of tears. "I'm… I'm not whole, James. I'm broken, shattered into a million pieces. And I'm terrified that once you see that, once you realize how damaged I am… you'll leave."

James' eyes widened, a flicker of pain flashing across his face. "Oh, Peter…"

He pulled Peter into his arms, cradling him against his chest as if he were something precious, something to be cherished. Peter couldn't hold back the tears any longer, his body shaking with silent sobs as he clung to James like a lifeline.

"Listen to me, Peter," James murmured, his lips brushing the shell of Peter's ear. "You are not broken. You are not damaged. You are the most beautiful, the most incredible person I have ever met."

Peter shook his head, burying his face in the crook of James' neck. "But my memories, my past… I don't even know who I am, James.

How can you want to be with someone like that?"

James pulled back slightly, cupping Peter's face in his hands and forcing him to meet his gaze. "I want to be with you because of who you are, Peter. Not because of who you were or what you remember. The person you are right here, right now… that's the person I care about. That's the person I want to be with."

Peter's heart swelled, a fragile hope blossoming in his chest. "Really?"

James smiled, brushing a stray tear from Peter's cheek with his thumb. "Really. We'll figure out your past together, Peter. But no matter what we discover, no matter what secrets come to light… it won't change how I feel about you."

Peter let out a shaky breath, a hesitant smile tugging at his lips. "Thank you, James. For being here, for… for seeing me. The real me."

James leaned in, pressing a gentle kiss to Peter's forehead. "Always, Peter."

They sat like that for a long moment, wrapped in each other's arms, the silence broken only by the soft sound of their breathing. Peter felt a sense of calm wash over him, a feeling of safety and acceptance that he hadn't known he craved.

Slowly, almost hesitantly, James tilted Peter's chin up, his blue eyes searching Peter's face for any sign of uncertainty. "Peter, I… I want you. All of you. But only if you're ready, only if it's what you want too."

Peter's heart raced, desire and nerves tangling together in his chest. He knew, with a certainty that took his breath away, that he wanted this - wanted James - more than he had ever wanted anything in his life.

"I want you too, James," he whispered, his voice trembling slightly. "I… I've never been more ready for anything."

James smiled, a soft, tender thing that made Peter's heart ache with longing. He leaned in, capturing Peter's lips in a kiss that started sweet and gentle but quickly deepened, becoming something hungry, something desperate.

Peter melted into the kiss, his hands fisting in James' shirt, pulling him closer. He needed to feel James' skin against his own, needed to be as close to him as possible.

As if reading his mind, James broke the kiss just long enough to tug his shirt over his head, tossing it carelessly to the floor. Peter drank in the sight of him, all tanned skin and toned muscle, his fingers itching to trace every line and curve.

"You're beautiful," he murmured, his hands skimming over James' chest, marveling at the way his skin pebbled with goosebumps at his touch.

James grinned, a wicked glint in his eye. "Not nearly as beautiful as you."

He tugged at the hem of Peter's shirt, a silent question in his eyes. Peter nodded, raising his arms to allow James to slip the fabric over his head. For a moment, he felt a flicker of self-consciousness, a fear that James would find him lacking.

But the look in James' eyes as he took in the sight of Peter's bare chest - a look of awe, of reverence, of pure, unadulterated desire - chased away any lingering doubts.

"Peter," James breathed, his fingers ghosting over Peter's skin, leaving trails of fire in their wake. "You're perfect. Absolutely perfect."

Peter blushed, ducking his head to hide his smile. "I'm really not, James. I'm just... me."

James shook his head, cupping Peter's face in his hands and forcing him to meet his gaze. "Don't you see, Peter? That's what makes you perfect. You, exactly as you are."

Peter's heart swelled, tears pricking at the corners of his eyes. He surged forward, capturing James' lips in a searing kiss, pouring all the emotion, all the longing he couldn't put into words into the press of their mouths.

Clothes were shed with fumbling fingers and breathy laughs, each new expanse of skin explored with reverent touches and worshipping kisses. When they finally came together, skin to skin, heart to heart, it was like two halves of a whole finally clicking into place.

They moved together slowly, savoring each gasp, each moan, each shudder of pleasure. James was gentle, almost unbearably so, his every touch a whispered promise, a silent vow of devotion.

Peter lost himself in the sensation, in the feeling of James moving inside him, around him, filling him up in ways he hadn't even known he needed. It was more than just physical pleasure, more than just the joining of two bodies. It was a connection, a bond forged in the heat of passion and the tenderness of true intimacy.

When they finally reached their peak, it was with James' name on Peter's lips and Peter's name on James', a shared cry of ecstasy that seemed to echo through the very fabric of the universe.

Afterwards, they lay tangled together, sweat-slicked and panting, exchanging soft kisses and even softer words. Peter traced idle patterns on James' chest, marveling at the way their bodies fit together, like two puzzle pieces finally snapping into place.

"That was…" he started, trailing off as he struggled to find the words to encompass the magnitude of what he was feeling.

"Amazing? Incredible? Earth-shattering?" James supplied, a teasing grin on his kiss-swollen lips.

Peter laughed, swatting at James' chest. "All of the above. And then some."

James' expression softened, his fingers combing gently through Peter's hair. "For me too, Peter. I've never… I've never felt anything like that before. Like I was finally whole, finally complete."

Peter's heart clenched, a lump forming in his throat. "Me neither, James. It's like… it's like I've been searching for something my whole life, and I finally found it. Found you."

James pulled him closer, pressing a kiss to the top of his head. "I'm here, Peter. I'll always be here. No matter what happens, no matter what we have to face… we'll face it together."

Peter nodded, burrowing deeper into James' embrace. "Together," he echoed, the word a promise, a prayer, a declaration of the unbreakable bond they shared. And they drifted off to sleep

In the hazy depths of slumber, Peter found himself standing in a void of swirling shadows. The darkness was thick, tangible, pressing against his skin like a living thing. He shivered, wrapping his arms around himself, a sense of unease prickling at the back of his neck.

Suddenly, a figure emerged from the shadows, a silhouette that was both familiar and utterly foreign. As it drew closer, Peter's eyes widened in shock. It was… him. But not him. This version of Peter was cloaked in darkness, his eyes glittering with a malevolent red light.

"Hello, Peter," the shadow purred, his voice a twisted echo of Peter's own. "I've been waiting for you."

Peter took a step back, his heart pounding in his chest. "Who… who are you? What do you want?"

The shadow laughed, a sound like shattering glass. "Who am I? I'm you, Peter. The real you. The you that's been buried beneath the lies and the false memories."

Peter shook his head, confusion and fear warring in his gut. "I don't understand. What are you talking about?"

The shadow stepped closer, his movements fluid and predatory. "You've been living a lie, Peter. Your past, your identity… it's all been hidden from you. But I can change that. I can give you the power to unlock your true potential, to reclaim what's been stolen from you."

Peter's mind raced, a flicker of temptation sparking in his chest. The chance to finally know the truth, to fill the aching void in his memories… it

was almost too good to resist.

But something held him back, a whisper of warning that cut through the haze of desire. This was wrong. This... thing, this dark reflection of himself... it couldn't be trusted.

"No," he said, his voice trembling but resolute. "I don't know who or what you are, but I won't let you tempt me. My past, my memories... I'll find the truth on my own terms, not through some dark bargain."

The shadow's face twisted into a snarl, the darkness around them pulsing with malevolent energy. "Fool," it hissed, its voice dripping with venom. "You're too weak to grasp the power I offer. But you'll come around, in time. You can't escape your destiny, Peter. Sooner or later, you'll come to me. And when you do... I'll be waiting."

With a final, chilling laugh, the shadow melted back into the darkness, leaving Peter alone and shaking in the void.

He jolted awake with a gasp, his heart racing, his skin slick with sweat. For a moment, he couldn't remember where he was, the dream still clinging to the edges of his consciousness like a sticky web.

Then strong arms tightened around him, a sleepy murmur of concern brushing against his ear. "Peter? You okay, love?"

Peter turned, burying his face in the solid warmth of James' chest. The steady thrum of James' heartbeat, the scent of his skin... it chased away the last lingering tendrils of the nightmare, grounding him in the here and now.

"Y-yeah," he mumbled, his voice muffled against James' skin. "Just a bad dream. It's nothing."

James' fingers carded gently through Peter's hair, his touch soothing and tender. "Do you want to talk about it?"

For a moment, Peter was tempted. To pour out the fear and confusion, to share the burden of the shadow's dark promises. But something held him back, a flicker of protectiveness, a need to shield

James from the darkness that seemed to dog Peter's every step.

"No, it's okay," he said, forcing a small smile. "It was just a silly nightmare. Nothing to worry about."

James studied his face for a long moment, concern etched in the furrow of his brow. But he didn't push, just pulled Peter closer, dropping a soft kiss on his forehead.

"Alright. But I'm here, Peter. Always. If you ever need to talk, about anything... I'm here."

Peter's heart clenched, a rush of gratitude and affection threatening to overwhelm him. "I know, James. Thank you."

They lay like that for a long while, Peter's head on James' chest, James' fingers tracing soothing patterns on Peter's back. But even as the comfort of James' presence chased away the last of the dream's chill, Peter couldn't shake the feeling of unease, the sense that something dark and dangerous was lurking just out of sight.

He closed his eyes, trying to will away the whispers of doubt, the echo of the shadow's mocking laughter. He had James. He had his friends, his new life in Willowbrook. Whatever the shadow was, whatever it wanted... he wouldn't let it win.

13

Shadows

James

The first light of dawn filtering through the curtains woke him up. He turned to see Peter still sleeping peacefully beside him, his tousled hair falling across his face. James' heart ached remembering the pain in Peter's eyes as he'd opened up last night about his lost memories and feelings of not belonging.

He wished he could take away all of Peter's hurt, but for now, he settled on a small gesture to brighten his spirits.

Quietly, James slipped out of bed and padded to the kitchen. He packed a wicker basket with fresh croissants, fruit, and cheeses, along with a thermos of coffee and orange juice. He folded a soft blanket and tucked it under his arm. With a small smile, he made his way back to the bedroom.

Peter was just starting to stir when James sat on the edge of the bed. "Good morning, sunshine," James said softly.

Peter blinked up at him blearily. "Morning. What time is it?"

"Early still. I thought we could go on a little adventure, just the two of us. A beach picnic to get away from…everything for a bit. What do you say?"

Peter pushed himself up, eyes widening as he noticed the basket. "You planned all this? For me?"

James felt a pang at the surprise in Peter's voice, as if he wasn't used to someone doing kind things just for him. "Of course, Peter. I want to do something special for you."

A slow smile spread across Peter's face, chasing away the shadows that lingered there. "That sounds perfect. Thank you, James."

They got ready quickly, Peter practically bouncing with excitement as they made their way out of the cozy cottage and toward the shore. James tangled their fingers together as they walked, marveling at how well they fit, like two puzzle pieces snapping into place.

The beach was empty this early, the sand cool and untouched. They made their way to a secluded little cove, the gentle crash of waves and calls of seagulls a soothing melody. James spread out the blanket and they settled down, digging into the simple but delicious breakfast.

For a while, they just enjoyed each other's company, trading stories and jokes between bites. But James noticed when Peter's gaze drifted to the horizon, a wistful, almost pained expression flitting across his features.

"Hey," James said gently, brushing a hand down Peter's arm. "What's going on in that head of yours?"

Peter was quiet for a long moment, but James waited patiently. Finally, he spoke, voice soft and pained. "When I first woke up in that hospital in New York, no idea who I was…I was so lost. So alone. The only thing I had was this necklace." His fingers drifted to the pendant resting against his chest. "I didn't know what it meant, but I clung to it like a lifeline."

James rested a hand over Peter's, a silent promise. He held his tongue, giving Peter space to gather his thoughts.

"I tried to build a life there, but it always felt…hollow. Like I was playing a role, going through the motions. I smiled and joked and pretended everything was fine, but inside…I was drowning, James." Peter's voice cracked. "I didn't know how to find my way to the surface. Until I met you."

James' heart clenched. He cupped Peter's face, brushing away the single tear that had escaped down his cheek. "Peter, I…I can't imagine how hard that must have been, feeling so adrift and alone. But you're not alone anymore. You have me, and this whole crazy wonderful town. We're your anchors now. Your safe harbor."

Peter leaned into the touch, eyes fluttering closed for a moment. When he opened them again, they shone with gratitude and something deeper, stronger. "I don't know what I did to deserve you, James. But I'm so glad the universe saw fit to bring us together."

"I'm the lucky one," James whispered fiercely. "You, Peter, are a marvel. Brave and kind and so incredibly strong, even when you don't feel it. I'm in awe of you, every single day."

A watery laugh bubbled out of Peter. "Okay, sap. You're going to make me cry again and then where will we be?"

"Right here," James said simply. "Together. And that's all that matters."

Peter surged forward, capturing James' lips in a searing kiss, pouring all the feelings he couldn't quite name into the press of their mouths. James responded just as fervently, wrapping Peter tight in his arms as if he could pour every ounce of comfort and care directly into his very soul.

They broke apart, foreheads pressed together as they caught their breath. The shadows in Peter's eyes had receded, replaced by a tentative but genuine peace.

"Thank you, James. For this, for everything."

"Anytime, anywhere. I've got you, Peter. Always."

They settled back on the blanket, Peter tucked securely under James' arm as they watched the waves roll in. The road ahead was still uncertain, with mysteries to unravel and a curse to break. But in this perfect pocket of time, none of that mattered. They had each other, a connection soul-deep and unshakeable. And that was enough. More than enough.

As the sun climbed higher and the beach began to fill, James packed up their picnic, pulling Peter to his feet with a mischievous grin. "What do you say we explore a bit? I hear there's a hidden sea cave around here with a resident octopus that gives great relationship advice."

Peter laughed, bright and uninhibited. "Lead the way, captain."

As they walked hand in hand along the shore, James felt a swell of emotion. Peter's openness about his pain and isolation tugged at his heart, and he knew it was time to share his own story.

"You know," he began softly, "growing up, I always felt a little different, too."

Peter glanced over, curiosity mingling with the vulnerability in his gaze. "Really? How so?"

James huffed a laugh, memories playing behind his eyes. "Oh, you know, the usual. Too tall, too gangly, too prone to getting lost in my own head. I was the kid who always had his nose buried in a book, dreaming of far-off adventures."

Peter bumped their shoulders together playfully. "Why do I get the feeling those adventures usually featured you as the dashing hero?"

"Naturally," James grinned. "But in all seriousness, I struggled to find my place. To feel like I truly belonged. It wasn't until I left home, started to explore the world, that I began to come into my own."

As they continued walking, James' thoughts drifted to his past, to the time when he was the Conqueror of the Seas. He remembered the clashes with Peter on the high seas, the flash of swords and the crackle of magic. But beneath the surface of their battles, James had always felt a spark of something more, a connection he hadn't been ready to acknowledge.

Even as they fought, James knew it was all for show. A carefully choreographed dance where neither truly wanted to hurt the other. There had always been something about Peter that drew him in, like a moth to a flame.

But James kept these thoughts to himself.

Instead, he focused on the present, on the feel of Peter's hand in his and the warmth of his presence by his side. He silently vowed to help Peter unravel the mysteries of his forgotten life, to break the curse that held his memories hostage. Together, they would face whatever challenges lay ahead.

As they walked, James couldn't help but marvel at the rightness he felt with Peter, the bone-deep certainty that this was meant to be. Even with the uncertainties of the future, he knew he would fight for this, for them.

But suddenly, the air around them shifted, a prickling sense of warning dancing along James' skin. He tensed, his senses on high alert as he scanned their surroundings.

"James?" Peter asked, concern lacing his voice. "What's wrong?"

Before James could respond, a group of menacing shadow creatures emerged from the treeline, their dark forms flickering and pulsing with malevolent energy. They moved with unnatural speed, their eyes glowing an eerie red as they fixed their sights on Peter.

"Stay behind me," James commanded, positioning himself between Peter and the advancing threat. His own magic surged to the surface, humming beneath his skin. With a flash of silver, his prosthetic hand transformed into his signature hook, the metal gleaming wickedly in the fading light.

Peter's eyes widened, confusion and fear warring on his face. "James, what's happening? What are those things?"

"I don't know," James gritted out, his focus never wavering from the shadow creatures. "But I won't let them hurt you. When I give the signal, I need you to run, Peter. Run as fast as you can and don't look back."

"I'm not leaving you!" Peter protested, his voice trembling but fierce.

James spared a glance over his shoulder, his heart clenching at the determination in Peter's eyes. "I'll be right behind you, I promise. But I need you safe. Please, Peter."

Something in James' tone must have conveyed the urgency of the situation, because Peter gave a sharp nod, his jaw clenched tight.

The shadow creatures lunged, their movements a blur of darkness. James met them head-on, his hook slashing through their insubstantial forms. But for every one he cut down, two more seemed to take its place.

"Peter, run!" James shouted, desperation coloring his voice.

Peter hesitated for a split second, his eyes locked on James, before he turned and sprinted towards the safety of the town. But one of the shadow creatures slipped past James' defenses, its sights set on Peter's retreating form.

"No!" James roared, fear and fury mixing in his veins. He tried to give chase, but the remaining creatures blocked his path, their claws tearing at his skin.

But just as the lone shadow creature was about to reach Peter, something incredible happened. Peter spun around, his hand outstretched, and a shimmering shield of shadows burst to life around him. The creature slammed into the barrier, dissolving into wisps of smoke on impact.

James stood stunned, his mind reeling. Peter's powers were manifesting, even without his memories. A surge of pride, wonder and dread momentarily overwhelmed the adrenaline pumping through his system.

The momentary distraction cost him. Sharp claws raked down his back, drawing a pained grunt from his lips. James whirled, his hook flashing as he renewed his attack with a vengeance.

One by one, the shadow creatures fell beneath his onslaught, until only a few tattered wisps of darkness remained, quickly dissipating in the breeze. James stood amidst the carnage, his chest heaving and his hook dripping with inky ichor.

His gaze snapped to Peter, who was still surrounded by the flickering shadow shield. But as James watched, the barrier wavered and collapsed, leaving Peter swaying on his feet, his face ashen.

James was at his side in an instant, catching him just as his knees buckled. "I've got you," he murmured, cradling Peter against his chest. "You're safe now, it's okay."

Peter clung to him, his whole body trembling. "What…what was that?" he asked, his voice small and lost. "Did I do that? The shield?"

James smoothed a hand down Peter's back, trying to calm the racing of his own heart. "You did. You protected yourself, Peter. Your magic…they're starting to come back."

Peter pulled back slightly, his eyes wide and confused, with a spark of tentative wonder. "I have magic?"

"You do," James confirmed softly. "Incredible ones. And they're still in there, even if you don't remember yet."

Peter shook his head, overwhelmed. "I don't understand any of this. Those creatures, magic…I'm scared, James. I'm really scared."

It broke James' heart to hear the tremor in Peter's voice, to see the fear and confusion clouding his usually vibrant eyes. He cupped Peter's face in his hands, his touch gentle but grounding.

"I know you're scared, and that's okay. This is a lot to take in. But you're not alone, Peter. I'm right here, and I'm not going anywhere. We'll figure this out together, I promise."

Peter leaned into the touch, his eyes fluttering closed for a moment. When he opened them again, some of the fear had eased, replaced by a fragile trust that stole James' breath.

"Okay," Peter whispered.

James pressed a tender kiss to Peter's forehead before gathering him close again. He could feel the adrenaline starting to ebb, the pain from his injuries making itself known. But he pushed it aside, his focus solely on the man in his arms.

"We need to get somewhere safe," he said, his mind already racing. "I know a place, not too far from here. Do you think you can walk?"

Peter took a shaky breath, then nodded. "I think so. Just...don't let go, okay?"

"Never," James vowed, meaning it with every fiber of his being.

With an arm securely around Peter's waist, James led them away from the shore, towards the outskirts of town. As they walked, he kept up a steady stream of soft reassurances, trying to distract Peter from the shock of what had just transpired.

James gently placed Peter into the car who fell unconscious after a while and before long, a stately manor came into view, its windows glowing with warm, welcoming light. James felt a wash of relief as he carried an unconscious Peter through the iron gates and up the winding path.

The door swung open before they even reached it, revealing Adrian's concerned face. "James? What happened? Is that...Peter?"

James nodded wearily. "We were attacked. Shadow creatures. Peter's magic manifested, but he's in shock. We need a place to regroup, to keep him safe."

Adrian stepped aside without hesitation, ushering them into the foyer. "Of course, come in. You're both safe here."

James followed Adrian into the manor, his arm securely around Peter's waist. The events of the beach had taken their toll, and Peter was barely clinging to consciousness, his head lolling against James' shoulder.

"There's a guest room just down the hall," Adrian said, his voice low and concerned. "You can lay him down there."

James nodded gratefully, carefully maneuvering Peter through the elegant corridors. When they reached the room, he gently lowered Peter onto the plush bed, his heart clenching at the sight of his pale, drawn face.

Peter stirred slightly, his eyelids fluttering. "James?" he mumbled, his voice thick with exhaustion.

"I'm here," James soothed, brushing a stray curl from Peter's forehead. "You're safe now. Just rest, okay?"

Peter sighed, leaning into the touch before his eyes drifted shut again, his breath evening out as he slipped into a deep sleep.

James sat on the edge of the bed for a long moment, just watching the rise and fall of Peter's chest. The urge to protect, to shelter, was almost overwhelming, a fierce ache in his bones.

A soft knock at the door drew his attention. Adrian stood in the doorway, his expression a mix of worry and curiosity.

"Is he alright?" he asked, nodding towards Peter's sleeping form.

James ran a hand over his face, suddenly feeling the weight of the day's events. "I think so. Just shaken up and exhausted. It's been...a lot."

Adrian opened his mouth to respond, but before he could, the sound of hurried footsteps echoed down the hall. Benjamin burst into the room, his face etched with concern, Jimmy the black cat hot on his heels.

"What happened?" Benjamin demanded, his gaze darting between James and Peter. "I could sense the disturbance from across town."

James took a deep breath, trying to gather his thoughts. "We were attacked. On the beach. Shadow creatures, unlike anything I've ever seen before."

Adrian and Benjamin exchanged a grim look. "Shadow creatures?"

Adrian repeated, his voice tight. "In Willowbrook? You mean just like the last one we saw in the same place?"

James nodded. "They came out of nowhere. Went straight for Peter. I fought them off, but…" He swallowed hard, the memory of Peter's fear a bitter taste on his tongue "Peter's magic…they resurfaced. He created a shield, made of shadows. Took out one of the creatures that slipped past me."

The room fell silent, the weight of James' words hanging in the air. Benjamin was the first to break it, his voice uncharacteristically solemn.

"It seems Willowbrook has become a magnet for trouble these past months," Benjamin said, absently stroking Jimmy's sleek fur. "First Malachai and Dominic's stepmother and now shadow creatures bold enough to attack in broad daylight."

Adrian's jaw clenched, a flicker of something ancient and powerful in his eyes. "We need to get to the bottom of this. Figure out what's drawing these forces to our town."

James looked back at Peter, his heart twisting at the thought of him facing more danger, more uncertainty. "I just want to keep him safe," he murmured, more to himself than the others.

A gentle hand landed on his shoulder, startling him from his thoughts. Benjamin stood beside him, his eyes soft with understanding.

"We all do, James. Peter's one of us now, whether he likes it or not. We'll do everything in our power to protect him."

James managed a small, grateful smile. "Thank you. Both of you. I don't know what we would do without your help."

Adrian waved a dismissive hand. "Nonsense. You're family. Both of you. And family sticks together, no matter what."

The words wrapped around James like a warm blanket, easing some of the tension from his shoulders. He knew the road ahead would be difficult, fraught with unknown dangers and challenges.

Well, James had to believe they could face anything. That they could unravel the mysteries plaguing their town and keep the ones they care about safe.

His gaze drifted back to Peter, to the man who had captured his heart so completely. The man he would move mountains for, fight legions of shadow creatures for, without a second thought.

14

Hurtful Truths

Peter

He woke with a gasp, his heart racing and his mind a jumbled mess of fractured images. Shadow creatures, glowing eyes, the crackle of dark energy - it all swirled together in a dizzying kaleidoscope of fear and confusion.

He bolted upright, his breath coming in short, sharp bursts. The last thing he remembered was the beach, the attack, and the strange creatures.

"Peter? Hey, it's okay, you're safe."

The familiar voice cut through the haze of panic, warm and soothing. Peter turned, his eyes wide and wild, to see James sitting beside him, his face etched with concern.

"James?" he croaked, his throat dry and tight. "What...where are we?"

James reached out, his hand hovering for a moment before gently resting on Peter's arm. The touch grounded him, a lifeline in the churning sea of his emotions.

"We're at Adrian's manor. After the attack, I brought you here. It's protected, warded against dark magic."

Dark magic. The words sent a shiver down Peter's spine. He shook his head, trying to clear the cobwebs, to make sense of the impossible.

"I don't…I don't understand," he whispered, hating the tremor in his voice. "Those creatures, the things I did…it's not possible. Magic isn't real. It can't be."

James sighed, a sad, knowing sound. "I know it's a lot to take in. But Peter…magic is very much real. It's all around us, woven into the fabric of Willowbrook itself."

Peter stared at him, searching for any hint of deception, any sign that this was all some elaborate prank. But James' eyes held only truth and a deep, aching sympathy.

"I feel like I'm losing my mind," Peter confessed, his voice small and lost. "Like I've stepped into some fantasy world where nothing makes sense. I don't…I don't know how to handle this, James."

James shifted closer, his presence a solid, comforting warmth at Peter's side. "You're not losing your mind, Peter. And you're not alone. I'm here, and I'll help you navigate this new reality in any way I can."

Peter leaned into him, drawing strength from the contact. His mind was still reeling, questions and fears tumbling over each other in a dizzying dance. But with James beside him, he felt a flicker of something like hope amid the chaos.

"I need to understand," he said, the words spilling out in a rush. "The shadow creatures…all of it. I can't just hide from this, James. I need to know what's happening to me."

James hesitated, concern warring with understanding in his eyes. "I know you do. And I promise, I'll tell you everything I can. But Peter, you've been through a lot. You need to rest, to give yourself time to process."

Peter shook his head stubbornly. "I can't rest, not with all these questions burning in my brain. Please, James. I need this. I need to make sense of my world again."

There was a long, weighted pause. Then, with a sigh of acceptance, James nodded. "Alright. But we take it slow, okay? And the moment it becomes too much, you tell me."

Relief bloomed in Peter's chest, chasing away some of the icy fear. "Thank you," he breathed, meaning it with every fiber of his being.

James smiled softly, his thumb tracing soothing circles on Peter's wrist. "Okay. Let's start with the basics. Magic, in its purest form, is the energy that flows through all living things. It's a part of nature, a part of us."

Peter frowned, trying to wrap his mind around the concept. "But why have I never seen it before? Why is it only showing up now?"

"Willowbrook is...special," James explained, choosing his words carefully. "It's a nexus, a place where the lines between the mundane and the magical are thinner. People with magical abilities are drawn here, like moths to a flame."

A shiver ran through Peter at the words. Special. Magical abilities. It all sounded so fantastical, so far removed from the life he thought he knew.

"And the shadow creatures?" he asked, almost afraid to hear the answer. "What were they?"

James' face darkened, a flicker of something ancient and powerful in his eyes. "Manifestations of dark magic. Malevolent entities that feed on fear and chaos. They're not...common, even in a place like Willowbrook."

Peter swallowed hard, the memory of those glowing red eyes sending a fresh wave of fear through him. "But why were they after me? Why did I have...magic?"

There was a long, heavy pause. For a moment, Peter thought James wasn't going to answer. But then, with a sigh of resignation, he spoke.

"I wish I had all the answers, Peter. But the truth is, there's still so much we don't understand."

Peter's heart sank, a leaden weight in his chest. "So what you're saying is, I'm some kind of freak. An anomaly."

"No!" The word burst from James, fierce and vehement. He gripped Peter's shoulders, his gaze boring into him with an intensity that stole his breath. "You are not a freak, Peter. You're special, yes. Unique. But that's not a bad thing."

Peter wanted to believe him. Wanted to cling to the conviction in James' voice like a lifeline. But the doubt, the fear, was a living thing, coiled tight around his heart.

Peter wanted to believe him. Wanted to cling to the conviction in James' voice like a lifeline. But the doubt, the fear, was a living thing, coiled tight around his heart.

"But what if I hurt someone?" he blurted out, the words tasting like ash on his tongue. "What if I can't control myself and I become a danger to everyone around me?"

James' grip on his shoulders tightened, his gaze fierce and unwavering. "That won't happen, Peter. I won't let it. We'll learn to control your abilities together, one step at a time."

Peter shook his head, a bitter laugh bubbling up in his throat. "You make it sound so simple. But James, I don't even know what I'm capable of. I don't know what I am."

"You're Peter," James said, the words ringing with a certainty that made Peter's heart ache. "You're the same kind, brave, wonderful person you've always been. These powers, they don't define you."

Peter wanted to believe him. Wanted to let the words sink into his skin, to chase away the icy tendrils of fear that gripped his heart. But the more he learned, the more lost he felt, like he was drifting further and further away from the life he thought he knew.

"I feel like I'm losing my mind," he confessed, his voice small and broken. "Like everything I thought I knew was a lie. I don't...I don't know how to trust myself anymore."

James was silent for a long moment, his eyes searching Peter's face. When he spoke, his voice was soft, almost hesitant.

"Do you trust me, Peter?"

The question caught Peter off guard, his heart stuttering in his chest. He stared at James, at the man who had been his rock, his anchor in the storm of confusion and fear.

"Yes," he whispered, the word feeling like a vow, a promise. "I trust you, James. More than anything."

A small, tender smile curved James' lips. "Then trust that I will be here, every step of the way. That I will never let you face this alone."

Peter swallowed hard, emotion clogging his throat. He had so many questions, so many fears still swirling in his mind. But there was one that rose above the rest, demanding to be voiced.

"James, do you...do you have magic too?"

James blinked, surprise flickering across his face. Then, slowly, he nodded. "I do. I can control and manipulate magnetic fields."

Peter's eyes widened, a spark of wonder momentarily eclipsing the fear. "That's...that's incredible. Can you show me?"

James hesitated, then held out his hand. Peter watched, transfixed, as the metal bed frame began to tremble and shake. Slowly, one of the posts detached, floating through the air to hover above James' palm.

"Wow," Peter breathed, awe and disbelief warring in his chest. "That's...I don't even know what to say."

James let the bedpost drop back into place, a wry smile tugging at his lips. "It took me years to learn to control it. To not be afraid of what I could do. I know exactly how you're feeling, Peter."

Peter stared at him, a sudden, desperate hope blooming in his chest. "You do?"

"I do," James said softly, his eyes distant with memory. "When my abilities first manifested, I was terrified. I thought I was a monster, a freak of nature. I pushed everyone away, too scared to let them close."

Peter's heart clenched, a lump rising in his throat. "What changed?"

James' gaze refocused on him, warm and tender. "I met people who understood. Who showed me that my powers weren't a curse, but a gift. That I wasn't alone."

Tears pricked at the corners of Peter's eyes, hot and stinging. "I want to believe that. I want to believe that I'm not...broken. But it's so hard, James. I'm so scared."

And then he was in James' arms, the dam inside him finally breaking. Sobs tore from his throat, raw and aching, as he clung to James like a lifeline. James held him, murmuring soft, soothing words against his hair, his touch gentle and grounding.

"It's okay, Peter. Let it out. I've got you. I'm here."

Peter cried until he was spent, until the storm of emotion had passed, leaving him feeling raw and hollowed out. But beneath the exhaustion, there was a flicker of something else. Something like hope.

"Thank you," he whispered, his voice hoarse and scratchy. "For everything. I don't...I don't know what I would do without you, James."

James' arms tightened around him, a fierce, protective embrace. "You never have to find out. I'm not going anywhere, Peter. I promise."

They stayed like that for a long moment, just breathing each other in. And then, softly, hesitantly, Peter spoke.

They stayed like that for a long moment, just breathing each other in. And then, softly, hesitantly, Peter spoke.

"James, did we...did we know each other before? Before I lost my memories?"

James stiffened, his arms tightening around Peter for a brief, almost painful moment. Peter could feel the tension thrumming through him, the sudden heaviness in the air.

"I..." James began, his voice rough and hesitant. "Yes. We did know each other, Peter."

Peter's heart stuttered in his chest, a dizzying mix of shock and something like betrayal rushing through him. He pulled back, just enough to see James' face, to search those eyes for the truth.

"Why didn't you tell me?" he whispered, hating the way his voice shook. "All this time, you knew, and you never said a word?"

James closed his eyes, a pained expression etched across his features. "I wanted to, Peter. God, you have no idea how much I wanted to. But I couldn't. I'm…I'm bound by higher powers, oaths I can't break."

Peter shook his head, anger and confusion warring in his chest. "Higher powers? What are you talking about, James? What could possibly be more important than the truth?"

"Your safety," James said softly, the words heavy with a weight Peter couldn't understand. "Your life, Peter. There are things at play here, forces beyond your understanding. Beyond mine."

Peter laughed, the sound harsh and bitter in the quiet room. "My life? My safety? James, I don't even know who I am anymore. I have magic I can't control, memories I can't access. How am I supposed to feel safe when everything I thought I knew is a lie?"

"It's not a lie, Peter. Your life here, the person you are…that's real. That's always been real."

"But our past, our…connection. That's real too, isn't it? And you kept it from me."

James' shoulders slumped, defeat and guilt written in every line of his body. "I'm sorry, Peter. I'm so sorry. I never wanted to hurt you. I was just trying to protect you."

Peter wanted to, no, needed to move just so he could put some distance between himself and James. But his body was still too weak.

"Protect me from what, James? From the truth? From myself? How can I trust you, how can I trust anyone, when everyone seems to know more about my life than I do?"

James held his hands held out in a placating gesture. "Peter, please. I know this is a lot to take in. I know you're hurt and confused. But you have to believe me when I say that everything I've done, every secret I've kept…it's been for you."

Peter whirled on him, hot tears pricking at the corners of his eyes. "For me? How can you say that, James? How can hiding the truth from me, lying to me, be for me?"

"Because the truth is dangerous, Peter. Because there are people, powerful people, who would stop at nothing to keep the secrets of your past hidden. People who would hurt you, use you, if they knew what you were capable of."

Peter stared at him, a cold, sinking feeling settling in the pit of his stomach. "What I'm capable of? James, what are you saying?"

James shook his head, a look of anguish crossing his face. "I've said too much already, Peter. I wish I could tell you more, wish I could make you understand. But I can't. Not yet. Not until I know it's safe."

Peter felt like he was going to be sick, the room spinning around him in a dizzying whirl.

"I can't…I can't do this, James. I can't handle any more secrets, any more lies. I feel like I'm losing my mind, like I'm drowning in a sea of questions and no one will throw me a lifeline."

James took a step forward, his hand outstretched, but Peter flinched away. The hurt that flashed across James' face was like a knife to the heart, but Peter couldn't bring himself to close the distance between them. Not now. Not with the weight of betrayal still heavy on his shoulders.

"Peter…" James whispered, his voice thick with emotion. "Please. Don't push me away. I know I've hurt you, I know I've broken your trust. But I'm still here. I still care about you, more than you could possibly know."

Peter closed his eyes, hot tears spilling down his cheeks. "I care about you too, James. That's what makes this so hard. But I can't…I can't be around you right now. I need time, space, to try and make sense of all this."

"I understand," James said softly, the pain in his voice echoing the ache in Peter's chest. "Take all the time you need, Peter. I'll be here when you're ready. Always."

Peter nodded, not trusting himself to speak. He heard James' footsteps, the soft click of the door opening and closing, and then he was alone.

Alone with his thoughts, his fears, his shattered sense of self. He curled in on himself, hugging his knees to his chest as sobs wracked his body. He cried for the life he'd lost, the memories he couldn't reach. He cried for the trust broken, the secrets kept.

But most of all, he cried for James. For the pain he'd seen in those eyes, the fear and desperate need to protect. He didn't understand, couldn't make sense of the higher powers James had spoken of, the dangers that lurked in the shadows of his past.

But he knew, with a certainty that scared him, that his feelings for James were real. That the connection between them, the bond that had been there from the moment they met, was more than just a trick of fate.

Peter lay there, staring at the ceiling, his mind a whirlwind of thoughts and emotions. Time seemed to stretch and warp, minutes bleeding into hours as he grappled with the revelations of the day. The betrayal, the secrets, the love that still burned bright despite it all.

He didn't know how long he'd been there, lost in the labyrinth of his own mind. But when he finally turned his head, the sky outside the window was an inky black, stars twinkling in the distant heavens.

A sudden thought struck him, a jolt of panic lancing through his chest. Was James still here? In the manor, just a few rooms away? The idea of facing him, of seeing those blue eyes filled with guilt and pain, was too much to bear.

No, Peter decided, a grim determination settling over him. He couldn't stay here, couldn't let himself drown in the secrets and lies that seemed to permeate every inch of this town. He needed to get away, to find solid ground beneath his feet.

He needed to go back to New York.

The thought brought a pang of longing, of homesickness for a life he wasn't even sure was real. But it was the only thing that made sense, the only path forward he could see.

Shaking himself, Peter rose from the bed, his limbs heavy and aching. He dressed quickly, pulling on the same clothes he'd worn on his date with James. The memory of that perfect, shining moment seemed like a lifetime ago now, a dream he'd been rudely awakened from.

Quietly, he slipped out of the room, his heart pounding in his chest. The manor was vast, a labyrinth of corridors and staircases that seemed designed to confuse and disorient. Peter felt like a mouse in a maze, scurrying through the shadows in search of an exit.

"Peter?"

The voice made him jump, a yelp of surprise escaping his lips. He whirled around to see Benjamin standing there, his brow furrowed in concern.

"Are you okay?" Benjamin asked, taking a step closer. "What are you doing up and about? Should I call James?"

"No!" The word burst from Peter's lips, sharp and panicked. He took a deep breath, trying to calm the racing of his heart. "No, please don't. I just...I need to get out of here, Benjamin. I need to go back to New York."

Benjamin's frown deepened, confusion and worry warring on his face. "New York? But why? I thought you were happy here, with James."

Peter closed his eyes, the lie burning on his tongue. "I am. I was.

But I just…I have things I need to take care of back home. Loose ends I need to tie up."

It was a flimsy excuse, and from the look on Benjamin's face, he wasn't buying it. But to Peter's relief, he just nodded slowly, a glimmer of understanding in his eyes.

"Alright. If that's what you need, then I won't stop you. Come on, I'll take you to Mr. Johnson. He can drive you to the inn, and from there…well, I guess New York awaits."

Peter felt a rush of gratitude, a lump rising in his throat. "Thank you, Benjamin. Really. I know this must seem crazy, but I just…I need some time. Some space to think."

Benjamin clapped a hand on his shoulder, a gesture of comfort and support. "I get it, Peter. Better than you know. Just…don't stay away too long, okay? This place, these people…they have a way of getting under your skin. In the best way possible."

Peter managed a small, watery smile. "I'll keep that in mind."

Together, they made their way through the manor, the silence heavy but not uncomfortable. When they reached the front door, Benjamin pulled out his phone, tapping out a quick message.

"Mr. Johnson will meet you out front. He'll make sure you get to the inn safe and sound."

Peter nodded, a sudden tightness in his chest. This was it. He was really doing this, really leaving behind the only world that made sense, the only person who made him feel whole.

But he knew, deep in his bones, that it was the right thing to do. The only thing he could do, if he had any hope of finding himself again.

"Thank you, Benjamin. For everything. Tell James…tell him I'm sorry. And that I'll be back. When I'm ready."

Benjamin's smile was sad, but understanding. "I will. Take care of yourself, Peter. And remember, you've always got a home here. No matter what."

With a final nod, Peter stepped out into the night, the cool air a balm on his feverish skin. Mr. Johnson was waiting by a sleek black car, his face impassive as he held the door open.

Peter slid into the backseat, his heart a lead weight in his chest. As the car pulled away, he watched the manor recede in the rear view mirror, until it was nothing more than a distant light in the darkness.

He was on his way. Back to New York, back to the life he'd left behind.

But even as the miles stretched out before him, even as the familiar skyline of the city came into view, he knew, with a certainty that both thrilled and terrified him, that he'd left his heart behind. In a little town called Willowbrook, in the hands of a man named James.

15

Weight of Secrets

James' footsteps echoed through the quiet streets of Willowbrook, a relentless staccato that matched the pounding of his heart. He moved with single-minded focus, his destination clear in his mind: Adrian's Manor, where he had left Peter.

Hours that felt like an eternity, each minute stretching out into an age of uncertainty and regret.

James couldn't shake the image of Peter's face from his mind, the devastation and confusion that had clouded those beautiful eyes as he processed the revelation of their shared past. The way he had looked at James, like he was a stranger, a puzzle he couldn't quite solve. It tore at James' heart, a physical ache that settled deep in his bones.

He should have been more careful, should have guarded his words and his heart more closely. But with Peter, it was like all his carefully constructed walls came crumbling down, leaving him raw and exposed and utterly vulnerable.

And now, Peter knew the truth. Or at least, a part of it. The part that James had been holding close to his chest, a secret he'd sworn to keep until the time was right.

But the time would never be right, not really. Not when the truth held such danger, such potential for destruction. James had seen firsthand the forces that lurked in the shadows of their world, the powers that would stop at nothing to keep the secrets of the past buried.

Powers that would see Peter as a threat, a weapon to be wielded or a pawn to be sacrificed.

The thought made James' blood run cold, a shiver of fear racing down his spine. He had sworn, from the moment he'd first laid eyes on Peter in this new life, that he would protect him. That he would keep him safe from the darkness that threatened to swallow them both.

But now, with the truth laid bare between them, that promise seemed more fragile than ever.

James shook his head, trying to clear the doubts and fears that clouded his mind. He couldn't afford to waver, not now. Not when Peter needed him, needed the strength and certainty that only James could provide.

As he approached the manor, a sense of unease washed over him, a prickling at the back of his neck that set his nerves on edge. Something wasn't right, a discordant note in the usual harmony of the place.

He quickened his pace, his heart pounding in his chest as he hurried up the front steps and pushed through the heavy wooden doors. The foyer was dimly lit, shadows dancing across the walls like ghostly specters.

"James."

He whirled around to see Adrian and Benjamin standing there, their faces etched with concern and a hint of apprehension. They looked like they'd been waiting for him, bracing themselves for the storm they knew was coming.

"Where is he?" James demanded, his voice rough with emotion. "Where's Peter?"

Adrian stepped forward, his hands held out in a placating gesture. "James, listen to me. You need to calm down, give him some space…"

But James was already pushing past him, a sinking feeling in his gut. He couldn't explain it, but he knew, with a certainty that chilled him to the bone, that Peter was gone.

He took the stairs two at a time, his footsteps echoing through the silent halls. When he reached Peter's room, he didn't bother to knock, just flung the door open with a force that sent it crashing against the wall.

The room was empty. The bed was neatly made, the curtains drawn tight against the night. There was no sign of Peter, no trace of his presence save for the faint scent of his cologne lingering in the air.

James felt like he'd been punched in the gut, all the air rushing out of his lungs in a painful whoosh. He staggered back, his hand gripping the door frame for support.

"No," he whispered, the word a broken plea. "No, he can't be gone. He can't…"

"James." Adrian's voice was gentle, but firm. "He's not here. He left last night."

James whirled on him, a sudden fury rising up to replace the despair. "And you just let him go? You didn't try to stop him, to make him see reason?"

Benjamin met his gaze steadily, unflinching in the face of James' anger. "It wasn't my decision to make, James. Peter's a grown man, and he made his choice. We have to respect that."

James shook his head, a bitter laugh escaping his lips. "Respect it? How can I respect a decision born out of fear and confusion? How can I just let him walk away, when I know the dangers that await him out there?"

Benjamin stepped forward, his eyes soft with sympathy. "James, I know this is hard. But you have to trust Peter. Trust that he knows what he needs right now, even if it's not what you want."

James closed his eyes, fighting back the sting of tears. He knew they were right, knew that he couldn't force Peter to stay, to face the truth of their past before he was ready.

But the thought of losing him again, of watching him walk out of his life just when he'd found him…it was more than James could bear.

"I can't lose him," he whispered, his voice raw with emotion. "Not again. Not after everything we've been through, everything we've sacrificed…"

Adrian's hand landed on his shoulder, a comforting weight. "You won't lose him, James. He's just too scared and confused to see things clearly right now. But you have to give him time, give him space to come to terms with it all."

James nodded, a single tear slipping down his cheek. He knew Adrian was right, knew that he had to be strong, to trust in the bond he shared with Peter.

But it was the hardest thing he'd ever had to do, standing there in that empty room, the silence pressing in on him like a physical weight.

"Where did he go?" he asked, his voice barely above a whisper. "Did he say anything, give any clue as to where he might be heading?"

Before Adrian or Benjamin could reply, the doors to the living room burst open, revealing a disheveled and frantic woman who James recognised. Mr. Prattle trailed behind her, his face a mix of apology and exasperation.

"I'm sorry, sir," he said to Adrian, his tone slightly breathless. "I tried to stop her, but she insisted on seeing you immediately."

James stared at Lyra, shock and confusion warring in his mind. What was she doing here, in Willowbrook? And why did she look like she'd just run a marathon, her hair wild and her eyes wide with urgency?

Lyra's hands flew in a flurry of signs, her movements sharp and agitated. Benjamin, stepped forward, his brow furrowed in concentration that James assumed to help translate what she was saying.

"She says Peter's gone," he translated, his voice tight with concern. "He left, went back to New York to try and make sense of everything on his own."

James felt like he'd been punched in the gut, all the air rushing out of his lungs in a painful whoosh. Peter was gone, out there in the world without him, without anyone to protect him from the dangers that lurked in the shadows.

A wave of fear and guilt crashed over him, threatening to drag him under. How could he have let this happen? How could he have failed Peter so completely, so utterly?

He closed his eyes, fighting back the sting of tears. He had to be strong, had to focus on the task at hand. He couldn't afford to fall apart, not now. Not when Peter needed him more than ever.

Lyra's hands were moving again, her expression grave and urgent. Benjamin's eyes widened as he translated her rapid-fire signs.

"She says that she will have to go after him, to bring him back to Willowbrook. Now that his memories and powers are manifesting, his Shadow Self will start wreaking havoc."

James tensed, a cold dread seeping into his bones. "What do you mean, his Shadow Self? What are you talking about, Lyra?"

Lyra's shoulders slumped, a look of defeat and sorrow crossing her face. Her hands moved more slowly now, as if weighed down by the burden of her words.

"When Peter was captured in Tír na nÓg," Benjamin translated, his voice soft and heavy, "there was a witch who tried to take his magic for herself. But Peter was smart, he was able to counteract the ritual. But the witch…she still managed to separate his shadow from him, creating a new entity. One as powerful as Peter was before they took him to the mortal realm."

James clenched his fists, anger and guilt warring within him. "And when they brought him to the mortal world, the curse of those who leave Tír na nÓg under the Dagda's rule took hold. His memories were stripped away, leaving him lost and vulnerable."

Adrian frowned, confusion etched on his face. "But why weren't you two affected by the curse?"

James sighed, running a hand through his hair. "That's because we weren't under the Dagda's authority. The curse only applies to those who are bound to him, who owe him allegiance. Peter, being one of his subjects, wasn't so lucky."

Benjamin's eyes widened, realization dawning. "So when they took him to the mortal world, they knew what would happen. They knew he'd lose his memories, his sense of self."

James nodded grimly, a bitter taste in his mouth. "It was a cruel fate, one I wouldn't wish on anyone. To be stripped of your identity, your past, your very essence…it's a violation of the highest order." He then turned back to Lyra. "Who was the witch?" he demanded, his voice rough with emotion. "Did you see her face, Lyra? Do you know who she is?"

Lyra shook her head, a look of frustration and regret on her face. Her hands moved in a quick, apologetic gesture.

"She can't remember," Benjamin said, his voice tinged with sympathy. "Their faces were masked, hidden from view."

James ran a hand through his hair, a gesture of helplessness and desperation. He felt like he was drowning, like the weight of the world was pressing down on him from all sides.

But he couldn't afford to break, to let the fear and the guilt consume him. Not when Peter was out there, alone and vulnerable, with a dark shadow dogging his every step.

He took a deep breath, squaring his shoulders and setting his jaw with determination. He had to be strong, had to be the rock that Peter needed him to be.

James' mind reeled with the revelations Lyra had shared, a dizzying mix of fear and confusion swirling in his head. A Shadow Self, a dark reflection of Peter's power, born from a witch's twisted ritual. It was a terrifying thought, one that sent a shiver of dread down his spine.

But beneath the fear, a fierce determination burned in his veins. He had to find Peter, had to bring him back to safety before the Shadow Self could cause any more harm. He couldn't bear the thought of Peter out there alone, vulnerable to the forces that sought to tear them apart.

"I'm coming with you," he said to Lyra, his voice brooking no argument. "To New York. I can't just sit here while Peter's in danger."

But Lyra was already shaking her head, her hands moving in a firm, resolute gesture. Benjamin, ever the faithful translator, spoke her words aloud.

"She says you need to stay here, James. Give Peter some space, let him process everything on his own terms. She'll message us if anything happens, if she needs our help."

James wanted to argue, to insist that his place was by Peter's side, no matter the cost. The thought of being separated from him, of not being there to protect him, was like a physical ache in his chest.

But as he looked into Lyra's eyes, saw the fierce determination and unwavering loyalty shining there, he knew she was right. Peter needed time, needed space to come to terms with the truth of his past and the reality of his powers.

And much as it pained him to admit it, James knew his presence would only complicate matters, would only add to the turmoil and confusion Peter was surely feeling.

"Okay," he said at last, the word feeling like a surrender, a white flag waved in the face of his own desperate need. "I'll stay. But Lyra...

promise me you'll keep him safe. Promise me you'll bring him back to me."

Lyra's face softened, a glimmer of understanding shining through the worry. Her hands moved in a gentle, reassuring gesture, a silent vow that spoke louder than words ever could.

James felt a lump rise in his throat, a wave of gratitude and affection washing over him. He didn't know what he'd done to deserve a friend like Lyra, a soul who understood him better than he understood himself at times.

But he knew, with a certainty that burned bright in his heart, that he would never take her for granted. Never forget the sacrifices she'd made, the risks she'd taken, to keep Peter safe and bring them back together.

As Lyra turned to leave, a sudden thought struck James, a question that had been nagging at the back of his mind since she'd arrived. "Lyra, wait," he called out, his voice laced with concern. "Your wings…what happened to them? You're a fairy, aren't you?"

Lyra paused, a flicker of pain crossing her face. Her hands moved slowly, hesitantly, as if the words were difficult to form. "My wings don't work anymore," Benjamin translated, his voice soft and somber. "She used up a lot of magic to track Peter down. That was the price."

James felt a pang of guilt, a heavy weight settling in his chest. Lyra had given up so much, had sacrificed her very essence, to help him and Peter. And what had he done in return? How could he ever repay such a selfless act of love and loyalty?

But before he could voice his thoughts, Benjamin spoke up, a glimmer of excitement in his eyes. "I might be able to help with that," he said, a grin tugging at the corners of his mouth. "Lyra, would you be willing to let me try something?"

Lyra shrugged, a gesture of acquiescence and trust. She nodded, stepping forward to stand in front of Benjamin.

James frowned, a flicker of unease stirring in his gut. "What are you going to do?" he asked, his voice tight with concern.

Benjamin's grin widened, a mischievous glint in his eye. "My magic," he explained, a note of pride in his voice, "basically allows me to change reality at will. It's powerful stuff, but I rarely use it. Whatever I do to Lyra, it'll just be temporary, until her own magic recovers."

James watched, transfixed, as Benjamin reached up and removed the necklace he always wore. In his hands, it shimmered and shifted, transforming into a staff that James had seen him wield once before, in a battle that seemed like a lifetime ago.

Benjamin raised the staff, a look of intense concentration on his face. There were no incantations, no spells or rituals. Just pure, raw magic, a force of will that seemed to radiate from every pore of his being.

Light began to envelop Lyra, a shimmering cocoon that lifted her off the ground. She floated there, suspended in a halo of radiance, her face peaceful and serene.

James watched, his heart pounding in his chest, as the light faded and Lyra drifted gently back to earth. She opened her eyes, a look of wonder and disbelief on her face.

"Try letting your wings out," Benjamin urged, a note of excitement in his voice.

Lyra closed her eyes, a look of intense concentration on her face. And then, with a soft rustle of feathers, her wings unfurled.

But they weren't the delicate, gossamer wings James had seen before, the ones that shimmered with a golden light. These wings were pure white, each feather gleaming like freshly fallen snow.

Lyra's eyes flew open, a look of shock and dismay on her face. Her hands flew in a flurry of signs, too fast for James to follow.

But Benjamin just laughed, a sound of pure, unbridled joy. "She says she looks like a bloody chicken," he translated, his eyes sparkling with mirth. "And that she's going to curse Peter for making her go through all this trouble."

Despite himself, James felt a grin tugging at his own lips. It felt good to laugh, to feel something other than the weight of his own fear and guilt.

"You look beautiful, Lyra," he said, meaning every word. "Like an angel. Peter's lucky to have a friend like you."

Lyra rolled her eyes, but James could see the glimmer of pleasure in her gaze. She reached into her pocket and pulled out a small pouch, pressing it into James' hand.

"Fairy dust," Benjamin explained, his voice soft and reverent. "Her last supply. So we can find her when we need to."

James felt a lump rising in his throat, a wave of emotion threatening to overwhelm him. He clutched the pouch tightly, feeling the weight of Lyra's trust, her love, her sacrifice.

"Thank you," he whispered, the words feeling inadequate in the face of such a gift. "I promise, I won't let you down. I won't let Peter down."

Lyra smiled, a soft, gentle curve of her lips. Her hands moved in a slow, deliberate gesture, a promise and a benediction all in one.

"She says she knows you won't," Benjamin translated, his voice thick with emotion. "She says she believes in you, James. In both of you."

16

Price of Running

Peter

He stood behind the counter of the bustling coffee shop, his hands moving on autopilot as he prepared drink after drink. He'd been back in New York for a couple of days now, trying to slip back into the familiar routine of his old life. But no matter how hard he tried, he couldn't shake the feeling that everything had changed.

"Peter, you okay?" His coworker, Sarah, sidled up next to him, her brow furrowed with concern. "You seem a little…off today."

Peter forced a smile, shaking his head. "I'm fine," he said, the lie tasting bitter on his tongue. "Just tired, I guess."

Sarah raised an eyebrow, clearly unconvinced. "You sure? Because you just put soy milk in that latte instead of almond."

Peter cursed under his breath, quickly dumping the ruined drink and starting over. "Sorry," he muttered, his cheeks burning with embarrassment. "I'll pay more attention."

But even as he said the words, he knew it was a promise he couldn't keep. His mind, no matter how hard he tried to focus, kept drifting back to Willowbrook. To James, and the way he'd looked at Peter with such softness, such devotion, even as Peter had pushed him away.

The guilt was a constant ache in his chest, a weight that seemed to grow heavier with each passing hour. He knew he'd hurt James, had seen the pain and confusion in those hazel eyes as he'd begged Peter to stay.

But he'd run anyway, too scared and overwhelmed to face the truth of his past, the reality of his life. And now, here he was, back in the city he'd once called home, feeling more lost and alone than ever.

"Order up!" The barista called, snapping Peter out of his reverie. He grabbed the cup, turning to hand it to the waiting customer.

But in his distraction, he stumbled, the hot liquid sloshing over the rim and onto his hand. He yelped in pain, nearly dropping the cup in his haste to set it down.

"Whoa, you alright?" The customer asked, her eyes wide with concern.

"Fine," Peter gritted out, cradling his burned hand to his chest. "Just a little clumsy today, I guess."

The customer frowned, looking unconvinced. "Maybe you should take a break," she suggested gently. "You look like you could use a minute."

Peter shook his head, a bitter laugh bubbling up in his throat. A minute? He could take a whole year, and it still wouldn't be enough to sort through the tangled mess of his thoughts, his emotions.

"I'm okay," he said, forcing a smile. "Really. Just a little off my game."

The customer nodded, taking her drink and heading for the door. But Peter could feel her gaze on him, could sense the pity and concern radiating off her in waves.

It was the same look he'd been getting from his coworkers all day, the same whispered conversations that stopped abruptly whenever he walked into the room. They knew something was wrong, could sense the turmoil that was eating him up inside.

But how could he even begin to explain it to them? How could he put into words the feeling of having his entire world turned upside down, of discovering that he was something more than human, something powerful and dangerous and utterly terrifying?

"Peter." The manager's voice cut through his thoughts, sharp and impatient. "Can I see you in the back for a minute?"

Peter's heart sank, a cold dread seeping into his veins. He knew that tone, had heard it directed at other employees just before they were let go.

He followed the manager into the small office, his stomach churning with nerves. The door clicked shut behind them, the sound ominous in the sudden silence.

"Peter, I'm going to be frank with you," the manager said, his face serious. "Your performance lately has been…subpar. Mistakes on orders, spills, daydreaming on the job. It's not like you."

Peter swallowed hard, his mouth suddenly dry. "I know," he said, his voice barely above a whisper. "I'm sorry. I've just been…dealing with some personal stuff."

The manager's face softened slightly, a glimmer of sympathy in his eyes. "I understand that life can be challenging sometimes," he said, not unkindly. "But when you're here, I need you to be fully present. Our customers deserve your full attention and care."

Peter nodded, shame burning hot in his cheeks. "I know. I'll do better, I promise."

The manager sighed, leaning back in his chair. "Look, Peter, I like you. You're a good employee, and you've been a reliable one. But I can't keep overlooking these slip-ups. One more mistake, and I'm going to have to let you go."

The words hit Peter like a punch to the gut, knocking the air from his lungs. He'd known this was coming, had seen the writing on the wall. But somehow, hearing it out loud made it all too real, all too painful.

"I understand," he said, his voice hollow. "It won't happen again."

The manager nodded, a note of finality in the gesture. "See that it doesn't. Now, why don't you take the rest of the day off? Get your head on straight, come back tomorrow ready to work."

Peter mumbled his thanks, stumbling out of the office in a daze. He grabbed his coat and bag, ignoring the curious stares of his coworkers as he hurried out the door.

The cold New York air hit him like a slap in the face, shocking him back to reality. He walked aimlessly, his feet carrying him through the familiar streets and alleys, his mind a whirlwind of thoughts and emotions.

He'd thought coming back to the city, back to the life he'd known before Willowbrook, would help him make sense of everything. Would give him the space and clarity he needed to sort through the tangled web of his past.

But all it had done was make him feel more lost, more alone. More like a stranger in his own skin, a ghost wandering through a world that no longer made sense.

He thought of James, of the love and acceptance he'd found in those strong arms, those gentle eyes. He thought of the way James had looked at him, like he was something precious, something worth fighting for.

And he thought of the way he'd run, the way he'd pushed James away in a moment of fear and confusion. The way he'd broken both their hearts, shattered the fragile trust they'd built.

The guilt was a physical ache in his chest, a weight that seemed to grow heavier with each passing step. He knew he needed to go back, needed to face the truth of who he was and what he meant to James.

But the fear was still there, the overwhelming sense of being lost in a world he didn't understand, a world he wasn't sure he belonged in.

Peter's phone buzzed in his pocket, startling him out of his thoughts. He pulled it out, surprised to see a text from Lyra flashing on the screen.

"Hey Peter, can you come over to my place? I think we should talk."

Peter stared at the message, a mix of emotions swirling in his chest. He'd known Lyra was in New York, had seen her a few times since he'd been back. But the idea of talking, of really opening up about everything that had happened…it scared him.

Still, he found himself typing out a response, his fingers moving almost of their own accord.

"Sure, I'll be there soon."

Part of him was touched, deeply moved that Lyra had followed him, had sought him out even after he'd pushed her and everyone else away. But another part of him felt undeserving, unworthy of her loyalty and support.

He made his way to her house, his steps heavy with the weight of his thoughts. When he reached her apartment, he hesitated, his hand hovering over the doorbell. But before he could ring it, the door swung open, revealing Lyra's smiling face.

"Peter," she signed, her movements fluid and graceful. "Come in, please."

He stepped inside, feeling a sudden rush of warmth and comfort wash over him. Lyra's apartment was cozy and inviting, filled with soft colors and gentle light. It felt like a sanctuary, a haven from the chaos of his own mind.

"I'm sorry," Peter signed, his hands shaking slightly as he formed the words. "For leaving, for pushing you away, for…everything."

Lyra shook her head, her expression soft and understanding. "You don't need to apologize," she signed back, her movements graceful and fluid. "I know this has been overwhelming for you, Peter. It's okay to take time to process everything."

Peter felt a lump rise in his throat, tears pricking at the corners of his eyes. "I just…I don't know what to do, Lyra," he signed, his hands moving frantically. "I feel so lost, so confused. Like I don't know who I am anymore, or where I belong."

Lyra gestured for him to sit, sinking down onto the couch beside him. "That's understandable," she signed, her face etched with sympathy. "You've been through a lot, Peter. Your whole world has been turned upside down. It's natural to feel the way you do."

Peter nodded, swallowing hard. "I told you about what happened with James," he signed, his movements slower now, more deliberate. "How he revealed that we had a shared past. It's just…it's a lot to take in, you know? I feel like I'm scrambling to make sense of everything, to figure out who I am and what I want."

Lyra reached out, taking his hand in hers. Her touch was gentle, comforting, like a lifeline in the midst of a storm. "I understand, Peter," she signed with her free hand. "It's not easy, having your whole world shifted like that. But you're not alone in this. You have people who care about you, who want to support you."

Peter felt a flicker of warmth in his chest, a spark of hope amidst the darkness. "I know," he signed, a small smile tugging at his lips. "And I'm grateful for that, truly. But I can't help feeling like I'm letting everyone down, like I'm running away from my problems instead of facing them head-on."

Lyra squeezed his hand, her eyes fierce with conviction. "Peter, listen to me," she signed, her movements sharp and insistent. "You're not letting anyone down. You're taking the time you need to process everything, to figure out what you want and need. That's important, and it's brave."

Peter felt tears spill down his cheeks, a sob catching in his throat. "I want to believe that. I do," he signed, his hands trembling. "But I'm scared, Lyra. Scared of facing James, of trying to make sense of our past. Scared that he won't understand why I left, or that he'll realize I'm not worth the trouble."

Lyra's brow furrowed, concern etching itself across her features. "Peter, James cares for you," she signed, her movements slow and deliberate. "That kind of thing doesn't just disappear because things get complicated. He'll understand, if you give him the chance. And he'll be there for you, no matter what."

Peter nodded, wiping at his tears with the back of his hand. "I know," he signed, his movements growing steadier. "Deep down, I know that. It's just…it's hard, you know? Hard to trust in that, when everything feels so uncertain."

Lyra smiled, her expression soft and understanding. "I know it's hard, Peter," she signed, her hands moving gently. "But you're not alone in this. You have me, and James, and everyone else who cares about you. We're here for you, no matter what. And when you're ready, we'll be here to help you face whatever comes next."

Peter felt a rush of gratitude, a wave of love and relief that threatened to sweep him away. He leaned forward, pulling Lyra into a fierce hug, feeling her arms wrap around him in a tight, protective embrace.

"Lyra," he said finally, his voice hesitant. "Do you…do you believe in magic?"

Lyra's brow furrowed, confusion flickering across her features. "What do you mean?" she signed, her movements slow and deliberate.

Peter took a deep breath, steeling himself. "I mean…I think I might have magic, Lyra. Abilities that I can't explain, that scare me. And I don't know what to do, or who to talk to about it."

Lyra's eyes widened, surprise and something like understanding dawning on her face. "Magic?" she signed, her expression carefully neutral. "What kind of magic?"

Peter shook his head, frustration welling up inside him. "I don't know, exactly. James and I were attacked near the Lighthouse in Willowbrook by some shadow creatures. And I somehow conjured up this shield the blocked the creatures' attack. I know I must sound crazy but when have I ever lied to you.."

Lyra leaned forward, her gaze intense. "Show me," she signed, her movements sharp and insistent.

Peter hesitated, fear and uncertainty warring in his chest. But something in Lyra's eyes, in the gentle encouragement of her smile, made him want to try.

He closed his eyes, reaching deep within himself, searching for that flicker of power he knew was there. He felt it, a warm, pulsing energy that seemed to flow through his veins, his very being.

But when he tried to grasp it, to bring it to the surface…nothing happened. He opened his eyes, disappointment and frustration washing over him.

"I'm sorry," he said, his voice rough with emotion. "I thought I could show you, but…I don't know how. I don't know how to control it, or even what it is."

Lyra reached out, taking his hand in hers. Her touch was gentle, comforting, a lifeline in the midst of his inner turmoil.

"It's okay," she signed with her free hand, her movements slow and soothing. "I believe you, Peter. And I'm here for you, no matter what."

Peter felt a rush of gratitude, a warmth that spread through his chest like honey. He squeezed Lyra's hand, trying to convey through touch what he couldn't find the words to say.

They sat like that for a while, just taking comfort in each other's presence. But eventually, the restlessness that had been building in Peter's bones all day became too much to ignore.

"I think I need to head home," he signed, an apologetic smile tugging at his lips. "Try to get some rest, clear my head."

Lyra nodded, understanding shining in her eyes. "Of course," she signed back, her movements gentle. "Take all the time you need, Peter. And remember, I'm always here if you need to talk."

Peter stood, pulling Lyra into a tight hug. He breathed in the comforting scent of her, letting it ground him in the moment.

"Thank you," he whispered, knowing she couldn't hear him but needing to say the words anyway. "For everything."

With a final squeeze, he pulled back, smiling softly at Lyra before turning to leave.

The walk back to his apartment was a blur, his mind too full of thoughts and emotions to take in the bustling city around him. He kept his head down, his hands shoved deep in his pockets, trying to make himself as invisible as possible.

When he finally reached his building, he took the stairs two at a time, suddenly desperate for the comfort and familiarity of his own space. But as he approached his door, a sense of unease prickled at the back of his neck.

Something was wrong. He could feel it, a disturbance in the air that set his teeth on edge.

With a shaking hand, he unlocked the door, pushing it open slowly. And as he stepped inside, his heart seized in his chest.

The apartment was in shambles. Furniture overturned, belongings scattered across the floor like confetti. It looked like a bomb had gone off, like a whirlwind of destruction had torn through the space.

"What the hell?" Peter breathed, his voice trembling. He took a cautious step forward, his eyes darting around the room, searching for any sign of the intruder.

But there was nothing, no trace of whoever had done this. Just an eerie silence, broken only by the pounding of his own heart.

He moved through the apartment slowly, taking stock of the damage. His laptop was gone, along with his camera and a few other valuables. But most of his things seemed to be accounted for, just tossed around like toys in a child's playroom.

It wasn't until he reached the bedroom that he noticed something strange. The closet door was ajar, the darkness within seeming to beckon him closer.

With a flicker of trepidation, Peter stepped forward, pulling the door open fully. And there, tucked away in the back corner, was a small compartment he had never noticed before.

His heart in his throat, he reached inside, his fingers brushing against something cool and metallic. He pulled it out, holding it up to the light.

It was an amulet, ancient and tarnished, with strange symbols etched into its surface. It seemed to pulse in his hand, an otherworldly energy that made his skin tingle. And beside it, a note. Written in a language he couldn't understand, the characters seeming to dance and shift before his eyes.

With trembling fingers, he unfolded the paper, his breath catching in his throat as he tried to make sense of the foreign words. But as he stared at the cryptic message, something strange began to happen. The amulet in his hand grew warm, almost hot, and suddenly, his mind was flooded with images.

Flashes of memory, of sensation, of a life he didn't recognize. A dark, shadowy figure, looming over him, its presence cold and malevolent. Whispers in the darkness, a language he couldn't understand but somehow knew was ancient, powerful.

And through it all, a sense of dread, of fear, of something lurking just beyond the edges of his consciousness.

With a gasp, Peter dropped the amulet, watching it clatter to the floor. His heart was racing, his breath coming in sharp, ragged bursts. He knew, with a certainty that chilled him to the bone, that the figure in his visions was connected to his past. To his powers, to the strange and terrifying things that had been happening to him.

And he knew, with a sinking sense of horror, that it may have followed him to New York.

Hands shaking, he picked up the amulet and the note, stuffing them into his pocket. He couldn't leave them here, couldn't risk someone else finding them.

But as he turned to leave the apartment, he couldn't shake the feeling that he was being watched. A prickling sensation at the back of his neck, a whisper of movement in the shadows.

He quickened his pace, his heart pounding in his ears as he fled the building. He didn't know where he was going, didn't have a plan or a destination in mind. All he knew was that he had to get away, had to put as much distance as possible between himself and the dark presence that seemed to be dogging his every step.

But even as he ran, even as he pushed himself to the brink of exhaustion, he couldn't escape the truth that was beginning to dawn on him. And now, by running away, by trying to hide from the truth.

He may have put everyone he cared about in danger.

17

Shadows and Moonlight

Peter

He trudged through the tranquil woodland, dappled sunlight filtering through the emerald canopy overhead. The earthy scent of moss and damp leaves filled his nostrils as his mind drifted, untethered.

He really didn't know how he ended up here. It was as if the forest had beckoned to him, an ethereal siren song luring him deeper into its verdant embrace.

With each step, the distant hum of traffic and chatter faded, replaced by the gentle rustling of leaves and the melodic chirping of unseen birds. Peter felt a growing sense of disconnection, the trappings of his everyday life seeming to belong to another world entirely. Out here, amidst the ancient trees and hidden glens, the concerns of work, bills, and social obligations held no sway.

And yet, Peter couldn't shake the prickling unease that crept up his spine. It was a feeling he couldn't quite put his finger on, a whisper of wrongness that threaded through the tranquil atmosphere like an discordant note in a symphony.

"Get it together, Peter," he muttered to himself, shaking his head as if to dislodge the intrusive thoughts. "You're just being paranoid. There's nothing out here but trees and squirrels."

But even as he spoke the words aloud, seeking to reassure himself, the feeling only intensified. The hair on the back of his neck stood on end, and a chill raced down his arms, raising goosebumps in its wake.

Peter stopped in his tracks, his heart beginning to thud against his ribs. "Okay, this is getting weird," he said, his voice sounding small and thin in the vast expanse of the forest. "I think it's time to head back."

He turned to retrace his steps, eager to leave behind the unsettling sensations that plagued him. But as he took his first step back towards the city, a sound shattered the tranquility of the woods—a chilling, inhuman cry that seemed to come from everywhere and nowhere at once.

Peter froze, his breath catching in his throat. The sound was unlike anything he had ever heard before, a wailing shriek that pierced him to his very core. It was a sound of anguish, of rage, of hunger. And it was close.

His eyes darted around the shadowed forest, searching for the source of the terrifying cry. But the trees remained silent and still, their branches swaying gently in a breeze that Peter could no longer feel.

"Who's there?" he called out, his voice trembling despite his efforts to keep it steady. "Show yourself!"

Silence greeted his words, broken only by the thundering of his own heartbeat in his ears. Peter strained his senses, desperate to catch any sign of movement or sound that might betray the presence of whatever had made that awful noise.

And then, from the corner of his eye, he saw it—a flicker of shadow, darting between the trees like a wisp of smoke. Peter whirled around, his eyes wide and his breath coming in short, sharp gasps.

"I know you're there," he said, his voice sounding braver than he felt. "Come out and face me!"

But the shadow vanished as quickly as it had appeared, leaving Peter alone once more in the suddenly oppressive stillness of the forest. He could feel eyes upon him, hidden gazes that seemed to bore into his very soul. The feeling of being watched was overwhelming, a physical weight that pressed down on him from all sides.

Peter's mind raced as he tried to make sense of what was happening. Was this some kind of prank? A hallucination brought on by stress and lack of sleep? Or was there truly something out there, lurking in the shadows, waiting to pounce?

He took a deep breath, forcing himself to calm down. "Okay, Peter," he said softly to himself. "You can do this. Just stay focused and get out of here."

With newfound determination, Peter began to pick his way through the forest once more, keeping a wary eye on the shadows that seemed to dance and flicker at the edge of his vision. Each snap of a twig beneath his feet made him flinch, his nerves stretched taut as bowstrings.

As he walked, Peter's mind drifted unbidden to James—beautiful, enigmatic James with his piercing eyes and secretive smile. What would James think if he could see Peter now, jumping at shadows like a frightened child?

The thought brought a wry smile to Peter's face despite his unease. James would probably just laugh that rich, warm laugh of his and pull Peter into his arms, chasing away all the darkness with the sheer force of his presence.

"I wish you were here, James," Peter murmured softly, his voice barely above a whisper. "I could really use one of your pep talks right about now."

As if in answer to his quiet plea, a breeze suddenly stirred the leaves around him—a warm, gentle wind that seemed to caress his skin like a lover's touch. Peter closed his eyes for a moment, letting the sensation wash over him, feeling some of his anxiety begin to melt away.

But then, just as quickly as it had come, the breeze died away, leaving him once more in the oppressive stillness of the forest. Peter's eyes snapped open, a renewed sense of dread settling in the pit of his stomach.

Peter's heart raced as the realization sank in. Something was wrong. Something was very, very wrong.

And so he had run. He had run faster than he ever had before, his feet pounding against the earth, his lungs burning with each gasping breath. But no matter how quickly he moved, the entity was always just behind him, its presence like a physical weight pressing down upon him.

Peter's mind raced as he ran, trying to make sense of what was happening. But there were no answers, only the relentless pursuit and the growing sense of dread that coiled in his gut.

As he ran, Peter began to tire, his legs growing heavy and his vision blurring at the edges. He stumbled over a root, nearly falling, but managed to catch himself at the last moment.

"Keep going," he muttered to himself, gritting his teeth against the burning in his muscles. "Just keep going."

But even as he pushed himself onward, he knew that he could not run forever. Sooner or later, he would have to face his pursuer—and when that moment came, he could only hope that he would be ready.

Suddenly, Peter burst into a clearing, the moonlight flooding down upon him in a pool of silver. He stumbled to a halt, his chest heaving as he fought to catch his breath.

And there, at the edge of the clearing, the entity emerged from the shadows.

Peter felt a thrill of fear run through him as he stared into those glowing eyes, so full of malice and hunger. But beneath the fear, there was something else—a flicker of recognition, a sense that he had seen those eyes before.

"What do you want from me?" he demanded, his voice raw and ragged from the chase.

The entity said nothing for a long moment, simply staring at him with that unnerving gaze. And then, it spoke, its voice like the whisper of dead leaves underfoot.

"You know what I want, Peter. You have always known."

Peter felt a chill run down his spine at the sound of his name on the creature's tongue. How could it know who he was?

"I don't know what you're talking about," he said, trying to keep his voice steady. "I've never seen you before in my life."

The entity laughed, a sound like the grating of bone against bone. "Oh, but you have, Peter. You see me every time you look in the mirror."

And with those words, Peter felt a sickening lurch in his stomach as realization dawned. He looked down at the ground, at the patch of moonlight where his shadow should have been.

But there was nothing there. Nothing but bare earth and the faint impression of footprints.

Peter looked back up at the entity, his eyes wide with shock and horror. "You're...you're my shadow," he whispered, his voice trembling. "But how? Why?"

The entity grinned, a terrible, twisted expression that made Peter's skin crawl. "I am the part of you that you have always tried to deny, Peter. The darkness that lurks within your heart, the hunger that gnaws at your soul. I am the truth that you have been running from all your life."

Peter shook his head, backing away from the creature. "No," he said, his voice cracking. "No, that's not true. I'm not like you. I'm not..."

But even as he spoke the words, he could feel the doubt creeping in, the certainty that the entity was right.

The entity took a step forward, its form seeming to grow and stretch, filling the clearing with its presence. "You cannot escape me, Peter," it hissed, its voice like venom in his ears. "I am a part of you, whether you like it or not. And now, it is time for you to embrace your true nature."

Peter's heart raced as he stared into those glowing, malevolent eyes. Fear coursed through his veins, but beneath it, a flicker of determination sparked to life. He wouldn't let this thing win, this dark manifestation of his own deepest fears and doubts. He was more than his shadows, more than the darkness that lurked within.

Gritting his teeth, Peter reached deep within himself, desperately searching for something, anything, to help him in this dire moment. He had never been in a situation like this before, never faced an enemy that seemed to know him better than he knew himself.

As he searched his soul, Peter suddenly became aware of a strange sensation, a warmth that seemed to emanate from his very core. It was unfamiliar, yet somehow comforting, like a long-forgotten memory stirring from the depths of his being.

Instinctively, Peter latched onto this feeling, this glowing ember hidden within. He didn't understand what it was, but in this moment of desperation, he knew he had to try something, anything, to save himself.

With a defiant cry, more a plea than a command, Peter thrust out his hand toward the advancing entity. He willed this newfound warmth to come forth, to manifest in some way that could strike down his foe.

But nothing happened.

Peter's eyes widened in shock and disbelief as he stared at his outstretched hand, waiting for some kind of reaction, some rush of energy or crackle of arcane might. But there was only silence, and the mocking laughter of the entity before him.

"What's this?" the shadow taunted, its voice dripping with cruel amusement. "The little lost boy thinks he has power? Thinks he can stand against me with some pathetic, untrained magic?"

Peter's heart sank as the realization hit him. Magic. That's what this feeling was, this ember glowing within him. But he had no idea how to use it, how to shape it into something tangible and powerful.

Panic rose in his throat as the entity drew closer, its dark form looming over him. Peter's mind raced, desperately grasping for some way to tap into this power, to make it obey his will.

But he was untrained, unprepared. He had never even known he possessed magic until recently, and now, when he needed it most, it lay dormant and unresponsive within him.

The entity's laughter grew louder, more mocking, as it savored Peter's helplessness. "Foolish child," it hissed, raising a shadowy claw to strike. "You have no power here. You have no chance against me."

Peter's breath came in ragged gasps as he stared death in the face, his untapped magic a taunting reminder of his own inadequacy. He had failed, and now he would pay the ultimate price.

But even as despair threatened to consume him, a tiny spark of determination flickered to life in Peter's heart. No. He would not give up. He would not let this monster, this twisted reflection of his own fears, triumph over him.

He might not know how to use his magic, but he would keep trying, keep fighting, until his last breath. For James, for his friends, for himself - he would not go down without a fight.

With a roar of defiance, Peter leapt to his feet, his eyes blazing with a resolve he hadn't known he possessed. He would meet his fate head-on, magic or no magic.

"Time to die, little mage," it hissed, raising one clawed hand to strike.

But even as the blow fell, something deep within Peter's core ignited. A spark of light, small but fierce, burst into life, flooding his veins with sudden, glorious power.

With a desperate, defiant cry, Peter flung out his hand, and this time, his magic answered. A bolt of pure, shadow energy exploded from his palm, slamming into the entity's chest and sending it reeling back with a howl of pain and rage.

Peter stared at his hand in amazement, hardly daring to believe what he had just done. But there was no time to marvel at his own power, for the entity was already recovering, its eyes blazing with fury.

"You'll pay for that, you little bastard," it snarled, gathering itself for another attack.

But before it could strike, a new voice cut through the night air, sharp and cold as a blade.

"Finish him quickly, you imbecile! Stop toying with him and end it!"

Peter whirled around, searching for the source of the voice. But there was no one there - only the shadows, and the entity still advancing upon him.

He turned back to face his foe, his heart pounding in his chest. He had to end this now, before whoever had spoken could interfere.

Reaching out with his senses, Peter suddenly knew what to do like it was second nature to him. He felt for the shadows around him - the deep, cool pools of darkness that lurked beneath the trees and in the hollows of the earth. He could feel them stirring, responding to his call.

With a surge of will, he commanded them to rise up, to take form and shape. And to his amazement, they obeyed.

Tendrils of inky blackness rose from the ground like spectral serpents, weaving and twisting through the air. They converged upon the entity, wrapping around its limbs, its torso, its throat.

The creature thrashed and struggled, but the shadows held fast, tightening their grip with each passing second. Peter could feel the strain upon his own mind as he fought to maintain control, pouring all of his strength and focus into the effort.

"Impossible!" the entity howled, its voice thin and strained.

Peter gritted his teeth, sweat beading upon his brow as he redoubled his efforts. "I am more than you know," he ground out, his voice low and fierce.

The shadow laughed, a chilling sound that echoed through the clearing. "You think you can stop me, boy?" it taunted, its form rippling and shifting as it strained against the shadowy tendrils that held it. "I am the darkness within you, the part of you that you can never escape."

With a sudden burst of strength, the entity tore free from the shadows' grasp, sending inky fragments scattering through the air. Peter stumbled back, his eyes wide with shock and exhaustion. He could feel his energy waning, his newfound magic sputtering like a candle in the wind.

But he couldn't give up. Not now, not when everything he loved was at stake. Gritting his teeth, Peter reached out once more, trying to summon the shadows to his aid. He could feel them responding, sluggishly, reluctantly, but he didn't know how to shape them, how to make them obey his will.

The entity lunged forward, its claws slashing through the air. Peter barely managed to dodge, feeling the whisper of shadow against his skin. He couldn't keep this up much longer. His body ached, his mind reeled, and his magic felt like a distant, unreachable thing.

"Is that all you've got?" the shadow mocked, circling him like a predator toying with its prey. "You're pathetic, Peter. Weak. Just like you've always been."

Peter's heart clenched at the words, tears of frustration and despair stinging his eyes. Maybe the shadow was right. Maybe he was weak, maybe he had always been destined to fail.

But then, just as despair threatened to consume him, Peter heard a sound that made his heart leap with sudden, desperate hope. The beating of wings, strong and steady, growing louder with each passing second.

He looked up, hardly daring to believe it. But there, descending from the sky like an angel of light, was a figure he knew as well as his own reflection.

Lyra.

Lyra alighted on the ground, her wings shimmering with an otherworldly glow. The gust of her arrival sent leaves swirling through the air, momentarily breaking the shadow's focus.

Peter stumbled towards her, relief and gratitude welling up within him. "Lyra," he gasped out, his voice ragged. "You're here. How did you—"

But Lyra wasn't looking at him. Her eyes, fierce and determined, were fixed on the shadow. With a swift, decisive gesture, she signed to Peter: "Stay back."

Peter blinked, surprised by the command in her movements. Lyra, gentle, playful Lyra, looked like a warrior ready for battle.

The shadow, too, seemed taken aback by her appearance. But then its shock turned to a sneer, its eyes glinting with malicious recognition.

"You," it hissed, its voice dripping with contempt. "I should have known you'd show up, fairy. Always meddling in things that don't concern you."

Lyra's expression remained impassive, but her wings flared brighter, the golden glow intensifying until it was almost painful to look at. She raised her hands, and Peter felt the air crackle with energy, with a power older and deeper than anything he had ever known.

The shadow recoiled, its form flickering and wavering under the onslaught of light. It hissed and spat, lashing out with tendrils of darkness, but Lyra's glow burned them away like mist beneath the sun.

Peter watched, awestruck and bewildered, as his best friend and his worst nightmare battled before him. He didn't understand how Lyra could be here, how she could wield such magic, or why the shadow seemed to know her.

But right now, none of that mattered. All that mattered was that she was here, fighting for him, protecting him as she always had.

With a final, wrenching effort, Lyra thrust her hands forward, and a wave of blinding light exploded from her, engulfing the shadow in its radiant embrace. The entity screamed, a sound of rage and anguish that seemed to shatter the very air.

But even as the light consumed it, the shadow's voice rang out, defiant and menacing. "This isn't over!" it hissed, its words echoing in Peter's mind. "You can't banish me forever. I am a part of you, and I will always be there, waiting in the darkness."

Peter felt a chill run down his spine at the shadow's words, fear and doubt creeping back into his heart. But Lyra's light only grew brighter, her wings flaring with a power that seemed to fill the entire clearing.

The shadow let out a final, despairing wail as the light consumed it entirely, its form dissipating like smoke on the wind.

And then, as suddenly as it had appeared, the shadow was gone, banished by the power of Lyra's light.

In the sudden, ringing silence that followed, Peter felt his knees give way. He collapsed to the ground, his body shaking with exhaustion and delayed shock.

Lyra was at his side in an instant, her wings folding behind her as she knelt beside him. Her hands moved in rapid, urgent signs, her expression a mix of concern and relief.

But Peter could barely focus on her words. His mind was reeling, trying to make sense of everything that had just happened. The magic that had awakened within him, the shadow's taunting words, Lyra's unexpected appearance and incredible power...

It was all too much. He felt like he was drowning, like the world was spinning out of control and he couldn't find his footing.

Lyra's hands grasped his, her touch warm and grounding. She signed to him, slowly and deliberately, forcing him to focus on her words.

"Peter," she signed, her eyes locked on his. "I know you're confused. I know you're scared. But you're not alone. You've never been alone."

Peter felt tears welling up in his eyes, hot and stinging. He clung to Lyra's hands like a lifeline, feeling the weight of his own inadequacy pressing down on him.

"But I failed," he signed back, his movements clumsy and shaky. "I couldn't control my magic. I couldn't beat the shadow. If you hadn't come..."

Lyra shook her head fiercely, her expression stern. "You didn't fail, Peter," she signed. "You faced your darkness. You fought back. That takes more strength than you know."

Peter swallowed hard, wanting desperately to believe her. But the shadow's words still echoed in his mind, taunting him with his own weakness.

"What if it comes back?" he signed, his hands trembling. "What if I can't stop it next time? What if I'm not strong enough?"

Lyra's gaze softened, her hands moving to cup his face. "You are strong, Peter," she signed. "Stronger than you realize. And you're not facing this alone. You have me. You have James. You have all of us."

At the mention of James' name, Peter felt a pang of longing so sharp it took his breath away. He thought of warm brown eyes, of gentle hands and a smile that could chase away any shadow.

God, he missed James. He missed all of them even he haven't knew for long. And that was the last thing he remembered thinking after everything turned black.

18

Love Despite Being Hurt

Sitting at the head of the conference table, his brow furrowed as he tried to concentrate on the financial reports spread out before him. The numbers seemed to blur together, his mind constantly drifting to thoughts of Peter and the unresolved tension that hung between them.

It had been days since their last conversation, since Peter had walked out the door with hurt and confusion in his eyes. James knew he should have gone after him, should have tried harder to explain, but his own pride and fear had held him back.

Now, as he sat in this stuffy boardroom, surrounded by the trappings of his corporate empire, all he could think about was Peter. His gentle smile, his kind heart, the way he made James feel like anything was possible.

A sudden commotion outside the office snapped James out of his reverie. He glanced up sharply, exchanging a look of concern with Adrian.

"What the hell is going on out there?" James muttered, pushing back from the table and striding towards the door. Adrian followed close behind, his expression grim.

As they stepped out into the hallway, James felt his heart stop. There, in the center of the chaos, was Lyra. Her face was etched with worry, her delicate fairy wings fluttering anxiously as she cradled an unconscious figure in her arms.

A figure that James would know anywhere.

"Peter!" he cried, rushing forward. Panic and guilt warred within him as he took in Peter's battered form, his clothes torn and his skin marred with bruises and cuts.

Lyra looked up at James, her eyes wide and pleading. With one hand, she signed frantically, her movements sharp and urgent.

"Shadow…attacked…woods…barely got him out…"

James felt his blood run cold. James Hadn't been there to protect the man he loved more than life itself.

With shaking hands, he reached out and gathered Peter into his arms, cradling him gently against his chest. He could feel the faint rise and fall of Peter's breathing, the weak flutter of his heartbeat, and it was both a relief and a terror.

He looked down at Peter's pale, still face, feeling tears sting his eyes. "I'm sorry," he whispered, his voice cracking. "I'm so sorry, Peter. I should have been there. I should have protected you."

Beside him, Lyra placed a gentle hand on his arm. When James glanced at her, she signed slowly, deliberately, making sure he understood.

"Not your fault. Peter chose to face this alone. He didn't want to put you in danger."

James shook his head, anger and frustration welling up within him. "But that's just it, isn't it?" he said, his voice raw. "He shouldn't have had to face it alone. I should have been there, Lyra. I should have been by his side, no matter the danger."

Lyra's expression softened, her eyes filled with understanding. "You're here now," she signed. "That's what matters. Peter needs you, James. He needs all of us."

James swallowed hard, nodding. She was right. As much as he wanted to wallow in his own guilt and self-recrimination, Peter needed him to be strong now. Needed him to be the rock, the anchor in the storm.

Lyra's hands moved urgently, her signs sharp and insistent. "We need to get him somewhere safe, somewhere he can heal, away from prying eyes and potential threats."

James' mind raced, trying to think of a place that could offer the privacy and protection Peter needed.

"I know where we can go," he said, already gathering Peter into his arms once more. "My rental house. It's secure, and I have a room there that's completely off the grid."

Lyra nodded, relief flickering across her face. "Good. Let's go, quickly."

As they hurried out, James' mind was already racing ahead. He needed to contact Simon, to make sure he had everything they might need to treat Peter's injuries.

With one hand, he fumbled for his phone, awkwardly typing out a message while still cradling Peter close.

"Simon, it's James. I need you to meet us at the house, as soon as possible. Bring any medical supplies you can find. It's an emergency."

He hit send, praying that Simon would understand the urgency, would drop whatever he was doing and come to their aid.

The journey to the rental house seemed to take an eternity, every second stretching out in agonizing slow motion. James held Peter tightly, murmuring words of comfort and reassurance, even though he knew Peter couldn't hear him.

"Stay with me, Peter," he whispered, pressing a gentle kiss to Peter's forehead. "Stay with me."

When they finally arrived, James wasted no time. He carried Peter inside, heading straight to his bed room. It was a small, cozy space, with a comfortable bed and all the amenities they might need.

Gently, he laid Peter down on the bed, his hands shaking as he tried to arrange him in a position that might ease his pain. Lyra was at his side in an instant, her own hands moving with a healer's precision as she checked Peter's vital signs.

"His breathing is steady," she signed, her face etched with concern. "But he's still unresponsive. We need to clean and dress these wounds, and fast."

James nodded, already moving to gather supplies. He had never been more grateful for his paranoid streak, for the way he had always kept this room stocked with medical equipment and emergency rations.

Just as he was laying out bandages and antiseptic, there was a knock at the door. James tensed, his hand instinctively reaching for the weapon at his hip.

But then a familiar voice called out, muffled by the heavy wood. "James? It's Simon. I got your message."

James let out a shaky breath, relief flooding through him. He hurried to the door, ushering Simon inside.

Simon's eyes widened as he took in the scene - Peter lying pale and still on the bed, Lyra hovering over him with worry written all over her face.

"My god," Simon breathed, already reaching for his medical bag. "What happened?"

"His shadow attacked him," James said, his voice tight. "The damn thing that's been haunting him and Lyra managed to get him out."

Simon nodded grimly, moving to Peter's side. "Let me take a look."

Together, the three of them worked to clean and dress Peter's wounds. James poured every ounce of his focus, his love, into each gentle touch, each careful bandage.

He couldn't shake the feeling that this was his fault, that he should have been there to protect Peter. The guilt gnawed at him, a constant ache in his chest.

But he pushed it down, forced himself to concentrate on the task at hand. Peter needed him now, needed his strength and his support.

As the hours ticked by and Peter remained unconscious, James felt fear clawing at his throat. What if Peter never woke up? What if the shadow had done some kind of irreparable damage, something beyond the reach of medicine or magic?

He couldn't lose Peter. Couldn't even bear the thought of it. Peter was his heart, his soul, the one bright spot in a life that had been filled with so much darkness.

Lyra seemed to sense his spiraling thoughts. She reached out, placing a comforting hand on his arm.

"He's strong, James," she signed, her eyes fierce with conviction. "He's a fighter. He'll come back to us. He's just drained."

James managed a nod, blinking back the tears that threatened to fall. "I hope you're right," he whispered. "I don't know what I'd do without him."

Simon finished tying off the last bandage, his face grim. "We've done all we can for now," he said. "The rest is up to him."

James swallowed hard, reaching out to take Peter's hand in his. It felt so cold, so lifeless. Nothing like the warm, vibrant touch he had come to know and crave.

As he sat there for a couple of hours, lost in his own thoughts and fears, a soft knock at the door startled him. He looked up to see Lyra entering the room, her face etched with concern.

"How is he?" she signed, her movements gentle but urgent.

James took a deep breath, trying to steady himself. "I think... I think I can feel his body starting to heal," he said, his voice rough with emotion. "It's slow, but it's happening."

Lyra nodded, relief flickering across her face. James watched her hands intently as she signed, trying to piece together the meaning. His sign language was still rudimentary at best, but he knew Lyra well enough to grasp the general gist of her words.

Suddenly, Lyra's expression shifted. She reached into her pocket and pulled out an object, holding it up for James to see.

James' eyes widened as he recognized the amulet, its surface covered in intricate symbols and runes. A tracking amulet, designed to locate and monitor its wearer.

"Where did you get that?" he asked sharply, fear and suspicion warring in his chest.

Lyra set the amulet down on the bedside table, then reached into her pocket again. This time, she pulled out a folded piece of paper, worn and yellowed with age.

James took the paper with shaking hands, unfolding it carefully. The words that stared back at him were written in ancient Gaelic, a language he had studied in his youth but had never fully mastered.

"What does it say?" he asked, looking up at Lyra with desperate eyes.

Lyra shook her head, her own frustration evident. She pointed to the amulet, then to Peter, her signs becoming more emphatic.

"You found these on Peter?" James asked, dread coiling in his gut. "In his pocket?"

Lyra nodded, her face grim.

"Do you have any idea how he got them?" James pressed, his mind racing with possibilities, each more terrifying than the last.

Again, Lyra shook her head. She pointed to the amulet once more, then made a quick, slashing motion with her hand.

"You destroyed it," James said, relief and gratitude washing over him. "Thank god. But... if they were tracking him..."

He didn't need to finish the thought. The implications were clear. Whoever had given Peter these items, whoever was trying to monitor his movements... they would know he was in Willowbrook now. They would be coming for him.

James felt a wave of exhaustion wash over him, the events of the past few hours finally catching up to him. He slumped back in his chair, his hand still clasping Peter's.

"We'll deal with it," he murmured, more to himself than to Lyra. "Whatever comes, we'll face it together. We'll keep him safe."

Lyra placed a gentle hand on his shoulder, her touch a silent promise of support. James managed a weak smile, gratitude welling up in his chest.

"Thank you," he signed clumsily, hoping she would understand. "For everything."

Lyra smiled, her eyes soft with understanding. She gestured to the bed, then mimed sleeping, her meaning clear.

James hesitated, torn between his need to stay awake, to keep watch over Peter, and the bone-deep exhaustion that threatened to drag him under.

But in the end, his body made the decision for him. His eyelids grew heavy, his head nodding forward until it came to rest on the bed beside Peter's hand.

Just before sleep claimed him, James found himself gazing at Peter's sleeping form, his heart swelling with a mix of love and regret. The words tumbled from his lips, soft and sincere in the quiet of the room.

"Peter," he whispered, his voice barely audible even to his own ears. "I don't know if you can hear me, but there's something I need to say."

He took a deep breath, his hand tightening around Peter's.

"Our friendship, it's… it's evolved into something more. Something deeper. And I've been too blind, too stubborn, to see it until now."

He closed his eyes, memories of their time together flashing through his mind. The laughter, the shared glances, the electricity that seemed to crackle between them whenever they touched.

"I thought… I thought what I felt for you was just a fluke. A momentary lapse in judgment. But I realize now that it was so much more than that."

A single tear slipped down his cheek, landing softly on the bedsheets.

"I love you, Peter. I think I've loved you for a long time. And I'm so sorry it took me this long to see it, to acknowledge it."

He brought Peter's hand to his lips, pressing a gentle kiss to his knuckles.

"I promise you, when you wake up, things will be different. I'll be different. I'll be the man you deserve, the partner you've always needed me to be."

His voice cracked, exhaustion and emotion finally overtaking him.

"Just… just come back to me, Peter. Come back to me, and I'll spend the rest of my life showing you how much you mean to me."

19

Echo of the Past

James

There was a slight movement beside him pulling him from the depths of sleep. His eyes flew open, his heart pounding in his chest as he turned to look at the bed.

Bathed in the soft glow of the bedside lamp, was Peter. His eyelids were fluttering, his breathing growing deeper and more even as he gradually regained consciousness.

James felt a wave of relief and joy crash over him, so powerful that it stole his breath. He leaned in closer, his hand shaking as he gently brushed Peter's hair back from his forehead.

"Peter?" he whispered, his voice thick with emotion. "Can you hear me?"

Slowly, Peter's eyes opened, blinking up at James with a mix of confusion and pain. "James?" he croaked, his voice hoarse from disuse. "What happened? Where am I?"

James felt tears welling up in his eyes, his heart swelling with love and gratitude. He took Peter's hand in both of his own, bringing it to his lips for a gentle kiss.

"You're safe now," he murmured, his voice trembling with the depth of his feelings. "You're in my room, and I'm here. I'm not going anywhere."

Peter's eyes widened as he took in his surroundings, realization dawning on his face. "You brought me here?" he asked softly, wonder and gratitude mingling in his tone. "You took care of me?"

James nodded, a watery smile spreading across his face. "Lyra brought you back here." he said, his voice low and fervent. "I'll always take care of you, Peter. No matter what happens, I'll always be here for you."

Peter's eyes filled with tears, and he reached up with his free hand to touch James' face, his fingers trembling against James' cheek. "I'm sorry," he whispered, his voice breaking. "I'm sorry for running away, for pushing you away. I was just so scared, so confused…"

James shook his head, leaning into Peter's touch like a man starved for affection. "You have nothing to apologize for," he said firmly, his eyes locking onto Peter's. "I understand, Peter. I really do. And I'm sorry too, for not being there when you needed me, for not being able to tell you everything."

Peter's breath hitched, his eyes searching James' face with a desperate intensity. "What are you saying, James?" he asked, his voice barely above a whisper.

James took a deep breath, gathering all of his courage and all of his love. "I'm saying that I love you, Peter," he said, his voice strong and clear despite the tears streaming down his face. "I've loved you for longer than I can remember, and I'll love you until the end of time. You're my everything, Peter. My heart, my soul, my home."

Peter let out a sob, his own tears spilling over as he surged forward, capturing James' lips in a kiss that felt like coming home, like the first breath of air after being underwater for too long.

They clung to each other, pouring all of their love and longing into the kiss, their tears mingling on their cheeks as they finally, finally let themselves feel the depth of their connection.

When they finally broke apart, breathless and overwhelmed, James rested his forehead against Peter's, his eyes closed and his heart full to bursting. "We're going to figure this out," he whispered, his voice fierce with determination. "Together. No more secrets, no more running. Just you and me, side by side, always."

Peter nodded, a small, hopeful smile curving his lips. "Together," he echoed, the word a promise.

They simply held each other, basking in the warmth and comfort of their embrace. But as the seconds ticked by, James felt a flicker of unease stirring in his gut.

James looked at Peter, taking in the pallor of his skin and the dark circles under his eyes. Even in his weakened state, Peter was still the most beautiful sight James had ever seen. But he needed to know what had happened, needed to understand the dangers they were facing.

"Peter," he said softly, hesitantly. "I know you're tired, but… do you think you're well enough to tell me what happened? Before Lyra found you?"

Peter took a deep breath, wincing slightly at the movement. "I… I think so," he said, his voice still hoarse. "It's all a bit of a blur, but… I remember walking towards my apartment and saw that the door was slightly opened."

He trailed off, his eyes growing distant as he lost himself in the memory. James squeezed his hand gently, bringing him back to the present.

"Take your time," he murmured, his thumb stroking soothing circles on Peter's skin. "I'm here, and you're safe."

Peter nodded, swallowing hard before continuing. "When I went to investigate, I found my place had been ransacked. Drawers emptied, furniture overturned… it was a mess."

James felt a flash of anger at the thought of someone violating Peter's space, invading his privacy. But he pushed it down, focusing on Peter's words.

"I was about to call the police when I found it. The letter, and the amulet." Peter's hand went to his pocket, his face crumpling in confusion when he found it empty.

"I have them," James said quickly, reaching over to the bedside table and picking up the items Lyra had given him. "Lyra found them on you, after... after she saved you."

Peter took the amulet with trembling fingers, his eyes widening as he examined the intricate symbols etched into its surface. "What... what is this?" he whispered, fear and awe mingling in his voice.

James sighed, running a hand through his hair. "It's an ancient tracking amulet," he explained, his voice low and serious. "Whoever gave it to you, they were using it to monitor your movements, to keep tabs on you."

Peter's face paled, his grip on the amulet tightening. "But why?" he asked, his voice small and scared. "Why would someone do that?"

James shook his head, frustration and fear warring in his chest. "I don't know," he admitted. "But Lyra destroyed it before they could do any more harm. She made sure they can't use it to find you again."

Peter let out a shaky breath, relief and gratitude flashing across his face. "Lyra..." he murmured, a small smile tugging at his lips. "I owe her so much."

James nodded, his own smile bittersweet. "We both do," he said softly. "She's an amazing friend."

For a moment, they were both silent, lost in their own thoughts. Then Peter spoke again, his voice hesitant and unsure.

"There's something else," he said, his eyes fixed on the bed sheets. "After I found the amulet, I... I went for a walk. To clear my head, to try and make sense of everything."

James felt a flicker of unease stir in his gut. He had a feeling he knew where this was going, but he stayed silent, letting Peter continue at his own pace.

"I ended up in the woods, and that's when... when it attacked me." Peter's voice was barely above a whisper, his hands clenching into fists. "The shadow."

James' heart clenched, anger and fear and helplessness washing over him. "Peter..." he breathed, reaching out to pull him into a tight embrace. "I'm so sorry. I'm so sorry I wasn't there."

Peter shook his head against James' chest, his tears soaking into James' shirt. "It's not your fault," he mumbled, his voice muffled. "You couldn't have known."

James just held him tighter, pressing fierce kisses into his hair. "Tell me what happened," he said softly, when Peter's sobs had subsided. "If you can."

Peter took a deep, shuddering breath, pulling back slightly to meet James' eyes. "It... it was like it knew me," he said, his voice trembling. "Like it had been waiting for me. It said... it said I belonged to it, that I couldn't escape."

James felt a chill run down his spine at Peter's words. The thought of that creature, that dark manifestation of Peter's fears, claiming ownership over him... it made James' blood boil with protective rage.

"I tried to fight it off," Peter continued, his eyes growing distant once more. "I tried to use my...magic, but... but it wasn't working. It was like I was powerless against it."

He paused, his brow furrowing as he struggled to remember. "And then... then I heard a voice. A woman's voice, ordering the shadow to... to finish me off."

James' eyes widened, shock and dread washing over him. "A woman?" he repeated, his mind racing. "Did you recognize the voice?"

Peter shook his head, frustration and fear evident in his expression.

"No," he admitted. "But it was cold, and cruel, and… and it scared me more than the shadow itself."

James pulled Peter close once more, his heart aching with the need to protect him, to shield him from all the horrors of the world.

They stayed like that for a long time, simply holding each other, drawing strength and comfort from the solidity of their embrace. James relished the feeling of Peter's heartbeat against his own, the warmth of his skin, the soft puffs of his breath against James' neck.

He knew they couldn't stay like this forever, knew that the world outside was waiting, with all its dangers and mysteries. But for now, in this perfect, precious moment, all that mattered was Peter, safe and alive and in his arms.

Eventually, Peter pulled back, his eyes red-rimmed but clear. "James," he said softly, hesitantly. "I… I need you to do something for me."

James frowned slightly, a flicker of uncertainty crossing his face. "Anything," he said immediately, meaning it with every fiber of his being. "What is it?"

Peter took a deep breath, his gaze locking onto James' with an intensity that stole James' breath. "I need you to make me forget," he whispered, his voice rough with emotion. "Just for a little while. I need to feel something other than fear, and pain, and… and helplessness."

James' heart stuttered in his chest, a wave of desire and love and protective instinct washing over him. "Peter…" he breathed, his hand coming up to cup Peter's cheek. "Are you sure? You're still healing, and I don't want to hurt you…"

Peter leaned into the touch, his eyes fluttering closed for a moment. "You could never hurt me, James," he murmured, turning his head to press a soft kiss to James' palm. "And I'm sure. I need this. I need you."

James swallowed hard, desire and love and a hint of nervousness swirling in his gut. "Okay," he whispered, leaning in to capture Peter's lips in a gentle, reverent kiss. "Okay."

Slowly, carefully, he laid Peter back against the pillows, his hands roaming over Peter's body with gentle reverence. He took his time, mapping out every inch of Peter's skin with his lips and fingers, worshipping him with every touch, every sigh, every whispered word of love and devotion.

And when they finally came together, moving as one in a dance as old as time itself, James poured everything he had, everything he was, into the act. He let his love, his fierce, unshakable love, flow through every thrust, every caress, every breathless moan and whispered plea.

He made love to Peter slowly, tenderly, cherishing every moment, every sensation. And when they reached their peak, crying out each other's names in a moment of perfect, blissful union, James knew that he would spend the rest of his life loving this man, protecting him, fighting for him.

No matter what challenges lay ahead, no matter what demons they had to face, James knew that they would face them together. Always together, side by side, heart to heart.

In the afterglow, as they lay tangled together beneath the sheets, James pressed soft, lazy kisses to Peter's hair, his heart full to bursting with love and contentment.

"I love you, Peter Naps," he murmured, his voice low and rough with emotion. "More than anything in this world or any other."

Peter smiled against his chest, his fingers tracing idle patterns on James' skin. "I love you too, James Crane," he whispered back, tilting his head up to meet James' eyes. "Always and forever."

And there, in the warm cocoon of their love, the outside world and all its dangers felt very far away. They knew the road ahead would be long and perilous, knew that there were still so many questions left unanswered.

But they also knew that as long as they had each other, as long as they held fast to the unbreakable bond between them, they could face anything.

Together, they were strong. Together, they were whole.

James was drifting in that hazy space between sleep and wakefulness, his body sated and his heart full, when a sharp knock at the door jolted him into full alertness. Beside him, Peter stirred, a small frown creasing his brow.

"Shh, it's okay," James murmured, pressing a soft kiss to Peter's forehead. "I'll see who it is. You stay here and rest."

Peter mumbled something incoherent, already slipping back into sleep as James slid out of bed. He grabbed his robe, shrugging it on as he padded to the door.

When he opened it, he was surprised to see Simon standing there, his face grave. "Simon?" James asked, his voice rough with sleep. "What's going on?"

Simon glanced over James' shoulder, his eyes flicking to Peter's sleeping form before returning to James. "We have visitors," he said, his voice low and serious. "You'd better come downstairs."

James felt a flicker of unease stir in his gut, but he nodded. "Give me a minute," he said, turning back to the bed.

Peter was awake now, his eyes heavy-lidded but alert. "James?" he asked, his voice rough. "What's happening?"

James sat on the edge of the bed, taking Peter's hand in his own. "I'm not sure," he admitted, his thumb stroking soothing circles on Peter's skin. "But Simon says we have visitors. I need to go see what's going on."

Peter struggled to sit up, wincing slightly at the movement. "I'll come with you," he said, determination shining through the exhaustion in his eyes.

James shook his head, gently pushing Peter back against the pillows. "No, love," he said softly, the endearment slipping out naturally. "You need to rest. I won't be long, I promise."

Peter looked like he wanted to argue, but something in James' expression must have convinced him. He nodded, sinking back into the bed. "Okay," he murmured, his eyes already fluttering closed. "But be careful."

James leaned down, capturing Peter's lips in a soft, sweet kiss. "Always," he whispered against Peter's mouth. "I'll be back before you know it."

With one last lingering look at Peter's sleeping form, James followed Simon out of the room and down the stairs. As they approached the kitchen, James could hear the murmur of voices, the clink of cups and spoons.

When he stepped into the room, he was greeted by a surprising sight. Lyra was there, her hands flying as she signed rapidly to a huge, hulking man with a shock of red hair. Adrian was leaning against the counter, his arms crossed and his expression thoughtful. And there, sitting at the table with a steaming mug in front of him, was Benjamin.

James cleared his throat, drawing everyone's attention. "What's going on?" he asked, his voice calm despite the unease churning in his gut.

Benjamin stood, gesturing to the redheaded man. "James, this is Merin," he said, his voice solemn. "He's a seer, and he told us that he had a vision."

James felt a flicker of mistrust at the word 'seer'. He had never put much stock in fortune-tellers and soothsayers, finding their predictions vague and often self-fulfilling. But something in Merin's eyes, a depth of wisdom and sorrow, made him pause.

"A seer?" he repeated, his gaze flicking to Benjamin. "And you trust him?"

Benjamin nodded, his expression grave. "I do," he said simply. "Merin has proven himself to me many times over. If he says he has information, I believe him."

James sighed, running a hand through his hair. "Alright," he said, turning to Merin. "What do you know?"

Merin leaned forward, his huge hands wrapped around his mug. "Is Peter able to join us?" he asked, his voice deep and rumbling. "What I have to say concerns him greatly."

James bristled, a protective instinct rising up within him. "Peter needs to rest," he said firmly, his jaw clenching. "He's been through a lot, and he's still healing."

But even as the words left his mouth, a movement at the kitchen door caught his eye. He turned, his heart leaping into his throat as he saw Peter standing there, leaning heavily against the doorframe.

"Peter!" he exclaimed, rushing to his side. "What are you doing up? You should be in bed!"

Peter shook his head, a determined glint in his eye. "I'm fine, James," he said, though the pallor of his skin and the tremor in his voice belied his words. "If this concerns me, I need to hear it."

James wanted to argue, wanted to sweep Peter up in his arms and carry him back to bed. But he knew his lover's stubbornness, knew that Peter would not rest until he had heard what Merin had to say.

With a sigh of resignation, he wrapped an arm around Peter's waist, supporting him as they made their way to the table. He eased Peter down into a chair, taking the seat beside him and lacing their fingers together.

20

Visions of Fate

Peter

As he looked around at the faces gathered in the cozy kitchen, he couldn't help but marvel at the incredible diversity of the individuals who had come together to support him.

There was Lyra, she signed rapidly to Merin, her face animated with concern and determination. Peter's heart swelled with love and gratitude for his best friend, who had risked so much to save him from the shadow's clutches. But beneath the warmth, there was a flicker of confusion and hurt. Why had Lyra never told him about her true nature? What other secrets might she be keeping?

Beside her, Merin sat with an air of ancient wisdom, his eyes holding secrets that Peter could only begin to imagine. The hulking redhead was an imposing figure, but there was a gentleness to his demeanor that put Peter at ease. Still, Peter couldn't shake the feeling that there was more to Merin than met the eye. The way he spoke of visions and prophecies, the knowing glint in his gaze… it was both comforting and unnerving.

And then there was Benjamin and Adrian, the enigmatic strangers who had become an unexpected ally in their quest for answers. Peter found himself drawn to their quiet strength. But there was something otherworldly about them, a sense of power that seemed to radiate from him like a physical force. Peter couldn't quite put his finger on it, but he knew that they were no ordinary men.

"Peter?" James' voice cut through his thoughts, soft with concern. "Are you alright?"

Peter blinked, realizing that he had been staring off into space. He turned to James, offering a small, reassuring smile. "Yeah, I'm okay," he said, though his voice sounded unconvincing even to his own ears. "It's just… a lot to take in, you know?"

James nodded, his hand finding Peter's under the table and giving it a gentle squeeze. "I know," he murmured, his eyes soft with understanding. "But you're not alone in this, Peter. We're all here for you, no matter what."

Peter swallowed hard, feeling a lump rising in his throat. He knew that James meant well, that he truly believed in the support and loyalty of the people gathered around them. But Peter couldn't shake the feeling that he was still an outsider, a newcomer stumbling blindly into a world he barely understood.

"I'm sorry for my delayed arrival," Merin said, his deep voice rumbling through the room. "Margaret and I have been on a mission to create a seer council, to protect our kind from those who would seek to harm us."

James leaned forward, his curiosity piqued. "A seer council?" he asked, his brow furrowing. "I didn't even know there were other seers out there."

Merin chuckled, a sound like distant thunder. "We are a rare breed," he admitted, his eyes twinkling. "And we have faced many challenges over the years. Prejudice, persecution, the decline of our numbers as the world has grown more skeptical of the supernatural."

Peter felt a pang of empathy at Merin's words. He knew all too well the pain of being different, of feeling like an outsider in a world that didn't understand him. "That must be so hard," he said softly, his gaze meeting Merin's. "To have a gift that so few people appreciate or even believe in."

Merin nodded, a sad smile tugging at his lips. "It is a heavy burden to bear at times," he acknowledged. "But it is also a great honor, to be able to see beyond the veil and guide others on their paths."

Peter couldn't help but be moved by Merin's dedication, by the quiet strength that seemed to radiate from him. "And you think this council will help?" he asked, leaning back in his chair. "That it will make things better for seers?"

"I have to believe that it will," Merin said, his voice firm with conviction. "We cannot change the world overnight, but by coming together, by supporting each other and sharing our knowledge, we can start to build a brighter future for our kind."

Peter felt a flicker of hope at Merin's words, a sense that maybe, just maybe, there was a way forward for supernaturals like him. A way to find acceptance and understanding in a world that often feared and reviled them.

"It sounds like an incredible undertaking," James said from beside Peter, his hand finding Peter's under the table and giving it a gentle squeeze. "I can only imagine the challenges you must have faced in trying to bring seers together from all over the world."

Merin let out a rueful chuckle, shaking his head. "You have no idea," he said, his eyes sparkling with humor. "Try convincing a bunch of stubborn, independent-minded fortune-tellers to agree on anything, let alone form a council. It's like herding cats, if the cats could see the future and argue about it endlessly."

Lyra let out a silent laugh, her shoulders shaking with mirth. Peter couldn't help but grin, the image of Merin trying to wrangle a room full of bickering seers just too amusing to resist.

"But in the end, we all want the same thing," Merin continued, his voice growing serious once more. "To protect our own, to preserve our ways and our knowledge. And if that means putting aside our differences and working together, then that's what we'll do."

Peter felt a swell of admiration for Merin, for the quiet strength and determination that seemed to flow through him. He couldn't imagine the courage it must have taken to step up and lead a group of people who had been marginalized and persecuted for so long.

"I think it's incredible, what you're doing," he said softly, meeting Merin's gaze with a smile. "And I'm honored that you would take the time to come here and help me, with everything else you must have on your plate."

Merin reached across the table, his large hand engulfing Peter's in a gentle grip. "It is I who am honored, Peter," he said, his voice warm with sincerity. "To be able to use my gift to help someone as special as you… it is a privilege and a joy."

Peter felt tears prick at the corners of his eyes, overwhelmed by the kindness and acceptance he saw in Merin's face. He had spent so long feeling alone, feeling like an outsider even among his own kind. But here, in this room full of supernaturals who had come together to support him, he finally felt like he belonged.

"Thank you," he whispered, his voice thick with emotion. "Thank you all, for being here. For believing in me, even when I didn't believe in myself."

James wrapped an arm around Peter's shoulders, pulling him close. Peter leaned into James' embrace, feeling the warmth and strength of his love flowing through him.

"So," he said, straightening up and looking around the table with a determined grin. "What's our next move? How do we take down this big bad darkness that's coming for me?"

Merin leaned back in his chair, a glint of mischief in his eyes. "Whoa there, Peter," he said, a smirk tugging at his lips. "I admire your enthusiasm, but rushing headlong into battle isn't always the smartest move."

Peter felt a flush creep up his neck, but he refused to back down. "Hey, I may be new to this whole supernatural thing, but I'm not helpless," he said, a hint of a challenge in his voice. "And I'm not about to sit back and let some shadow monster take over my life."

Merin held up his hands in a placating gesture, his smirk softening into a genuine smile. "Hey, I get it," he said, his voice warm with understanding. "Believe me, I know what it's like to feel like the world is against you, to want to take control of your own fate."

Peter felt a flicker of surprise at Merin's words, a sense of kinship that he hadn't expected. "You do?" he asked softly, leaning forward in his seat.

Merin nodded, his eyes growing distant for a moment. "Yeah," he said, his voice tinged with a hint of melancholy. "I've had my fair share of battles, both with external threats and with my own inner demons. It's never easy, but it's always worth fighting for."

Peter felt a swell of emotion at Merin's words, a sense of validation that he had rarely experienced before. "Thanks," he said softly, ducking his head. "I just... I don't want to be a victim anymore. I want to fight back, to take control of my own destiny."

Merin reached across the table, clasping Peter's shoulder in a gesture of solidarity. "And you will, Peter," he said, his voice firm with conviction. "We all will. But we have to be smart about it, to approach this fight with strategy and caution."

Peter nodded, feeling a sense of determination settling over him. "Okay," he said, straightening up in his seat. "So what's our plan? How do we outsmart this darkness and keep it from taking over?"

Merin leaned forward, his expression growing serious. "Actually,

Peter," he began, his voice low and thoughtful. "There's something I haven't told you yet. About my vision."

Peter felt a flicker of unease at Merin's words, a sense that whatever was coming next would be momentous. "What is it?" he asked, his voice barely above a whisper.

Merin took a deep breath, his eyes distant as if he were seeing something far beyond the walls of the cozy kitchen. "In my vision, I saw a battle," he said, his voice taking on a strange, almost reverent tone. "A clash between light and darkness."

Peter's heart began to race, a mix of excitement and terror coursing through his veins. "And… and I was there?" he asked, his voice trembling slightly.

Merin nodded, his gaze snapping back to Peter's with an intensity that stole his breath. "You were at the center of it all, Peter,"

Peter felt a chill run down his spine, a sense of awe and fear at the prospect of his own potential. Could he really be capable of such power? Could he rise to the occasion when the moment came?

"Wait, hold on," Adrian interjected, his brow furrowed in confusion. "You're saying you saw Peter in your vision, but how did you know it was him?"

Merin shook his head, a rueful smile tugging at his lips. "Visions are funny things," he said, shrugging his shoulders. "They don't always come with nametags and introductions. It wasn't until I heard Peter's name from Benjamin that asked him for a picture that I realized he was the one I had seen."

Lyra's hands flew in a flurry of signs, her face alight with excitement and worry. "What else did you see?" she asked, her movements sharp and urgent. "Were there any clues about how to stop this darkness?"

Merin's expression grew thoughtful, his eyes unfocusing as he delved back into the depths of his vision. "There were symbols," he said slowly, his voice distant and dreamy. "Ominous shapes and cryptic warnings that I couldn't quite decipher."

Peter's mind raced with theories and possibilities, trying to make sense of the fragmented images. Could they be metaphors, hints at weaknesses or strategies they could use against their enemy?

"Okay, that's sufficiently creepy," Benjamin quipped, his voice laced with a forced lightness. "Any chance you could, I don't know, unscramble that mystical mumbo-jumbo into something a bit more actionable?"

Merin shot Benjamin a wry look, shaking his head. "If it were that easy, I'd be out of a job," he said, a hint of amusement in his tone. "Interpreting visions is more art than science. It takes time, contemplation, and a healthy dose of intuition."

James, who had been listening intently, leaned forward, his hand finding Peter's under the table and giving it a reassuring squeeze. "What about the woman's voice?" he asked, his tone low and serious. "The one that ordered the shadow to… to finish Peter off. Did you see anything about her in your vision?"

Merin's face grew grave, a flicker of fear passing behind his eyes. "I saw a figure cloaked in shadows," he said, his words slow and heavy. "A presence of immense power and malevolence. But I couldn't make out her face, couldn't hear her voice. It was like trying to grasp smoke with my bare hands."

Peter felt a shiver of dread at Merin's words, a sense of the immense challenge that lay ahead. This wasn't just a rogue shadow they were dealing with, but a mastermind of darkness, a foe of unimaginable strength and cunning.

Peter felt a shiver of dread at Merin's words, a sense of the immense challenge that lay ahead. This wasn't just a rogue shadow they were dealing with, but a mastermind of darkness, a foe of unimaginable strength and cunning.

"Are we talking about an all-out war here?" James asked.

Merin shook his head, his eyes distant and troubled. "I can't say for certain," he admitted, his words slow and heavy. "The outcome of the battle was shrouded in mist, the future still unwritten. But one thing was clear Peter was in the middle of it."

Adrian absorbed the information with a grim determination, his jaw clenching and his eyes hardening with resolve. Peter could practically see the gears turning in his head, the strategic mind already working on contingencies and battle plans.

Peter felt the weight of Merin's words bearing down on him, his mind racing with questions and fears. The enormity of the task before them threatened to overwhelm him, and he couldn't help but feel a creeping sense of doubt and uncertainty.

But as he sat there, his thoughts churning, a sudden realization struck him. He sat up straighter, his eyes widening with a glimmer of hope.

"The ancient text." he exclaimed, his voice cutting through the heavy silence. "The one from library, the one that seemed to hold some kind of key to my past."

The others turned to him, their expressions a mix of curiosity and confusion. But Benjamin's eyes widened with recognition, a spark of excitement flashing across his face.

"The book that Jimmy gave you?" he asked, his voice tinged with reverence.

"Yes…" he admitted, his brow furrowing. "I tried to read it but still couldn't understand what it says. But I never knew who wrote it."

Suddenly, a new voice chimed in, startling Peter from his thoughts. "The Dagda's book, you say?" The voice was smooth and velvety, with a hint of mischief.

Peter whirled around, his eyes widening in shock as he saw a sleek, black cat perched on the windowsill, its tail swishing lazily behind it.

"Did… did Jimmy just talk?" he sputtered, his voice rising in disbelief.

The cat chuckled, a distinctly human sound that sent shivers down Peter's spine. "Indeed I did," it said, its green eyes glinting with amusement. "And I've been around long enough to know a thing or two about ancient texts and powerful magic."

Peter gaped, his mind reeling with the revelation of a talking cat. But the others seemed unfazed, as if this were a perfectly normal occurrence.

"Jimmy," Merin said, his voice warm with familiarity. "It's good to see you, old friend. What do you know about this book?"

Jimmy leaped down from the windowsill, his movements fluid and graceful. "The Dagda's book is a powerful artifact," he said, his voice growing serious. "It's said to contain the secrets of the Dagda himself, the great king of the Tuatha Dé Danann. If Peter has seen it, even glimpsed its pages... it could hold the key to unlocking his memories, and his true potential."

Peter's heart raced, a mix of excitement and trepidation coursing through him. "But I don't have the book," he said, his voice tinged with desperation. "I left it back in New York, in my apartment."

Lyra, who had been listening intently, signed. "I can get it,"

"Thank you, Lyra." Peter said.

As the conversation continued, Peter could feel his exhaustion and lingering pain from his injuries starting to take their toll. His body ached, his head throbbed, and a creeping sense of weakness seemed to seep into his very bones.

He tried to hide his discomfort, not wanting to distract from the vital discussions at hand. But as he leaned forward to listen to Adrian's latest point, a sudden wave of dizziness washed over him, and he felt himself swaying in his chair.

"Peter?" James' voice cut through the haze, sharp with concern. "Are you alright?"

Peter blinked, trying to focus on his partner's face. "I'm... I'm fine," he mumbled, even as the room seemed to tilt and spin around him. "Just a little tired, that's all."

But James, ever attentive, wasn't buying it. He stood up, his chair scraping against the floor, and was at Peter's side in an instant. "I think you need to rest, love," he said softly, his hand coming to rest on Peter's shoulder. "You've been through so much, and your body needs time to heal."

Peter wanted to protest, to insist that he was fine, that he could push through the pain and fatigue. But as he looked up into James' eyes, he saw the depth of love and concern there, and he knew that he couldn't lie to him.

"You're right," he said, his voice rough with exhaustion. "I... I don't think I can keep going like this."

Lyra, who had been watching the exchange with worried eyes, signed quickly to the others. "We should take a break," she gestured, her face etched with concern. "Peter needs to rest, and we all need time to process what we've learned."

Adrian nodded, his expression softening. "Agreed," he said, his voice gentle. "We've made good progress today, but we won't be any use to anyone if we run ourselves into the ground."

As the others murmured their assent and began to gather their things, James helped Peter to his feet, his arm sliding around Peter's waist to support him. Peter leaned heavily into the touch, savoring the warmth and strength of his partner's body.

"Lean on me, love," James murmured, his breath tickling Peter's ear. "I've got you."

Peter nodded, too tired to speak, and let James guide him out of the room and up the stairs to their bedroom. He could feel the others' eyes on them as they left, could sense the silent vows of protection and support that hung in the air.

Once they were alone, the door closed softly behind them, Peter felt the last of his resolve crumble. He sagged against James, his knees buckling, and let out a shuddering breath.

"I'm scared, James," he whispered, his voice cracking with emotion. "I'm scared that I won't be strong enough, that I'll fail everyone when they need me most."

James gathered him close, his arms wrapping around Peter in a cocoon of warmth and safety. "You could never fail us, Peter," he said fiercely, his words ringing with conviction. "You are the strongest, bravest, most amazing person I have ever known. And you don't have to face this alone. We're all here for you, every step of the way."

Peter felt tears prickling at the corners of his eyes, and he buried his face in James' chest, breathing in the familiar scent of him. "But what if I can't do it?" he whispered, his voice muffled by James' shirt. "What if I'm not the hero Merin saw in his vision? What if I'm just… me?"

James pulled back slightly, his hands coming up to cup Peter's face. "Listen to me, Peter," he said, his eyes blazing with love and conviction. "You are not 'just' anything. You are everything. Everything to me, everything to our friends, everything to this world that we're fighting for."

He leaned in, pressing his forehead against Peter's, and spoke softly, his words a caress against Peter's skin. "You have a light inside you, Peter, a strength that shines brighter than any darkness. And no matter what happens, no matter what sacrifices we may have to make… that light will guide us through."

Peter felt a surge of love and gratitude so powerful that it stole his breath. He clung to James, his hands fisting in the fabric of his shirt, and let himself be held, be loved, be cherished.

And as he drifted off to sleep, his mind still reeling from Merin's revelations, he saw visions of his own. Fragmented images of battles yet to come, of shadows and light, of love and sacrifice.

But even in the midst of the darkness, he could feel James' presence, a constant warmth and comfort that anchored him, that reminded him of what he was fighting for.

213

21

Sacrifices

James

The room was quiet, the only sound the soft, even breathing of the man he loved more than life itself.

As he watched the gentle rise and fall of Peter's chest, James felt a wave of emotions wash over him. Worry, fear, love… they all tangled together in his heart, a bittersweet cocktail that left him feeling raw and exposed.

Gently, he reached out and brushed a stray lock of hair from Peter's forehead, marveling at the peace and innocence that graced his features in sleep. It was a rare sight these days, a fleeting glimpse of the carefree young man Peter had once been, before the weight of the world had settled on his shoulders.

James sighed, his heart heavy with the knowledge of all that Peter had endured, all that he had suffered. The lost memories, the attacks, the constant fear and uncertainty… it was enough to break even the strongest of men.

But Peter… Peter was different. He had a strength, a resilience, that never ceased to amaze James. No matter how hard things got, no matter how bleak the future seemed, Peter never gave up. He kept fighting, kept pushing forward, driven by a courage and determination that James could only marvel at.

And yet, even the bravest of heroes needed someone to lean on, someone to hold them up when the burden became too much to bear. And James knew, with a certainty that went soul-deep, that he would be that someone for Peter.

He would be the rock, the anchor, the unwavering support that Peter needed. He would stand by his side, no matter what challenges lay ahead, no matter what sacrifices had to be made.

Because Peter was worth it. Worth the sleepless nights and the constant worry, worth the danger and the heartache and the impossible odds. Worth everything.

James leaned forward, pressing a soft, reverent kiss to Peter's forehead. "I love you," he whispered, his voice barely more than a breath against Peter's skin. "I love you more than I ever thought possible. And I swear, on everything I hold dear, that I will do whatever it takes to keep you safe, to help you find the answers you seek."

With a final, lingering look at Peter's peaceful face, James reluctantly pulled himself away. As much as he wanted to stay by Peter's side, to watch over him and ensure his safety, he knew that there was work to be done.

He made his way back downstairs, his mind already churning with plans and possibilities. The others were gathered in the living room, their expressions grave and their voices low as they discussed the challenges ahead.

"How's Peter?" Lyra asked, her hands moving in a flurry of signs as soon as she saw James enter the room.

James sighed, running a hand through his hair. "He's resting," he said, his voice heavy with concern. "But I'm worried about him. He's been through so much already, and we still have so far to go."

Benjamin nodded, his eyes dark with understanding. "We need to be careful," he said, his words measured and thoughtful. "We can't push him too hard, too fast. His recovery needs to be our top priority."

James felt a surge of gratitude for Benjamin's words, for the care and concern he showed for Peter's well-being. "I agree," he said, his voice firm with conviction. "We need to balance our mission with Peter's needs. We can't risk losing him, not now, not ever."

The others murmured their agreement, their faces etched with worry and determination.

"So, what's our plan?" Adrian asked, leaning forward in his seat. "How do we move forward without putting Peter in danger?"

James thought for a moment, his brow furrowed in concentration. "We take turns," he said finally, his voice steady and sure. "We watch over Peter in shifts, making sure he's never alone, never vulnerable. And in between, we gather information, we plan our next moves, we do whatever it takes to stay one step ahead of our enemies."

Lyra nodded, her expression fierce with determination. "I'll take the first watch," she signed, her movements sharp and decisive. "Peter's my best friend, and I'll be damned if I let anything happen to him on my watch."

James felt a swell of affection for Lyra, for the unwavering loyalty and love she showed for Peter. "Thank you, Lyra," he said softly, his voice thick with emotion. "I know Peter is safe with you."

As the group continued to discuss their plans, their voices rising and falling in a symphony of strategy and concern, a sudden commotion outside the room interrupted them.

James was on his feet in an instant, his heart pounding and his senses on high alert. "What the hell was that?" he demanded, his voice tight with fear and adrenaline.

Before anyone could answer, a bone-chilling shriek rent the air, followed by the sound of shattering glass and splintering wood.

"We're under attack!" Benjamin yelled, his eyes flashing with a primal, predatory gleam. "Shadow creatures, at least a dozen of them!"

James felt a surge of terror and rage course through him, his mind immediately flying to Peter, vulnerable and alone upstairs. "Lyra, stay with Peter!" he barked, his voice brooking no argument. "The rest of you, with me! We need to hold them off, buy ourselves some time!"

As the shadow creatures swarmed the manor, the group sprang into action, their powers and abilities surging forth to meet the threat head-on.

"Benjamin, watch your flank!" James called out, his hands manipulating the metal in the room to send sharp projectiles hurtling towards the shadows. "Adrian, we need some crowd control!"

Benjamin nodded, his staff whirling in a blur of motion as he channeled his reality-altering magic. "I'm on it!" he yelled back, his brow furrowed with concentration. "Trying to thin their numbers, but they just keep coming!"

Adrian's eyes flashed with an icy blue light, his hands weaving intricate patterns in the air. "Leave it to me!" he shouted, his voice barely audible over the howling wind that suddenly filled the room. "Let's see how they like a little arctic blast!"

Merin, his arcane sight allowing him to perceive the weaknesses in the creatures' forms, called out to the others, his voice ringing with an otherworldly resonance. "Aim for the center mass!" he instructed, his gaze darting from one shadow to the next. "That's where their essence is concentrated!"

But despite their best efforts, the shadows kept coming, their numbers seemingly endless. James felt his strength beginning to falter, his magnetic hold on the metal objects wavering as he poured more and more of himself into the fight.

"We have to hold them off!" he gasped, his chest heaving with exertion. "We can't let them get past us!"

Suddenly, a massive shadow loomed up before him, its form twisted and grotesque. James barely had time to register the danger before a powerful blow struck him square in the chest, sending him flying backwards.

"James!" Benjamin's voice rang out, sharp with fear and concern.

James hit the ground hard, the air rushing from his lungs in a painful gasp. His head swam, his vision darkening as he struggled to stay conscious.

Dimly, he heard the others crying out his name, their voices distant and muffled. He tried to push himself up, to rejoin the fight, but his limbs wouldn't cooperate. He was too weak, too drained.

As the shadow creature loomed over him, its eyes glowing with a sickening, malevolent hunger, James felt a wave of despair wash over him. This was it. This was how he would die, failing in his duty to protect the man he loved.

But then, just as the creature's claws descended, a blast of searing, arcane energy erupted from behind James, engulfing the shadow in a supernova of icy brilliance.

"Back off, you overgrown inkblot!" Adrian snarled, his hands outstretched and his eyes blazing with cold fury.

The creature shrieked, its form freezing solid before shattering into a thousand glittering shards. And there, standing tall and proud, his chest heaving with exertion, was Adrian.

James struggled to his feet, his body aching and his mind reeling. He stumbled forward, his hand clasping Adrian's shoulder in a gesture of gratitude and relief.

"Thank you," he rasped, his voice rough with emotion. "I thought I was done for."

Adrian grinned, his icy blue eyes glinting with wry amusement. "Can't have you checking out on us now, can we?" he quipped, his tone light despite the gravity of the situation. "Peter would never forgive me if I let anything happen to you."

At the mention of Peter's name, James felt a pang of fear and longing shoot through him. He had to get back to him, had to make sure he was safe.

With a grunt of effort, he pushed himself fully upright, his jaw set with determination. "Let's finish this," he growled, his hands once again crackling with magnetic energy.

And with that, they threw themselves back into the fray, their powers and abilities working in perfect sync as they drove the shadows back, inch by hard-fought inch.

It was a battle unlike any they had faced before, a test of their strength, their courage, and their unwavering commitment to each other.

But in the end, as the last shadow fell and the manor stood silent once more, they knew that they had passed that test with flying colors.

"Well, that was a right mess," Benjamin panted, his staff clattering to the floor as he leaned heavily against the wall. "Let's not do that again anytime soon, yeah?"

Merin chuckled, his lined face creasing in a weary smile. "Somehow, I don't think we'll have much choice in the matter," he said wryly, his arcane sight already scanning the horizon for signs of further trouble.

James, his heart still pounding with the rush of battle, could only nod in agreement. "We'll be ready," he said softly, his gaze drifting towards the stairs that led to Peter's room. "We have to be."

As the others began to disperse, tending to their wounds and assessing the damage to the manor, James caught Simon's eye from across the room. With a slight jerk of his head, he motioned for the man to follow him, his expression grave and determined.

"Simon," James began, his voice low and urgent as they stepped into a quiet alcove. "I need you to do something for me. For Peter."

Simon's brow furrowed, his eyes searching James' face for clues. "Of course," he said, his tone serious. "Whatever you need, you know I'm here for you both."

James took a deep breath, his hand running through his hair in a gesture of nervous energy. "The ancient book," he said, his words heavy with significance. "I need you to retrieve it, and I need you to do it safely."

Simon nodded, his expression hardening with resolve. "Consider it done," he said, his voice firm. "I'll leave at first light, and I won't come back until I have that book in my hands."

But James shook his head, his grip on Simon's shoulder tightening. "No," he said, his tone brooking no argument. "You're not going alone. I want you to take Lyra with you."

At the mention of Lyra's name, Simon's eyes widened, a flicker of surprise and concern crossing his face. "Lyra?" he repeated, his brow creasing. "But she's Peter's best friend, his guardian. Shouldn't she stay here, with him?"

James sighed, his gaze drifting towards the stairs once more. "Trust me, there's nothing I want more than to keep Lyra by Peter's side," he said, his voice rough with emotion. "But this book... it's too important. We can't take any chances, can't risk it falling into the wrong hands. You need backup, Simon. You need Lyra."

For a long moment, Simon was silent, his eyes searching James' face for any sign of hesitation or doubt. But there was none to be found - only a steely determination and an unwavering commitment to Peter's safety.

"Alright," Simon said at last, his shoulders squaring with purpose. "We'll leave at dawn, and we won't come back without that book. I swear it, James."

James nodded, a wave of gratitude and relief washing over him. "Thank you, Simon," he said softly, his hand clasping the other man's in a gesture of profound appreciation. "I know I can count on you, on both of you."

As Simon turned to go, already making mental lists of the preparations he would need to make, James felt a sudden presence at his side. He turned, his heart skipping a beat as he found himself face to face with Merin, the arcane seer's expression grave and troubled.

"James," Merin said, his voice low and urgent. "There's something you need to know, something I've seen in my visions."

James felt a chill run down his spine, a sense of foreboding settling heavy in his gut. "What is it?" he asked, his words barely above a whisper. "What have you seen?"

Merin took a deep breath, his eyes distant and unfocused as he delved into the depths of his arcane sight. "The attack," he said, his voice taking on a strange, otherworldly cadence. "The battle that I saw… it will happen during the Summer Solstice."

James felt the breath leave his lungs in a rush, his mind reeling with the implications of Merin's words. The Summer Solstice… that was a couple of days away. They have three days to prepare, to train, to gather their allies and steel themselves for the fight of their lives.

"Three days," he whispered, his voice hoarse with shock and disbelief. "That's… that's not enough time. How are we supposed to be ready in just three days?"

Merin shook his head, his expression sorrowful. "I don't know," he admitted, his shoulders slumping with the weight of his own powerlessness. "But that is what I have seen, and I cannot change it."

For a long moment, James was silent, his mind racing with a thousand questions and fears. But one thought rose above the rest, sharp and accusing in its intensity.

"Why didn't you tell us this before?" he asked, his voice tight with barely restrained anger. "Why did you wait until Peter was gone, until he was out of earshot? He deserves to know, Merin. He deserves the truth."

Merin sighed, his eyes heavy with regret and understanding. "I know," he said softly, his hand coming to rest on James' shoulder in a gesture of comfort. "And believe me, there is nothing I want more than to be completely honest with Peter, with all of you. But James… he's already carrying so much, already shouldering a burden that would break lesser men. I didn't want to add to that, didn't want to pile on more stress and fear when he's already struggling to heal, to come to terms with his own powers and destiny."

James felt a flicker of understanding, a grudging acknowledgment of the truth in Merin's words. But still, the thought of keeping secrets from Peter, of withholding information that could be vital to their survival… it felt wrong, like a betrayal of the trust and love they had worked so hard to build.

"I don't like this," he said at last, his voice rough with conflicting emotions. "I don't like keeping things from Peter, even if it's with the best of intentions. He's my partner, Merin. My equal in every way. I can't… I can't lie to him, can't hide the truth from him."

Merin nodded, his eyes shining with a deep, sorrowful understanding. "I know," he said softly, his hand squeezing James' shoulder in a gesture of support. "And I would never ask you to lie to him, James. But maybe… maybe you can find the right moment, the right way to tell him. A way that doesn't add to his burdens, but instead helps him to shoulder them, to face them with the strength and courage that I know he possesses."

James was silent for a long moment, his mind churning with the weight of Merin's words. He knew, deep in his heart, that the seer was right. That Peter needed to know the truth, needed to be prepared for the battle that lay ahead.

But he also knew that he would have to be the one to bear that knowledge alone, at least for a little while. To carry the weight of that secret, that looming deadline, until the time was right to share it with the man he loved.

It would be a heavy burden, a constant ache in his chest and a shadow over his thoughts. But for Peter… for Peter, he would bear it gladly, would shoulder any weight and face any fear.

Because that was what love was, in the end. Not just the joy and the laughter and the stolen moments of bliss, but the hard choices and the painful truths and the unwavering commitment to stand together, no matter what the future might hold.

With a deep, steadying breath, James squared his shoulders, his jaw set with determination. "Alright," he said, his voice low but filled with a quiet, unshakable strength. "I'll find the right moment, the right way to tell him. And until then… until then, I'll carry this knowledge for both of us, will bear the weight of it so that he doesn't have to."

Merin nodded, his eyes shining with a mix of understanding and admiration. "You are a strong man, James," he said softly, his hand resting briefly on James' shoulder. "Peter is lucky to have you by his side."

James managed a tight smile, the weight of Merin's words settling heavy on his heart. He knew that the road ahead would be difficult, that the sacrifices and secrets he would have to bear would take their toll. But for Peter… for Peter, he would endure anything.

With a final nod to Merin, James turned and made his way back to the others, his mind already churning with plans and possibilities. As he entered the room, he could feel the tension and uncertainty hanging thick in the air, the gravity of their situation weighing on every face.

"So," Adrian said, breaking the heavy silence. "The Summer Solstice. That's our deadline, then?"

James nodded, his expression grim. "According to Merin's vision, yes. We have until then to prepare, to gather our strength and our allies."

Lyra's hands flew in a flurry of signs, her face etched with worry. "But that's barely three days away!" she gestured, her movements sharp and urgent. "How are we supposed to be ready in such a short time?"

Benjamin leaned forward, his elbows resting on his knees as he fixed James with a steady gaze. "We prioritize," he said, his voice calm and measured. "We focus on what's most important. We can't afford to waste time or resources on anything else."

James felt a flicker of doubt, a nagging sense that they were missing something crucial. "But what if there's more to it than that?" he asked, his brow furrowed in thought. "What if there are other pieces of the puzzle we haven't uncovered yet, clues that could help us understand what we're up against?"

Adrian nodded, his eyes narrowing. "You're right," he said, his fingers drumming a restless rhythm on the arm of his chair. "We can't just rely on Merin's vision, as powerful as it may be. We need to dig deeper, to explore every possible angle."

James felt a surge of determination, a renewed sense of purpose. "I'll reach out to my contacts in the supernatural world," he said, his mind already racing with possibilities. "See if they've heard any rumors or whispers about the coming attack."

Lyra's face lit up, her hands moving in a flurry of excitement. "I can help with that!" she signed, her eyes sparkling with eagerness. "I've been doing some research of my own, and I think I might have found some leads worth pursuing."

James felt a swell of pride and gratitude, a warmth blooming in his chest at the sight of his friends' unwavering dedication. "Thank you," he said softly, his gaze sweeping the room. "All of you. I know this isn't going to be easy, but with you by my side... I believe we can do this. We can find a way to keep Peter safe, to stop this attack before it ever begins."

The others nodded, their expressions a mix of determination and solemnity. They knew the stakes, knew the sacrifices that lay ahead. But they also knew that they had each other, that they were bound by a love and loyalty that went deeper than blood.

22

Secrets of the Ancient Text

Peter

He stirred from his slumber, his eyes fluttering open to the sight of James sleeping beside him. James' head rested on the edge of the bed, his hand clasped tightly around Peter's, as if even in sleep, he couldn't bear to let go.

A wave of emotion wash over him, a mixture of love, gratitude, and awe at the unwavering devotion James had shown him. He took a moment to simply appreciate the sight, his heart swelling with affection for the man who had become his rock, his anchor in the stormy seas of his life.

Gently, Peter reached out and ran his fingers through James' hair, marveling at the peace and vulnerability that softened his features in sleep. It was a rare sight, to see James so unguarded, so free from the weight of responsibility and worry that he carried on his shoulders.

Peter's mind drifted to the challenges they had faced together, the seemingly insurmountable obstacles they had overcome through sheer force of will and the strength of their bond. From the moment they had met, there had been an undeniable connection between them, a

226

sense of rightness and belonging that defied explanation.

James began to stir, his eyes fluttering open and his hand tightening around Peter's. He sat up immediately, his expression a mix of relief and concern as he scanned Peter's face for any sign of pain or distress.

"Peter," he breathed, his voice rough with sleep and emotion. "How are you feeling? Are you in any pain? Do you need me to get you anything?"

Peter couldn't help but smile at the barrage of questions, at the earnest worry in James' eyes. "I'm okay, James," he said softly, squeezing James' hand in reassurance. "A little sore, maybe, but nothing I can't handle."

James let out a shaky breath, his shoulders slumping with relief. But then his expression clouded, a flicker of guilt and self-recrimination passing over his features. "I'm so sorry, Peter," he whispered, his voice cracking with emotion. "I should have been there, should have protected you. If anything had happened to you, I don't know what I would have done."

Peter felt his heart clench at the raw pain in James' voice, at the weight of responsibility he carried. He sat up, ignoring the twinge of discomfort in his battered body, and cupped James' face in his hands.

"James, we've been over this already but listen to me," he said firmly, his gaze locked on James' troubled eyes. "You have nothing to apologize for."

James opened his mouth to protest, but Peter silenced him with a gentle finger to his lips. "No, let me finish," he said, his voice soft but unyielding. "You have been my rock, James. My constant support, my unwavering ally. I couldn't have made it through any of this without you." He leaned in, resting his forehead against James', and let his words pour out in a heartfelt whisper. "You are my strength, James. My courage, my hope. And I know, with every fiber of my being, that as long as we're together, there's nothing we can't face, nothing we can't overcome."

James let out a shuddering breath, his eyes shining with unshed tears. "I love you, Peter," he whispered, his voice raw with emotion. "More than I ever thought possible. And I swear, I will always be here for you, always stand by your side, no matter what comes our way."

Peter felt a rush of emotion, a love so powerful it stole his breath. He leaned in, capturing James' lips in a soft, sweet kiss that held all the promises and declarations he couldn't put into words.

And there, in the quiet sanctuary of their bedroom, wrapped in each other's arms and lost in the depth of their connection, Peter knew that they would find a way through this. That they would unravel the mysteries of his past, would face the coming battles with courage and conviction.

Because together, they were invincible. Together, they could face anything, could emerge stronger and more united than ever before.

As they broke apart, Peter couldn't help but grin, a mischievous sparkle in his eye. "You know," he said, his tone light and playful, "if this is the kind of wake-up call I get after something happens, I might have to start picking fights more often."

James let out a bark of laughter, the sound warm and rich and full of love. "Don't you dare," he growled, pulling Peter close and pressing a fierce kiss to his forehead. "I've had enough heart attacks to last a lifetime, thank you very much."

Peter chuckled, snuggling deeper into James' embrace. "Fine, fine," he said, his voice muffled against James' chest. "I'll try to be more careful. But only because you asked so nicely."

They lay there for a long moment, content in each other's presence, the worries of the world temporarily held at bay.

"We should probably head downstairs," he said reluctantly, pulling back to meet James' gaze. "The others will be wondering where we are, and we have a lot to discuss."

James sighed, the weight of responsibility settling over his features once more. "You're right," he said, his jaw set with determination. "We have a battle to plan, and not a lot of time to do it."

He took a deep breath, his shoulders relaxing slightly as he turned to face Peter fully. "But before we do that, there are some things you need to know. Things that happened while you were resting."

Peter felt a flicker of unease at James' words, a sense that whatever he was about to hear would change everything. But he pushed down his apprehension, focusing instead on the relief and gratitude that shone in James' eyes.

"Tell me everything," he said softly, his hand finding James' and squeezing in encouragement.

And so James did. He spoke of the battle that had raged while Peter slept, of the bravery and skill their friends had shown in the face of overwhelming odds. He described the way Lyra had fought like a warrior queen, her wings shimmering with power as she blasted the shadow creatures with bolts of pure energy. He spoke of Adrian's icy prowess, of the way he had frozen the very air around them, turning the battlefield into a glacial wasteland.

"Sounds like I missed all the fun." Peter said.

"Trust me, none of it was fun. I'd rather be here with you."

He reached out, cupping James' face in his hands and forcing him to meet his gaze.

James leaned into his touch, his eyes fluttering closed for a moment as he drew strength from Peter's words. But when he opened them again, there was a flicker of hesitation, a guardedness that made Peter's heart sink.

A sudden knock at the door startled them both. They pulled apart, eyes wide and hearts racing, as the door swung open to reveal Simon and Lyra, their faces alight with excitement.

"Sorry to interrupt," Simon said, his tone apologetic but his eyes sparkling with anticipation. "But we have news. Big news."

Peter blinked, his mind struggling to process the sudden shift in conversation. "What are you talking about?" he asked, his brow furrowing in confusion.

Lyra stepped forward, her hands flying in a flurry of signs. "The book, Peter," she gestured, her face alight with eagerness. "The one you left behind in New York, the one that might hold the answers to everything. Simon went back and retrieved it."

Peter felt a jolt of shock, a surge of hope and fear and desperate, aching curiosity. "You did?" he whispered, his voice hoarse with emotion.

Simon grinned, a touch of pride in his expression. "We have our ways," he said, his tone light and playful. "Let's just say that being your friend has its perks. I know how important this is to you, to all of us."

Peter couldn't help but laugh, a burst of joy and relief that bubbled up from somewhere deep within him. "I could kiss you right now," he said, his eyes shining with gratitude.

James cleared his throat, a mock-stern expression on his face. "I'd rather you didn't," he said, his tone dry but his eyes sparkling with amusement. "I'm the jealous type, you know."

Peter grinned, leaning over to press a quick, soft kiss to James' cheek. "Don't worry, my love," he murmured, his voice low and intimate. "My heart belongs to you and you alone."

Lyra made a gagging noise, her face scrunched up in exaggerated disgust. "Okay, okay, enough with the sappiness," she signed, her movements sharp and playful. "We have a world to save, remember?"

Peter laughed, a feeling of lightness and hope suffusing his entire being. "Right, of course," he said, his tone growing more serious. "So, where's the book now? How do we figure out what it's trying to tell us?"

Simon reached into his bag, pulling out a small, leather-bound tome.

"I thought we might head over to the diner," he said, his tone thoughtful. "Benjamin's dads are there, and they might be able to help us decipher some of the more arcane bits of the text."

Peter nodded, a flicker of excitement and trepidation racing through him. "Okay," he said, his voice steady and determined. "Let's do it."

* * *

Willow was quiet when they arrived, the usual bustle of customers and staff replaced by a hushed, almost reverent silence. Benjamin was waiting for them, his face drawn and his eyes shadowed with worry.

"Did you get it?" he asked, his voice low and urgent. "The book?"

Simon nodded, setting the small tome down on one of the empty tables. "It's here," he said, his tone solemn. "But we're going to need help figuring out what it says."

Benjamin nodded, a flicker of understanding passing over his features. "I'll go get my dads," he said, his tone brisk and businesslike. "If anyone can make sense of this, it's them."

As Benjamin hurried off, Peter and the others gathered around the table, their eyes fixed on the worn, leather-bound book that lay before them.

"I still can't understand any of the text that's in the book," he said, his voice small and lost. "In my head, I could read them but the meaning of the words are just lost on me."

James reached out, his hand finding Peter's and squeezing gently. "We'll find a way," he said, his tone soft but fierce with conviction. "We've come this far, and we're not giving up now."

Lyra nodded, her face set with determination. "James is right," she signed, her movements sharp and decisive. "We've faced impossible odds before, and we've always found a way through. This is just one more challenge, one more obstacle to overcome."

"Okay," he said, his voice growing stronger with each word. "Okay, let's do this. Let's figure out what this book is trying to tell us, and let's use that knowledge to save the world."

He looked up to see Benjamin's dads approaching the table, their faces etched with a strange, knowing expression.

"May we?" Larry asked, gesturing to the book with a gentle smile.

Peter nodded, pushing the tome towards them with a flicker of hope. "Please," he said, his voice barely above a whisper. "If you can make any sense of this, we would be forever in your debt."

The two men exchanged a glance, a silent conversation passing between them in the space of a heartbeat. And then, with a reverence that made Peter's breath catch in his throat, they began to read.

Their eyes widened as they scanned the pages, their fingers tracing the intricate symbols with a familiarity that bordered on the uncanny. Peter watched, his heart in his throat, as they seemed to absorb the book's secrets like water into a sponge.

"How…" James breathed, his voice thick with awe and confusion. "How is this possible? How can they understand a language that's been lost for centuries?"

Peter shook his head, his mind racing with possibilities. "Maybe they've seen something like this before," he offered, his tone hesitant. "Or maybe… maybe they have some kind of magic that allows them to decipher ancient texts."

Lyra's hands flew in a flurry of signs, her face alight with excitement. "I bet they're secretly linguists," she gestured, her movements sharp and playful. "You know, the kind who spend their weekends holed up in dusty libraries, poring over dead languages."

Simon snorted, a grin tugging at the corners of his mouth. "Or maybe they're just really, really good at charades," he quipped, his eyes sparkling with mirth.

But Benjamin, who had been watching his dads with a strange, pensive expression, suddenly spoke up. "They're not linguists," he said softly, his voice heavy with a weight that made Peter's heart ache. "They're celestials. Fallen angels, sent to protect me and guide me in my own magical journey."

A stunned silence fell over the group, broken only by the soft rustling of pages as Benjamin's dads continued to read. Peter felt a jolt of shock, a sudden, dizzying realization that the world was so much bigger, so much stranger, than he had ever imagined.

"Celestials?" he whispered, his voice hoarse with wonder.

Benjamin nodded, a small, hesitant smile tugging at his lips. "I've always known there was something different about them," he admitted, his gaze distant and unfocused. "The way they seemed to know things before they happened, the way they could heal even the most serious injuries with just a touch. But I never knew... I never realized the full extent of what they were."

He couldn't imagine what it must be like, to discover that your parents were literal celestial beings, with powers beyond mortal comprehension.

Benjamin's dads looked up from the book, their faces grave and their eyes shining with a strange, otherworldly light.

"We know what this is," Steve said, his voice soft but filled with a quiet intensity.

Larry leaned forward, his eyes shining with a mixture of curiosity and concern. "What is it that you seek from this ancient tome?" he asked, his gaze sweeping over the assembled group. "What knowledge do you hope to gain?"

Benjamin cleared his throat, his expression serious. "We're looking for a way to restore Peter's memories," he explained, his voice steady despite the weight of the request. "He's lost a crucial part of himself, and we believe this book may hold the key to getting it back."

The two celestials exchanged a glance, a silent communication passing between them. Then, with a nod, they began to carefully flip through the pages, their fingers skimming over the ancient symbols with a practiced ease.

Peter watched, his heart pounding in his chest, as they searched for the answer they so desperately needed. He could feel James' hand in his, a steady anchor in the midst of the chaos, and he drew strength from that touch, from the unwavering love and support it represented.

After what felt like an eternity, the celestials paused, their eyes widening with recognition. "Here," the shorter one said, his finger tapping against a particular passage. "To restore memories that have been lost, you must find the person's other half and trap it, then perform a ritual to absorb its essence."

Peter felt a jolt of shock, a sudden, sickening realization of what that meant. "My shadow," he whispered, his voice hoarse with dread. "We have to trap my shadow."

Larry nodded, his expression grave. "It will not be easy," he warned, his tone heavy with the weight of centuries. "Your shadow is a part of you, a manifestation of your deepest fears and doubts. Trapping it will require great strength, both of will and of magic."

Peter swallowed hard, his mind racing with the implications of what they were suggesting. "But how?" he asked, his voice trembling slightly. "How are we supposed to trap something that's literally a part of me?"

The celestials smiled, a knowing, almost mischievous glint in their eyes. "With this," Steve said, reaching out to tap the necklace that hung around Peter's neck. "We can sense its power, the magic that thrums within it. It may be the key to your success."

Peter's hand flew to his necklace, his fingers closing around the warm, pulsing stone. He had always known it was special, had always felt a strange, inexplicable connection to it. But to think that it could be the answer to his prayers, the key to unlocking his lost memories…

Lyra's hands suddenly flew into motion, her signs sharp and excited. "The fairy dust!" she gestured, her eyes wide with realization. "There's still some left in the necklace, from when I gave it to you. Maybe we can use that, combine it with the necklace's power to create a trap for your shadow!"

Peter felt a flicker of hope, a sudden, dizzying rush of possibility. He looked around at the faces of his friends, his family, and saw the same fierce determination reflected back at him.

"Okay," he said, his voice growing stronger with each word. "Okay, let's do this. Let's find my shadow, trap it, and get my memories back. Together."

23

Decisions, Dilemmas and Deliberations

Peter

Peter felt a growing sense of dread, a heavy weight that seemed to settle into his very bones. He knew they were worried about him, could see the concern in their eyes and the hesitation in their gestures. But he couldn't bring himself to burden them with his fears, couldn't bear to see the pity or the helplessness in their expressions.

James, of course, refused to let him suffer in silence. He was a constant presence at Peter's side, always ready with a gentle touch or a comforting word. But even his love and support couldn't chase away the darkness that seemed to be consuming Peter from the inside out.

"Peter, please talk to me," James pleaded one evening, his eyes searching Peter's face for some sign of the man he loved. "I know you're hurting, I know you're scared. But you don't have to face this alone. I'm here for you, we all are."

Peter forced a smile, but it felt brittle and false on his face. "I'm fine, James," he lied, his voice hollow even to his own ears. "Just tired, that's all. With everything that's going on, it's no wonder I'm a little stressed."

James frowned, his brow furrowing with concern. "Peter, you're not fine," he said firmly, his hand reaching out to cup Peter's cheek. "You're having nightmares, and you're barely eating. This isn't healthy, love. Please, let me help you."

Peter felt a surge of irritation, a sudden, irrational anger that made his hands clench into fists. "I don't need your help, James," he snapped, jerking away from his touch. "I'm not some fragile flower that needs to be coddled and protected. I can handle this on my own."

The hurt that flashed across James' face made Peter's stomach twist with guilt, but he pushed it down, burying it beneath the layers of fear and self-doubt that seemed to be suffocating him.

"I just need some space," he muttered, turning away from James and heading for the door. "I'm going for a walk. I'll be back later."

He could hear James calling after him, but he didn't stop, didn't look back. He just kept walking, his feet carrying him through the quiet streets of Willowbrook, his mind lost in a haze of dark thoughts and painful memories.

It wasn't until he found himself at the edge of the woods, staring into the shadows that seemed to beckon him closer, that he realized where he was. The same woods where he had first encountered his shadow, where he had nearly lost his life to the darkness that lurked within.

A shiver ran down his spine, a cold, creeping dread that made his heart race and his palms sweat. He knew he should turn back, should run as far and as fast as he could in the opposite direction. But something held him there, a morbid fascination that wouldn't let him look away.

"You can't escape me, Peter." The voice was a whisper, a sibilant hiss that seemed to come from everywhere and nowhere at once. "No matter how hard you try, no matter how far you run… I will always be with you."

Peter whirled around, his eyes wide and his breath coming in short, sharp gasps. But there was nothing there, just the empty woods and the lengthening shadows of the evening.

"I'm not afraid of you," he whispered, his voice trembling despite his best efforts. "I'm going to beat you, do you hear me? I'm going to trap you and absorb your essence, and then I'll be whole again. I'll be free."

The laughter that echoed through the trees was cruel and mocking, a sound that made Peter's blood run cold. "Oh, Peter," the voice purred, "you have no idea what you're up against. The darkness inside you, the power that I represent… it's beyond your wildest imagining. And when the time comes, you will see just how weak and helpless you truly are."

Peter felt tears stinging his eyes, a lump rising in his throat. He wanted to scream, to rage against the injustice of it all, to deny the truth of the shadow's words. But deep down, in the darkest corners of his heart… he knew it was right.

He was weak. He was helpless. And no matter how hard he tried, no matter how much he wanted to be strong for his friends, for James… he knew that he was fighting a losing battle.

With a choked sob, Peter sank to his knees, his hands clutching at his head as he tried to block out the sound of his shadow's laughter. He didn't know how long he stayed there, lost in a haze of despair and self-loathing, but when he finally looked up, the sun had long since set, and the woods were dark and silent around him.

Slowly, painfully, he dragged himself to his feet, his body aching with the effort. He knew he should go back, should face his friends and try to explain his behavior. But the thought of seeing the worry and the disappointment in their eyes was more than he could bear.

He made his way to the diner, each step feeling like a monumental effort. As he approached the familiar building, he could see the warm glow of the lights inside, could hear the murmur of voices and the clink of dishes.

For a moment, he hesitated, his hand hovering over the door handle. He didn't feel ready to face them, didn't feel strong enough to put on a brave face and pretend that everything was alright. But he knew he couldn't hide forever, couldn't keep running from the truth of what he was feeling.

Taking a deep breath, he pushed open the door and stepped inside, bracing himself for the worry and the questions he knew were coming.

But to his surprise, the scene that greeted him was not one of tension and concern, but of excitement and discovery. Lyra and the celestials were huddled around the ancient book, their faces alight with a new understanding.

"Peter!" Lyra signed, her movements sharp and eager. "You're just in time. We think we may have found something, a ritual that could give us an edge in the battle against your shadow."

Peter felt a flicker of hope, a tiny spark that chased away some of the darkness that had been clouding his mind. "What kind of ritual?" he asked, his voice hoarse from disuse.

Larry looked up, his eyes shining with a mixture of excitement and apprehension. "It's a powerful one," he said, his voice low and serious. "One that requires courage."

Peter's heart leapt at the thought, at the idea of facing his shadow with the strength and support of his loved ones at his side. But then the celestial's words fully registered, and a cold sense of dread settled into the pit of his stomach.

"And if it's not done correctly?" he asked, his voice barely above a whisper.

Larry's expression grew grave, his eyes shadowed with a deep, ancient sadness. "If you are not courageous enough then the ritual will fail." he said softly. "And there will be a chance that your mind will not be able to handle it and permanently lose all of you memories."

Peter felt the world tilt around him, felt the air rush from his lungs as if he had been punched in the gut. The responsibility, the weight of what they were suggesting… it was too much, too heavy for him to bear.

"But what if I'm not ready?" he whispered, his voice small and broken. "What if I'm not strong enough to face my shadow, to defeat the darkness inside me?"

Steve stepped forward, his eyes shining with a gentle, ancient wisdom. "Peter," he said softly. "Strength comes not from an absence of fear, but from the courage to face that fear head-on. And you, my dear boy, have more courage in your little finger than most people have in their entire being."

He looked around at the faces of the people around him, and saw the same fierce, unshakable belief reflected back at him.

"Okay," he said, his voice growing stronger with each word. "Okay, let's do this. Let's set a trap for my shadow, weaken it before the final battle. Together."

Over the next few hours, they worked tirelessly, brainstorming ideas and strategies, each member contributing their unique knowledge and abilities. Lyra, with her keen fairy senses and quick thinking, suggested a secluded location deep within the forest, a natural clearing ringed by ancient trees that thrummed with an inherent magic.

James, ever the tactician, devised a complex system of snares and wards, designed to trap and hold the shadow once it was lured into the open. Adrian and Merin, their powers complementary and potent, worked to create a series of illusions and distractions, hoping to disorient and confuse their enemy.

As the sun began to set, casting long shadows across the forest floor, they made their way to the chosen location, each step heavy with the weight of what was to come. Peter could feel the tension in the air, could see it in the set of his friends' shoulders and the tightness around their eyes.

As they reached the clearing, they quickly set to work, each member falling into their assigned roles with a grim determination. James and Lyra worked to set the snares, their hands moving in perfect synchronicity as they wove the delicate strands of magic and silver into a gleaming web of entrapment.

Adrian and Merin, their faces etched with concentration, began to weave their illusions, conjuring shadowy figures and eerie whispers that danced at the edges of the clearing, tempting and taunting the enemy that lurked just beyond sight.

And Peter, his heart in his throat and his palms slick with sweat, took his place at the center of it all, a living bait for the shadow that had haunted his every waking moment and plagued his dreams with visions of darkness and despair.

For a long, tense moment, there was nothing, only the sound of their own ragged breathing and the rustling of leaves in the breeze. And then, like a nightmare given form, Peter's shadow emerged from the trees, its eyes glowing with a malevolent hunger and its form writhing with an otherworldly wrongness.

"Well, well, well," it purred, its voice a twisted mockery of Peter's own. "Look who finally decided to come out and play. I was starting to think you'd forgotten about me, Peter."

Peter felt a shiver of fear run down his spine, but he pushed it down, squaring his shoulders and meeting his shadow's gaze with a defiant glare. "I could never forget you," he spat, his voice dripping with contempt. "You've made damn sure of that, haven't you?"

The shadow laughed, a sound like the grating of bones and the shattering of glass. "Oh, Peter," it crooned, "you have no idea what I've done, what I'm capable of. But you will, soon enough. You'll see the truth, the reality that you've been running from all this time."

It took a step forward, its form shimmering and shifting like smoke on the wind. And then, in a blur of movement too fast for the eye to follow, it lunged, its claws outstretched and its maw gaping wide in a silent scream of hunger.

But Peter was ready, his body moving on instinct as he dove to the side, rolling to his feet and summoning every ounce of his power in a desperate, defiant burst of light. The shadow recoiled, hissing in pain and rage as the magic seared its shadowy flesh, leaving wisps of darkness curling in the air like acrid smoke.

Around him, Peter could hear the sounds of battle, could feel the crackle of magic and the clashing of wills as his friends fought with everything they had. James, his face a mask of grim determination, wielded his sword with a deadly precision, the blade flashing in the fading light as he drove the shadow back with a relentless onslaught of strikes and parries.

Lyra, her wings shimmering with an otherworldly iridescence, darted and wove through the air like a glittering comet, her fairy magic leaving trails of sparkling light in her wake as she rained down bolts of searing energy upon the enemy.

Adrian and Merin, their powers intertwined in a dizzying display of elemental fury, unleashed a barrage of ice and wind, the air crackling with the force of their combined magic as they sought to trap and contain the shadow within a prison of frozen time.

And Peter, his heart pounding and his blood singing with the rush of battle, poured every ounce of his strength and determination into the fight, his shadow magic flaring and pulsing in a dazzling display of light and darkness that left the very air humming with power.

For a moment, it seemed as if they might win, as if their combined might would be enough to overwhelm the shadow and trap it within the snares they had so carefully laid. But then, in a moment of horrifying clarity, Peter saw the trap begin to unravel, the strands of magic and silver snapping like gossamer threads under the weight of the shadow's malevolent power.

And in that instant, he knew that something had gone terribly, horribly wrong.

It happened in a heartbeat, a blur of movement and a scream of agony that tore through the clearing like a knife. One moment, Lyra was there, her wings flaring with an incandescent light as she dove towards the shadow, her magic gathered in a searing bolt of energy. And the next, she was falling, her body limp and broken as she plummeted towards the ground like a puppet with its strings cut.

Time seemed to slow, the world narrowing to a single, horrifying point of focus as Peter watched his best friend, his sister in all but blood, crumple to the forest floor in a tangle of shattered wings and shimmering fairy dust. He felt a scream building in his throat, a howl of rage and despair that threatened to tear him apart from the inside out.

But before he could give voice to his anguish, before he could rush to Lyra's side and gather her broken body in his arms, he felt a presence at his back, a cold, creeping dread that froze the blood in his veins and turned his limbs to lead.

"You see, Peter?" the shadow whispered, its voice a sibilant hiss that echoed in the sudden, horrified silence of the clearing. "This is the price of your defiance, the cost of your futile resistance. You cannot win, cannot hope to stand against the darkness that dwells within you."

Peter felt a wave of despair wash over him, a crushing weight of guilt and self-loathing that threatened to drag him down into the depths of his own personal hell. He had done this, had brought this pain and suffering upon the people he loved most in the world. It was his fault, his weakness, his failure.

But even as he spiraled into the abyss of his own misery, he felt a flicker of something else, a tiny spark of defiance that refused to be extinguished. He thought of James, of the love and devotion that shone in his eyes every time he looked at Peter. He thought of Lyra, of her fierce, unwavering loyalty and the way she had always stood by his side, no matter the cost.

And he knew, with a sudden, blazing certainty, that he could not let them down, could not let their sacrifices be in vain.

With a roar of fury and determination, Peter surged to his feet, his heart pounding with a newfound strength. He could feel the shadow recoil, could sense its confusion and fear as he advanced upon it, his eyes blazing with a fire that seemed to burn away the very darkness itself.

"No," he growled, his voice low and dangerous, thrumming with a power that surprised even himself. "No, you're wrong. I am not weak, am not helpless in the face of your darkness. I have the strength of my friends, the love of my family, the unbreakable bonds that tie us together. And with them at my side, there is nothing, nothing, that I cannot overcome."

With a final, defiant cry, he pushed forward, his very essence seeming to pulse with a light that cut through the shadows like a beacon in the night. He didn't know how to wield this newfound magic, didn't know how to control the raw, untamed energy that coursed through his veins.

He had to try. For his friends, for his family and for everything he held dear.

When the light faded, when the spots had cleared from his vision and the ringing in his ears had subsided, Peter found himself standing alone in the center of the clearing, the shadow nowhere to be seen. For a moment, he dared to hope that it was over, that he had somehow, miraculously, managed to defeat his darkest self and banish it back to the depths from whence it came.

But then, like a whisper on the wind, he heard its voice, cold and mocking and filled with a malevolent glee.

"Oh, Peter," it crooned, its words echoing in his mind like the tolling of a funeral bell. "Did you really think it would be that easy? Did you truly believe that you could defeat me with a single, paltry display of power?"

Peter felt a chill run down his spine, a creeping sense of dread that settled in the pit of his stomach like a leaden weight.

"If you want to end this, once and for all," the shadow continued, its voice growing louder and more insistent with each passing second, "then you know what you have to do. Come to me, Peter. Come to the heart of the forest, where the darkness runs deep and the shadows never sleep. Come alone, and face me as you were meant to, as equals in the dance of light and dark."

Peter swallowed hard, his mouth dry and his heart pounding with a sickening, relentless rhythm.

"And if you don't," the shadow purred, its voice dripping with a cruel, malicious satisfaction, "then I will hunt down every last one of your precious friends, every person you have ever loved or cared for, and I will make them suffer in ways that will make even your darkest nightmares seem like child's play."

Peter felt a wave of nausea wash over him, a sickening, gut-wrenching horror at the thought of his loved ones in the clutches of this monster, this twisted reflection of his own darkest desires and deepest fears.

He knew, with a sudden, terrible certainty, that he had no choice, that he could not risk the lives of those he held most dear, no matter the cost to himself.

And so, with a heavy heart and a mind clouded with dread, Peter made his decision.

He would go to the heart of the forest, would face his shadow alone and unaided, and he would end this, once and for all.

Even if it meant sacrificing his own life in the process.

246

24

Shadowstep

Peter

The journey back to James' house was a blur of pain and guilt for Peter, his mind replaying the horrifying moment of Lyra's injury over and over again. The sight of her broken body, the sound of her scream - they echoed in his head like a twisted, relentless symphony of suffering.

As they stumbled through the door, exhausted and battered, Peter couldn't meet anyone's eyes, couldn't bear to see the accusation and blame that he was sure must be written across their faces. He had done this, had brought this pain and danger upon them all.

"Peter." James' voice, soft and gentle, cut through the haze of self-recrimination. "Look at me, love."

Slowly, reluctantly, Peter raised his gaze, steeling himself for the condemnation he was sure he would find in James' eyes. But all he saw was love, pure and unwavering, tinged with a deep, aching concern.

"This isn't your fault," James said firmly, his hands coming up to cup Peter's face, his thumbs brushing away the tears that Peter hadn't even realized were falling. "None of this is your fault, do you hear me?"

Peter felt a sob rise up in his throat, a desperate, wrenching thing that tore at his very soul. He flung himself into James' arms, burying his face in the crook of his neck and clinging to him like a drowning man to a life raft.

"I'm so sorry," he whispered, his voice muffled and broken. "I'm so sorry for all of this, for putting you all in danger, for not being strong enough to stop it."

"No more apologizing, yeah?" James said.

James just held him tighter, his hands rubbing soothing circles on Peter's back as he let him cry, let him pour out all the fear and guilt and pain that had been eating away at him for so long.

Around them, the others moved quietly, tending to their wounds and making plans for the battles to come. Lyra, her wings bandaged and her face pale but determined, signed rapid-fire instructions to Benjamin and Adrian, her movements sharp and urgent.

Simon and the celestials huddled together, poring over ancient texts and muttering in low, urgent tones. They were searching for answers, for some way to turn the tide against the darkness that threatened to consume them all.

Eventually, the others began to trickle out and James and Peter were left alone, the silence of the house settling around them like a comforting blanket.

"Stay with me tonight," James murmured, his lips brushing against Peter's temple. "Let me hold you, let me show you how much I love you."

Peter nodded, unable to speak past the lump in his throat. He let James lead him upstairs, let him undress him with gentle, reverent hands. And when they came together, skin to skin and heart to heart, it was like coming home, like finding a piece of himself that he hadn't even known was missing.

Peter gazed into James' eyes, seeing the love and devotion shining back at him. In that moment, all the fear and guilt melted away, replaced by a profound sense of connection and belonging.

James' hands roamed over Peter's body, each touch igniting sparks of pleasure that danced across his skin. Peter arched into the caress, a soft moan escaping his lips.

"I need you," he whispered, his voice rough with emotion. "I need to feel you, to know that this is real, that we're real."

James smiled, a tender, understanding curve of his lips. "I'm here, love," he murmured, his breath ghosting over Peter's ear. "I'm right here, and I'm not going anywhere."

He captured Peter's lips in a kiss, deep and passionate, pouring all of his love and reassurance into the press of their mouths. Peter responded eagerly, his hands tangling in James' hair, pulling him closer, ever closer.

They undressed each other slowly, reverently, taking the time to explore every inch of newly revealed skin. James traced the lines of Peter's body with his fingertips, his touch leaving trails of fire in its wake.

"You're so beautiful," he breathed, his eyes dark with desire. "Sometimes I look at you and I can't believe you're mine, that I get to love you like this."

Peter felt tears prick at his eyes, overwhelmed by the depth of emotion in James' words. "I'm yours," he whispered, his voice trembling. "Always and forever, in this life and the next. I love you, James, more than I ever thought possible."

James' answer was a kiss, fierce and claiming, as he lowered Peter back onto the bed. Their bodies aligned, fitting together like two halves of a whole, and Peter gasped at the perfection of it, at the rightness he felt in James' arms.

They moved together, slowly at first, savoring each touch, each shared breath. But soon the heat between them grew, the need becoming more urgent, more demanding.

"James," Peter panted, his nails digging into the muscled expanse of James' back. "Please, I need... I need..."

"I know, love," James rasped, his own voice tight with desire. "I've got you, I'll give you everything you need."

He reached between them, taking Peter in hand, and Peter cried out at the sensation, at the exquisite pleasure that coursed through his veins. He rocked up into James' touch, chasing the bliss that hovered just out of reach.

And then James was moving faster, thrusting deeper, and Peter was lost, drowning in a sea of sensation and emotion. He clung to James like a lifeline, anchoring himself in the solid strength of his body, in the unwavering love that poured from every touch.

"Let go, Peter," James urged, his hand moving in time with his thrusts. "Let go and let me catch you. I'll always catch you."

And with a broken cry, Peter did, his release crashing over him in waves of ecstasy. James followed a moment later, Peter's name a reverent prayer on his lips.

In the aftermath, they held each other close, trading soft kisses and whispered words of love. Peter had never felt so safe, so cherished, so completely and utterly at peace.

"Thank you," he murmured, his face tucked into the crook of James' neck. "For loving me, for believing in me, even when I can't believe in myself."

James' arms tightened around him, a silent promise of protection and devotion. "Always," he whispered fiercely. "No matter what happens, no matter what we have to face, I will always love you, always believe in you. You're my heart, Peter. My everything."

Peter felt a warmth bloom in his chest, a feeling of love and belonging so profound that it brought tears to his eyes. He nestled closer to James, savoring the feel of his strong, steady heartbeat against his cheek.

For a long moment, they lay in contented silence, their breathing gradually slowing as the exhaustion of the day caught up with them. But just as Peter was about to drift off, lulled by the warmth and safety of James' embrace, his lover spoke again, his voice soft and wistful.

"I've been thinking," James murmured, his fingers tracing idle patterns on Peter's bare shoulder. "About the future, about what we'll do when all of this is over."

Peter tilted his head, meeting James' gaze with a curious smile. "Oh? And what have you been thinking?"

James hesitated, a flicker of uncertainty crossing his handsome face. "I know it might sound silly," he said, his voice tentative. "But I can't help but dream of a life here, in Willowbrook. A quiet, simple life, filled with love and laughter and lazy Sunday mornings in bed."

Peter's breath caught in his throat, his heart swelling with a rush of emotion. He had never dared to hope for such a thing, had never allowed himself to imagine a future beyond the constant struggle and danger of their current situation.

But hearing James speak of it now, with such longing and conviction… it made something come alive inside of Peter, a yearning for a life he hadn't even known he wanted.

"It's not silly at all," he whispered, his hand coming up to cup James' cheek. "In fact, it sounds like heaven to me. A little cottage, maybe, with a garden and a porch swing. Somewhere we can make our own, somewhere we can build a life together."

James' eyes shone with love and gratitude, a soft, wondering smile playing at the corners of his mouth. "You really mean that?" he asked, his voice rough with emotion. "You'd really want that, with me?"

Peter leaned in, capturing James' lips in a tender, lingering kiss. "I want everything with you, James Crane," he murmured against his mouth. "I want lazy mornings and cozy evenings, I want laughter and tears and every little moment in between. I want a lifetime of loving you, in whatever form that takes."

James made a soft, choked sound, his arms tightening around Peter as he buried his face in the crook of his neck. "I love you," he whispered, his voice muffled and trembling. "I love you so much, Peter. And I swear, I will do everything in my power to give you that life, to make all of our dreams come true."

Peter smiled, feeling a sense of peace and contentment wash over him, even in the midst of the chaos and uncertainty that surrounded them. "I know you will," he said softly, running his fingers through James' hair. "And I'll be right there with you, every step of the way. Together, we can face anything."

James' answer was a soft, sleepy hum of agreement, his body growing heavy and pliant in Peter's arms. Peter held him close, listening to the sound of his breathing evening out, feeling the steady rise and fall of his chest against his own.

But even as he reveled in the warmth and comfort of James' presence, Peter couldn't shake the weight that had settled in his heart, the cold, creeping dread that whispered in the back of his mind.

The shadow's threat echoed in his thoughts, a cruel, taunting reminder of the danger that lurked just beyond the safety of this moment. He thought of Lyra, broken and bleeding, of the pain and suffering he had already caused to those he loved most.

And he knew, with a sickening, sinking certainty, that he could not let it happen again. He could not risk the lives of his friends, his family, for his own selfish desires. He had to end this, once and for all, even if it meant sacrificing his own chance at happiness.

Carefully, so as not to wake James, Peter extricated himself from his lover's embrace. He stood beside the bed for a long moment, drinking in the sight of James' peaceful, slumbering face, committing every beloved feature to memory.

"I'm sorry," he whispered, his voice breaking on the words. "I'm so sorry, my love. But I have to do this. I have to keep you safe, even if it means losing you."

With trembling hands, he dressed quickly, his movements stiff and mechanical. He scribbled a hasty note, his vision blurred with tears, and left it on the pillow beside James' head.

And then, with one last, longing look at the man who held his heart, Peter slipped out into the night, his feet carrying him towards the forest, towards the final confrontation with his shadow.

The journey to the heart of the forest seemed to pass in a blur, Peter's mind consumed with thoughts of James and the life they had dreamed of together. He clung to those images like a lifeline, drawing strength from the love and happiness they represented.

But as he stepped into the clearing, the sight that greeted him drove all thoughts of the future from his mind. There, waiting for him with a cruel, triumphant smile, was his shadow. And beside it, stood a figure that made Peter's blood run cold.

A woman, tall and regal, with eyes that glittered with malice and power. She wore a cloak of deepest black, and in her hand, she held a staff topped with a glowing, pulsing orb.

"Welcome, Peter," she purred, her voice like silk and poison. "I've been waiting for you."

Peter felt a shiver of fear run down his spine, but he forced himself to stand tall, to meet her gaze with a defiance he didn't quite feel. "Who are you?" he demanded, his voice rough and shaking. "What do you want with me?"

The woman laughed, a sound like the shattering of glass. "Oh, my dear boy," she crooned, "I am Wanda, the mistress of shadows and the weaver of fates. And as for what I want... I want you, Peter. I want your magic, your potential, your very soul."

Peter's mind reeled, a sickening sense of dread washing over him. He had never seen this woman before, had never heard her name. And yet, there was something about her, a terrible familiarity that made his skin crawl.

"I don't understand," he whispered, his voice small and lost. "How do you know me? What do you mean, my magic?"

Wanda smiled, a cold, cruel thing that made Peter's heart twist in his chest. "Oh, Peter," she sighed, shaking her head in mock pity. "There is so much you don't know, so much you have forgotten. But I remember. I have been watching you, guiding you, shaping your destiny from the shadows."

She took a step forward, her eyes boring into Peter's with a terrible intensity. "You are special, Peter," she hissed, her voice low and urgent. "You have a power within you, a potential for greatness that few can even imagine. And with my help, with the strength of your shadow at your side… you could be unstoppable."

Peter felt a flicker of something, a terrible, treacherous temptation that whispered in the back of his mind. To be strong, to be powerful, to never feel weak or afraid again… it was a seductive thought.

But then he thought of James, of the love and light that he brought into Peter's life. He thought of Lyra, of her unwavering loyalty and fierce, protective spirit. He thought of all the people who believed in him, who fought for him, who loved him just as he was.

And he knew, with a sudden, blazing certainty, that he could never betray that love, could never give in to the darkness that Wanda offered.

"No," he said, his voice ringing with conviction. "No, I won't join you. I won't let you use me, twist me into something I'm not. I am more than my shadow, more than the darkness inside me. And I will fight you, with every last breath in my body."

Wanda's face contorted with rage, her eyes flashing with a terrible, searing power. "So be it," she snarled, raising her staff high. "If you will not join me, then you will die, and your power will be mine to command."

And with that, the battle began.

It was like nothing Peter had ever experienced, a whirlwind of shadow and light, of pain and fury and desperate, clawing hope. His shadow lashed out at him, its claws tearing at his flesh, its voice whispering poisonous doubts in his mind.

Peter fought back with all his might, calling upon every scrap of strength and courage he possessed. He reached for his shadow magic, the untrained power that surged through his veins, but it was wild and unpredictable, slipping through his grasp like water.

Again and again, he tried to bend the shadows to his will, to turn them against his foes. But each time, the magic rebelled, twisting and writhing out of his control, lashing back at him with a vengeance.

Wanda's laughter rang out, cruel and mocking, as she watched Peter struggle and fail. "You see?" she taunted, her voice dripping with disdain. "You are nothing, a pitiful creature fumbling in the dark. Your power is wasted on you, a mere vessel for a force you cannot hope to comprehend."

Peter's shadow pressed its advantage, driving him back with a relentless onslaught of blows. Peter's body screamed in agony, his mind reeling with the pain and the despair of his own impotence.

He thought of James, of the life they had promised each other, of the love that bound them together across time and space. He tried to draw strength from those memories, to find the courage to keep fighting.

But it wasn't enough. With a final, devastating blow, Peter's shadow sent him flying, his body crumpling to the ground in a broken, bleeding heap.

Wanda loomed over him, her face twisted with a terrible, triumphant glee. "And so it ends," she hissed, her staff pointed at Peter's heart. "The great Peter Naps, brought low by his own weakness, his own fear.

Pathetic."

Peter's vision blurred, his breath coming in ragged, painful gasps. He knew he was dying, could feel his life slipping away with each passing second.

But even as the darkness closed in, even as the last of his strength deserted him, Peter's thoughts turned to James. To the man who had loved him, believed in him, fought for him.

"I'm sorry," he whispered, his voice a broken, desperate thing. "I'm so sorry, my love. I tried... I tried so hard. But I wasn't strong enough, wasn't good enough. Please, please forgive me."

25

Summer Solstice

James

His arm instinctively reached out for Peter, seeking the warmth and comfort of his lover's body. But instead of the familiar heat and softness, his hand met only cold, empty sheets.

Confusion and unease prickled at the edges of his consciousness, and he sat up, his eyes bleary and his mind still foggy with the remnants of slumber.

"Peter?" he called out, his voice rough and thick. "Love, where are you?"

Silence greeted him, heavy and oppressive, and a cold knot of dread began to form in the pit of his stomach. James threw back the covers, his heart starting to race as he searched the room for any sign of his missing partner.

And then he saw it. A note, propped up on the pillow beside him, his name scrawled across the front in Peter's familiar handwriting.

With shaking hands, James unfolded the paper, his eyes scanning the words with a growing sense of horror and disbelief.

"My dearest James," it began, the words already blurring with the tears that filled his eyes. *"I'm sorry. I'm so sorry for what I'm about to do, for the pain I know it will cause you. But I can't let anyone else get hurt because of me, can't risk the lives of the people I love most in this world."*

James' heart clenched, a physical pain that stole his breath and made his chest ache. He read on, each word like a knife to his soul.

"I have to face my shadow, have to end this once and for all. And I have to do it alone. Please, don't try to follow me. Don't put yourself in danger for my sake. I couldn't bear it if something happened to you."

A sob tore from James' throat, raw and desperate. How could Peter do this? How could he just leave, without a word, without a chance for James to stop him, to protect him?

"I love you, James. More than life itself. And I will carry that love with me, into the darkness and beyond. Please, forgive me. And know that, no matter what happens, you will always be the light that guides me home."

The note slipped from James' numb fingers, fluttering to the floor like a broken promise. For a moment, he couldn't move, couldn't breathe, couldn't think past the overwhelming surge of panic and fear that gripped him.

But then, like a switch being flipped, he sprang into action, his mind whirring with desperate, half-formed plans. He had to find Peter, had to stop him before it was too late. He couldn't lose him, not like this, not ever.

James threw on his clothes, his hands shaking so badly he could barely button his shirt. He raced out of the room, his heart pounding and his breath coming in short, sharp gasps.

He nearly collided with Simon, who was emerging from his own room, his face creased with sleep and confusion. "James?" he asked, his voice groggy and concerned. "What's going on? Is everything alright?"

James couldn't speak, couldn't force the words past the lump in his throat. He thrust the note at Simon, his eyes wild and pleading.

Simon scanned the words, his face paling with each passing second. "Oh, no," he breathed, his voice thin and strained. "Oh, Peter, what have you done?"

Something in James snapped, a dam bursting under the weight of his fear and frustration. "What have you done?" he snarled, rounding on Simon with a fury that surprised even himself. "You were supposed to be watching him, supposed to be keeping him safe! How could you let this happen?"

Simon flinched, his eyes wide and hurt. "James, I... I didn't know. I'm sorry, I never meant..."

But James wasn't listening, too lost in his own spiral of anger and guilt. "Sorry isn't good enough!" he shouted, his voice cracking with the force of his emotions. "Peter is out there, alone and in danger, and it's all your fault!"

The words hung in the air between them, heavy and harsh, and James immediately regretted them. He saw the pain and shock on Simon's face, the way he seemed to shrink under the weight of James' accusation.

"I'm sorry," James whispered, his anger draining away as quickly as it had come, leaving him hollow and exhausted. "I shouldn't have said that. It's not your fault, Simon. It's mine. I should have been there for him, should have seen this coming."

Simon shook his head, his expression soft with sympathy and understanding. "No, James," he said gently, reaching out to lay a comforting hand on James' shoulder. "It's not your fault, either. Peter made his choice, and as much as it hurts, we have to respect that."

James closed his eyes, fighting back the tears that threatened to overwhelm him. "I can't lose him, Simon," he choked out, his voice small and broken. "I can't. He's everything to me, my whole world. I have to find him, have to save him."

Simon squeezed his shoulder, his grip firm and grounding. "We will, James," he said, his voice ringing with conviction. "We'll find him, and we'll bring him home. But we have to be smart about this, have to think with our heads and not just our hearts."

James nodded, drawing in a deep, shuddering breath. Simon was right. He couldn't let his emotions cloud his judgment, couldn't rush off half-cocked and risk making things worse.

But even as he tried to calm his racing heart, to focus on the task at hand, James couldn't shake the sense of urgency that thrummed through his veins. He paced the room, his steps quick and agitated, his mind whirring with possibilities and fears.

Where could Peter have gone? What was he thinking, facing his shadow alone? And then, with a sickening lurch of his stomach, James remembered the date. The Summer Solstice. The day they had been dreading and preparing for, the day when the veil between worlds was at its thinnest and the shadows at their strongest.

"Oh, God," he whispered, his voice hoarse with dread. "Simon, today is the Solstice."

Simon's eyes widened, understanding and horror dawning on his face. "Shit," he breathed, running a hand through his hair. "Shit, shit, shit. James, we have to find him. We have to stop him before it's too late."

James nodded, his jaw clenched with determination. "I know," he said, his voice tight with fear and resolve. "But we can't do this alone, Simon."

He paused, his mind racing, and then a thought struck him like a bolt of lightning. "Adrian," he said, his voice thrumming with sudden certainty. "We have to go to Adrian and Benjamin's manor. They might know something that could help us find Peter, or have resources we can use."

Simon nodded, already reaching for his jacket and keys. "You're right," he said, his voice grim but determined. "Adrian's knowledge of magic and the supernatural is unparalleled. If anyone can help us, it's him and Benjamin."

They raced through time, the familiar streets and landmarks blurring past the windows, James couldn't shake the sense of dread that coiled in his gut. Every second that ticked by was another second that Peter was out there, alone and in danger, facing a threat that none of them truly understood.

When they arrived at the manor, James was out of the car before it had even come to a complete stop. He raced up the steps, his heart pounding and his breath coming in short, sharp gasps.

He pounded on the door, his fist striking the heavy oak with a desperate, frantic rhythm. "Adrian!" he called out, his voice raw and ragged. "Benjamin! Please, open up! It's James, and it's an emergency!"

For a moment that seemed to stretch into eternity, there was only silence, a heavy, oppressive stillness that made James' skin crawl with unease. But then, like a miracle, the door swung open, revealing Adrian's concerned face.

"James?" he said, his brow furrowed with worry. "What's going on? What's happened?"

James felt his composure crumble, the desperate, aching fear that he had been holding back finally breaking free. "It's Peter," he choked out, his voice cracking with emotion. "He's gone, Adrian. We have to find him, have to stop him before it's too late."

Adrian's eyes widened, a flicker of something ancient and unfathomable passing behind his gaze. He stepped aside, ushering James and Simon into the manor with a sense of grim urgency.

"Come in," he said, his voice low and serious. "Tell me everything. We'll find him, James. We'll bring him back, no matter what it takes."

As they entered the manor, James felt a flicker of hope, a desperate belief that here, among friends and allies, they would find the answers they so urgently needed. But even as Adrian led them into the heart of the house, even as Benjamin emerged from the shadows with a look of grave concern on his face, James couldn't shake the sense of urgency that thrummed through his veins.

"Adrian," he said, his voice tight with barely contained panic, "please, we need to know. How much time do we have? How long until the Solstice reaches its peak?"

Adrian exchanged a glance with Benjamin, a silent communication passing between them in the space of a heartbeat. And then, from the depths of the room, a new voice spoke, a low, rumbling purr that seemed to echo from the very walls themselves.

"Mere hours," said Jimmy, the wise and mysterious cat, as he emerged from the shadows with a fluid grace that belied his years. "The alignment will be complete before the sun sets, and then... then the shadows will be at their strongest."

James felt his heart sink, a leaden weight of despair settling in the pit of his stomach. Hours. They had only hours to find Peter, to save him from the darkness that sought to claim him. It seemed an impossible task, a race against time and fate itself.

Beside him, Simon let out a low, shuddering breath, his face pale and drawn in the flickering light of the candles. "Shit," he whispered, his voice hoarse with dread. "How are we going to find him in time? How are we going to stop this?"

But James couldn't accept defeat, couldn't let himself succumb to the hopelessness that threatened to overwhelm him. He thought of Peter, of the love that bound them together, of the unbreakable bond that had brought them through so much darkness and pain.

And he knew, with a sudden, blazing certainty, that he would not fail. That he would find Peter, would bring him back from the brink, no matter what it took.

"We'll find a way," he said, his voice ringing with conviction. "We have to. Peter is counting on us, and I won't let him down. Not now, not ever."

Adrian nodded, his eyes glinting with a fierce, determined light. "James is right," he said, his voice low and serious. "We have faced impossible odds before, and we have always found a way through. This time will be no different."

James felt a flicker of hope, a desperate belief that with his friends by his side, they could do anything, could face any challenge and emerge victorious. But even as he opened his mouth to speak, to voice his gratitude and his determination, the door burst open with a bang, and Lyra came rushing into the room, her face pale and her eyes wide with fear.

"What's happening?" she signed frantically, her hands moving in a blur of motion. "Is everyone okay? Is Peter...?"

She trailed off, her expression tightening with dread as she took in the grim faces around her. James felt his heart clench, a wave of guilt and despair washing over him as he realized that he would have to be the one to break the news, to shatter the fragile hope that still shone in Lyra's eyes.

"Peter's gone," he said, his voice rough and heavy with emotion. "He left in the middle of the night, left a note saying he was going to face his shadow alone. We have to find him, Lyra. We have to bring him back before it's too late."

For a moment, Lyra was silent, her face a mask of shock and disbelief. And then, like a dam bursting, the tears began to fall, streaming down her cheeks in a silent, heartbroken flood.

"No," she signed, her movements sharp and jagged with grief. "No, he can't... he can't be gone. He promised, he swore he would never leave us. How could he do this, how could he be so stupid?"

James felt his own eyes stinging, his throat tight with the effort of holding back his own tears. He stepped forward, gathering Lyra into his arms and holding her close, letting her sob into his chest as he stroked her hair with a shaking hand.

"I know," he whispered, his voice cracking with the weight of his own pain. "I know, Lyra. But we're going to find him, okay? We're going to bring him back, no matter what it takes."

Lyra pulled back, her face streaked with tears but her eyes blazing with a fierce, determined light. "I think I know how," she signed, her movements sharp and urgent. "Peter's necklace, the one I gave him. It has fairy dust in it, dust that acts as a tracking device. If I can tap into its magic, I might be able to find him, to lead us to where he's gone."

James felt a surge of hope, a desperate, clawing thing that threatened to overwhelm him. "You can do that?" he asked, his voice rough with emotion. "You can find him, even if he's far away?"

Lyra nodded, her expression grim but determined. "I can try," she signed, her hands moving with a fluid, practiced grace. "But it will take time, James. Time we may not have."

But before she could finish, a sound like thunder ripped through the air, shaking the very foundations of the manor. James stumbled, his heart pounding and his mind reeling as he tried to make sense of what was happening.

And then Dominic barged in with a vampire that James didn't recognise, his face pale and his eyes wide with fear. "The town square…it is under attack!" he gasped, his voice tight with urgency.

James felt his heart lurch, a sickening sense of dread washing over him. The town square, the heart of Willowbrook, under attack. And Peter, lost and alone in the darkness, facing a threat that none of them truly understood.

"Lyra," he said, his voice low and urgent, "I need you to focus all your efforts on finding Peter. Use every scrap of magic, every ounce of power you possess. Find him, and come to us as soon as you have a location, no matter what."

Lyra nodded, her face set with a grim, unwavering resolve. "I won't let you down, James," she signed, her movements sharp and precise. "I'll find him, I swear it. And I'll bring him back to you, no matter what it takes."

James felt a surge of gratitude, a fierce, aching love for this brave, loyal fairy who had become like a sister to him. "Thank you," he whispered, his voice rough with emotion. "Thank you, Lyra. I don't know what I would do without you."

Lyra smiled, a small, sad thing that barely touched her eyes. "You'll never have to find out," she signed, her hands moving with a gentle, reassuring grace. "Now go, James. Go and save our town, our home. And trust that I will find Peter, and bring him back to you."

James nodded, his jaw set with a grim, unyielding determination. He turned to the others, his eyes sweeping over their faces, taking in the fear and the resolve, the love and the loyalty that shone in their gazes.

"We have to buy Lyra time," he said, his voice ringing with the weight of command. "We have to hold off whatever is happening in town. We have to protect the people of Willowbrook until Peter can be found. It won't be easy, and it won't be without sacrifice. But we have faced impossible odds before, and we have always found a way through. This time will be no different."

Adrian nodded, his hand finding Benjamin's and squeezing tight. "We're with you, James," he said, his voice low and fierce. "Until the end, no matter what happens."

Benjamin smiled, a small, fierce thing that made James' heart ache with love and pride. "Let's show these bastards what happens when they mess with us," he growled, his eyes glinting with a savage, protective light.

Jimmy purred, a low, rumbling sound that seemed to fill the room with a gentle, comforting warmth. "We will hold the line," he said, his ancient eyes shining with a wisdom that took James' breath away. "We will give Lyra the time she needs."

James felt a lump rise in his throat, a surge of emotion so powerful that it nearly brought him to his knees. He had always known that he had friends, had allies in this fight. But to see them here, ready to stand with him against the very forces of darkness itself... it gave him a strength he hadn't known he possessed.

"Then let's go," he said, his voice ringing with a fierce, unyielding conviction. "Let's show these monsters what happens when they dare to threaten the people we love."

With grim determination, they made their way to the town square, the heart of Willowbrook. As they approached, the sounds of chaos and destruction grew louder, the acrid smell of smoke and fear hanging heavy in the air.

The scene that greeted them was one of utter devastation. The once-charming buildings lay in ruins, their windows shattered and their walls crumbling. Fires raged unchecked, casting an eerie, flickering light over the carnage. And everywhere, the shadows swarmed, their twisted forms writhing and shrieking as they tore through the town like a plague.

For a moment, James and his companions could only stare in horror, their hearts sinking at the sight of their beloved home reduced to rubble. But then, a fierce, unquenchable anger began to rise within them, a determination to protect what was theirs, to defend the people they loved with every ounce of strength they possessed.

And with a roar of defiance, a battle cry that seemed to shake the very foundations of the earth, they charged out into the night, their hearts pounding and their weapons at the ready.

The battle was fierce, a whirlwind of magic and steel, of blood and sweat and desperate, clawing hope. James lost himself in the rhythm of the fight, his sword flashing in the moonlight as he cut down shadow after shadow, monster after twisted, shrieking monster.

Beside him, Adrian and Benjamin fought like demons, their powers intertwined in a dazzling display of elemental fury. Ice and wind, fire and earth, all of it swirling together in a maelstrom of destruction that left their enemies reeling, their ranks shattered and broken.

And through it all, James could feel the steady, unwavering presence of Jimmy at his back, the ancient cat's magic thrumming through the air like a heartbeat, a pulse of pure, unadulterated power that seemed to fill them all with a strength they hadn't known they possessed.

Just as the tide of battle seemed to turn in their favor, just as James began to dare to hope that they might emerge victorious after all… Lyra appeared, her face pale and her eyes wide with a terror that made James' blood run cold.

"I found him," she signed, her hands shaking so badly that James could barely make out the words. "I found Peter. But James… it's bad. It's really, really bad."

James felt his heart stop, a sickening, gut-wrenching sense of dread washing over him. "Where?" he demanded, his voice raw and ragged with fear. "Where is he, Lyra? Take me to him, now."

Lyra nodded, her face set with a grim, unyielding determination. And together, they raced through the night, their feet pounding against the earth as they followed the delicate, shimmering thread of fairy magic that would lead them to Peter.

They found him in a small, ramshackle house deep in the heart of the woods, a place that seemed to pulse with an aura of darkness and despair. James felt his heart lurch as they burst through the door, his eyes scanning the room with a desperate, frantic intensity.

There, lying on the floor in a pool of his own blood, was Peter. His body was broken, his face pale and still, and for a moment, James was sure that they were too late, that he had lost the love of his life forever.

But then he saw the rise and fall of Peter's chest, the faint, fluttering pulse at his throat, and he felt a surge of hope, a desperate, clawing thing that threatened to consume him whole.

"Peter," he breathed, his voice cracking with emotion as he fell to his knees beside his everything. "Peter, I'm here. I'm here, and I'm going to save you, I swear it."

But even as he reached out, even as his hands found Peter's cold, clammy skin… a voice rang out from the shadows, a voice that made James' heart stop in his chest.

"Oh, I don't think so," purred the voice, a feminine lilt that dripped with malice and cruel amusement. "You're too late, James. Peter is mine now, body and soul. And there's nothing you can do to stop me."

James' head snapped up, his eyes widening in shock and disbelief as he searched the darkness for the source of the voice. And then, like a nightmare given form, two figures stepped out of the shadows, each one more horrifying than the last.

The first was Peter's shadow, a twisted, malevolent thing that seemed to pulse with an aura of darkness and despair. Its eyes glowed with a sickly, red light, and its mouth was twisted in a cruel, mocking grin.

But it was the second figure that made James' blood boil with rage and disgust. It was Wanda, the witch who had always set his teeth on edge, the one person in all of Tír na nÓg that he had never trusted.

"You," he snarled, his voice low and deadly with the force of his anger. "I should have known it would be you behind this, you backstabbing bitch. I always knew there was something off about you, something twisted and wrong."

Wanda laughed, a cold, cruel sound that made James' skin crawl with revulsion. "Oh, James," she crooned, her voice dripping with mock sympathy. "You poor, foolish boy. Did you really think you could keep Peter safe from me? Did you really believe that your love, your pathetic, mortal love, could stand against the power of the darkness itself?"

She gestured to Peter's shadow, her lips curling in a cruel, triumphant smile. "With this creature at my side, with the power of Peter's own darkness coursing through my veins... there is nothing that can stop me now."

James felt a roar of fury building in his chest, a white-hot rage that threatened to consume him whole. He surged to his feet, his sword leaping into his hand as he faced down the woman who had betrayed them all, the monster who had stolen the light from his world.

"You're wrong," he snarled, his voice low and deadly with the force of his anger. "Peter will never be yours, Wanda. He is strong, and brave, and good, and he will fight you with every last breath in his body. And I will be there with him, every step of the way, until we banish you back to the hell that spawned you."

Wanda's eyes flashed with a cruel, mocking light, and she threw back her head and laughed, a sound that made James' skin crawl with disgust.

"Such brave words," she taunted, her voice dripping with disdain. "But in the end, they are just that. Words. And words have no power against the darkness that I command, the shadow that I have claimed as my own."

She raised her hand, and James felt a surge of power, a wave of malevolent energy that slammed into him like a physical blow. He staggered back, his sword falling from his nerveless fingers as he fought to keep his footing, to stay standing in the face of Wanda's onslaught.

But even as he struggled, even as he felt his strength beginning to fail... he knew that he would not give up. That he would fight for Peter, for the man he loved, for the life they had built together, no matter the cost.

Because in the end, that was what love was. A force stronger than any darkness, any evil, any shadow that dared to stand in its way.

26

Shadowplay

Peter

He drifted in a haze of pain and confusion, his mind struggling to make sense of the chaos that surrounded him. He could feel the cold, hard floor beneath his back, the sticky wetness of his own blood seeping through his clothes. Every breath was agony, every twitch of his muscles a fresh wave of torment.

But even through the fog of his suffering, he could hear the sounds of battle raging nearby. The clashing of steel against steel, the sizzling crackle of magic unleashed, the grunts and cries of exertion and pain. It was a symphony of violence, a cruel and relentless melody that pounded against his skull like a drumbeat.

And then, cutting through the din like a knife, came a voice. A woman's voice, melodic and otherworldly, whispering in his mind with a gentle insistence.

"Peter," the voice called, soft and urgent. "Peter, you must wake up. You must fight. Your friends need you, your love needs you. You cannot let the darkness win."

Peter groaned, his eyelids fluttering as he struggled to obey the voice's command. It was like trying to swim through molasses, his body heavy and unresponsive, his mind clouded with exhaustion and despair.

But slowly, painfully, he managed to open his eyes, blinking against the sudden brightness that assaulted his vision. And what he saw made his heart lurch with a sickening mixture of fear and awe.

There, locked in a fierce and desperate battle, were James and Wanda, their forms illuminated by the flashes of spells and the gleam of weapons. James was a whirlwind of steel and fury, his sword flashing in the dim light as he parried and thrust with a skill born of years of training and an unshakeable determination.

But Wanda was a force of nature, her magic crackling and sizzling around her like a living thing. She moved with a fluid grace, her body twisting and weaving as she unleashed blast after blast of dark energy, her eyes glinting with a cruel and malicious glee.

And there, hovering at the edges of the fight like a malevolent specter, was Peter's own shadow. It watched the battle with a hungry intensity, its form shifting and writhing as if eager to join the fray, to sink its claws into the flesh of its enemies.

Peter felt a surge of panic, a desperate need to help James, to stand by his side and face this threat together. He tried to rise, his arms shaking with the effort as he pushed himself up from the floor.

But his body betrayed him, his legs buckling beneath him like twigs in a storm. He collapsed back onto the ground with a cry of pain and frustration, tears of helpless rage burning in his eyes.

"James," he croaked, his voice barely a whisper.

He didn't know if James could hear him over the chaos of the battle, didn't know if his words would even make a difference. But he had to try, had to let the man he loved know that he was still here, still fighting, even if his body refused to cooperate.

And then, as if in answer to his desperate plea, he heard James' voice, strong and fierce and filled with a love that took Peter's breath away.

"Peter," he called, his words ringing out like a clarion call. "Peter, hold on. Hold on, my love. I'm here, and I won't let them take you. I won't let them win."

Slowly, painfully, he began to drag himself forward, inch by agonizing inch. His body screamed in protest, his wounds sending bolts of white-hot agony through his veins with every movement. But he didn't stop, didn't falter, his eyes fixed on James' form as he fought with a fierce and unflagging courage.

"I'm coming," Peter whispered, his voice hoarse with pain and determination.

Even as his body screamed in protest, even as his vision blurred and his knees buckled beneath him, Peter held on. He clung to that spark of hope, that flicker of light that refused to be extinguished, no matter how hard the darkness tried to snuff it out.

"I won't let you win," he gritted out, his voice raw and ragged with pain and determination. "I won't let you take everything I love away from me. Not again, not ever."

He felt his magic rising up, felt it engulfing him in a blinding, searing light that chased away the shadows and left only clarity and strength in its wake.

He didn't know how he was doing it, didn't understand the power that now thrummed through his veins like a living thing. But he knew, with a bone-deep certainty, that he was exactly where he was meant to be, doing exactly what he was meant to do.

And as he stood there, Peter knew that he had finally found his place in the world. He had found his magic, his purpose, his reason for being.

But then, just as the last embers of his hope threatened to gutter out, he felt a presence beside him. A warm, comforting aura that seemed to chase away the chill of despair and fill him with a gentle, steady strength.

Peter turned his head, his breath catching in his throat as he saw Lyra her face etched with a mixture of concern and relief. She reached out, her hands gentle as she helped him sit up, supporting his weight as if he were made of spun glass.

With a gentle breath, she blew the particles over Peter's skin, watching as they settled on his wounds like a healing balm. And as they did, Peter felt a strange, wondrous sensation - a warmth that spread through his veins like liquid sunlight, chasing away the pain and the weakness that had held him in their grip for so long.

He gasped, his eyes flying open as he felt strength flooding back into his limbs, his mind clearing like a sky after a storm. He stared at Lyra in amazement, his voice rough with wonder when he finally managed to speak.

"Lyra," he croaked, his hand finding hers and squeezing tight. "Thank you. Thank you so much, I don't know what I would have done without you."

But Lyra just shook her head, a flicker of fond exasperation crossing her features. "You shouldn't have left in the first place, you big idiot," she signed, her movements sharp and scolding. "Do you have any idea how worried we've been? How scared?"

Peter felt a pang of guilt, a sudden, sickening realization of the pain he had caused, the fear he had sown in the hearts of those he loved most. He hung his head, unable to meet Lyra's gaze as he struggled to find the words to make things right.

"I'm sorry," he whispered, his voice cracking with emotion. "I'm so sorry, Lyra. I thought... I thought I was protecting you, all of you. I thought I could face this alone, could spare you the danger and the heartache. But I was wrong. I was so, so wrong."

Lyra's expression softened, her hand coming up to cup Peter's cheek with a gentleness that made his heart ache. "I know," she signed, her eyes shining with understanding. "I know you were trying to do the right thing, Peter. But you have to remember - we're in this together. Always. No matter what happens, no matter how hard things get… we face it as one. As a family."

Peter felt tears welling up in his eyes, a sudden, fierce rush of love and belonging that threatened to overwhelm him. He nodded, his throat too tight to speak, and let Lyra pull him into a fierce, bone-crushing hug.

"Guys, a little help here would be nice!" James growled.

He pulled back, his jaw set with a grim, unyielding determination. "We have to trap my shadow," he signed, his movements sharp and urgent. "We have to end this, once and for all. Before it's too late, before it can hurt anyone else."

Lyra nodded, her own face hardening with resolve. "Then let's go," she signed, her hands moving with a fluid, deadly grace. "Let's finish this, together."

He turned his attention to the battle raging before them, his eyes scanning the chaos for any sign of James or his shadow.

And then he saw it - a flicker of movement, a blur of darkness that seemed to materialize out of nowhere, lunging towards James' unprotected back with a speed and ferocity that made Peter's heart stop in his chest.

"No!" he screamed, the word tearing from his throat in a ragged, desperate cry. And before he even realized what he was doing, before he had time to think or plan or strategize, he felt his own magic surging forth, a blast of pure, unadulterated shadow energy that slammed into his doppelganger like a physical blow.

The shadow staggered back, its form flickering and wavering as if struck by a gale-force wind. James whirled around, his eyes wide with shock and confusion, and for a moment, their gazes locked across the battlefield.

In that instant, Peter saw a flicker of something in James' eyes - a mixture of surprise and gratitude, of love and fierce, unshakable determination. And then James nodded, a small, almost imperceptible gesture that seemed to say everything that needed to be said.

They were in this together. They always had been, and they always would be.

With a roar of defiance, Peter flung himself into the fray, his shadow magic crackling and sizzling around him like a living thing. He could feel Lyra at his side, her own powers intertwining with his in a dazzling display of light and darkness, of hope and fury and unbreakable resolve.

And there, on the other side of the battlefield, was James - his sword flashing in the dim light, his face set with a grim, unyielding determination as he fought to hold back the tide of Wanda's malevolent magic.

For a moment, Peter was struck by the sheer, breathtaking beauty of it all - the way they moved together, the way their powers and skills complemented each other so perfectly. It was like a dance, a symphony of violence and grace, of love and loyalty and the unshakable bonds that held them together.

"Is that all you've got?" James taunted, his voice ringing out over the chaos of the battle. "I've seen tougher shadows in a kindergarten play!"

Wanda snarled, her face contorting with rage as she redoubled her efforts, her magic lashing out like a whip of pure, searing agony. But James just laughed, a wild, reckless sound that made Peter's heart soar with sudden, giddy hope.

"You think you can beat us with cheap tricks and petty illusions?" James shouted, his sword whirling in a blur of steel and shadow. "We've faced worse than you, witch. And we've always come out stronger, always come out on top."

Beside him, Lyra grinned, her hands moving in a flurry of signs that Peter couldn't quite make out. But he didn't need to - he could feel the essence of her words, the fierce, unshakable confidence that radiated from her like a physical force.

They were going to win this. They were going to beat back the darkness, banish Wanda and his shadow to the depths from whence they came.

And then, in a moment of perfect clarity, Peter saw it - a flicker of vulnerability, a chink in his shadow's armor that seemed to call out to him like a beacon in the night. It was a tiny thing, a split-second opening that most would have missed.

But Peter wasn't most people. And he knew, with a bone-deep certainty, that this was his chance. His one shot at ending this battle, once and for all.

"Now!" he cried, his voice ringing out over the chaos of the fight. And with a surge of effort, a wrenching, soul-deep push that seemed to drain the very marrow from his bones, he channeled every last scrap of his power into a final, devastating attack.

It was like nothing he had ever felt before - a rush of pure, unadulterated magic that flooded through his veins like liquid fire, scorching away the last of his doubts and fears and leaving only a fierce, unshakeable determination in its wake.

He could feel his shadow's resistance, could sense its desperate, clawing attempts to break free from the net of energy that Peter had woven around it. But it was too late, too weak, its power drained by the relentless onslaught of Peter's assault.

With a final, wrenching cry, Peter's magic enveloped his shadow completely, trapping it within the confines of the necklace that hung around his neck. The stone flared with a brilliant, blinding light, and for a moment, Peter thought he could hear his shadow's anguished howl echoing in the depths of his mind.

But then it was gone, vanished into the ether like a bad dream banished by the first rays of the morning sun. And Peter was left standing there, his chest heaving and his body trembling with the aftershocks of his exertion.

"You did it," James whispered, his voice rough with awe and exhaustion as he staggered to Peter's side. "Peter, you brilliant, beautiful bastard. You actually did it."

Peter managed a weak, lopsided grin, his hand finding James' and squeezing with a strength he didn't know he still possessed. "Told you I would," he murmured, his words slurring slightly as the last of his energy began to drain away. "Didn't doubt me, did you?"

James laughed, a breathless, giddy sound that seemed to chase away the last of the shadows that clung to the edges of Peter's vision. "Never," he said fiercely, his hand cupping Peter's cheek with a tenderness that made Peter's heart ache. "I never doubted you for a second, my love."

But even as they reveled in their victory, even as they clung to each other with a desperate, fierce joy... a scream of rage and frustration tore through the air, shattering the moment like a hammer through glass.

Wanda stood before them, her face a mask of pure, unbridled rage. Her eyes blazed with a malevolent fire, her lips curled back in a snarl that was more beast than human. The air around her crackled with dark energy, a palpable aura of hatred and madness that made the very earth tremble beneath their feet.

"You," she spat, her voice dripping with venom as she pointed a gnarled finger at Peter. "You think you've won? You think you can defeat me with your pitiful little parlor tricks?"

Peter stood tall, his chin lifted in defiance. "It's over, Wanda," he said, his voice ringing with a strength and conviction that surprised even himself. "Your ally is gone. You have nothing left to fight for."

But Wanda only laughed, a chilling sound that sent shivers down their spines. "Oh, you foolish boy," she crooned, her lips twisting into a cruel, mocking smile. "You have no idea what I'm capable of. No idea of the true depths of my power."

With a flick of her wrist, Wanda summoned a swirling vortex of dark magic, a whirlwind of shadows and crackling energy that grew larger and larger with each passing second. It tore through the clearing like a hurricane, ripping trees from the ground and sending debris flying in all directions.

James and Lyra sprang into action, their own magic flaring to life in a dazzling display of light and color. James's magnetic mastery allowed him to manipulate the metal in the earth, forming a barrier of iron and steel that deflected the worst of Wanda's attack. Lyra's fairy magic, meanwhile, wove a shimmering shield of iridescent light around them, a gossamer barrier that pulsed with ancient, protective power.

But even with their combined strength, they were no match for the sheer, overwhelming force of Wanda's magic. She hurled bolt after bolt of crackling energy at them, each one more powerful and devastating than the last. The ground shook and split beneath their feet, the air sizzling with the stench of ozone and burnt flesh.

Peter, however, refused to back down. With a roar of defiance, he unleashed his own magic, a blinding burst of shadow energy that slammed into Wanda like a physical blow. She staggered back, her eyes widening in shock and pain as the force of his attack sent her reeling.

But she recovered quickly, her face contorting with an almost inhuman rage. "You dare strike at me?" she shrieked, her voice rising to a fevered pitch. "You, a pathetic whelp who knows nothing of true power?"

She redoubled her efforts, her magic swirling and writhing around her in a maelstrom of darkness and chaos. The very air seemed to warp and twist, reality itself bending to her will as she poured every ounce of her hatred and fury into the attack.

They fought back with everything they had, their magic intertwining and merging in a dazzling display of raw, primal power. They wove shields of shimmering light, hurled bolts of searing energy, and summoned walls of rock and earth to block Wanda's onslaught.

Peter tensed, his hand tightening around James' as he braced himself for the impact. He could feel Lyra at his side, her own magic thrumming through the air like a living thing, ready to defend and protect at a moment's notice.

But the blow never came. Instead, just as Wanda was about to unleash her attack, a shimmering force field appeared around her, blocking the killing blow and trapping her within its iridescent confines.

For a moment, there was only silence - a ringing, deafening silence that seemed to stretch on for an eternity. And then, like a figure stepping out of a dream, a man appeared before them, his form materializing out of a swirling portal that hung in the air like a tear in the fabric of reality itself.

He was tall and imposing, with a presence that seemed to command the very air around him. He wore a tailored suit of the finest cut, and carried a cane that glinted with a malevolent intelligence in the dim light of the room. But it was his eyes that caught Peter's attention - cold, calculating eyes that seemed to see straight through to the heart of him, stripping away every last defense and leaving him feeling exposed and vulnerable.

"Wanda," the man said, his voice a low, silken purr that made Peter's skin crawl with unease. "I am disappointed in you, my dear. I thought I had made myself clear - failure is not an option."

Wanda flinched, her face paling as she shrank back from the man's gaze. "I'm sorry," she whispered, her voice trembling with a fear that

Peter had never heard before. "I tried, I swear I did. But they were too strong, too…"

The man's hand lashed out, striking Wanda across the face with a force that made Peter wince in sympathy. "Excuses," he snarled, his lips curling in a sneer of disgust. "I do not tolerate excuses, Wanda. You know this."

He leaned in close, his face mere inches from Wanda's as he spoke his next words with a quiet, deadly intensity. "You still have a role to play in my plans, my dear. Do not forget that. And do not forget the consequences of failing me again."

Wanda nodded, her eyes wide with terror as she shrank back into the shadows, her form seeming to flicker and waver like a candle flame in the wind.

The man turned his attention to Peter, James, and Lyra, his gaze sweeping over them with a kind of detached, clinical interest. "Well," he said, his voice dripping with a mocking sort of amusement. "It seems congratulations are in order. You have defeated my little pet, and captured your wayward shadow. Quite the accomplishment, I must say."

Peter felt a chill run down his spine at the man's words, a sense of foreboding and uncertainty washing over him like a cold, creeping tide. "Who are you?" he demanded, his voice rough with exhaustion and fear. "What do you want with us?"

The man chuckled, a low, sinister sound that made the hairs on the back of Peter's neck stand on end. "Who I am is not important, But that is a conversation for another time, I'm afraid. For now, I must bid you all farewell."

With a mocking bow, the man raised his hand, and the portal behind him began to swirl and churn with a renewed intensity. "Until we meet again." he called, his voice echoing strangely in the sudden stillness of the room. "And trust me… we will meet again."

And then, before any of them could react, the man stepped back into the portal, taking Wanda with him in a flash of blinding, searing light. The room seemed to shudder and convulse around them, the very air trembling with the aftershocks of the man's departure.

And then, as suddenly as it had appeared, the portal vanished, winking out of existence like a snuffed candle flame. In its place, lying on the ground like a taunting reminder of the mystery they now faced, was a single business card.

With shaking hands, Peter reached out and picked it up, his eyes widening as he read the words printed in a neat, precise script across the front.

"The Deal Maker," he murmured, his voice barely above a whisper. "What the hell does that mean?"

Beneath the name, etched in a strange, indecipherable script, were a series of symbols and glyphs that seemed to dance and shimmer before Peter's eyes, their meaning tantalizingly out of reach.

He looked up at James and Lyra, seeing the same confusion and apprehension mirrored in their faces. "I don't understand," he said, his voice small and lost in the sudden, oppressive silence of the room. "Who was that man?"

James shook his head, his jaw tight with worry and frustration. "I don't know," he admitted, his hand finding Peter's and squeezing with a fierce, protective intensity. "But whatever it is, whatever he's planning… we'll face it together. We'll find a way to stop him, to keep you safe."

Lyra nodded, her hands moving in a flurry of signs that Peter could barely follow in his exhausted, addled state. "He's right," she gestured, her face set with a grim, unyielding determination. "We won this battle, Peter. But the war… the war is just beginning."

Peter felt a shiver run through him at her words, a sense of foreboding and uncertainty that settled deep in his gut like a lead weight. She was right, he knew. They had emerged victorious today, had beaten back the darkness and captured his shadow.

But the man in the suit, the one who called himself The Deal Maker… he represented a threat that none of them fully understood, a mystery that could unravel everything they had fought so hard to protect.

And as Peter stood there, the business card clutched tight in his trembling fingers, he knew that their journey was far from over. That the true nature of the enemy they faced was still shrouded in shadows, waiting to be revealed.

27

Memories

Peter stumbled through the streets of Willowbrook, his body aching and his mind reeling from the battle he had just fought. Beside him, James and Lyra walked in silence, their faces grim and their eyes haunted by the horrors they had witnessed.

As they made their way back to the town square, Peter couldn't help but feel a sense of dread settling in the pit of his stomach. He knew that the fight was far from over, that the mysterious Deal Maker still lurked in the shadows, plotting and scheming. But for now, all he wanted was to see his friends, to make sure that they were safe and whole.

When they finally reached the square, Peter felt his heart sink at the sight that greeted them. The once-bustling heart of Willowbrook was now a scene of destruction and chaos, with buildings reduced to rubble and wounded civilians lying on the ground, their faces twisted in pain.

But even amidst the devastation, there was a sense of relief in the air, a feeling of triumph that seemed to pulse through the crowd like a living thing. People were hugging and crying, their voices rising in a cacophony of joy and disbelief.

"We made it," Peter heard someone say, their voice cracking with emotion. "We actually made it through."

As he picked his way through the debris, Peter's eyes scanned the crowd, searching for any sign of his friends. And then, like a miracle, he spotted them - Adrian, Benjamin, and Dominic, their faces bruised and battered but their smiles wide and genuine.

"Peter!" Adrian called out, his voice hoarse with exhaustion and relief. "Thank god you're alright. We were so worried."

Peter felt a rush of emotion at the sight of them, a sense of gratitude and love that threatened to overwhelm him. Without a second thought, he rushed forward, pulling them into a fierce, tight hug that seemed to last for an eternity.

"I'm sorry," he murmured, his voice muffled against Adrian's shoulder. "I'm so sorry for putting you all through this, for dragging you into my mess."

Benjamin pulled back, his eyes shining with a fierce, protective light. "Don't you dare apologize," he said, his voice rough with emotion. "You're family, Peter. We would go to the ends of the earth for you, fight any battle, face any danger. That's what family does."

Dominic nodded, his hand finding Peter's and squeezing with a gentle, reassuring pressure. "He's right," he said softly, his lips quirking in a small, wry smile. "Besides, it's not like we had anything better to do today. Fighting off an army of shadow monsters? Just another Tuesday in Willowbrook."

Peter let out a choked laugh, feeling some of the tension and fear that had been coiled in his chest start to unravel. "You guys are insane," he said, shaking his head in wonder. "Certifiably, utterly insane."

Lyra grinned, her hands moving in a quick, playful series of signs. "Pot, meet kettle," she gestured, her eyes sparkling with mirth. "We learned from the best, after all."

For a moment, they all just stood there, basking in the warmth and comfort of each other's presence. But then Peter remembered the necklace, the tiny, pulsing light that held the key to their victory.

With a shaking hand, he reached up and unclasped the chain from around his neck, holding it out for the others to see. "It's over," he said, his voice rough with exhaustion and relief. "We did it. We trapped my shadow, and Wanda… she's gone."

The others gathered around, their eyes wide with wonder and awe as they stared at the necklace, at the flickering, dancing light that seemed to pulse with a life of its own.

"You can rest easy now," Adrian breathed, his fingers hovering just above the stone's surface.

But even as the words left his mouth, Peter felt a flicker of unease, a sense that their troubles were far from finished. He thought of the Deal Maker, of the cryptic warning he had left behind, and felt a shiver run down his spine.

The celebration around him seemed to fade away, the laughter and cheers becoming muted and distant as a cold, creeping dread began to settle in the pit of his stomach. He knew, with a bone-deep certainty, that the Deal Maker's parting words had been more than just a taunt, more than a empty threat.

They were a promise, a declaration of intent that chilled Peter to his very core.

As if sensing his thoughts, Lyra stepped forward, her face grave and her hands moving with a sense of urgency that cut through the haze of fear and uncertainty that clouded Peter's mind.

"We need to do the ritual," she signed, her movements sharp and precise, each gesture imbued with a sense of purpose and determination. "Before the sun sets, before it's too late."

Peter felt a flicker of fear at her words, a sense of trepidation that made his heart stutter in his chest. He knew what the ritual entailed, knew the risks and the dangers that came with facing his shadow head-on.

But he also knew that Lyra was right, that this was the only way to truly end this, once and for all. The only way to ensure that the Deal Maker's plans, whatever they might be, would never come to fruition.

"Okay," he said, his voice rough with emotion as he met Lyra's gaze with a nod of understanding. "Okay, let's do it. Let's end this, here and now."

Adrian stepped forward, his brow furrowed in thought as he surveyed the group with a calculating eye. "We'll need a place of power to perform the ritual," he said, his voice low and serious. "Somewhere safe, somewhere protected. And I think I know just the spot."

He turned to James, a small, knowing smile tugging at the corners of his mouth. "The lighthouse," he said, his voice ringing with a quiet conviction. "It's been a beacon of hope and strength for Willowbrook for generations. If there's anywhere that can give us the power we need, it's there."

James nodded, his hand finding Peter's and squeezing with a reassuring strength that made Peter's heart swell with love and gratitude. "It's a good idea," he said, his voice low and steady, a rock in the storm of Peter's emotions. "We'll be safe there, and the light... it will guide us home."

Peter felt a lump rising in his throat at James' words, a sense of belonging and purpose that filled him with a warmth and strength he hadn't known he possessed. He looked around at the faces of his friends, at the love and determination that shone in their eyes, and felt a surge of hope rising in his chest.

They could do this. They could face this final challenge, this last battle, and emerge victorious. As long as they had each other, as long as they stood together... there was nothing they couldn't overcome.

"Then let's go," he said, his voice ringing with a newfound conviction. "Let's finish this, once and for all."

Together, leaning on each other for support and strength, they made their way to the lighthouse, their steps heavy with exhaustion but their hearts full of hope and determination.

As they climbed the winding stairs, each step a struggle against the fatigue that threatened to overwhelm them, Peter couldn't help but feel a sense of awe and wonder at the history that surrounded them, at the countless generations that had come before, seeking guidance and protection in the steadfast light of the beacon.

And now, as they reached the top and stepped out onto the observation deck, he knew that they were adding their own chapter to that story, their own tale of courage and sacrifice in the face of unimaginable odds.

Lyra wasted no time, her hands moving with a fluid grace as she began to prepare for the ritual. With deft, practiced movements, she drew a complex circle on the floor, her fingers tracing intricate patterns of salt and chalk that seemed to shimmer and dance in the fading light of the setting sun.

"Peter," she signed, her face serious and her eyes intense as she beckoned him forward. "Stand in the center, and hold the necklace in your hands."

Peter nodded, his throat tight with emotion as he stepped into the circle, the cool, smooth surface of the necklace a comforting weight in his palm. He could feel the power emanating from it, the pulse of his shadow's essence thrumming against his skin like a second heartbeat.

Lyra's hands moved again, her signs sharp and urgent as she met Peter's gaze with a fierce, unwavering intensity. "When the barriers are up," she gestured, her movements precise and deliberate, "open the necklace. And no matter what happens, no matter what you see or feel... don't break. Don't let go."

Peter swallowed hard, a flicker of fear and uncertainty dancing in his chest. He knew that facing his shadow, facing the darkest parts of himself, would be the hardest thing he had ever done. That it would take every ounce of his strength, every shred of his courage, to see this through to the end.

But he also knew that he was ready, that he had been preparing for this moment his entire life, even if he hadn't realized it until now. With a deep, steadying breath, he nodded, his voice ringing with a quiet, unshakeable conviction.

"I won't let go," he said, his words a vow, a promise to himself and to the people he loved. "I won't break. I'll see this through, no matter what."

As the ritual began, Peter felt a surge of power building within him, a rush of energy that seemed to fill every cell of his body with a bright, burning light. It was like nothing he had ever experienced before, a sensation that was both exhilarating and terrifying in its intensity.

He closed his eyes, focusing on the feeling of James' hand in his, on the love and strength that flowed between them like an unbreakable bond. He could feel the others around him, their presence a steady, comforting anchor in the maelstrom of magic and emotion that swirled through the air.

And then, with a deep breath and a silent prayer, he opened the necklace, releasing his shadow into the circle.

At first, there was nothing, just a faint, pulsing darkness that seemed to hover at the edges of his vision. But then, like a thunderclap, his shadow exploded outward, its form twisting and writhing as it took shape before him.

It was a sight that made Peter's blood run cold, a horrifying, twisted reflection of himself that seemed to embody every dark thought, every secret fear that had ever haunted his dreams. Its eyes glowed with a malevolent, hungry light, and its mouth curled in a sneer of cruel, mocking laughter.

"Well, well, well," it hissed, its voice a sibilant, grating whisper that made Peter's skin crawl. "Look who finally decided to face me. The scared little boy, the weak, pathetic excuse for a hero."

Peter felt a flicker of fear, a moment of doubt that threatened to overwhelm him. But he pushed it down, squared his shoulders, and met his shadow's gaze with a fierce, unwavering determination.

"I'm not scared of you," he said, his voice ringing with a conviction he hardly recognized. "Not anymore. You're a part of me, but you don't control me. And I won't let you hurt the people I love."

The shadow laughed, a harsh, grating sound that made Peter's teeth ache. "You think you can stop me?" it sneered, its form shifting and changing like smoke on the wind. "You're nothing, Peter Naps. Nothing but a scared little boy playing at being a hero."

And with that, it attacked, its form exploding outward in a whirlwind of darkness and fury. Peter felt the impact like a physical blow, a searing, agonizing pain that tore through his body and mind like a thousand burning knives.

But even as he reeled from the assault, even as he felt his strength beginning to waver, he heard James' voice, cutting through the chaos like a beacon in the night.

"Don't listen to it, Peter!" he cried, his words fierce and urgent. "It's lying, trying to break you. But you're stronger than it is, stronger than you know. Fight back, my love. Fight back with everything you have."

Peter felt a surge of warmth and love and gratitude washing over him, a tidal wave of emotion that made his heart swell and his eyes sting with unshed tears. He clung to James' words like a lifeline, letting them fill him with a strength and a courage he hadn't known he possessed.

And with a roar of defiance, a primal, wordless cry that seemed to shake the very foundations of the lighthouse, he pushed back against the darkness, against the shadows that sought to claim him as their own.

What followed was a battle unlike any Peter had ever known, a war waged not with swords or spells, but with the very essence of his being. He could feel his shadow's anger, its fear, its desperate, clawing hunger for power and control.

But beneath that, buried deep within the twisting, writhing darkness… he could sense something else. A flicker of pain, of loneliness, of desperate yearning for acceptance and love.

And as he stood there, his body shaking with the effort of holding himself together, he began to understand. His shadow was not his enemy, not some dark, twisted thing to be feared and hated. It was a part of him, a reflection of his own deepest fears and desires.

"I see you," he whispered, his voice soft and trembling with emotion. "I see your pain, your loneliness. And I'm sorry. I'm sorry for pushing you away, for trying to pretend you didn't exist."

The shadow faltered, its form flickering and wavering like a candle flame in the wind. "You… you're sorry?" it whispered, its voice small and uncertain.

Peter nodded, tears streaming down his face as he reached out, not to fight his shadow, but to embrace it, to welcome it back into himself with open arms and an open heart.

"I am," he said, his words ringing with a quiet, unshakeable conviction. "You're a part of me, and I accept that now. I accept you. And I promise, from this day forward, I will never push you away again."

And with those words, with that simple, powerful act of love and acceptance… the battle was won.

Peter felt a rush of memories flooding back, a tidal wave of images and emotions that threatened to sweep him away. He saw himself as a child in Tír na nÓg, running through fields of wildflowers with James at his side.

He saw Lyra, her wings shimmering in the sunlight as she taught him the secrets of fairy magic, her laughter ringing out like a bell across the endless green hills.

He saw his own power, his own potential, shining like a beacon in the darkness. A light that had always been there, waiting to be uncovered, waiting to be embraced.

And he saw James. Always James, his closest friend, his constant companion, the one person who understood him better than anyone else.

He saw their adventures in Tír na nÓg, the mischief they would get into, the laughter they shared. Peter, the carefree, eternal child, and James, the more serious and grounded of the two, balancing each other out perfectly.

He saw the games they would play, Peter always one step ahead, a twinkle of mischief in his eye as he led James on another wild chase through the enchanted forests of their homeland.

He saw the quiet moments too, the times when they would sit together by the babbling brooks or under the shade of ancient trees, talking about their hopes and dreams, their fears and doubts.

He saw the unbreakable bond of friendship that had held them together through all their adventures, through all the challenges and changes that life in Tír na nÓg could bring.

And he saw the moment when everything changed, when their relationship shifted from the innocent playfulness of childhood friends to something deeper, something more powerful than either of them had ever known.

Peter felt a sob rising in his throat, a rush of emotion so powerful that it threatened to bring him to his knees. But he held on, clinging to James' hand like a lifeline as the ritual ended and the barriers fell away.

And then he was collapsing, his body and mind exhausted but his heart full to bursting. He felt James' arms around him, strong and steady and so achingly familiar, holding him close as he wept and laughed and marveled at the sheer, overwhelming joy of being whole again.

"Peter," he said softly, his voice almost hesitant. "The ritual... did it work? Do you... do you remember?"

Peter's eyes filled with tears, a smile of pure, unbridled joy spreading across his face. "I remember," he whispered, his voice trembling with emotion. "I remember everything, James. Our life together, our love, our destiny."

He reached out, cupping James' face in his hands as he gazed into those beloved eyes. "You never gave up on me," he said softly, his thumbs brushing away the tears that streamed down James' cheeks. "Even when I couldn't remember, even when I pushed you away, you never stopped fighting for us."

James let out a choked sob, his arms tightening around Peter as he buried his face in the crook of his neck. "I never could," he murmured, his voice muffled against Peter's skin. "You're my heart, Peter. My soul. I would have searched for you across a thousand lifetimes if that's what it took to bring you back to me."

Lyra, her own eyes glistening with tears, wrapped her arms around them both, her wings fluttering with joy and relief. "You did it, Peter," she signed, her hands moving with a fierce, proud energy. "You broke the curse, you saved us all. You're a hero, you know that?"

Peter laughed, a watery sound that was half sob, half giggle. "I don't know about that," he said, shaking his head in wonder. "But I do know one thing: I'm the luckiest man in the world to have you both by my side."

And then he was collapsing, his body and mind exhausted but his heart full to bursting. He felt James' arms around him, strong and steady and so achingly familiar, holding him close as he wept and laughed and marveled at the sheer, overwhelming joy of being whole again.

"You did it, my love," James whispered, his own tears mingling with

Peter's on their cheeks. "You faced your shadow, and you won. I'm so proud of you, so in awe of your strength and your courage."

Peter shook his head, a watery smile tugging at the corners of his mouth. "I couldn't have done it without you," he said, his voice rough with emotion. "Without any of you. You gave me the strength to keep fighting, to believe in myself when I thought all was lost."

Lyra grinned, her hands moving in a series of quick, playful signs. "That's what family's for, you dork," she gestured, her eyes sparkling with mischief and affection. "We'll always be here to kick your ass and keep you in line."

Peter laughed, a real, genuine laugh that seemed to chase away the last of the shadows that clung to his heart.

"I don't doubt it for a second," he said, his gaze sweeping over the faces of his friends, his chosen family. "I love you all so much. More than I could ever put into words."

Adrian smiled, his eyes soft with understanding. "We love you too, Peter," he said, his voice warm and sincere. "And we always will, no matter what challenges lie ahead."

Peter nodded, a sense of peace and contentment settling over him like a warm, comforting blanket. He knew that their journey was far from over, that there would be more battles to fight, more obstacles to overcome.

But he also knew that he was ready for whatever lay ahead. That with James by his side, with the love and support of his family to guide him... there was nothing he couldn't face, nothing he couldn't conquer.

The Summer Solstice was upon them, and with it, a chance to celebrate the light, to revel in the joy and magic of the season.

"Come on," he said, pulling back from James with a grin. "We can't miss the festival. Not after everything we've been through to get here."

James laughed, his eyes sparkling with mischief and affection. "I thought you'd never ask," he said, taking Peter's hand and tugging him towards the stairs. "Let's go show Willowbrook how to really celebrate."

As they made their way into the heart of the town, Peter couldn't help but marvel at the resilience and joy of the people around him. Despite the recent battles and hardships, despite the scars that still lingered on their hearts and minds, they had come together with a spirit of unity and celebration that took his breath away.

The streets were lined with colorful banners and twinkling lights, the air filled with the scents of sizzling meats and sweet, spiced desserts. Music and laughter echoed from every corner, mingling with the excited chatter of the crowds as they wandered from stall to stall, sampling the wares and reveling in the festive atmosphere.

"Can you believe it?" Peter asked, leaning in close to James as they wove their way through the throng. "After everything that's happened, they still managed to put together the most incredible Solstice celebration I've ever seen."

James grinned, his arm slipping around Peter's waist and pulling him closer. "That's Willowbrook for you," he said, his voice warm with pride and affection.

As the sun began to set and the bonfires were lit, Peter and James made their way to the central square, where their friends were waiting for them with open arms and wide, beaming smiles.

"About time you two showed up!" Dominic said, his face alight with mischief. "We were starting to think you'd gotten lost in each other's eyes again."

Peter laughed, a blush heating his cheeks as he signed back, "Can you blame me? Have you seen this man?"

James chuckled, pressing a kiss to Peter's temple. "Flatterer," he murmured, his breath warm against Peter's skin.

As the music started up and the dancing began, Peter felt a sense of joy and belonging wash over him, a feeling of rightness and purpose that he had never known before. He joined hands with James and their friends, forming a circle around the flickering flames as they moved to the beat, their laughter and voices rising into the night sky like a prayer of thanksgiving.

"I love you all so much," he said, his eyes shining with tears of happiness. "I don't know what I did to deserve you, but I am so grateful to have you in my life."

Dominic grinned, reaching out to ruffle Peter's hair. "You're stuck with us now." he said, his voice gruff with emotion. "We're family, and that means we're in this together, no matter what."

As the fireworks burst overhead, painting the sky in dazzling colors and bathing them all in shimmering light, Peter turned to James, his heart so full that he thought it might burst.

"Thank you," he whispered, leaning in to rest his forehead against James'. "Thank you for never giving up on me, for loving me even when I couldn't love myself."

James smiled, his hand coming up to cup Peter's cheek. "That's my job," he said softly, his eyes shining with adoration. "To love you, to believe in you, to fight for you, always. And I will, Peter. I will love you and fight for you until the end of time."

And as their lips met in a kiss that held all the promises of a lifetime, as the cheers and laughter of their friends washed over them like a joyous tide, Peter knew that he had finally found his place in the world. His home, his family, his purpose.

And with James by his side, with the love and support of the incredible people around him, he knew that he could face anything that the future might bring.

Because he was Peter Naps, wielder of magic and master of his own destiny. And he was exactly where he was meant to be.

Epilogue

In the days that followed the Summer Solstice celebration, as Willow-brook began the slow, steady process of rebuilding and healing, Peter found himself walking hand in hand with James through the streets of the town, basking in the simple joy of being together.

It was strange, in a way, to think of how far they had come. From the early days of their friendship, when Peter had been the mischievous, carefree spirit and James the more grounded, responsible one, to the battles they had fought side by side, the challenges they had faced and overcome together.

But through it all, one thing had remained constant: the love that bound them together, the unbreakable connection that had seen them through even the darkest of times.

As they walked, they talked about everything and nothing, their words flowing easily in the warm summer air. They spoke of their pasts, of the adventures they had shared in Tír na nÓg and the trials they had faced in Willowbrook. They spoke of their futures, of the life they wanted to build together, the dreams they hoped to make reality.

And always, always, they found themselves drawn back to the lighthouse, to the spot where they had first pledged their love, their devotion, their unending commitment to each other.

It was there, on a warm evening as the sun began to set over the ocean and the stars started to appear in the sky, that James took Peter's hand and led him to the top of the lighthouse once more.

Peter's heart raced as they climbed the winding stairs, his mind filled with memories of all the moments they had shared in this place. The first time James had brought him here, when he had been lost and confused and desperate for answers. The night of the ritual, when they had faced their darkest fears and emerged stronger, more united than ever before.

And now, as they stepped out onto the observation deck and the world stretched out before them, Peter felt a sense of anticipation, of excitement and nerves and a love so deep that it took his breath away.

James turned to face him, his eyes shining with a warmth and tenderness that made Peter's heart skip a beat. "Peter," he said softly, his voice thick with emotion. "There's something I need to ask you, something I've been waiting to ask for a long time now."

Peter swallowed hard, his mouth suddenly dry as he watched James reach into his pocket and pull out a small, velvet box. "James," he whispered, his voice trembling. "What are you…?"

But before he could finish, James was sinking to one knee, the box open in his hand to reveal a ring that glinted in the fading light of the sun. It was simple, elegant, a band of silver with a single, shimmering stone that seemed to capture all the colors of the ocean and the sky.

"Peter," James said again, his voice steady and strong despite the tears that shone in his eyes. "You are my everything. My love, my life, my reason for being. From the moment I first saw you, all those years ago in Tír na nÓg, I knew that you were special. That you were the one I was meant to be with, the one I would love for all of my days."

He took a deep breath, his gaze never leaving Peter's. "We've been through so much together, you and I. We've faced challenges and dangers that would have broken lesser men, that would have torn apart weaker bonds. But through it all, we've only grown stronger, more united, more deeply in love."

Peter felt tears welling up in his own eyes, a lump rising in his throat as he listened to James' words. He thought of all the moments they had shared, all the laughter and tears and whispered promises in the dark. He thought of the way James made him feel, the way he challenged him and supported him and loved him with a fierceness that took his breath away.

"I want to spend the rest of my life with you, Peter," James continued, his voice rough with emotion. "I want to build a future with you, to create a family and a home and a life that we can be proud of. I want to wake up every morning to your smile, to fall asleep every night with you in my arms. I want to be yours, wholly and completely, for all the days of my life."

He took another deep breath, his hand trembling slightly as he held out the ring. "Peter Naps, wielder of magic and master of shadows, love of my life and keeper of my heart… will you marry me?"

For a moment, Peter couldn't speak, couldn't breathe, couldn't do anything but stare at the man before him with a heart so full of love that it felt like it might burst. And then, with a sob of joy and a smile that lit up his whole face, he was falling to his knees and throwing his arms around James, holding him close as the tears streamed down his cheeks.

"Yes," he whispered, his voice thick with emotion. "Yes, James, a thousand times yes. I love you so much, more than I ever thought possible. And I want nothing more than to spend the rest of my life with you, building the future we've always dreamed of."

James let out a shaky laugh, his own tears mingling with Peter's as he slipped the ring onto his finger. It fit perfectly, the cool metal warming quickly against Peter's skin, and he knew in that moment that he would wear it proudly for the rest of his days.

They stayed like that for a long time, kneeling on the floor of the lighthouse and clinging to each other like they would never let go. And when they finally rose to their feet, their hands clasped tightly together and their eyes shining with love and joy, Peter knew that this was just the beginning.

The beginning of their happily ever after, the beginning of a love that would never, ever end.

As the days turned into weeks and the weeks into months, Peter and James threw themselves into planning their wedding, their excitement and anticipation growing with each passing day. They knew they wanted the ceremony to be held at the lighthouse, the place that had meant so much to them throughout their journey, and they worked tirelessly to transform the space into a magical, enchanted wonderland.

Lyra was a constant presence at their side, her hands flying in a flurry of signs as she helped with the preparations. She insisted on creating the flower arrangements herself, weaving delicate blooms and shimmering fairy lights into stunning displays that took Peter's breath away.

"Lyra, these are incredible," he signed to her one day, his eyes wide with wonder as he took in the riot of color and beauty that filled the lighthouse. "You have such a gift, such an eye for beauty and magic."

Lyra grinned, her cheeks flushing with pleasure at the praise. "Anything for you, Peter," she signed back, her movements soft and sincere. "You and James deserve the most beautiful, most perfect wedding day possible. And I'll do everything in my power to make sure you have it."

Peter felt tears prickling at the corners of his eyes, his heart swelling with love and gratitude for this incredible fairy who had become like a sister to him. He pulled her into a tight hug, pouring all of his affection and appreciation into the embrace.

As the big day drew nearer, Peter found himself thinking more and more about Tír na nÓg, about the magical land that had been his home for so long. He knew that he could never truly go back, that his place was here in Willowbrook with James and the family they had built together.

But still, there was a part of him that longed for the endless green hills, the babbling brooks and ancient forests of his youth. A part of him that missed the carefree adventures and mischievous games he had shared with James, the bond of friendship that had been the foundation of their love.

And so, on the morning of their wedding day, as he stood in front of the mirror in his suit and tie, his hair tamed and his face glowing with happiness, Peter closed his eyes and whispered a silent prayer to the spirits of Tír na nÓg.

"Thank you," he murmured, his voice soft and reverent. "Thank you for the magic, for the wonder, for the love that you brought into my life. Thank you for leading me to James, for giving us the strength and the courage to fight for each other, to never give up on our dreams."

He took a deep breath, a smile playing at the corners of his lips. "I may not be the boy I once was, the eternal child who never wanted to grow up. But I promise you, I will never forget the lessons you taught me, the joy and the light that you brought into my world."

With a final nod of gratitude, Peter opened his eyes and turned to face the door, his heart racing with excitement and love. It was time, time to take the next step in his journey, to pledge his heart and his life to the man who meant everything to him.

And as he walked down the aisle, his eyes locked on James' shining face, he knew that he was exactly where he was meant to be. Here, in this moment, surrounded by the people he loved most in the world, ready to start the next chapter of his story.

Their story, the tale of Peter and James, the boy who never wanted to grow up and the man who taught him the meaning of true love. The story that would be told for generations to come, the legend of a love that had conquered shadows and curses and the very fabric of time itself.

And as they spoke their vows, as they promised to love and cherish each other for all of their days, Peter felt a sense of peace and rightness settle over him, a certainty that this was the path he was meant to walk, the future he was meant to build.

With James by his side, with the love and support of their family and friends to guide them, he knew that they could face anything that lay ahead. That they could weather any storm, overcome any challenge, as long as they had each other.

And so, with a kiss that held the promise of forever, Peter and James sealed their love, their commitment, their unending devotion to each other. And as the cheers and applause of their loved ones washed over them, as the sun set over the ocean and the stars began to appear in the sky, Peter knew that he had finally found his happily ever after.

His heart, his home, his reason for being. The other half of his soul, the missing piece that made him whole.

James, his husband, his partner, his love. For now, and for always.

Thank you and Please Leave a Review!

Dear Readers,

As we come to the end of this wild and whimsical journey with the third book of Willowbrook, I want to take a moment to express my deepest gratitude. Thank you for joining us on this adventure filled with laughter, love, and a touch of the supernatural.

It's been an absolute joy to share this story with you, and I hope their antics brought a smile to your face and warmth to your heart. Writing their tale has been an incredible experience, and I'm so grateful for the opportunity to share it with all of you.

If you enjoyed our story, please consider leaving a review. Your feedback means the world to me, and it helps other readers discover our book and join in on the fun.

Thank you again for your support, your laughter, and your love. Here's to many more adventures together!

With heartfelt appreciation,
Ken Sanchez

About the Author

Ken Sanchez, the visionary behind spellbinding M/M romance-fantasy worlds where love and magic entwine in a mesmerizing dance. With a heart devoted to the art of LGBTQ+ romance and an unbounded imagination,

Please sign up for my newsletter to get my new releases and get some freebies! And join my Facebook group for more updates!

You can connect with me on:

https://www.facebook.com/groups/1071310280763009

Subscribe to my newsletter:

http://eepurl.com/iJMYvA

Also by Ken Sanchez

Enter my world of Fantasy and Romance.

Enchanted (Willowbrook Book One)
In the enchanting town of Willowbrook, a young man named Benjamin discovers a remarkable power—the ability to bring stories to life. When he encounters a reclusive Beast named Adrian, cursed to shift between a fearsome ice dragon and a human form that freezes everything he touches, their destinies entwine.

As Benjamin and Adrian navigate a treacherous journey filled with love, friendship, and the transformative power of stories, they must break Adrian's curse to save Willowbrook from an eternal winter. With the town's magical essence slowly fading, time is running out.

Discover a captivating tale of redemption, acceptance, and the enduring magic of true love. Uncover the secrets hidden within the enchanted library and witness how love can rewrite even the darkest of stories. Join Benjamin and Adrian in "Enchanted" and experience the magic within your reach.

"Enchanted" is a captivating gay retelling of a timeless legend of Beauty and The Beast.

This is a standalone and can be read in any order. Unlock the Magic Within, and Let Love Rewrite the Story.

Stormweaver (Willowbrook Book Two)

In the enchanted town of Willowbrook, where supernatural forces intertwine, a storm is brewing, threatening to shatter the delicate balance between magic and reality. Weather witch Dominic Reed seeks solace in his bakery, Glimmer, but his haunted past and tumultuous family dynamics refuse to fade.

Enter Christian Belgrade, heir to a vampire coven, whose scarred history and possessive nature are eclipsed only by his mysterious powers. When their worlds collide at Christian's club, a revelation unfolds, setting off a chain of events that will test their strengths, unravel their vulnerabilities, and force them to confront the shadows that lurk in the magical underbelly of Willowbrook.

As the connection deepens between Dominic and Christian, they must navigate the treacherous waters of Elder Eros Grim's vendetta and Dominic's malevolent stepfamily. Will love be enough to weather the storm that threatens to consume them, or will the secrets of their pasts tear them apart?

In this enthralling sequel to Willowbrook, immerse yourself in a tale of redemption, passion, and the enduring power of love. Stormweaver will sweep you away into a world where the supernatural meets the deeply human, leaving you breathless and craving more.

This is book two in the Willowbrook Series and can be read as a stand alone. This is also a gay retelling of Cinderella.

Echoes of Destiny (Shadowguards Book One)

Eryx, a gifted musician, channels haunting melodies that echo his forgotten godly lineage. When a sinister encounter alters his reality, he finds solace in an enigmatic guardian named Alex, whose alluring presence sparks an inexplicable connection.

Unbeknownst to Eryx, Alex is Hades, sentinel of the Underworld. As he guides Eryx through their intertwined destinies, an undeniable attraction forms, challenging the fabric of their worlds.

Amidst mysticism in contemporary New York, ancient prophecies resurge with encroaching darkness. Their bond becomes a beacon of hope as Eryx's ancestry awakens and their love deepens. The duo embarks on a quest that will test their resolve, unravel hidden truths, and decide humanity's fate.

Shadowguards is a gay urban fantasy that marries the ordinary with the extraordinary. Where music and shadows converge and the line between mortal and divine blurs, this spellbinding tale explores the complexities of destiny and the unbreakable ties that bind us.

Light Redeemed (Shadowguards Book Two) the line between mortal and divine blurs as an ancient threat resurfaces, determined to plunge New York into chaos. Eryx Ross, now fully embracing his destiny as Apollo's vessel, must navigate his burgeoning powers and deepening bond with the enigmatic Alexander Knight, the mortal embodiment of Hades. Together, they face an unconventional challenge that will test their love and the very fabric of their world.

Amidst the gathering darkness, Eryx and Alex's souls entwine on a cosmic scale, their love a beacon of hope against the sinister machinations of the Order. They rally allies both old and new, gods and mortals alike, to stand against the rising tide of evil. But the Order holds a terrifying trump card – a mimic with the power to steal magic – threatening to unravel all they hold dear.

With destiny hanging in the balance, Eryx must embrace his godly light, and Alex must confront the shadows of his past. Only together can they hope to triumph over the forces that would tear them asunder and redeem the future for all. Immerse yourself in this spellbinding tale of star-crossed love, found family, and the unbreakable ties that bind us, even across the boundaries of life and death. "Light Redeemed" is an emotional rollercoaster that will leave you breathless and yearning for more in this next chapter of the Shadowguards saga.